PAGE STAINS

OK

W9-BTO-010

Delafield Public Library
Delafield, WI 53018

SKELETON CREW

Other books by Beverly Connor in the
Lindsay Chamberlain Series:

A Rumor of Bones

Questionable Remains

Dressed to Die

SKELETON CREW

A LINDSAY CHAMBERLAIN NOVEL

BEVERLY CONNOR

CUMBERLAND HOUSE
NASHVILLE, TENNESSEE

Delafield Public Library
Delafield, WI 53018

To Harriette Austin

Copyright © 1999 by Beverly Connor

All rights reserved. Written permission must be secured from the publisher to use or reproduce any part of this work, except for brief quotations in critical reviews or articles.

Published by Cumberland House Publishing, Inc., 431 Harding Industrial Drive, Nashville, TN 37211-3160.

The characters and events in this book are fictitious. Any similarity to real persons, living or dead, is coincidental and not intended by the author.

Jacket design: Gore Studio, Inc.

Library of Congress Cataloging-in-Publication Data
Connor, Beverly, 1948–
    Skeleton crew : a Lindsay Chamberlain novel / Beverly Connor.
        p.   cm.
    ISBN 1-581-82042-9 (alk. paper)
        I. Title.

PS3553.O5138 S56 1999
813'.54—dc21
                                                                    99-046311

Printed in the United States of America
1 2 3 4 5 6 7—05 04 03 02 01 00 99

Acknowledgments

Thanks to Diane Trap, Judy and Takis Iakovou, Marie and Richard Davis, Julia Cochran, and Nancy Vandergrift for their criticism and advice.

A special thanks to my husband Charles Connor whose encouragement and support never waver.

Author's Note

The barrier island of St. Magdalena is a fictitious composite of characteristics from several of Georgia's barrier islands.

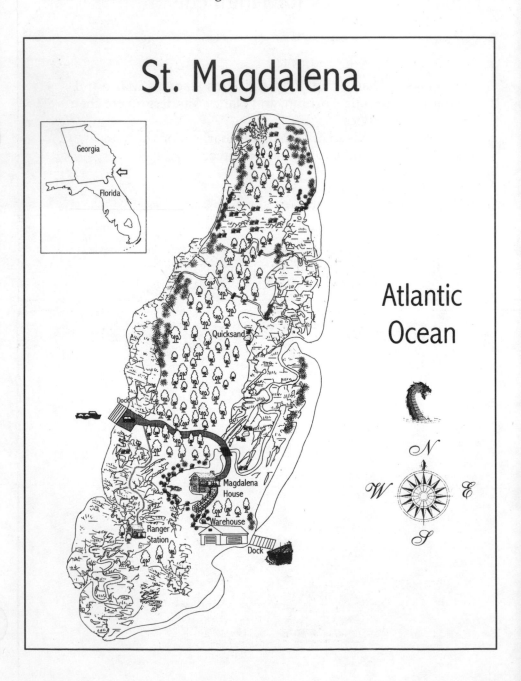

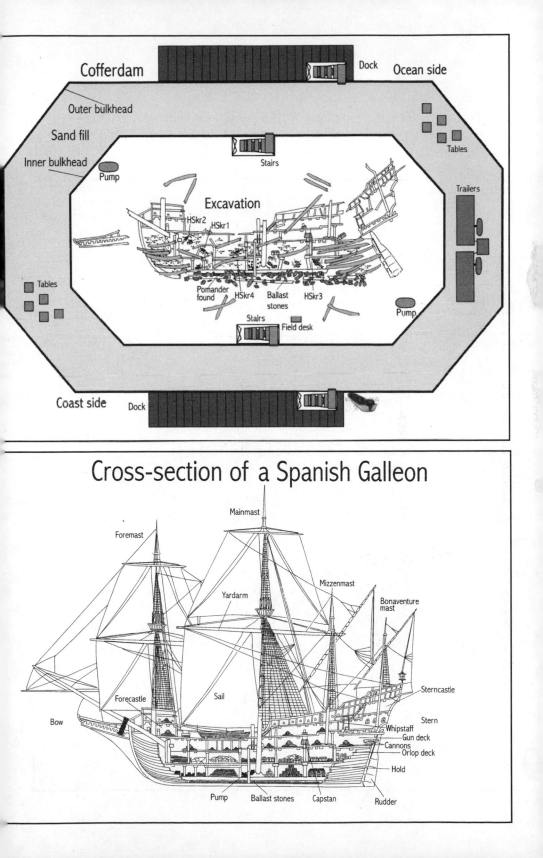

Cofferdam — Dock — Ocean side

Outer bulkhead

Sand fill

Inner bulkhead

Pump

Tables

Trailers

Excavation

HSkr2

HSkr1

Stairs

Pomander found

HSkr4

Ballast stones

HSkr3

Tables

Stairs

Field desk

Pump

Coast side — Dock

Cross-section of a Spanish Galleon

Mainmast

Foremast

Mizzenmast

Yardarm

Bonaventure mast

Forecastle

Sail

Sterncastle

Bow

Stern

Whipstaff

Gun deck

Cannons

Orlop deck

Hold

Pump

Ballast stones

Capstan

Rudder

SKELETON
CREW

Chapter 1

A Passenger's Diary: Part I

From a voyage on the Spanish Galleon
Estrella de España, c. 1558
—Translated by Harper Latham

*W*HEN I SAW the *Estrella de España* wafting on the water beside the dock, I almost turned to go back to the House of Trade and tell them, "No. I can't. I cannot get on this wooden thing that looks like it carries the crosses of Calvary on its back and sail across the sea."

While I pondered how I was going to refuse this mission, my trunk was taken from the wagon that brought me to the docks and hoisted onto the ship by a rope attached to one of the long arms extending from the great mast. I was not consulted for my permission. Do they never have passengers who change their minds? Does everyone who comes down here intending to cross the Atlantic board without a second thought? The decision was made for me. With a sigh, I wove amid the noisy and stinking animals, wagons, and dockworkers to a plank that led from the dock to the ship.

The deck of the ship reminded me of an anthill—crawling with busy sailors. The only person to greet me from among the mass of laboring bodies was a page—a lad of about ten. He grinned at me, showing a smile with missing front teeth, and led me down narrow steps to the deck below and to a small cabin that was already occupied by someone with an affinity for maps, for they were spread about on the single table and weighted down with a heavy compass. Before I could ask any question, the lad scampered off to some other task.

11

I came to learn that my quarters are with Bellisaro, the navigator and pilot of our ship. He is a knight of the Order of Santiago, as I, and a laconic, brooding fellow—and a lucky fellow by my accounting. Bellisaro was injured in a battle with the French. He received both a broken arm and leg, injuries that in many would require amputation. He was, however, found by a peasant family who had no knowledge of current healing practices. They straightened his limbs and tended his wounds, and he recovered with only a slight limp. Not long after, he discovered that he has a great aptitude for navigation and embarked on a career at sea. Indeed, his skill was demonstrated almost at once, for I understand that the Guadalquivir is the most difficult of rivers for large ships such as this one to navigate. She was actually loaded at Las Horcadas where I boarded her rather than Seville, because to navigate such a length down the Guadalquivir from Seville is too treacherous. I'm grateful that we were already out to sea and under way when I was told by the steward that many ships our size, even at high tide, fail to pass the sandbar at Sanlúcar where the river's mouth joins the ocean. Bellisaro, he says, is a good pilot.

Our cabin is small and dark with a low ceiling. We have two cots low on the floor and the one table. Bellisaro takes most of the space in our small cabin, but I do not begrudge him. He needs space to spread out his maps to guide our course through these waters—which look all the same to me. He will tell me nothing about his skills, no matter how often I ask.

For the beginning of our journey, the sky was concealed day and night by a blanket of clouds. For a full week the gray canopy has hung over us. Knowing that a navigator needs the sun and stars, I worry. Evidently, my worrying is enough for both of us, for Bellisaro is unaffected. He has his compass, which I know points north always. But even I in my ignorance figure that a more precise measure is needed if we are to find our way across the vast ocean to some exact spot. I watch him as he drops a rope tied to a lead weight off the side of the ship at some regular interval. He will soon pull it up, as if hauling in a fish, and examine the mud dredged up by the weight. He will rub the mud between his hands and nod his head. I don't know what or how he reads from the bottom of the ocean, but I am impressed.

Sharing the cabin with the capable Bellisaro does much to calm my nerves. I have heard many tales among the crew of storms at sea and ships that disappear into the depths of the ocean—as there are also stories of raids by corsairs upon the peaceful vessels of commerce on the sea, and rumors of disputes and conflicts between ships of our beloved Spain and fleets of the great seafaring states of England and France. Though I am reassured by the size and strength of the ships in our convoy, I am daily reminded of the perils that can befall us. The sea has great beauty, but I do not want it to be my final resting place.

⚓

Cofferdam Site off the Coast of Georgia, c. 2000

THE SUN WAS just high enough that it made a diffuse golden avenue across the glittering blue-green ocean as the boat Lindsay rode in approached the cofferdam. The oval dam, five miles out in the Atlantic Ocean off the coast of one of Georgia's barrier islands, was a structural marvel that held back the ocean and allowed archaeologists to work on the ocean floor as if it were dry land.

The boat docked outside the dam where a young Native American held out his hand and helped her onto the dock. Luke Youngdeer, his nametag read.

"Dr. Chamberlain, welcome aboard." He grinned at her with even white perfect teeth, and nodded toward the pilot of the boat. "He'll take your luggage to the barge."

Lindsay looked up at the metal outside wall of the dam extending some nine feet above the waterline. "Wow, this is big."

"Wait until you get inside," Luke said.

Lindsay climbed a metal staircase to the top of the dam and stood on the wide ring of sand like an oval racetrack that filled the space between the two steel bulkheads of the cofferdam. The structure reminded her of the walls of a castle, protecting the keep within from the rising surge of water without. She looked down into the dry center of the dam at a large pump that, like the fifth Chinese brother who could hold the ocean in his mouth, had sucked out the water and revealed the ocean bottom and its wondrous treasures.

The Spanish galleon *Estrella de España*, once 123 feet from stem to stern, lay on her side, buried in the ocean bottom. When they had first uncovered her, she could have been a giant creature that had been laid to rest in a flexed position with the frames as ribs and keel as a backbone. Now, with layers of silt, sand, and her hull removed, she looked like any other archaeological excavation, with grid squares and walkways. But it was not hard for Lindsay to visualize the ship upright and new, in full sail gliding across the water.

The remains of the ship and its cargo were criscrossed with scaffolding that kept the weight of the crew and equipment off the fragile wreck as it was being excavated. Several crew were already stretched out on the planks, working under the tall roof shading the site. Trey Marcus, University of Georgia underwater archaeologist and principal investigator of the site, looked up and waved at Lindsay. She returned the wave and started to climb down the ladder.

"Rabbit, I see you're still wearing my hat," a voice came from behind her.

Lindsay whirled around and faced John West. His long black hair was pulled back in a low ponytail and covered with a hat identical to hers. She smiled, absently touching the bill of the West Construction cap he had given her a couple of years ago to replace her Atlanta Braves one. "John, it's good to see you, though I'm surprised you have stooped to working with archaeologists."

He took off his sunglasses and hung them on the neck of his white T-shirt. "Anything to encourage you guys to dig up your own ancestors instead of mine. You just get here?"

She looked around at the huge dam and the two support barges anchored nearby. "Yes, I'm trying to take it all in."

"Me, too, and I built the thing."

Lindsay rubbed her bare arms. She was already getting sticky from the salty ocean breeze. She nodded toward the ladder she had just climbed from the dock to the top of the dam. "That young guy, Luke, on the dock checked me in. He said he'd store my gear on the barge. I guess that's where I'll be staying?"

As she spoke, John reached for the binoculars around his neck and stared out across the ocean. Lindsay, shading her eyes, followed his gaze to several ships near the horizon. "Shrimp boats?" she asked.

"Some. Two are pirates."

She whipped her head back to face him. "Excuse me, pirates?"

He let down his binoculars but continued to stare out to sea. His lips and even white teeth were somewhere between a snarl and a grin. "That's what I call them. One belongs to Hardy Denton. He thinks this job should have gone to him and not to some upstart redskin. That schooner belongs to Evangeline Jones, who's anything but good news."

"Sounds familiar."

John gave a little laugh and looked at her. "It should. She's a world-class pothunter, and she seems to have gotten herself a whiff of Spanish gold."

"Eva Jones. I remember. She's supposed to have looted the *Madre de Jesus* off the coast of Africa just two years ago." Lindsay squinted her eyes at the tiny sailing ship on the horizon.

"And the Byzantine wreck in the Mediterranean before that. She's been going through Greece and Turkey like an anteater. It's rumored that she stole and sold that *T. rex* discovered last year."

"How do you know so much about a pothunter?" Lindsay tucked a few tendrils of hair under her cap that the wind had whipped into her face.

"She has a reputation with your marine archaeologist friends here."

"What do you think she's doing here?"

John shrugged. "Spanish galleons mean treasure to a treasure hunter."

At that moment a diver dressed in spandex shorts and tank top and a bright yellow vest climbed over the outside wall of the dam and began stripping himself of his air tank.

"Here's one of my divers. Talk to you later." John turned and trotted off before Lindsay could ask him anything else.

She looked out at the vast ocean surrounding the tiny man-made island. In one direction she could see only blue-green ocean all the way to the arc of the horizon. In the opposite direction the distant land was a thin strip between sky and sea. She took a deep breath and climbed down the metal scaffolding staircase into the middle of the dam where Trey Marcus and the other crew members were excavating on the ocean floor.

The interior of the cofferdam was enormous. Lindsay guessed about a hundred and fifty by eighty feet, perhaps larger. Damp metal walls loomed thirty-five feet above her head. It was like being in a giant well, but a reverse well in which the water is on

15

the outside and the hole is dry. A metal roof sheltered the excavation like an umbrella a good twenty feet above the top of the walls. Large lights nullified the shadows made by the roof—it was a bright well. The excavation itself was surrounded by a generous path of ocean floor. A musty fishy smell wafted through the air. As she walked toward the site proper, she caught whiffs of sunscreen and perspiration.

Lindsay grinned and held out her hands to Trey as he stepped off the planked walkway. "I'm impressed," she said.

Trey beamed and took her hands. "If you aren't, then I give up." He looked around at the interior of the dam as if for the first time. "This is something, isn't it?"

"Francisco Lewis wanted his arrival in the Archaeology Department to be spectacular, and I reckon it is. As hard as we all work to come up with the few thousand dollars we do get for archaeology, he manages to wrangle a couple of million in a flash."

"It does help to be a political animal. I really do think his becoming division head of Anthropology and Archaeology will be a good thing in the long run," Trey said, as she followed him onto the walkway that stretched over excavation units latticed with stakes and string. "Come on over and let me introduce you to some of the folks."

"We're ready," shouted a square-set bearded man with his hand on the rope at the end of a boom.

"We're just about to take up some more of the ship's timber," Trey said, nodding toward the man and a companion who had joined him. "Because she's on her side, everything's a jumble."

Lindsay watched as he helped two crew members secure a huge waterlogged beam to ropes on the end of a boom, then steady the beam as it rose slowly from their reach and swung to the deck of the dam. From there, others would lower it into a vat on the deck of the waiting barge and cover it with wet burlap to keep it from drying. At the end of the day, the barge would carry the soaking timbers to waiting tanks of brine located in a lab on one end of the island of St. Magdalena—a place Lindsay was dying to visit.

Trey turned back to Lindsay. "This is Steven Nemo." He pointed to one of the men who helped with hoisting the timber. "He's in charge of the ship's timbers."

Lindsay's lips twitched into a small smile. He removed a glove and held out a hand to her. "I've heard every joke several times," he said, so stern-faced that Lindsay had to laugh.

"I'll bet you have."

"Juliana Welton is working Unit 3 over here. She's a student at FSU," Trey continued. A woman stretched out on the planks lifted her head long enough to wave, then bent over her work again. Her long braid swung down in the mud and she shoved it back with a mild curse.

Trey introduced Gina Fairfax, a student from North Carolina recently transferred to Georgia, and Jeff Kendall, a Ph.D. candidate from Virginia. Gina smiled and said hello. Jeff ignored them all—totally absorbed in his work. "Some of the others are up top," Trey said. "If you need a break, we have a couple of trailers with couches and stocked refrigerators."

Trey pointed to the area vacated by the timber. "You can work in this unit." He stood facing her on the narrow pathway and grinned broadly. "We have a pool going on for who will be the first to find a human skeleton. We have twenty-five dollars so far. Want to contribute?"

"Sure," said Lindsay. "I'll put in another twenty-five." All heads turned toward her, even Jeff's.

Trey gasped in surprise. "That's very generous of you."

"Not really," said Lindsay, not taking her eyes from his. "I win."

Trey leaned forward, raising his eyebrows. "What?"

Lindsay squatted on the plank and pointed out a shaft of bone to the surprised crew who all came over to have a look.

"I don't believe it," said Trey, peering at the bone.

"It has to be human to win," Jeff said, squatting beside her, looking at the protruding bone.

"It's the proximal end of a human left radius," Lindsay said, gently stroking the bone with her fingers. "And looks to be in very good condition."

"I'll leave it to your capable hands, then." Trey gave her a pat on the back and he and Steven resumed the mapping that had been interrupted by the removal of the timber and Lindsay's arrival. The others went back to their uncomfortable prone positions over their excavation units.

Lindsay stretched out on her belly on the narrow plank and began uncovering the muck from the bone—going from the known to the unknown with a wooden tongue depressor, occasionally using her trowel. She worked her way up the shaft of bone, gently loosening and removing the damp soil that clung to it. She put the dirt in one of the several buckets nearby for that purpose, later to be hauled to the top and taken to one of the barges where it would be screened for artifacts. Halfway up the shaft of humerus she discovered matter that on close inspection revealed a weave. Textile. Exciting, but it slowed her work as she carefully separated the mud from the fabric.

Around her she could hear the sounds of the pump, the waves splashing against the dam, and the creaking of the interlocking panels that held back the ocean. Now and then she looked over at the walls, saw water trickling down the sides, and was reminded that the pump was still pumping water—water that leaked into the dam. She took a slow, deep breath and went back to her work.

Near the skeleton's shoulder, Lindsay uncovered part of the lower jaw. The skeleton lay with his head tilted, chin resting on the clavicle. The same fabric partially covered the facial bones. Lindsay wiped the sweat from her face with her forearm, smiling at her find, working as quickly as she could to uncover the face.

"I saw you looking at the walls." Lindsay almost jumped at the voice. She looked up from her work to see Gina. "Sorry, didn't mean to startle you. Just stretching my legs, taking a break."

"That's all right." Lindsay changed positions, stretching her own muscles.

"I noticed you have a West Construction hat. You know them?"

"I know John West. I met him on a dig a couple of years ago." Lindsay sat cross-legged on the plank and massaged her tired shoulder.

Gina sat down in front of her. Her bare legs were caked with sandy mud, and she had a smear across her forehead from pushing her hair out of her eyes. "He talked to us when we first got here. Told us how the cofferdam works. The greater the pressure from the outside, the tighter the walls fit together. It's a matter of structural geometry." Gina smiled, shrugged her shoulders, and looked around at the walls. "Isn't it funny that such a big place can make you feel claustrophobic?"

"Structural geometry not withstanding, when you think that these walls are holding back the whole Atlantic Ocean—"

"Yeah, boggles the mind." Gina stood up. "Better get back to work. See you around lunchtime. You know we have lunch catered, don't you?"

"Catered?" Lindsay lay back down on her stomach and started back to work.

"This place on the coast packs us fresh sandwiches, cakes, and fruit every day. Not bad, really." Gina looked over Lindsay's shoulder at the skeleton under excavation. "Our first victim of the wreck of the *Spanish Star*. Exciting."

Lindsay teased a dirt-encrusted layer on the frontal bone of the skull with her trowel and sprayed it with water, gently rinsing away some of the mud. "No. I suspect that he was already dead before the ship sank."

Trey, who stood only a plank away, and some of the others close by looked over at Lindsay. "You aren't that good," Trey said, grinning at her.

"Yes, I am." She turned her head and smiled back at him. "I've found fabric, and it looks like he was sewn into sailcloth. Isn't that what they did with the dead on ships before burial at sea?"

"Fabric? Let me see." Juliana rose and pushed past Gina to see the skeleton.

"Jeeze, Juli—" Gina caught herself before she fell off the plank.

Juliana squatted down beside Lindsay. "Yes, it's fabric. It could be his clothes."

"Could be," said Lindsay, "but this particular piece looks like it covers his skull and part of his face. We'll see when it's finished."

Trey and some of the others crowded on the narrow plank looking down on the mud-stained skeleton. The skull, arm, and shoulder were beginning to stand out in relief. Half the skull and portions of the shoulder were obscured by a brown textured veneer.

Later, when they broke for lunch, Lindsay was surprised at the sense of relief she felt as she emerged from the well of the cofferdam into the open sea air. She stood next to the outer bulkhead, letting the breeze cool her body, watching ships that seemed miniature in the distance.

"Better have a sandwich before they're all gone." A brown paper bag appeared in front of her face. It was attached to a suntanned arm. She took the bag and looked at the giver. It was the silent Jeff. "When the diving crew gets here, they'll scarf down what's left."

"Thanks," Lindsay said, digging into the bag. She found a sandwich, Twinkies, potato chips, a pear, and two towelette packets. She fished out the sandwich and gave it a sniff. Tuna fish.

"They're all tuna fish," he said. "I hope you like it. The caterer said they'd have to charge extra to fix different kinds of sandwiches every day. Tomorrow it'll be something else."

"Lucky for me I like tuna." Lindsay tore open one of the small packets and wiped her hands with the moist antiseptic towel. Nice touch, she thought.

"You know, you'd think after spending millions on this dig, they could spring for a little extra so we could have a choice." He bit into a pear. "Can I ask you a question?" He looked in his late twenties, but the tone of his voice made him sound like a kid.

"Sure," she said and took a bite of the sandwich. The tuna salad was made with celery, raisins, and small chunks of apple. Jeff didn't have any cause for complaint, she thought.

"Exactly why do they call you the Angel of Death?"

Chapter 2

"WHO CALLS ME the Angel of Death?"

"People. You know. From digs."

"What do they say? That I portend death or that I kill people?" Lindsay grinned, but she saw that the brooding Jeff merely waited for an answer.

Lindsay waited, too, taking another bite of her sandwich.

"They say that people die at the sites you visit." He stared at her with unblinking eyes.

"Was this at night around a campfire?" Lindsay shook her head. "Two sites I worked on were associated with crimes, and I was not the only archaeologist who worked at both sites. I suppose they associate me with them because I was involved in the solutions. I've worked on lots of sites where no one died—at least not in several hundred years."

"I see. You were just unlucky."

"Or the victims were, depending how you look at it." Lindsay watched one of the crew spread a beach towel on the sand and stretch out in the sun. The scent of suntan oil drifted her way.

She turned back to Jeff. He had finished his pear and was throwing the core into the ocean.

"I need to talk to Trey. Thanks for picking up my lunch." She walked off toward one of the trailers before he had a chance to say anything else. "Angel of Death, indeed," she muttered.

Trey stepped out the trailer door, followed by a woman in crisply pressed khaki shorts and a white tank top. She walked easily beside him with her hands in her pockets, laughing, as if sharing a joke. Trey caught sight of Lindsay and waved a notebook at her.

"Here's your copy of the journal," said Trey. "And this is the translator, Harper Latham."

Harper stuck out her hand and Lindsay took it. "I'm glad to meet you. This the same journal you told me about—the one by the passenger on the *Estrella*?"

Trey nodded. "Harper is absolutely the world's greatest translator." He touched the journal with his forefinger. Harper laughed and raised her eyebrows at Lindsay as if Trey had told a joke.

"The passenger wrote in his own archaic Spanish and Latin shorthand. I'm having to decode the thing as well as translate it," Harper said in a cheery voice.

"That must be very difficult," Lindsay said. "You certainly have my admiration."

"It's the most challenging thing I've done, and I love it."

"It's slow," Trey added. "But we're hoping that between this, our other documentation, and what we find here, we can positively identify this as the *Estrella*."

"You don't know that yet?"

"We're pretty sure, because of the ship's manifest and from documentation we found in the Spanish archives. But this journal is a rare find and will add a lot to this project. It details the life of the crew on board ship. Other than the Salazar letter and the Diego journal, there's almost nothing like it. And to be able to attach it to a ship under excavation is nothing short of amazing."

"The journal was almost lost forever," Harper said. "I don't know if you've heard how it was discovered."

"No, I haven't," Lindsay said.

"A UGA alum inherited an estate in St. Augustine, Florida. She was doing some renovation and found trunks full of really old stuff walled up in the attic. She had no way of knowing what any of it was, so she shipped it to a UGA librarian friend to look through it. The librarian happened to be an archivist with some knowledge of Spanish documents. She couldn't believe her eyes when she came upon it. If that archivist hadn't recognized what it was, it probably would have ended up in a trash heap or a garage sale."

Trey shook his head. "It's amazing how often fate plays a part in science. Francisco Lewis wants to put excerpts from the diary in the newspaper, like a serial. I think it might be a good idea. Public support is a good thing."

"Trey said you just arrived today," Harper said to Lindsay. "What do you think of his little operation here in the middle of the ocean? Pretty spectacular, huh?"

"It's like the eighth wonder of the world. I was just looking at the ocean all around the dam."

"Yeah, great, isn't it?" Trey obviously wasn't suffering any of the feelings of anxiety and vulnerability that the dam was producing in Lindsay. He was definitely in his element.

"If you can think about it without being scared, it's quite wonderful to be able to walk on the bottom of the ocean," Lindsay agreed.

Trey motioned Lindsay to one of the tables and chairs not far from the outer bulkhead and the three of them sat down. It was like an outdoor café with an ocean view. Several of the crew were sitting, eating their lunches. One person had binoculars, looking out at the ships at sea. Lindsay guessed they'd have to eat somewhere else on windy days. She could imagine the waves coming up over the walls nine feet above the ocean. Even on this pleasant day, she felt an occasional spray from the waves splashing against the bulkhead wall.

"Scared?" Trey gave her forearm a reassuring grip. "Oh, it's safe here. West and his crew maintain a constant presence." Lindsay looked over to the West Construction barge not far away. John and some of his crew were having lunch. She waved but she didn't think he saw her.

"I've hired meteorologists just for this project. They watch the weather minute by minute. Lewis got us enough money to do this right. Speaking of which, he'll be here in the next few days to do a little trowel work himself. I think he's bringing a television crew."

Lindsay laughed out loud. "He's such a show."

"Don't laugh too hard. Publicity gets us money."

"And pothunters, too, I'll bet."

"Some, but it also educates the public on what we're doing and why it's important."

"John mentioned Eva Jones," Lindsay said, pulling a Hostess Twinkie from her bag.

"Yeah, she has a yacht out there somewhere. There're rumors flying around about the *Estrella* being a Spanish treasure ship. I hear she's got her crew searching the ocean bottom. I've tried to put the word out that the *Estrella* was heading from Spain, and wouldn't have treasure, only supplies for the mission colonies. But you know, the *Atocha* was found just down the coast of Florida, and Blackbeard's *Queen Anne's Revenge* was found a little ways from here off the coast of North Carolina. When word got out that we had found a Spanish galleon, I guess gold fever kind of took over." He squinted at the horizon. "I think that may be her out there." He pointed at a tiny sailing ship on the horizon.

Harper and Lindsay shaded their eyes, looking toward the ship.

"Fancy boat," said Harper. "Who is this chick?"

"Depends on who you ask," answered Trey. "Some call her a looter, others a collector, and some call her names I won't mention."

"She sounds intriguing." Harper stood. "I guess I'd better get back to my translating." Trey started to stand up and Harper put a hand on his shoulder. "I'll find my way down to the dock. See you this evening. Nice to have met you, Lindsay. Come by my apartment sometime and visit." She winked at Trey and made her way to the ladder.

"Isn't she great?" Trey said, watching her go.

"We look a little smitten," Lindsay teased.

Trey's cheeks turned a little darker under his tan as he smiled and nodded to Lindsay. "Maybe."

"She does seem like a delightful person and a very talented translator."

"She's both of those." Trey spread his own lunch on the table and unwrapped his sandwich. "Harper is—well, I've never met anyone like her."

Lindsay watched Trey and smiled inwardly. Yeah, she thought, he's smitten. "Did I understand you two are going out this evening? Is there a place on the island? I thought it was only a research facility."

"We'll take my boat and go up the coast to a restaurant on St. Simons or Sea Island."

"Where does the crew eat, by the way?" Lindsay looked around as if perhaps there were a restaurant on the dam she had missed.

"We have a cook on the barge, and there's a café on St. Magdalena that's not bad. It's actually a break room, but it's kept stocked with soup and sandwiches. Occasionally, some of the crew take a boat and go to one of the restaurants along the coast. You're welcome to come with us," he said. "It's your first night and—"

Lindsay shook her head and laughed. "I think Harper would be a little disappointed. I'd like to poke around the island a bit." She gestured toward the sailing ship. "Jones must have some credible evidence of treasure. I can't imagine her spending money chasing a wild rumor."

Trey finished his sandwich and took a Twinkie out of the bag. "For one thing, she's being egged on by Hardy Denton. Denton would like to cause us trouble."

"Why?"

"He wanted this contract."

"Surely he's lost bids before." Lindsay finished everything but the pear. She held it in her hand, wondering whether to finish it now or save it for later.

"I'm sure he has, but he's a little bigoted, for one thing." Trey lowered his voice and Lindsay had to lean forward to hear him over the wind and waves. "Another thing, his was the lowest bid, and I'm sure he suspects it. But his was too low. He couldn't have met all the safety precautions with the numbers he had in his proposal, and his design was inferior. West Construction was actually the middle bid of the three. The third was a company called King-Smith-Falcon from Florida. They're the oldest maritime construction company in North America, and one of the biggest. Good proposal, but too high. John's was the best. He has a lot of good ideas."

Lindsay wasn't surprised. She had had a brief look at the proposals, but not the budgets that went along with them. She bit into the pear and some of the juice ran down her arm. "So you think this Denton fellow is just using Jones to aggravate us? That seems like a waste of time he could spend somewhere else making money."

Trey threw up his hands. "I know it sounds improbable and a little paranoid, but unless something has leaked—"

"Leaked?"

Again Trey lowered his voice to almost a whisper. "This is to be kept absolutely secret. The Spanish archives spoke of another ship, one of the silver galleons going back to Spain that sunk a year before the *Estrella*. It shouldn't have been this far up the coast, but—"

He was cut off by loud voices and clanging coming up the ladder from the dock on the ocean side of the dam.

"That son of a bitch. Jesus—"

Two divers, a male and a female, climbed onto the sand from the boat dock. The man held a hand to his upper arm as the woman helped him. Lindsay could see blood seeping from between his fingers and running down his arm.

Chapter 3

"Sit down, Nate, and let me look at your arm." The female diver looked around for a chair. Steven hurried over with one from his table.

"That sorry bastard—"

"Sit down and shut up." Nate's companion pushed him down in the chair.

Trey raced to the trailer and came out with a first-aid kit.

"How bad is he hurt, Sarah?" Trey asked.

"It's not that bad," Nate answered. "The water's making it bleed."

"Where's the nurse?" Trey demanded.

"She's seasick today," Gina told him.

Lindsay knelt by the bleeding diver. "I'm certified by the American Red Cross in emergency first aid—" She slipped on a pair of latex gloves from the first-aid kit.

Gina, Jeff, and others who were topside stood back watching. Jeff's narrow-eyed glare in her direction suggested to Lindsay that he blamed her.

Bobbie Lacayo, one of Lindsay's students, came up the ladder. Her swimsuit and yellow windbreaker told Lindsay she had been with the diving party. The grim set of her mouth broke into a smile when she saw Lindsay.

"You all right?" Lindsay asked her.

Bobbie nodded. "A little scared. Good to see you, Dr. Chamberlain."

"What happened, Nate?" asked Trey.

"One of those sorry treasure hunters shot me with a harpoon gun. Can you believe it?"

"What?" asked Trey. "On purpose?"

"Do I look like a fish?"

"Steven, call the Coast Guard," Trey ordered.

Lindsay gently pulled Nate's hand away and looked at the wound. There was an open gash in his flesh two inches long and a half inch deep. The edges were clean and straight. Lindsay put a dry square of clean gauze over it and held it tight. The blood soaked through, and she put another one over it.

"When this stops bleeding, someone needs to take you into town—wherever that is—and get it stitched up."

"You can't do it?" Lindsay looked up to see Nate half smiling at her. Wet ringlets of brown hair hung in his face.

"My doctor's degree will only let me do this much," she said, and he laughed.

Steven Nemo came out of the trailer and trotted over to them. "Guard's on its way."

"Sarah," Nate said, "dig in my pouch and get that thing I found for Nemo."

Sarah Donovan fished an object from the pouch around Nate's waist and handed it to him.

"Here, Nemo, it's a nautilus. I figure you lost it. Sorry about the blood."

Steven took the spiraled shell and rolled his eyes, the others laughed. Nate laughed the hardest, then started coughing.

"Are you all right?" Sarah asked.

Nate waved her away. "I'm fine. Just mad as hell."

"How fast did you come up?" asked Trey.

Nate waved his question away. "We weren't down deep or long. I'm all right."

Trey looked at Sarah and Bobbie for confirmation and they nodded. He turned to Steven. "You take Nate to the hospital." Sarah opened her mouth to protest. "You and Bobbie have to stay here and talk to the Coast Guard," he said.

The bleeding had stopped, and Lindsay wrapped Nate's arm with a gauze bandage. "Apply pressure if it starts up again."

"Sure thing, Doc. Thanks." Nate winked at her as he disappeared behind the bulkhead, following Steven down the ladder to the dock.

Trey turned to Sarah and Bobbie. "Okay, what happened?"

Lindsay didn't stay to hear. She stripped off the gloves and went to the trailer in search of a place to wash telltale spatters of

Nate's blood off her hands and arms. At the door, she looked at her hands, grimaced, and turned to ask someone to open it. Jeff stood a few feet away eyeing her.

Great, she thought. I must look like Lady Macbeth to this nut. "Would you open the door for me?" Jeff hesitated a moment then came to her aid. "Thanks," she said and stepped into the trailer.

The 25-by-12-foot trailer was cool, which surprised Lindsay. Principal investigators are not known for their attention to comfort. Then she realized it probably held sensitive equipment. Two old stuffed maroon couches sat along the walls in the living room. Several chairs, from brand-new to almost dilapidated, were arranged more or less around a large table covered with a giant map of the site. Other maps papered the walls. It looked like a war room. The stove in the kitchenette off the living room had been removed to make room for an extra refrigerator.

The blood was drying on Lindsay's hands and getting sticky. She walked down the narrow hallway and found the bathroom. It was the typical small trailer bathroom with a sliding door, small bathtub, toilet, and sink. She washed her hands and watched Nate's blood go down the drain in a pink froth of soapy water. Lindsay wondered briefly where the water drained to—not into the ocean, surely. For that matter, where did the water come from? She turned off the tap quickly. It obviously had to be boated in and put in a tank—probably the one behind the trailer.

Lindsay dried her hands on a paper towel and peeped inside the bedroom next to the bathroom. There was no bed. Instead, an old desk sat under an uncurtained window. A laptop computer, printer, and stacks of books and papers littered the surface. By the other wall stood a copy machine.

Maps of the ocean floor made from the various magnetometer surveys decorated the walls. Different colored points of ink marked the spots for anomalies on the ocean floor. On one map, the cofferdam site was outlined with a black marker with small x's pinpointing places where other artifacts presumably belonging to the Estrella de España had been found. She looked at the labels to see what some of the finds were. Two cannons had been discovered ten and fifteen miles away, an anchor a mile from the site.

On the far side of the room, stretching across the width of the trailer, a closet with no doors was filled neatly with well-used diving gear. It contrasted with the shiny new tanks that Lindsay had brought with her. For the better part of a year she had taken diving lessons in preparation for this dig, after Trey had invited her to be a member of the archaeology crew. Her lips turned up in a smile as she thought about his excitement in telling her about the find, and his further elation at discovering that the new division head, Francisco Lewis, was willing to raise the money to build a cofferdam, rather than having divers dig blindly in the murky waters. Lindsay turned and left, reminding herself as she stepped outside and heard the waves breaking on the bulkheads that this was a grand adventure.

From the ocean side of the dam came the deep bass sounds of a marine engine, and she turned to see a white boat displaying the emblem of the U.S. Coast Guard pulling up to the dock. Trey met a Coast Guard officer at the ladder and led him to Sarah and Bobbie, who were sitting restlessly at the table. Lindsay was about to climb back down to the excavation with the rest of the crew when Trey stopped her.

"I'd like you to stay. You've had some experience dealing with authorities, and I understand a lot of them know you."

"Sure," said Lindsay. Angel of Death, at your service, she thought. She followed him to the table and pulled up one of the chairs. Trey introduced her to the officer in charge, a Lieutenant Damon.

"We were about twenty-five miles out from shore—near an artificial reef," Sarah was telling him. "Nate and I were surveying some of the magnetometer anomalies, looking for artifacts. It's hard to survey around the artificial reefs because of the many recently sunk ships and tanks that make up those reefs. We were working slowly and carefully because we knew that the newer objects on top could be masking older artifacts underneath. Archaeologists have been known to pass over ancient wrecks for years by thinking the anomalies they knew about were from a more recent ship known to be there."

"Exactly what happened next?" Lieutenant Damon clearly wasn't interested in their methodology.

Sarah frowned, took a sip of water and ran her fingers through the tangles of her half-dry curly red hair. "The water's not real clear," she said. "You can't see far. They just appeared. Two of them. We thought they were fishing at first, but—" She hesitated. "I don't know. There was something about them. Some kind of purpose or aggressiveness as they came toward us. We motioned to them, and they motioned back, warning us away. When we didn't move, one of them shot at us. God, I was terrified. I've never been shot at before."

"Why did they do it?" asked Lieutenant Damon.

"Why? I don't know why. Ask them." Sarah still had a smudge of blood on her freckled arm. She started to cry when she looked down and saw it.

"Did they think they were being threatened?" Lieutenant Damon handed her a handkerchief.

"With what? Our Marshalltowns? We're archaeologists."

The lieutenant looked up at Trey, a question on his face.

"Trowels," Trey explained. "The trowels that we use for excavation are made by a company called Marshalltown."

"You don't carry weapons for sharks?" Damon asked.

"No. It was a short dive. They aren't usually a problem. They aren't as aggressive as people think."

Lieutenant Damon raised his eyebrows. "But you carry a diving knife, don't you?"

"Yes, a small one, for diving. We didn't threaten anyone. We were doing our survey, and these guys came at us. Nate was hurt."

"I'm just trying to get a clear picture. Who do you think shot at you?"

"Nate thinks it was the pirates."

"The pirates?"

"Pothunters . . . looters. You know," said Bobbie, "those vultures out there looking for treasure."

"But you don't know for sure? Did you recognize either one of them?" Sarah shook her head. "Did Nate?"

"I don't know, really. He thought they were the treasure hunters. Their boat was out there."

"Did you see the attackers?" the lieutenant asked Bobbie.

"I was topside with the boat. I didn't know anything was wrong until Nate and Sarah surfaced."

"How close was the other boat you mentioned?"

"The *Painted Lady* was less than a quarter of a mile away, I guess," Bobbie answered.

"But you don't know if they came from the *Painted Lady*? Was that the only boat near you?"

Bobbie shook her head and several strands of her long black

Delafield Public Library
Delafield, WI 53018

hair came loose from her casual French twist. She pushed the strands behind her ear. "No, there were some fishing boats farther away. But who else would do this? Not the fishermen, for heaven's sake. For what reason?"

"Does Nate have any enemies?" he asked Sarah. "Or do you?"

Sarah scowled at him. "You mean who would come gunning for us in the ocean? No."

"Can you give me a description of what they looked like?"

"I think one had blond hair. The other one a darker color. Both were about as big as Nate and muscular. They wore black vests and trunks. I didn't see the brand of diving equipment."

"You are sure they weren't people you met someplace else?"

"No. I told you. I don't know who they were."

The lieutenant turned his attention to Trey. "Have you had any other trouble?"

Trey shook his head. "Not at this site. West Construction, who built and maintains the cofferdam, has a twenty-four-hour security team guarding the place. They have their own divers."

"Could it have been one of them, thinking you were looters?" Damon asked.

"No—" answered Sarah. "No. This was miles away from the dam. West isn't guarding the whole ocean. Besides, the West divers wear distinctive yellow vests."

Lindsay could see Sarah was having trouble keeping her temper. The questions Lieutenant Damon asked could not be called hostile, but they did seem to Lindsay to be unnecessarily suspicious. She was accustomed to local authorities being suspicious of archaeology crews, but she would have thought that with a project of this size and cost, they would be more solicitous.

"We have a very professional security team," Trey added. "They wouldn't shoot at anyone in that way."

"We'd like to talk to them," said Lieutenant Damon, ". . . and Nate when he gets back."

"Sure," said Trey. He took his phone from his pocket, called West Construction, and left word for the members of the security team to join them.

"You said 'Not at this site.' You've had trouble elsewhere?" the lieutenant asked Trey.

"We're not sure. Carolyn Taylor, our conservation supervisor, believes that someone has come in the lab on the island at night on more than one occasion. We don't know for sure. Nothing is missing, and we hired a security guard from the mainland just for the lab."

Lieutenant Damon wrote in his notebook.

"Have there been any other incidents or complaints from fishermen or divers?" Lindsay asked the lieutenant.

"Nothing unusual."

"What's usual?" she asked.

"People who go sailing and don't know how, complaints about unruly boaters. That kind of thing. The waters are usually safe. But complaints have gone up. The smell of gold brings out the worst in people."

That explains it, thought Lindsay. She smiled sympathetically at Lieutenant Damon. This dig had made more work for the Coast Guard. They were probably having to deal with drunken weekenders with gold fever. That's what she told Trey when the lieutenant left after he had interviewed John West.

"A lot of jerks come out of the woodwork at the mention of the word *treasure*," Lindsay told Trey. "I think that's probably what this was—guys just acting inappropriately territorial. And you may have to face the possibility that the rumor is out about the silver galleon."

"You think so? I hope not. We don't need that complication." Trey ran his hand over his short-cropped hair. "That rumor can't be allowed to get out. This would become a madhouse."

Lindsay lowered her voice. "About how much treasure are we talking about?"

Trey looked around them before he answered. "Several hundred million dollars, perhaps as much as a billion. This was a 1,600-ton, overloaded galleon."

Lindsay was speechless. The old saying that two can keep a secret if one is dead popped into her head. "How many people know about this?"

"Me, and now you, Francisco Lewis, and Frank Carter, of course. That's all."

That was six people, thought Lindsay. "Who discovered the information?"

"It was in the Spanish archives. Nate and I came across it when we were researching the *Estrella*."

"And who did the translations?" asked Lindsay.

"Frank Carter. He went with us. He's pretty good at ancient Spanish and archival research. Harper will do the final translations for the reports," he added.

Frank Carter, current chairman of the Archaeology Department at UGA, was a good friend of Lindsay's. She trusted him. "Frank can keep a secret. Does anyone else know?"

"Possibly one of the archivists we were working with."

"And you swore this person to secrecy?"

"He understood the need for secrecy."

Lindsay shook her head.

"What?" Trey asked.

"It's not a secret, you can forget that."

"What do you mean?"

"Okay. Lewis knows. He raised the money for the site. You can bet he told selected people."

"I think you're being a little unfair to him. I know you don't like—"

"That's not it. He's a political animal. They trade in secrets. You can bet the president of UGA knows, and the governor. If the governor knows, then probably one of his aides knows also. If an aide knows, then the person the aide sleeps with will know."

"I think you are being a little paranoid, don't you agree?"

"I'm just telling you how hard it is to keep a secret. And those are just the possibilities from Lewis."

"Okay, you're right." He rubbed his eyes with the heels of his hands. "Do you think those were treasure hunters who shot Nate?"

"Could have been anything. Maybe Nate and Sarah got too near someone's drug stash. I imagine that's what Lieutenant Damon really thinks. Even though he didn't mention it, stopping drug smuggling is a big part of what the Coast Guard does. They'll probably have divers looking around the artificial reefs now. Besides, I think a professional looter like Evangeline Jones would be more subtle."

"You're probably right again," sighed Trey. "Nate wants me to hire some more security guards for the island. Maybe I should. John protects the dam, but the island has only one guard." Trey wrinkled his brow, scanning the horizon as if trying to tell which of the myriad boats out there contained individuals who knew about the silver galleon.

Chapter 4

LINDSAY GRIPPED THE handrail of the creaking scaffold stairway on her return to the ocean floor. The others were already back at their tasks, working silently, their usual patter quelled by the sight of blood, no doubt. Two guys were hooking lines to one of the *Estrella*'s timbers to be lifted to the top of the dam. She stopped to store her field notebook in the desk at the bottom of the stairway. She opened the bottom drawer and saw that it contained a couple of spray bottles of asthma medication, a pair of gloves, and some papers. She found an empty drawer, stored away her things, and made her way among muted sounds of digging and scraping along the planks to her excavation unit, where the unfortunate sixteenth-century sailor grinned up at her.

She gently teased the mud away from the side of the skull. The sail, or whatever cloth covered part of his face, had rotted away. The long face and prominent browridge and jawline were characteristic of a male skull. She traced her finger along his teeth as she would the keys of a piano. They were all there, including his wisdom teeth. She wondered what he did on the ship. Would his job show in his bones? Would he be mentioned in the journal?

"I heard you found the first human skeleton." Lindsay looked up to see denim cutoffs over a black bathing suit. It was Bobbie Lacayo, smiling down at her, trowel in hand. "Can I help?"

"Sure. See the sustentaculum tali sticking up through the mud? Start there."

"Dr. Chamberlain, I haven't had your osteology class."

Lindsay smiled. "You can call me Lindsay if you like." She reached over with her trowel and pointed to a portion of bone protruding through the mud. "That's part of the calcaneus—the heel bone, which is the largest bone of the tarsus—the bones of the foot.

There's fabric covering this guy, so take care. Have you ever excavated fabric?"

"In the first unit we uncovered some sailcloth and a coil of rope."

"Great."

"Have you heard from Nate and Steven?" Gina asked, rising from her prone position and stretching.

Bobbie shook her head.

"The cut wasn't too bad," Lindsay replied. "I imagine he'll only need a tetanus and a few stitches."

"Makes me scared to go diving," Gina continued.

"I imagine the Coast Guard presence will scare off whoever it was."

"You dive, Lindsay?" asked Gina.

"I don't have much experience, but I've been looking forward to going on a survey with the divers."

"Wouldn't it be neat," Juliana said to no one in particular, "if the walls of the dam were glass and we could see the ocean?"

"It would if the water were clear," said Bobbie.

"You people are crazy," Jeff complained. "That wouldn't be neat, as you put it, at all. Have you ever heard the term 'storm surge'? You get twenty-foot waves out there and this hole will fill up like a fishbowl, only we'll be the fish."

"Jeff," said Juliana, "if this bothers you so much, why don't you work on the barge or, better yet, back at the lab with the artifacts?"

"Yeah, you'd like that, wouldn't you, so you could get all the glory."

Juliana looked down at her mud-covered body, ragged denim shorts, and halter top. "Glory? What glory?"

Lindsay watched Jeff go back to work, jabbing with his trowel around a piece of timber. He stood abruptly. "That's all there is in this hole, this damn heavy timber." He threw down his trowel and made his way to the stairway, stopping at the field desk to take something out of the drawer, then climbed to the top of the dam.

"He's really having a hard time down here," said Gina, staring after him. "I really think Trey should put him in the lab."

"He could at least have taken some of these buckets of fill to be hoisted over to the barge," Juliana grumbled.

"Why did he agree to work here?" Lindsay asked. Now that Jeff was gone, only Bobbie, Gina, and Juliana were near her section at the bow of the ship.

"He's a marine archaeologist, and this is the biggest find in this whole area," said Gina.

"But he really specializes in classical archaeology, and you know how squirrelly those guys are," Juliana added.

"I can see how being down inside these walls could get to some people," Lindsay said. "I had some apprehension before I got here, but now I don't think it's so bad down here on the bottom of the sea. I could get used to it."

"Did the Coast Guard say anything?" Gina was unwilling to let the diving incident go. She squatted down by Lindsay.

"No, but like I said, they'll probably keep a closer watch in the area. I don't think we'll have any more incidents like that one." Lindsay began working on the skeleton's right shoulder, which was overlaid with fabric. This was going to be slow work.

"Okay, Chamberlain," said Juliana. "Exactly what is this Angel of Death thing Jeff keeps muttering about?"

Bobbie looked at Lindsay and laughed. Lindsay sat up and looked from one face to the other, tempted to say that she sleepwalked and killed people in the dead of night. But both Gina and Juliana were grinning from ear to ear and her sudden irritation vanished. "I seem to attract dead people," she said after a moment's hesitation.

"Damn!" said Juliana. "We have something in common. That's the kind of dates I attract."

"Speaking of dates, is the West guy married?" Gina asked.

"No," said Lindsay.

"Girlfriend?"

"I don't know that."

"How about you, Bobbie? You from his tribe?"

Bobbie shook her head. "Nope. Never knew him before I came here."

"You ever date him?" Gina asked Lindsay.

Lindsay shook her head. "No, I'm afraid I'm not his type. We met when he protested a dig I was working on. He has strong feelings about having his ancestors excavated."

"Hmm, I guess I could tell him I work only on historical sites," said Gina. "Of course, I need to find some better duds. It's hard to attract guys when you're covered with mud."

"How about the guys working for him?" asked Juliana.

"I suppose I could ask and make a list," Lindsay offered, turning back to her skeleton.

"That'd be great."

Lindsay looked over her shoulder at Juliana, who was still grinning at her.

They returned to their tedious work with concentration. The unusual sounds of this dig—the groaning of the dam and the splashing of the waves—drifted to the background and merged with the familiar sounds of excavation—the clicking and scraping of the trowels, the voices, the footfalls. Lindsay found it best not to think about the trillion gallons of ocean a few feet away on all sides of her.

"I think I've found a shoe," said Gina.

Lindsay rose to take a look over Gina's shoulder at the emerging outline. "It looks like both the upper and the sole are intact," Lindsay observed.

"The cellular structure of the leather will be shot to hell," said Gina. "It's the water and muck that keep the shape."

Gina was quick and clean with her excavation. She motioned for Trey to come over and take a reading of its placement in the ship. That shoe had survived for almost four hundred and forty years in the anaerobic environment of the ocean mud. Now that it was exposed to the air, it would deteriorate quickly. Once artifacts were uncovered, it was important to get them out of the ground and into an environment where they could be stabilized.

Lindsay moved back to her excavation unit to allow the photographers and the mappers freer access to Gina's find. For her part, she needed to get the skeleton out of the ground as quickly as she could. Everything about this dig was urgent—especially with the feel of the ocean around them. Summer was the best season to do the excavation, but it was also hurricane season. Like a bad tune you can't keep out of your mind, Jeff's mention of the term "storm surge" kept creeping into Lindsay's thoughts. What would happen if . . .

"Who's that?" asked Bobbie.

They all looked up to see John West escorting a woman with long blonde hair down the scaffolding stairs. The first thing Lindsay thought was that the woman was going to get her white silk blouse and beige linen slacks dirty.

"Well, damn," whispered Trey. "I believe it's Evangeline Jones."

Chapter 5

ALL HEADS JERKED up as Trey stepped across the planking toward the visitor. She stuck her hand out to him and introduced herself as Eva Jones. John West stood beside her with his arms folded. He caught Lindsay's gaze and winked at her.

"I'll get to the point," Eva Jones said, loud enough for all to hear. "It was none of my crew who shot your guy today, and I don't know who it was. It was stupid, and I don't hire stupid people."

"I'm glad to hear it," Trey replied. "My crew said the *Painted Lady* was not more than a quarter-mile from where my divers were surveying."

"It was. I'm doing my own looking. It's a big ocean, Marcus. Big enough for all of us. I don't need the kind of trouble that shooting divers would bring me. I can account for the whereabouts of all my divers. They were nowhere near yours."

"How do you know where mine were?" asked Trey.

Eva Jones smiled. "I don't. But my divers were alone. I keep track of them." She looked around at the site. "So, we're on the ocean floor. Damn, I'm impressed." She turned to go, then abruptly turned back to Trey. "I'll keep my people away from yours, and I assume you'll do the same. I don't want trouble."

"We are conducting an archaeological survey in Georgia waters," Trey said. "My divers will go where the artifacts lead them. I'm assuming you're looking for the recreation of it and don't intend to loot any of Georgia's historical resources."

Lindsay watched a smile play around Eva Jones's lips, but it never made it to her dark eyes. "I'm really weary of arguing with you archaeologists who think that everything that is ever lost in this world has to either stay where it fell or wait for you to pick it up. I operate within the law. That's all you need to know." She turned and left. John followed her out. They all watched her until she was out of sight over the dam walls.

"Well, what do you make of that?" asked Lindsay.

"The Coast Guard paid her a visit and she didn't like it," Trey said.

"What's she looking for out there?" asked Juliana.

Trey seemed deep in thought as he shook his head in reply.

⚓

The day ended for Lindsay and the crew at three o'clock. Discounting the hour she had for lunch, with only brief breaks, she had been lying on the narrow plank for eight hours. She stood and stretched her tired muscles. Bobbie stood beside her and yawned, covering her mouth with a clean spot on her forearm. Lindsay wanted to rub her eyes, but she had removed her gloves for the intricate parts of the excavation and her hands were covered with dark gray sandy muck. Instead, she closed her eyes tight, then opened them to see people coming down the scaffolding like an invading force. They were the night crew. They arrived early to be shown by the day crew what had to be done during the next shift.

Lindsay was loath to give up her skeleton to someone else, but she understood the need to excavate the site as quickly as possible. Her replacements were a couple of Trey's new graduate students whom she had seen around the department. She showed them how to proceed from where she and Bobbie had left off. One of the guys was a little defensive about being told how to do his job. The other was happy to be working on such an interesting find. Lindsay wondered how well they would work together. Satisfied that they knew what to do, she and Bobbie left them to it. Lindsay retrieved her notebook from the field desk and climbed the stairway to the top of the cofferdam.

"You'll be rooming with me. I hope you don't mind," said Bobbie.

"No. That'll be nice. We have a cabin on one of the barges, is that right?"

"Yes. I hope you don't get seasick. If you do, they can find a place for you in the lab on the island. A few of the crew stay there."

"I think I'll adjust." Lindsay stood in the sand at the top of the dam with Bobbie and the rest of the crew and looked down into the pit where the night crew continued the excavation. She could see little difference from when she had started that morning. Disentombing the *Estrella de España* would be a long and slow process.

The dock of the cofferdam had a gangplank leading to the barge *Winchester*. The barge wafted gently in the water, and Lindsay stood for a moment after coming aboard, adjusting to the movement, getting her sea legs. The barge had a large deck in comparison to its cabin area. Perfect for the kind of work they were putting it to.

She followed Bobbie past rows of the *Estrella's* timbers covered with sea-soaked blankets, past the screens used to separate artifacts from sand and mud, to a place where some of the crew were gathered rinsing their hands with a hose. Lindsay cleaned the mud from her hands, frowning at the grit under her nails.

Their boots were loud on the metal floor and the sounds of their footsteps echoed off the metal walls as Bobbie led her down a hatchway into a barely lit narrow hallway.

"We have the third room on the right."

Lindsay had to duck her head going into the small, sparse room, furnished only with two twin-size beds, a desk, a sink, and a single closet.

"I have the far bed, if that's all right?" asked Bobbie.

"Sure." Lindsay's bags had been put on the remaining stripped bed. She slid them under the bed and opened the single small closet. Her scuba gear was neatly stored beside Bobbie's. "So this is home."

Bobbie grinned. "You'll get used to it. You brought sheets and stuff, I hope."

"Yes, everything on Trey's list. Where's the—"

"Turn left out the door, to the end of the hall, and hang a right. It's the first door on the left. About half of us have to use it, so showers are quick."

"I imagine this time of day there's a line at the shower."

"Yep. If you have to go, the toilet has its own little closet."

Lindsay heard the barge's engine come to life and cover the noise of the ocean with a humming-puffing-tapping sound that settled into a rhythm. Gears ground as the capstan pulled up the anchors, and she felt the barge lurch gently as it moved away from the dock.

"Every day we take the timber and other artifacts to the lab on St. Magdalena. There's a big fabricated-metal warehouse with brine holding tanks for the timber. We have the end-of-the-day meeting in the lab from four till five, then we're through for the evening." Bobbie fished a towel and washcloth from her side of the closet and headed for the door. "We're sharing lab space on St. Maggie with the biologists. Don't expect them to be friendly. This is a research preserve, and Lewis came in with big bucks and kind of took over a lot of their space."

Lindsay lucked out. She was third in line to get a shower just behind Bobbie. The stall was small and plain, but it had running water. Lindsay knew how to take quick showers. Inside of seven minutes she was back in her cabin, clean and refreshed.

"Chamberlain, phone call." The voice was just outside the door.

"The phone's in the hall." Bobbie opened the door and pointed Lindsay to a recess a few feet from their door.

"Rabbit, this is John."

He hadn't needed to tell her who he was. John West was the only person in the world who called her Rabbit.

"You settled in?"

"Yes, the accommodations are quite nice, compared to many sites I've worked at."

"Why don't I take you to dinner? It's your first night. We can go up the intracoastal waterway to a seafood place I know near Fernandina."

"I'd like that. What should I wear?" There was silence for a long moment. John was evidently not prepared for a fashion consultation. Lindsay smiled into the phone. "Will slacks and a blouse be all right?"

"Fine. I'll meet you at St. Magdalena."

Bobbie's white halter top and khaki shorts contrasted well with her brown skin and black hair. She had pulled her still-damp hair up into a ponytail and was slipping her feet into a pair of brown sandals when Lindsay returned.

"So, going out to dinner with West?" Bobbie grinned. "Gina and Juliana are going to be envious."

"Well, it ought to be interesting. He really hates my work."

"Gives you something good to talk about."

"What are you doing this evening?"

"A group of us are going to eat on the barge and hang out with

Sarah. She's really spooked about what happened. And that guy from the Coast Guard didn't help, either."

"I imagine you're kind of spooked, too. Don't be too upset over the Coast Guard. Everything's probably old hat to them and they forget to be sensitive."

"He acted like we did it."

"I don't think he really thought that. This excavation has given him more work to deal with and he doesn't like it—"

"That's funny about the Jones woman showing up, isn't it?" Bobbie checked herself out in the mirror over the sink.

"I was kind of surprised." Lindsay put on an aquamarine cotton short-sleeved blouse and a pair of white slacks. "Is this all right for the restaurants along the coast? John wasn't able to help."

"Sure, that's fine. You look great."

"I think she was scoping out the place." Lindsay ran a brush through her long hair and pulled it up into a ponytail.

"For what? A raid?"

"Just to see what we're up to, to see maybe if we've found anything valuable. Or, to let us know that, if it was her men, it won't happen again."

Lindsay slipped on a pair of white leather sandals, grabbed a light sweater, and went up top with Bobbie. The barge was almost to the island. St. Magdalena was only five miles from the dam and, even though the barge moved very slowly, it took less than thirty minutes to reach the dock. Some of the crew were preparing to offload the timber to be taken to the brine tanks. Lindsay followed Bobbie down a wooden walkway toward the main building.

The Magdalena House was a large dark cedar three-story structure that fit into the flora of the island as if it had grown there. The first floor, largely concealed by the wraparound deck above it, sat on top of the ground. It was covered with stone and had only a small closed window and one door that Lindsay could see. The second story, the one they were about to enter, had large double doors and glass picture windows on at least two sides. The top-floor windows were regular size with closed rattan blinds. A satellite dish sat on the roof, pointing at some spot in the sky.

Beside the walkway, separated from them only by height and railing, was an alligator pond. Lindsay searched the surface of the pond and spotted the brow ridge, head, and back of an alligator, so still in the water it could have been a log.

"Guard dog?" Lindsay asked.

"Spooky, huh? Can't you almost hear the clock in his stomach ticking?"

Lindsay and Bobbie walked up the wooden ramp to the deck and entered a reception area decorated with racks of brochures, hanging plants, and prints of local flora and fauna. There was no receptionist. Lindsay suspected that Lewis had stopped most of the tours of the island until the excavation was finished. There weren't many anyway. This was one of the islands used as an experimental habitat for breeding colonies of several rare species of animals.

"The conservation lab is on the ground floor," said Bobbie. "There're some offices up here and a few apartments upstairs. The translator stays up there. You've met Harper, haven't you? I think Trey has a thing for her."

A woman rounded the corner and almost ran into them. "Oh, someone else," she said, looking at Lindsay. "I hope you don't intend to stay here. It's getting rather crowded."

"Tessa." Bobbie smiled. "Nice of you to greet us. This is Dr. Chamberlain. She's staying on the barge."

"Good. I think I should tell you that a group of us are signing a petition to get you all moved off the island. You can't just come here and take everything away from us. Our work is important—more important than yours." She paused, frustration clear on her angry face. "We were here first."

Bobbie cocked an eyebrow. "I'll tell you right now, that argument won't work. Look, this isn't going to be forever."

"Oh, you haven't heard?" She brandished a letter in their faces. "Lewis is planning to build a museum on the island. Listen, the environment won't be able to recover from the number of tourists that will be required to make such an enterprise pay off." Tessa's face had turned red, and Lindsay could see she was having to strain to hold back tears. "We have always worked well with you archaeologists. How could you do this to us—to the island? There aren't many untouched islands left."

"A museum?" asked Lindsay.

"Yes, and he wants to make the island a theme park." Tessa almost sobbed.

"I really doubt that. Whatever you think of Lewis, he's an archaeologist, not Walt Disney," Lindsay said, trying to get a look at the letter the woman held in her hand. It looked like a fax, but she couldn't see for sure.

Others from the barge came through the doors, talking and laughing. Tessa threw up her hands and started to leave, when they heard a splash and yells of distress just beyond the entrance.

Chapter 6

LINDSAY AND BOBBIE rushed outside. Several people leaned over the railing, looking into the pond and yelling at an elderly man who was splashing wildly, cursing, and clearly not listening to the profusion of advice from above.

"Oh, Christ, it's Boote. I'll bet he's drunk." The voice sounded like Tessa's, but Lindsay didn't look behind her, instead she hurried to the scene and saw that a piece of lower railing had come loose.

"We need to help him," Lindsay said. "If he is drunk, he probably can't help himself."

She looked over at the alligator. It was as still as a log in the same spot on the other side of the pond. She started to kneel down, but felt herself gently pushed aside.

"Boote, old man," said John West, kneeling and reaching out toward him. "Don't make me have to come in and drag you out of there. Swim toward me."

The alligator submerged and someone yelled. Boote, as if just realizing where he was, darted his head back and forth, looking, then panicked, flailed his arms, and went under.

"Well, shit," said John. He sat down on the walkway, dangled his legs over the side, and eased himself into the water.

The pond wasn't deep. It came only up to John's chest as he waded toward the spot were Boote went under. The old man surfaced, sputtering, and John grabbed him before he could go under again. He yelled and fought as if caught by the alligator. John put an arm across Boote's chest and glided him through the water the few feet to the walkway. Jeff and Nate, one arm in a sling, helped John haul the old man up.

"Don't get your arm wet with that muck," Jeff said to Nate. "It'll get infected."

John pulled himself onto the walkway, stood and looked down at his wet muddy clothes, and frowned. "Boote, you better have a good reason for falling into the swamp." He knelt beside Jeff and Nate, who were holding Boote in a sitting position with his head between his knees as he coughed.

"He seems to be all right," Nate said. "Just swallowed some water."

"That can't be good for him," said Jeff.

"Well, no, I don't reckon it is," said John.

"What happened?" asked Lindsay.

"Can't you see?" said Tessa. "He fell through the railing. It's your fault, all of you. Moving your equipment up the ramp here like a bulldozer, tearing up the railing."

She turned her attention to Boote, who had raised his head to look at her, squinting, trying to keep the dripping water out of his eyes.

"And you." Tessa pointed her finger. "You were told to stay away from here. Especially when you're drunk! Have you been out in your boat in that condition?"

"Now listen here, missy. I been bringing my boy here since he was little. You people come and run us off . . . studying my island. I could've told you 'bout my island, if you'd of asked."

Lindsay and Bobbie couldn't resist looking at Tessa under raised brows.

She jutted her chin forward. "It's not the same thing at all." She turned abruptly and hurried back up the walkway, brushing past Harper, who had just come through the double doors carrying a blanket.

"I thought he might need this." Harper placed the blanket around Boote's shoulders. "You all right, Mr. Teal?"

"Thank y' ma'am."

Nate pulled the blanket close under the old man's chin.

"I'll take you home," said John. "I have to go change clothes anyway." He put a hand on the old man's arm and guided him to his feet. "What are you doing here, anyway?"

"I was wondering if any of you seen Keith. He's good about looking in on me. He always brings me Sunday dinner. He didn't come Sunday last. I went over to the neighbors and used their phone to call some of his friends. They ain't seen him in about a week."

"Couldn't he have gone somewhere—Savannah or Atlanta maybe, and you forgot?" asked Nate.

The old man opened his eyes wide. "Atlanta. He has this girl he likes to visit in Atlanta sometimes."

"He's what, forty years old?" asked John. "I think he can probably take care of himself." John smiled at Lindsay, told her he'd be back, and guided Boote toward the dock. Lindsay watched the old man as he walked, unsteady on his feet, supported by John, trailing the blanket like an imperial robe.

"I take it you all know him," Lindsay said to Harper as they turned and walked back into the building.

"He comes around sometimes. He lives on the mainland near the coast somewhere. He and his son used to come here years ago to fish and prospect, before the state took it over and made it a preserve. He's a harmless old guy. Lonely, I think."

Bobbie and Harper led Lindsay through the lobby into a hallway. Lindsay peeked into rooms as she passed. In the first, several people around a table greeted her curious gaze with frowns. She assumed they were from the Biology Department.

"This is a private meeting," one of the men said.

"This is Dr. Chamberlain," introduced Bobbie, as if there were no hostile undercurrent. "This is Mike Altman. . . . He's Tessa's husband."

"Look," said Tessa. "What does it take to get through to you people? We aren't interested in being your friends."

Lindsay thought she noticed embarrassment on the faces of some of the others. She was glad she was staying on the barge.

The room across from them was filled with computers, printers, and an array of other electronic equipment, and a chessboard sitting on a table in one corner.

"This is where our two meteorologists keep track of the weather for us," said Bobbie. "They've got global positioning equipment and a lot of other neat stuff." She waved at a guy sitting at a terminal. "Good weather ahead?" she asked.

"So far, looks great," he answered.

"This is Dr. Chamberlain. She works with bones." Bobbie introduced two of the weather crew, Terry Lyons and William Kuzniak. After a few words about the weather, they continued down the hall.

At the end of the hallway, a stairwell led to the ground floor where the conservation crew did their work.

"We meet down here almost every day to debrief," Bobbie said. "You'll want to meet the conservators. The stuff they do is really interesting."

The head conservator, Carolyn Taylor, took Lindsay's hand, pumped it up and down, and introduced her to another conservator, Korey Jordan. Korey worked mainly with the iron objects and made technical drawings of all the artifacts.

"You should see his drawings. They're wonderful. Korey's had several showings of his work in New York."

Lindsay could almost see Korey's smooth, dark-chocolate skin blush under the praise Carolyn bestowed upon his work. His shoulder-length dreadlocks fell forward as he bowed his head, an unconscious effort to hide from her compliments. Carolyn slapped him on the back.

"He won't sing his own praises," she said. "Someone has to. I heard you found the first skeleton. We can't wait to get him—her?" Carolyn stopped, waiting for Lindsay's answer, a broad smile on her face.

"Him," Lindsay said, looking around at the various containers—giant glass aquariums, opaque tubs, and shallow trays—holding artifacts being treated. Carolyn had been working on a shoe with a dental tool. The shoe Gina found was evidently not the first. Before leather could be rendered stable enough to work with, it had to be treated, sometimes for several weeks, with a solvent to replace the water that permeated the tissues.

"Want to see some of the stuff we've found?"

Lindsay nodded and went from container to container looking at beads, pearls, a pewter cup and plate, a wooden pepper mill, a thimble, a caulker's mallet, carved ivory tools of some kind, large ceramic jars, sheets of mounted fabric soaking in what smelled like acetone, iron concretions waiting for Korey to pour a casting substance in them to make a mold of whatever iron object used to be inside.

"We have two barrels and a sea chest in tanks over at the warehouse where the ship's timbers are being taken. They weigh over a hundred pounds apiece. We put all the heavy stuff over there," Carolyn said. "We've already found enough artifacts to keep us busy for years."

"Is this an astrolabe?" asked Lindsay, pointing to an object in a tub of liquid. Both Korey and Carolyn nodded their heads vigorously.

"Cool, isn't it?" Korey smiled. "I don't envy you guys at the dam at all. This is the most fun part of the project."

Bobbie grinned back at them. "Maybe, but there is nothing like the feel of the initial find."

"I understand Lewis is going to build a museum?" asked Lindsay.

"I wouldn't be surprised. Cisco is backing this project to the hilt."

Cisco, thought Lindsay. Carolyn must be one of Francisco Lewis's people. Hardly anyone else ever called him that.

"Is he building a theme park?" Lindsay asked.

"A theme park?" Korey echoed. "You mean with rides? Where did you hear that?"

Carolyn laughed.

"Tessa thinks he is. She had a fax. I didn't see where it was from."

"Oh," said Carolyn. "Those people have a new rumor every day. Theme park. That's the stupidest one they've had yet."

"I understand we kind of usurped their space."

"Well," Carolyn said, "that's the breaks. It's not that those people haven't done it to us archaeologists enough times. You're from UGA campus, aren't you?" she said, changing the subject. "You know Gerri Chapman?"

"I've worked with her a couple of times," Lindsay said, eyeing Carolyn closely. Gerri Chapman was one of Francisco Lewis's favorites. She had preceded Lewis to campus and tried her best to get Lindsay's job as head of the osteology lab. Carolyn smiled, a knowing kind of smile. It wasn't an expression of disapproval, but one that said she would like to hear the story over a bottle of beer sometime. "She came to UGA with Lewis," Lindsay added—probably unnecessarily.

"Well, speak of the devil," Carolyn said, looking over Lindsay's left shoulder.

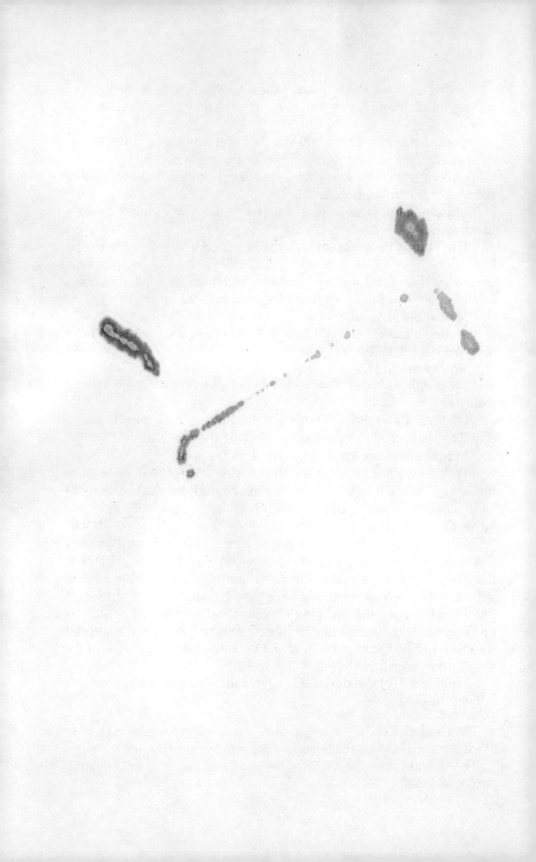

Chapter 7

LINDSAY TURNED AND came face-to-face with the hawkish countenance of Francisco Lewis.

"Dr. Chamberlain. Now that you've seen the dam, the lab, the crew, and the research plan, what do you think? Can I cook or what?" He grinned.

Lewis's teeth were so white, Lindsay was sure he must have them bleached regularly.

"I must give the devil his due."

Lewis laughed out loud, put an arm around her shoulders, and gave her a gentle shake.

"Trey tells me you found a human skeleton today. I knew you were right for this dig." His dark eyes glimmered and his mouth turned up in a slight, lopsided smile.

He knew I was right for the dig? Lindsay thought. Even though she had not been reassigned to a smaller office or lost the faunal lab, when her summer osteology courses were given to Gerri Chapman to teach, she had thought Lewis was beginning a campaign to ease her out and put in the person he brought with him. Instead, had he shifted the teaching load to Gerri and given Lindsay this plumb assignment? She couldn't imagine him choosing her over one of his pet people. Maybe Trey had talked him into it.

"Yes," Lindsay said. "He's in good condition, too."

"When do you think it will be ready to come up?"

"Tomorrow, perhaps. It depends on how much the night crew get done."

He nodded. Lindsay could almost see the wheels turning in his brain, so she was not surprised by the next statement.

"We'll want to make a cast of the skull right away. I understand you're an artist . . ."

"Well, I'm competent, but . . ."

"I hope you won't be offended," he went on as if she hadn't spoken. "I'm going to get a sculptor to do the face. You don't need to be spending time on that anyway. I would like the bone analysis to be finished as quickly as possible, especially on this first one."

This first one, thought Lindsay. Lewis was certainly optimistic.

"Frank tells me you're good at visualizing personal stories from a collection of artifacts. That's what I want here. Make it personal. We've got the journal, and I understand it's turning out to be quite interesting. I'd like you to match up the skeleton with the descriptions of crew members in the journal." He shook her again and grinned. "Glad to have you aboard." He turned and went to where charts and maps were hanging on the walls. It looked as if he would be conducting the debriefing.

"Energetic, isn't he?" Bobbie said.

"And optimistic."

"He likes you." Lindsay and Bobbie turned and faced Carolyn. "I bet that puts Gerri's nose out of joint." She looked as if that pleased her.

Lindsay and Bobbie sat down on a sofa next to one wall. Bobbie pulled up a dilapidated coffee table to prop their feet on. Slowly, members of the crew began filing into the room and taking seats wherever they could find them. Trey came in with Nate, who raised his fists in the air like a fighter, showing off his bandage. Everyone clapped and whooped.

"Eight stitches," he shouted.

Trey banged on the table with the edge of his clipboard. "OK, everybody. Let's get on with this. Some of us want to squeeze in a life while we're here. We've got Francisco Lewis with us. He'll be staying for a while and has a few things to say."

Lewis stepped forward. His slacks and shirt looked expensive, contrasting with the combination of torn blue jeans, shorts, and swimsuits the crew were wearing.

"I just wanted to say that I think you guys are doing a great job, and a fast job. I know archaeology is not meant to be a fast undertaking, but this is an unusual dig." He paused. "We've had an unfortunate incident with pothunters. I've spoken with Trey and John West, and we're taking steps to make sure nothing like what happened to Nate happens again. All of you know the problem sites have with pothunters when all that's at stake are ceramic pots and projectile points. You can imagine how the stakes are raised when people hear the words *Spanish galleon*. Please don't let today's incident disturb your work.

"As Trey said, I'm going to be here for a while." He grinned. "We're having a television crew—" There were groans from the crew, and Lewis raised his hands. "I know. They can be a pain, but publicity gets us money, and this is an expensive undertaking. So grin and bear it."

"Now, I understand Lindsay Chamberlain found the first human skeleton and wins the pool, which has a grand total of twenty-five dollars in it. I'm glad inflation hasn't hit the ranks of archaeology and we are still cheap." He got a laugh, not because he was funny, Lindsay thought, but because he was Lewis. "Come up, Lindsay. Trey has some cash for you."

Lindsay made a face, swung her feet off the table, reluctantly stood and walked to the front. Trey gave her the cash, and she waved it over her head to the applause of the crew and went back to her seat. Trey took over the meeting, and the focus went to the day's accomplishments and problems, illustrated on a map of the site and twenty miles of surrounding ocean. A quarter-mile east of the dam the scuba teams had found a few barrel hoops and another cannon similar to the first two. "We're not sure the cannons came from our ship," he said, "but we suspect they may have. The Spanish archives said only one ship of the 1558 fleet sank off the coast, and so far we haven't found any evidence to dispute that. We'll know more when the cannons are cleaned up."

Out of the corner of her eye, Lindsay noticed Lieutenant Damon of the Coast Guard at the doorway, holding a large plastic bag at his side. She wondered how long he had been standing there.

"Lieutenant, you have some information for us?" asked Trey.

Damon walked to the front of the room and removed what looked like a shattered piece of large plastic tubing from the bag.

"Our divers found this wedged in one of the wrecks that make up the artificial reef. It was in the vicinity of today's incident, and I wondered if it's yours."

"Oh, shit," whispered Bobbie.

"What is it?" Lindsay asked her.

Before Bobbie could answer, Trey cursed and threw his clipboard down on the table. Both he and Lewis looked furious. Nate jumped up. "Damn them," he sputtered.

"No," Trey told Lieutenant Damon. "It isn't ours. It's a piece of an airlift that's used to suck up sediment and small artifacts in an underwater excavation. The kind of airlift we use for survey work is small. At the depths we're working here, we never use one over three inches in diameter, and no archaeologist uses one over six inches. That one looks like it was nearly twelve. It would destroy the artifacts. The only people who use an airlift that size are treasure hunters looking for gold."

"What do you think they were looking for around the reef?" Damon asked.

Trey shrugged. "I don't know. We haven't found anything there."

"Thank you for your time," he said and left the room.

"Dammit, Trey," said Nate.

"Take it easy, Nate," Lewis cautioned. "That's why we're putting on extra guards. This won't happen again."

Trey wrapped up the debriefing quickly after Damon left, and everyone went on their way. Bobbie found Sarah and the others. Lindsay looked around for John West. Apparently he wasn't back yet. She took another quick tour of the lab and walked outside. While the meeting was going on, someone had repaired the railing. Lindsay looked for the alligator but didn't see him. A dragonfly lit on the shiny black water, causing a ripple in the smooth surface, and quickly disappeared beneath it. Lindsay bent down to examine the repair work. She shook the lower rail. It seemed solid. She spied something wedged between the planks of the walkway. It looked like a coin. She found a nail file in her purse and pried out a quarter with a hole punched neatly through the middle.

"What you got there, Rabbit?"

Lindsay rose from her haunches and held the quarter out to John. "Well, from what I hear, you are really raking in the money today. Maybe I'll get you to buy me dinner."

They walked to the dock where several large boats were moored. All were equipped with various kinds of winches, tanks, and mechanical devices. John led her to a large shiny white motor boat with the name *Sea Dragon* painted on the bow.

"Nice boat."

"Yeah. We've got a lot of nice stuff on this job."

John helped Lindsay in, started the engine at an idle, and untied the line. Lindsay stood beside him as he maneuvered the boat away from the dock. Something gently nudged the bottom of the boat, knocking Lindsay against him.

"What was that?" she asked.

John shrugged and put an arm around her shoulders. "Big fish, I suppose."

He piloted the boat out to the ocean, then picked up speed. The wind whipped her hair back and forth, and she had to shout to make herself heard over the roar of the engine and the sound of the waves against the boat.

"How's Boote?"

John didn't take his gaze away from the ocean, but turned his head slightly toward Lindsay. "He's okay. I left him at his house. A neighbor was home and I asked her to look in on him."

The boat seemed to leap and Lindsay grabbed hold of a rail.

"How far?"

"To the restaurant? About seventeen miles. It's just over the line in Florida."

She sat down and watched the shore go by. There was still a lot of daylight left and she could see the beach and the flora of Cumberland Island, the island next to St. Magdalena. Lindsay squinted her eyes to see if she could catch sight of one of the wild horses on Cumberland, but the only fauna she saw were birds. She turned her gaze to John's classic Indian profile, remembering their previous encounter at the dig and wondering about his asking her to dinner. He couldn't consider her too much of an enemy if he was willing to take her out.

It took only about thirty minutes to reach Fernandina Beach. John slowed the boat as he entered the intracoastal waterway and motored to a dock. As they shed their life jackets and climbed out, John stared into Lindsay's eyes for just a moment.

"It's just a few yards up here," he said finally, and walked arm-in-arm with her to the restaurant.

It was a popular place. The patrons looked like mostly tourists. Lindsay and John got a window seat where they could see the water several yards distant.

"So tell me about your business," she said, after John ordered a surf and turf and she a fisherman's platter. "I didn't realize it was so big."

"This is my biggest project. I've built cofferdams before, but for smaller projects—all bridge repair. Before I started West

Construction, I was one of the engineers for the Third Harbor Tunnel in Boston. We built the largest cofferdam in North America. I've done some oil rig work and some underwater construction in the navy. So, do you think that qualifies me to do this job?"

"I wasn't questioning your qualifications."

"But they surprised you."

"You aren't going to pick a fight with me, are you? I kind of figured as long as I'm not digging up your ancestors, we can be friends and not enemies."

John grinned and took her hand as she was about to reach for her iced tea.

"I'm not going to pick a fight with you."

The waitress came carrying their dinners, and John let go of her hand.

"That's a lot of food," Lindsay said.

"You work hard, you need to eat more than those little sandwiches they give you. You still seeing that guy—the one with the name like a piece of machinery?"

Lindsay laughed. "You mean Derrick? We see each other occasionally. No commitments."

"What does that mean?"

"It means we enjoy each other's company. Occasionally. Tell me more about your business. You must have been excited to have won the bid."

"That's an understatement. I stand to make a pot of money and gain a lot of reputation with this project. It means a lot to me and my family."

"I remember your sister and father well. Who else is in your family?" Lindsay tasted her stuffed crab. "This is good."

"That's why I brought you here. I have a son, Jason, twelve, a daughter, Shelly, in high school, and an ex-wife in Oklahoma."

"Your children live with you?"

John nodded. "They're with my father and sister while I'm here."

"Well, if it isn't the redskin."

Lindsay jerked her head toward the gravelly voice. It came from a stout man who looked to be in his early forties.

"Hardy Denton, don't you have some place to be?" John replied. His voice was calm, but Lindsay could see his hand was tight around his glass of iced tea.

Chapter 8

"LOOK, TONTO, I know I was the low bid. You know that, too, don't you?" Hardy Denton's words were slurred and he smelled like beer. "You got it because you're a damn Indian."

Lindsay looked beyond Denton and spotted Eva Jones sitting at a table with another couple, calmly looking in their direction, as if waiting for a movie to start. John saw her, too.

"I see you have a lady with you," John said. "Why don't you go back to your dinner with her?"

"Don't you patronize me, boy. I've got something to say. You got a job that's supposed to be mine. You ain't ever done a job like this before. You don't have the experience. I do. Don't tell me it wasn't rigged." Denton started shifting his weight from foot to foot.

"I'm not patronizing you. I think we should take this up some other time. Both of us have guests. Let's not subject them or the other diners to a disagreement."

"You're not getting rid of me until I've had my say, and I don't care who hears. Everyone needs to know what cheats you and those university people are."

Lindsay put down her fork and dabbed her mouth with the napkin. "We haven't met, and I don't want to. Go away."

Denton jerked his head in her direction as if she were a mannequin that had just spoken. He looked back at John. "Tell your squaw this don't have nothing to do with her."

John stood, but Lindsay was faster to her feet. By the look on Hardy's face, he was surprised at how tall she was.

"You go sit down or I'll call the manager," she said.

Denton stepped back and shifted his gaze to John. "My quarrel is with you."

Lindsay threw the napkin down on the seat. "We'll see." She marched over to Eva Jones and bent over her table. "Reel him back in. He's making you look suspicious."

Eva arched her brows, glanced over at her companions, winked at them, and looked back at Lindsay. "I don't know what you mean."

"Then I'm very disappointed in you. I'll spell it out to the Coast Guard, and they can enlighten you."

Eva shifted her gaze back to the man sitting with her as Lindsay turned and left. John stood with his arms folded over his chest. Denton was shaking a finger at him. Lindsay could see from the stony look on John's face that his patience wasn't endless. Out of the corner of her eye, Lindsay saw their waitress talking to the manager and he started toward them. Lindsay was about to speak to Denton when Eva and her companions rose and walked to their table.

"Come on, old boy." A man taller, stronger, and younger than Hardy gripped his arm. "I need to get back." His voice was friendly, but Lindsay noticed that his fingers bit into Denton's upper arm.

"Hey. I'm not finished. . . ," he yelped.

Eva turned to the approaching manager, a pale, gangly fellow who looked too young for the job, and handed him several bills.

"We need to be going. I think this will cover our meals. Give the rest to our waitress. She was great. So was the food."

Eva left with Denton between her and her male companion. The manager stood for a moment, money in hand, flashed an embarrassed grin at some of the customers who had interrupted their meal to watch, and returned to the wait station.

"Well," said Lindsay, "that was interesting."

John gave a short laugh. "That's not the word I'd use. What did you say to the Jones woman?"

"I hinted that Hardy Denton's harassment looked suspicious in light of Nate's getting shot. I don't think she wants to be in the spotlight with the Coast Guard."

"Rabbit jumping on the Tar Man again?" John shook his head and reached out to take her hand. "I'm sorry about this. I'd hoped for a quiet meal."

Lindsay squeezed his hand, rubbed her thumb across his knuckles, and met his gaze. "I'm enjoying this very much. I've never been taken to dinner by boat before. And this is the best seafood I've ever had. And . . ."

"And what?"

"And I like the company."

A corner of John's mouth turned up and after a moment they continued their meal.

"What's the story on Boote?" Lindsay asked after several pieces of shrimp.

"In the beginning, when the site was being surveyed, before most of the crew got here, Boote and his son, Keith, were—what do you archaeologists call them—informants? They know the coast and all the islands and have a collection of ancient stuff washed up on the beach over the years. Boote drinks a lot. So does Keith. I think they had some kind of falling-out with Trey and the others. Collectors and archaeologists don't get along for very long, I've noticed."

"Not surprising. We have such opposing philosophies." Lindsay glanced up from her food to John and saw from the look on his face that he disagreed—that he saw no difference between them at all. She started to speak, say something about archaeologists adding to the knowledge base, but put a fried oyster in her mouth instead. When John spoke it was to ask her about her family, and she was happy to drift into that conversational safe harbor.

They finished their meal. Lindsay waited outside on the porch while John paid, and the two of them walked arm-in-arm back to the boat. It was dark, but the dock was well lit. Lindsay couldn't help scanning the boats for one that might belong to Eva Jones, but she had no idea what a boat of hers would look like.

She climbed into their boat and sat down in the passenger seat next to her life preserver as John untied the ropes from the dock.

"I'm sorry about the things that Denton guy said," Lindsay told him.

"It's not your fault. A man with fire in his heart often has sparks fly out his mouth."

Lindsay laughed. "Is that an old Indian saying?"

John shook his head. "I heard it the other night on *Daniel Boone*."

Lindsay laughed again. "I didn't know you have a sense of humor, and I'm surprised you watch *Daniel Boone*."

John shrugged and grinned. "It was on and I was too tired to get out of bed and change the channel." He started the engine, moved away from the dock, and piloted the boat down the intracoastal waterway and out into the ocean.

Lindsay shivered, hunkered down in the seat trying to escape the wind, wishing she had brought a heavier jacket.

"I want to show you something," John shouted to her.

After several miles, he slowed and cut the engine. They bobbed in the ocean, and he surveyed the area before turning off the lights.

"Have a look at this," he said, taking her hand and pulling her up beside him.

The sliver of moon shining on the ocean cast enough light to make the velvet black water glitter as if it were covered with diamonds. Off toward the horizon the lights of ships shone like bright stars. The night was so dark it was hard to see where the ocean stopped and the sky began. Overhead, it looked as if every star in the Northern Hemisphere was visible. The rim of the galaxy cut a bright, dazzling path across the sky. Lindsay looked back down across the sea and saw in the distance a radiance shining up from the ocean. It took her a moment to realize it was the cofferdam, shining like a crown jewel among the glitter of the ocean and sky.

"What you think?" John whispered, his breath stirring her hair.

"It's breathtaking. I think it's the most beautiful sight I've ever seen."

"Yeah, I think so, too."

Lindsay couldn't see John in the darkness, but she felt his arm slip around her waist and was surprised that he so accurately found her lips in the dark, and was surprised again that he was so very good at kissing. Yes, breathtaking, she thought to herself. When his lips finally left hers, she wanted to pull him back. So she did.

Several minutes passed before John spoke. He sighed and said, "I have to turn the lights back on. If a boat comes along, they can't see us." He flipped a switch; Lindsay blinked at the brightness and looked at him. He touched her lips with the tips of his fingers. "If there was ever a perfect spot on earth to kiss a woman, this is it," he said and kissed her cheek before starting the engine.

⚓

"How was your date?" asked Bobbie.

Lindsay was tucked into bed, reading the journal of the ancient sailor when Bobbie came into their room.

"What? Oh. It was good. Very good."

Bobbie slipped out of her clothes and into a nightshirt. She climbed into her bunk and settled into the crib-like bed.

"Eva Jones and Hardy Denton were eating at the same restaurant."

"You're kidding. Where did you go?"

"All the way to Florida, can you believe it?" Lindsay told her about the encounter.

"Wow, do you think he's the one behind the attack on Nate and Sarah?"

"I don't know, but I think it is a possibility. He's very bitter about losing the contract, and he seems the reckless sort. How was your evening?"

"Uneventful. We had pizza and watched a pirate movie. The one where Geena Davis is the pirate."

"Keeping with the theme of the site, eh?" Lindsay murmured, drifting back to her reading.

"Yeah, we're making paper hats and wooden swords tomorrow evening. Have you read the journal yet?" asked Bobbie.

"I'm doing it now."

"How is it?"

"Fascinating."

Chapter 9

A Passenger's Diary: Part II

From a voyage on the Spanish Galleon
Estrella de España, c. 1558
—Translated by Harper Latham

*I*F LUISA HAD a gown like the night sky I see from this ship, made from the blackest of silk from the Orient, scattered by the hand of God with cut diamonds from Africa, a ruby here, an emerald there, perhaps a sapphire or two and one giant pearl, what glorious raiment she would have—and what sweet disposition.

But if Luisa had a sweet disposition, would I be on this wretched ship on this wonderful journey? I don't know.

I've found various places on the ship where I can observe and not get in the way of the crew performing the ceaseless repetition of activities required to sail the ship. (The ship is a mistress who must be constantly pampered and attended to or she can surely cause much misery.) For many tasks, success depends on the men working in unity. The community of seafarers have devised an ingenious way of working in unison without having to look at one another. They sing. Sing! I am quite amazed. Their voices cannot be said to bring to mind a heavenly chorus, but it is not quality of voice or the melody that is important, but the rhythm. And there is a song for every task.

The first leg of our journey has been very difficult. All of us, even the crew to one degree or another, became seasick until we got used to the constant rocking of the ship. It is with pride that I write that I was one of the least affected. The soldiers bound for Havana are not good sailors and spend much of the time with their heads bowed over the railings of the weather deck, emptying their stomach, and cursing the real sailors for wretches.

Father Hernando left his bed and joined us for meat for the first time in several days. He did not look hale, but the stew of salted pork seemed to sit well in his innards—which I took from the retching sounds coming from his quarters have been in no better shape than the ship's. I pity Carlos and José who share quarters with him.

We stopped at the Fortunate Isles this morning, anchoring in a quiet bay where the water was a wonderful blue. If I watched closely I could see the fish swimming near the ship.

The weather was fair for the first time since the voyage started and I had a clear view of the high, gently rounded mountains and distant green foliage. It was a place I would like to have visited, but the respite was to be brief, so I satisfied myself with breathing in the air and watching the scenery. It felt good.

Two boats rowed out to us. One contained large crates. The other carried two passengers. One, a man of wealth and authority, judging by his clothes and bearing, but I could not discern his nationality. The other man took his heritage from the Orient. He took great interest, as did his captain, with the loading of the crates.

We did not linger at the islands. As soon as the crates, fresh water, and firewood were loaded, the captain gave the order and the capstan rhythm began. The capstan is like a large wheel with a hub, six spokes, but no rim. The messenger rope—a smaller rope that is connected to the rather large anchor rope—is wound around the hub. The chanteyman, as the singer is called, starts a song and the sailors, four to a spoke, heave on the beat and turn the wheel. Thus one anchor after another is raised from the depths.

The pilot Bellisaro praises God and shouts directions to the crew. They scramble over the masts and yardarms with the mastery of squirrels scurrying over tree branches. They pull ropes and turn yardarms in a kind of dance. When the leader sings a phrase, the men chant oh, oh and at the same time pull one of divers ropes, and the sails are raised. It sounds thus:

> *Hoist sails—oh, oh—for God—oh, oh—will help us—oh, oh—for what we are—oh, oh—help us—oh, oh—or we die—oh, oh— well served—oh, oh—our faith—oh, oh—maintained—oh, oh— or the faith—oh, oh—of Christian—oh, oh—or Muslim—oh, oh—the pagan—oh, oh—to the bottom—oh, oh—and on . . .*

Working the sails is truly the most amazing and hazardous task of all they do. Each sail is heavy, requiring ropes and pulleys to manage. One slip and a man will fall to the deck or in the ocean. The crew praise God at every chance. Living so precarious a life as this one needs the goodwill of our heavenly Father.

We had an escort for two days after leaving the islands. Dolphins swam with us, providing the crew entertainment by leaping out of the water. Valerian, the passenger from the islands, stood with me and we watched the fish cavort.

"They are friendly and curious," he said, "like children. They are, I believe, my favorite fish in the sea."

"You've encountered them before?" I asked.

"Many times. They will play with the slightest provocation."

I was going to ask where he was when he played with them, when the captain, upon hearing our conversation, asked what they taste like.

"Oh, my friend, I haven't eaten them. I think that would be like eating a friend."

The captain, I could see, thought Valerian touched in the head and moved on to query Bellisaro. He missed seeing the whale that surfaced in the distance. They are quite large.

I sighted the *Nuestra Señora del Rosario* today. She is the *capitanas*—the lead ship in the convoy. What a majestic sight she is. Seeing her in full splendor, all sails filled with wind, sweeping through the ocean, I know now why some men desire to be mated to such a creature—only to find too soon what a difficult mistress she is. Much like my Luisa.

Pedro Acosta is the ship's captain. Bellisaro does not like him. For his part, Acosta, I think, resents the navigator. Acosta is a man who likes the last word. He has come to our cabin more than once arguing for a route different from the one Bellisaro chooses. "There is no wind there," Bellisaro tells him. The captain then yells and stomps off. In matters of the course of this ship, it is to Bellisaro the helmsman must listen. From my point of view, this is good, as the captain could find neither up nor down were not down the natural direction things fall.

We had guests today. The captain-general of the fleet came from the *Nuestra Señora del Rosario.* I have met him at court. He is a good man. I trust him. Like many men I've known with sweeping responsibilities, he is inclined to be remote to those who serve under him. But he tries to have a sense of humor. I think he only pretends, but that only makes it a greater courtesy. I was tempted to confide in him, but I did not.

Juan López, the king's general inspector, came aboard from the *Espiritu Viento.* He has a long face, eyes that droop at his lower lids, and dark hair that curls in ringlets. His countenance would look sad were it not for his jovial temperament. We were glad to see him. He seemed a little pale—not surprising, having been tossed about in such a small boat traveling from his ship to ours. We are a moving kingdom out here on the water. Instead of castles, we have ships. Instead of horses and wagons to travel from castle to castle, we have little boats. But we are no less connected to one another because we are not on land. We—I say we, I mean some—move from ship to ship as readily as we visit a neighbor and carry news of the others. However, in our kingdom we sometimes drift out of sight of our neighbor, or one neighbor is exchanged for another. It is an interesting community.

The captain told the cook to prepare a feast fit for a king. So the Captain-General, Acosta, Father Hernando, General-Inspector López, Bellisaro, Valerian, and I sat down at a table lain with six roasted chickens stuffed with rice, almonds, and raisins, broad beans and garlic, olives, honey cakes, and the best of the captain's wines. My stomach was joyful, so tired was it of dried fish, boiled pork, and dry biscuits.

López entertained us with many stories of his travels. He knows everyone. He is cousin to Father Hernando's sister-in-law; he is acquainted with Bellisaro's grandfather. He even knows my Luisa's sister.

"A delicious meal. The roast chicken, perfect," he spoke and slapped Bellisaro on the back. "Was generous of Captain Acosta, my friend, was it not, to tell the cook to prepare the chicken and not the pork?" The navigator nodded. I could have told López how useless it is to try and engage Bellisaro in conversation.

López continued to heap praises on our captain's hospitality and to dominate the conversation. I much wanted to hear from Valerian. I was sure he had more interesting stories to tell, but he is often disinclined to speak—as if he has to trust those to whom he speaks before engaging in conversation. I did learn that although Portuguese by birth, his mother was Moroccan, and he has since lived in many places. As he passed a platter of rice, I noticed his signet ring. It displays his initial and a falcon. I asked him about it. He told me that it isn't a family insignia, but his own. How fitting, I thought. I suspect that Valerian is as individual a man as I ever will meet.

When we finished, and the captain-general took leave to visit another of his ships, López stayed. He and Valerian went with the captain back to the captain's cabin. I was surprised. I would not have imagined Valerian and López to be friends. They do not seem to have ever met before this journey. It is easy to make me suspicious. It is why, I believe, that I may be well suited for this work.

Gaining enlightenment through overhearing the crew talk is not as easy for me as I had thought. It is not as if I do not have access to all parts of the ship. I can go where I will. It is the language. I am becoming accustomed to the accents, and I hear the words—but not the meaning. When I hear "Loosen the sheet," the pilot may be giving a command to do something or other with the sails, or he might just as well be asking for a cup! Cryptic speech can hide much.

Valerian came to my cabin this evening carrying a heavy case. Juan López followed him, spreading his jovial spirit over our small space. Bellisaro was resting in the corner on his cot.

"I hear that you play chess," said Valerian with a hopeful countenance.

"I do," I said, "but the ship . . . she will not allow it. Unless you have a board and pieces with those little pegs and holes."

Valerian, I discovered, is a man who devises contrivances, some of which are most useful, others quite fanciful. He carries with him one of the latter. He set a heavy chessboard with a clank on a table and grinned at me as he took pieces from a leather pouch and set them with a *clink, clink, clink,* on the board. When they were all arranged in their ranks, he gestured with a bow. The pieces stayed, defying the lurching of the ship. I picked up my queen and felt a slight tug as though she were reluctant to leave her square. The clever Valerian had inlayed the bottom of intricately carved ivory pieces with lodestone and made a board of iron. I laughed at his brilliance and we sat down and played. Juan López stayed and watched our play after turning to Bellisaro and making sure that we were not offending him.

"Of course not," said the pilot. But Bellisaro left the cabin and

I wondered if perhaps he was weary of the ever-jovial López. I, for one, am beginning to find his presence tiresome.

Valerian's servant, whose name is Jen, is a secretive fellow, but seems to get along well with the rest of the crew. He has no obligations except to Valerian, but he readily helps the crew with various tasks. He eats by himself, having his own cup and bowl. At first it was a cause for taunts from the crew. They eat from a common bowl and, I must add, as with dogs, this has on more than one occasion been the cause of fights. Sailors fight with knives, which they all carry for their work. They fight readily and cut one another viciously. They can just as easily make up. Have I mentioned that, also like dogs, the crew sleep where they can find a place on the deck, and usually in a different place each night? If the place where a man has chosen to lay his head is needed during the night, he must move. My own opinion is, every person needs a place of their own. Being a lowly sailor is a fate I would not wish on anyone. I don't know why anyone would choose it.

The sea has been smooth for the last few days and the winds favorable. By smooth, I don't mean like the still, mirrored surface of a lake. The ocean is never still. On the calmest of days, the sea has a sparkling, green-blue, coarse surface. The crew tend to repairing sails or washing the decks. During these tasks, which the men find monotonous, they sing, accompanied by Jen on the Veracruz harp. It surprises me that he plays a Spanish instrument. Not one of his ancestors seems to have come from Spain. The favorite entertainment for the crew, and I confess for me as well, is Valerian reading to us from books he has found in other lands about lost cities and strange creatures and quests for treasure. It is very easy to entertain a crew by talking about treasure. Valerian is clever enough to add many texts praising God, which I suspect are not in the book, but keep Valerian from being accused of blasphemy and allow the crew to listen without guilt.

I am becoming accustomed to our community here at sea. I do not mind the repetitive daily routine. It is a comfort. I believe it is López and the captain whom I need to overhear, but it is not easy. I am trying to make friends with López. One would think it would be easy. But it is not. He talks incessantly, but says nothing. He acts like your friend, but I sense it is false. Sometimes when I engage him in deep conversation during meals or in our cabins, I see Valerian eyeing me, not suspiciously, but knowingly. Sometimes it seems as if he can see through me. I want to know what secret he has with the captain and López—he is so very unlike them—and if it has anything to do with the business for which the House of Trade has sent me on this journey.

Today for all my attempts to listen to important conservation, quite by accident I overheard a fragment between the captain and López. It was early morning, the sun had not yet risen above the arc of the horizon. I stood on the weather deck at the stern of the ship, waiting for the golden sunrise, when quiet voices just below me rose, along with the steam and smoke from the galley hearth, through the grating. I heard what sounded to me like the captain saying something like, ". . . obstinate. I can't change him." Another voice that I am sure belonged to López, for it was clearer, said that there will be no obstacle in the way of their detour. That was all. I then heard footfalls and the voices stopped. I do not understand what they spoke of, nor am I sure how it fits with what I was sent to discover, but I know it was important. Moreover, talk of a detour fills me with fear.

A man fell from a yardarm to the deck today. I had awakened and come to the deck early as is my habit. The page was reciting our thanks to God and turning the sand clock. The sun was rising and the sky was bright red and the sea was quiet. It would be a fine day, I thought. But the sailors on duty grumbled to themselves. Acosta, the ship's captain, assembled the crew and reminded them that God is with us. (Not even in church do men beseech our Lord as often as they do on board ship.) Then he ordered the men fed. This surprised me. It was not a usual mealtime and the captain was unusually generous with the food. I mentioned this to Bellisaro, who had taken up his station. He answered that I might go down to our cabin. I shrugged and went to the forecastle deck to breathe in the fresh air.

"There's a storm coming." Valerian appeared beside me. He can be a very quiet man. "I heard you speak to Bellisaro," said he. "They feed the men before a storm, for there will be much work for them." I shivered as the first gust of wind blew across my face.

The wind increased, and Bellisaro ordered the topgallant sail to be furled. I watched several men scurry to the top. So tall is the mainmast that I had to crane my neck to see them. They loosened the bottom of the sail and were gathering it up to tie it to the yardarm when a gust of wind billowed it, knocking a sailor from his perch. I stood unable to move as he fell. I can barely remember his falling cry, but the sound of his body hitting the deck of the ship is forever in my head.

Valerian and I were the first to reach him. He was clearly beyond our help. The two of us, without waiting for an order, picked up his hands and feet and hauled him away. For my part, I wanted the sailors attending to the ship if a storm was coming. Valerian, however, is a man who does what needs to be done.

Valerian and I, followed by Father Hernando, took the poor soul down to the sailmaker, who quickly checked him over as Father Hernando prayed over him. The sailmaker removed the sailor's clothing and sewed him into sailcloth, the first stitch going through his septum. By the time the sailmaker finished, the ship's rocking had increased considerably. I prayed silently.

I went to my cabin to sit out the storm. Valerian kept me company. We talked at first, he telling me that it is good we are in the middle of the ocean, that there is greater danger nearer the coast. It was little comfort to me. At least nearer the coast I could swim to the shore.

The pitching of the ship became too violent for us to talk and we simply held on to whatever we could. I was glad that I had not eaten since the day before for surely it would not have stayed down. More than once was I slammed into the wall so hard I thought I would surely die. I pitied the poor men on deck and envied the man in the sailcloth.

I do not see how the ship withstood the fierce pounding of the ocean. The ocean is so vast and the ship so small. How could it possibly hold together? How in God's name could we survive? God help us, I whispered over and over.

"We are in good hands," Valerian yelled above the din to me. "Bellisaro is a good pilot. See, we pitch bow to stern, not side to side. This is good."

I hung on to his words as tightly as I hung on to the table leg, which was, thankfully, fastened to the floor.

We did survive. Abruptly, the heavy pitching of the sea stopped and we bobbed like a bottle of wine in the water. I was so relieved I forgot my aching body for the joy of finding myself alive and the ship whole. Valerian pulled himself up. "Thank God it's over," he said, and together we went up on deck to survey the damage. I thought I would find the men resting after such an ordeal, but they were busy pumping water from every deck and setting things right. A sailor must never rest. I pity them.

As it turned out, the storm was a harbinger of evil. The *Orgullo de España* was lost. There were but three survivors found clinging to pieces of broken mast floating in the water. The *Rosario* took in two of them, we the third—a sailor named Sancho.

Chapter 10

LINDSAY WAS UP early. She downed a glass of milk and had a sausage and biscuit from the mess before returning to the recovery of her unfortunate seafarer. Someone had brought a CD of sea chanteys, and she was greeted to the rhythmic strains of "What do you do with a drunken sailor?" She took up her spot beside her grid unit and removed the plastic covering. The night crew had finished the removal of the fill and the whole of the skeleton stood out in relief on the sea floor. His skull faced upward, his torso was twisted on its side so that the left set of ribs lay across the right set. His arms were at his sides—the right arm under the ribs and the left on top. The pelvis was slanted faceup like the skull, and the legs were extended. A yellow-brown textile covered half the face, part of the ribs, and upper legs. Fabric was also under the skeleton.

"Pretty interesting, isn't he?" The two members of the night crew were coming over, stepping across the planks. "We thought you would probably take him up first thing."

Lindsay nodded. "Nice job. He looks good. Lewis is here. He'll probably want to see him first."

As if on cue, Lindsay looked up and saw Lewis, followed by a television crew, descending the scaffolding.

"The ship's keel is 104 feet. That would make her main deck about 123 feet long. She was probably 37½ feet wide and, of course, had multiple decks. The *Estrella* was a big ship. If she had to wreck, we are lucky she wrecked off the coast of Georgia. Trey Marcus, the principal investigator and professor of marine archaeology at the University of Georgia, can tell you more."

Francisco Lewis was good. Lindsay had to concede that his voice and manner could make even the most mundane statistics

75

sound fascinating. In his jeans, khaki shirt, and tie, he looked ever the popular vision of an archaeologist. All he needed was a whip and a felt fedora.

The television crew had set up their equipment near the staircase, with the cameras pointing toward the dig and the crew as background. Lindsay shifted on the planks, wishing she could just take up the bones.

The interviewer turned to Trey. "How did you find the ship?"

"Two of my students were surveying in the area looking for a Civil War vessel and found a cannon. The cannon had on it an emblem suggestive of a much earlier Spanish ship. We went to Spain and found in their archives records of a ship named *Estrella de España* lost from a fleet of six ships on their way to Havana from Spain in 1558. The fleet lost sight of the *Estrella* during the night in good weather a few days away from their destination. Actually, we found that two ships were lost from the fleet, but the first ship was lost in the mid-Atlantic much earlier in the voyage."

"This sounds very mysterious. Was the ship in the Bermuda Triangle? Did that have something to do with her strange disappearance?"

Lindsay hoped her groan wasn't picked up by the sound equipment. She hated questions that assumed events in history were driven by aliens, lost tribes, and strange forces.

Trey paused for only a second. "The disappearance was a mystery, but not strange. The ocean is big and full of danger even today, and we have global positioning satellites and all kinds of sophisticated navigational equipment." He held up the instrument he had at his side. "This astrolabe, a compass, wind, brains, and muscle were all that got the ship across the ocean. It was easy to sail off course and become lost. As it happens, we believe this ship was sunk in a storm."

"How do you know that?"

"We've found three of what we believe to be her cannons several miles away, and so far we've found none in the excavation. Ships' captains often ordered the cannons and heavy cargo thrown overboard to lighten the ship when they ran into really serious trouble. We've also found anchor rope in a position that suggests they were desperately trying to save the ship from breaking up."

"So you can tell about her final days from what you find here?"

"Probably. We've already discovered plenty, and we've virtually only started."

"How about the crew? Do you expect to find any human remains?"

"As a matter of fact," said Lewis, "we have just finished excavating a human skeleton. Perhaps you would like to see it?"

"Oh, no," said Bobbie. "They're coming over here."

Trey helped them negotiate the walkways as they made their way to Unit 3 and HSkR1, as the skeleton was designated. The interviewer, blonde and in her mid-thirties, named Carma Grey, gingerly stepped over and peered at the remains as Trey introduced Bobbie and the two students.

"And this," he said, "is Dr. Lindsay Chamberlain. She's in charge of all the skeletal excavation at the site. Dr. Chamberlain is a professor of osteology at the University of Georgia. She also works occasionally with local law enforcement in identifying skeletal remains."

Lindsay stood, concentrating on not doing something dumb like smoothing her hair, tugging at her clothes, or looking at the man holding the camera on his shoulder. I hate this, she thought, hoping her sentiments didn't show on her face. She smiled.

"What can you tell me about this skeleton?"

"I can tell you he is definitely male. He did not die when the ship went down—"

"Oh, how do you know that?"

"He appears to be wrapped in sailcloth. That's what they did with passengers and crew who died aboard ship. They apparently didn't have time to give him a burial at sea, indicating that he probably died shortly before or during the storm. He could, for example, have fallen from a yardarm while trying to adjust the sails. Ships were hazardous places, especially during bad weather."

"Do you think you will be able to tell how he died?"

"There is a good chance."

"Will you be able to find out anything else about him?"

"We should be able to learn a lot about him. Human bones are not dead tissue. They are remodeled and changed throughout our lives, reflecting what we do, or have done to us. Our bones can speak very eloquently for us after we're gone."

"What happens to him now?"

"This morning we are going to take him up. It has to be done carefully, particularly because we have delicate fabric remains to protect. Then he will go to the lab and be put in a series of baths with decreasing percentages of seawater until his environment is gradually changed from salt water to fresh water."

"Why do you have to do that?"

"All these artifacts have been buried underwater for over 440 years," said Trey. "They have to gradually get accustomed to being out of water. The wood, for example, will always have to be kept in a climate-controlled environment, even after we rinse the salt water out, or it will disintegrate."

The interviewer turned to Lewis. "This dam, and everything that goes with it, is very expensive. What is going to come out of this that will be worth the money spent on it? We now have Tang because we went to the moon. What will we get from this?"

"If our own history is not of value, if discovering information about early nutrition and progression of diseases is not of value, if uncovering forgotten ways of building and manufacturing things is not of value, if the study of ocean currents and weather is not of value, if devising excavation techniques that can be generalized to, for example, underwater rescue, has no value, and if employing people and putting all this money into the regional economy has no value, then I suppose all we get from it is our curiosity satisfied."

Lindsay couldn't help but be reminded of the silver galleon and its possible value of hundreds of millions of dollars. It worried her.

The interviewer nodded and smiled as Lewis spoke, showing perfectly capped teeth.

"So you plan to glean a lot of information from this site?"

"Yes. Every time archaeologists dig a site, we hope to collect as much information as we can. It's how we add to our knowledge base. It's what we do. It's what makes us who we are."

The cameraman stayed and filmed Lindsay and her crew carefully placing the bones in plastic tubs and laying wet cloths over them. After a few minutes he moved on to film the hoisting of a large rib of the ship to the top of the dam.

"Well, I suppose it's good publicity." Lindsay carefully lifted each vertebra from the soil and laid it in the tub on a piece of wet cloth.

"Lewis wasn't half bad," Bobbie said.

"He handled the questions pretty well. Better than I would have, for sure," agreed Lindsay.

"I'd have told the broad to hang it up after that crack about the Bermuda Triangle," one of the night crew said with a snicker.

"Yeah," said the other, "they've always got to know what the monetary payoff is. Don't they care anything about knowledge? You want us to take these bones to the barge?"

Lindsay shook her head and stood up, stretching her legs. "No, put them by the field desk." If Trey and Lewis took the television crew to the lab, she might take the bones with her and get to work on them.

After the people from the night crew left, Lindsay gave her unit over to other members of the excavation crew, who troweled out the mud and put it into buckets. Lewis had come back and was working several feet away. Lindsay wondered if it was just for show. She watched him work on what appeared to be figurines. He did seem to know what he was doing. He lifted his trowel and one of the figurines came up with it, apparently hanging from the bottom of the trowel.

"What in the. . . ?" he said.

Lindsay squatted down to look. He took the object away from the trowel then put it back.

"It's a magnet," he said.

"It looks like a chess piece," said Lindsay.

He rubbed the piece gently, then asked for someone to bring him some water. Jeff handed him his canteen and Lewis washed off the piece, revealing a yellowed, detailed carving of a woman with a crown.

"You're right. A queen," he said.

Their talk caught the attention of one of the cameramen and he came to film what they were doing. Lewis picked another piece from the mud and washed it off. This one was a black horse with a rider.

"A knight," he said.

"Cool," said the cameraman.

"They played games on ships to pass the time," said Lewis. "I imagine this belonged to one of the officers. What's unusual is the magnet on the bottom."

"Why do you think they would have that?" he asked.

"So they wouldn't slide off the chessboard when the ship

rocked," said Lewis and Lindsay together.

"It's a unique find," Lewis said as he went back to work with enthusiasm.

No matter how high up you get on the ladder, thought Lindsay, the interesting find still brings out that feeling of excitement.

"Here is an ivory pawn," he said, washing off the piece.

Lindsay supposed that Jeff was going to have to forget about his canteen of water for a while.

"No," said Lindsay, when the piece was rinsed. "That's a first proximal phalange of a foot."

"I believe you are right," Lewis agreed, smiling up at her.

"Is it human?" the cameraman asked.

"Sure is," Lindsay replied.

"Was he the one playing chess?" he asked, zooming in on the bone in Lewis's hand.

Lewis and Lindsay briefly looked at each other.

Lindsay didn't see John that evening, but he sent a message asking her out to dinner the following night. She spent the remainder of the day with Carolyn, who took possession of the skeleton as if it were her relative, and began separating the bone from the fabric stuck to it. She took great care to handle the cranium upside down in case some brain tissue had survived in the anaerobic environment of the mud.

"I'll have the fabric separated in no time and you can look at the skull. I know Cisco wants the analysis done quickly. Just keep it wet."

"By the way," said Korey, "he left this for you. Said it was loaded with the latest."

He handed Lindsay a black laptop computer much like the one she had at home.

"Nice," said Lindsay, opening it up. "The guy knows how to give a girl a gift."

"You work for Cisco, you get good equipment," Carolyn said.

Lindsay examined her workstation for the first time and found it furnished with books, anthropometric measuring devices, a digital camera, cranial rests, and enough record forms for the entire crew of the ship if they were found. She plugged in the computer and Windows came up immediately. She looked at the programs available to her: word processing, a great statistical package, an artifact mapping program, a program for computing stature from long bones, and the latest software for recording and analyzing ethnic origin from skull measurements. She put in some numbers out of her head to see where on the map the program located the source. Not bad.

"The skull has quite a bit of damage under the textile," Carolyn called over to her.

Lindsay went over to see. There was a depression fracture of the left parietal on the temporal line, and two more depression fractures on the left side partially overlaying each other atop the lambdoidal suture—between the left parietal and the occipital.

Lindsay touched the indentations in the skull. She was, after all, a forensic anthropologist, and she recognized murder by blunt-force trauma to the head when she saw it.

Chapter 11

CAROLYN LOOKED AT the skull suspiciously. Lindsay could see it in her eyes. She wasn't sure, but it didn't look right. "Was that caused by a fall from the mast to the deck or something?" Carolyn asked, finally.

"No," Lindsay said. "Force was applied to an immobile head, not the other way around."

"You're saying something hit this guy?" Korey came to look. "Probably the lateen mizzen yard. They were head height and real killers on ships."

When Lindsay didn't say anything, they stared at her.

"You don't think that's it, do you?" Carolyn asked.

"I need to examine the skull thoroughly before I commit."

"Cisco is going to love this," Carolyn said, nodding her head.

"Let's not say anything to *Cisco* until I've had a go at the entire skeleton," Lindsay warned.

Carolyn cleaned the skull and, to their disappointment, there was no brain tissue remaining inside. She wrapped it in soft, wet cloths and handed it over to Lindsay. The undamaged face was long and thin with no healed breaks or unusual characteristics. The teeth were in good condition and not very worn. With the head spanner and calipers Lindsay recorded twenty-three different measurements on the face, cranium, and underside before setting the skull on the donut ring and placing the cloth over it. She keyed in the measurements and asked for the various indices and watched as the program located the ethnic origin on the matrix. She clicked a menu item and asked for a map. It placed the origin of HSkR1 as southern Spain.

Lindsay pushed aside the computer and again concentrated on the skull, examining the fractures. She ran her fingers over the arc of the semicircular indentation. With the calipers she measured the size, depth, and beveling angle of each fracture. She reached for the camera.

"You want me to take the photographs for you?" Korey's voice startled her. She hadn't known he was behind her. "I have a setup over here."

"That would be nice. I'd also like some detailed drawings of the fractures when you can get to them."

"Sure thing."

"Well?" asked Carolyn.

"Well, what?" Lindsay handed over the skull to Korey.

"Well, you know what," Carolyn countered.

"Yes, some unknown person hit him over the head." Furthermore, Lindsay thought she knew what the weapon was. If she was right, it was a tool still in common use today. In fact, she had a similar one in her shed at home.

"I knew it," Carolyn said, grinning and fairly jumping with excitement.

"Well, let's not spread this around."

"Can I see you a moment, Chamberlain?" Lindsay swiveled in her chair. She hadn't heard Trey come into the lab, hadn't realized it was quitting time at the site. Trey's voice had an edge to it. Had something else happened? Lindsay followed him to the far end of the lab.

"You weren't telling Taylor about the possibility of another galleon, were you?"

"No."

"What were you talking about with her just then? I heard you tell her not to tell anyone—about what?"

"We were talking about HSkR1. He was murdered. I didn't want it to become general knowledge. I was afraid it would attract too many curiosity seekers."

Trey put his head down. "Chamberlain, I'm sorry."

"It's all right. I'm sure his next of kin are all dead now."

"I'm glad you have a sense of humor."

"I don't. I'm wondering why you jumped to a conclusion like that."

"I'm sorry. I've been thinking about what you said—about how many people know about . . . you know, and it worries me. I have awful visions of this area becoming overrun with treasure hunters if the rumor of a silver galleon gets out. That TV interviewer—what was her name? Grey? She asked about treasure. I'm sure it was just because this was a galleon, and the discovery of the *Atocha* in Florida is still on everyone's mind, but—"

"You explained to her that it would have been unheard of for the Spanish government to send gold and silver over to the Indians?"

Trey's mouth quivered into half a smile. "I think I made her understand." He paused a moment. The tenuous uplift of his mouth fell back to a frown.

"Someone told King-Smith-Falcon that there were irregularities in the bidding process. They were the third bidder and are asking for an audit of the process. I imagine we have Hardy Denton to thank for that. If that isn't enough, Eva Jones had her lawyer send us a letter ordering us to stop harassing and slandering her . . . or else."

"Then she must be feeling heat from the Coast Guard."

"Must be." He cocked his head as if just hearing what she said about the skeleton. "You say he was murdered? Are you sure?"

"Unless the Spanish conducted executions by conking the condemned on the head—yes, I'm sure."

"Frank said you're good at this."

"Frank said I'm good at what?"

"Attracting anomalies, such as ancient murder victims. That's a rare talent."

"Yes, and I have to keep in practice."

"Maybe if we get people interested in this, they'll forget about the treasure angle."

"Don't count on it."

"I know. I wish I knew what Jones is up to—if she knows about the other galleon."

"Maybe she doesn't. Is there anything about this galleon, the *Estrella*, that has a lot of monetary value?"

Trey shook his head.

"How about mercury? Is it valuable? Didn't the Spanish send supplies of mercury to the New World for use in the mining of silver? Maybe she thinks there's some in the ship."

"Mercury does have value. I'm not sure, but I think we're talking about less than $7,000 a ton. That's not enough for someone like Jones."

"She collects artifacts, too. She may have buyers for astrolabes, bronze cannons, and olive jars," Lindsay offered.

"Maybe." Trey shrugged. "Look, I am sorry about what I said. It's not like me to be paranoid."

Lindsay patted him on the shoulder as she turned to go back to her desk and close down. "Maybe it's the effect of the Bermuda Triangle."

Lindsay hadn't seen the new warehouse that held the ship's timbers. Before that day's debriefing, she walked down to the dock to take a look at the huge brine tanks holding the beams and other wood artifacts. The metal fabricated building was like an airplane hangar—one large no-frills room. A front-end loader pulled the metal tanks out to the dock to receive the day's excavated timber, then took them back into the warehouse. They're going to need a large building if they plan to restore the whole ship, thought Lindsay. She had searched the Web for sunken ships and found a site showing the reconstructed *Mary Rose* in its environmentally controlled room. Something like that was probably what Francisco Lewis had planned for the *Estrella*. She would like to see that. She walked among the huge tanks, looking at the enormous pieces of timber stacked in them. One tank had a large sign that read: Some assembly required.

She walked the long distance to the other end near a wide double doorway that led out onto more decks. A tall, thin young man in cutoffs and rubber apron stood in front of a large metal-gray utility sink, not unlike the ones they had in the lab at Baldwin Hall on campus. He was chemically sorting soil samples from the site, looking for any plant remains.

"Finding much?"

He turned. "Hey, how you doing? Not a lot. A few charred beans, some seeds, your basic charcoal. The seeds we might be able to get to grow."

Lindsay noted the empty bags of sugar in the trash barrel. He nodded.

"Adding sugar to the water increases the specific gravity. Voilà—the plant remains float and we don't have to use chemicals toxic to the environment."

"Interesting. I hadn't heard of using sugar. I thought you were making whiskey."

He laughed. "It's a relatively recent method. A good thing for this place, otherwise we'd have to do the chemical floatation some-where else." He grinned. "The biology people are kind of picky about their island."

"I'll bet. By the way, I'm Lindsay Chamberlain."

"Isaac Jones, not related to the lady pirate. I heard she came to the site."

Lindsay nodded. "She has a presence, for sure. Where are you from?"

"University of South Carolina, same place as Nate and Sarah. You're from UGA. I've heard of you. Jeff calls you the Angel of Death."

"Yes, but I'm on holiday."

Isaac laughed and scooped out a sieveful of carbon remains and placed them on a drying rack.

Lindsay wandered a few feet to where three tanks sat by the wall. Two tanks contained a barrel each. They were whole, made with slats of wood with an iron hoop around the top and bottom. What was in them? Water? Wine?

In another tank was the sea chest. Lindsay guessed it was about two feet, by one foot, by one foot—not very big, but very heavy— about two hundred waterlogged pounds. She stooped down to get a closer look and peered through the brine. There was a carving on the lid—worn, beautiful, and faintly familiar—a crest perhaps? It looked like some kind of bird perched in the vee of a tree. And what was in this one? Lindsay wanted to reach in, open it, and dig through the contents. A paper taped to the tank indicated where it was from—the unit next to hers. It had been near where Lewis found the chess pieces.

"I'll bet you want to open it, don't you?"

Lindsay glanced sideways at Bobbie, who had come in from the dock. "You read my mind. What do you think's in it?"

"Probably decayed wet rags that used to be clothes," said Bobbie. "You think it could be gold coins or something?"

"I don't know. Could be anything. It has a crest, so it might belong to one of the officers."

They walked together to the house for the debriefing. Trey gave a summary of the day's progress and discoveries. Francisco Lewis himself uncovered the second human skeleton and, of course, the twelve chess pieces, each possessing a magnetic base.

"A chess set like this was described in the diary as belonging to a passenger on the *Estrella* named Valerian. All of us need to keep an eye out for this kind of matchup between the diary and our finds." He paused and grinned. "This is one of the things that makes this site so unique."

Trey also reported that the crew sifting the fill found amphibian bones, part of a comb, a thimble, glass beads, numerous undistinguishable pieces of wood, and hundreds of small iron concretions.

Steven Nemo reported that they had taken up several planks of deck and inner-wall timber in the stern.

"Considering the age of the ship, the timber is in remarkably good condition," he reported.

Nate Hampton, who was grounded from even being topside crew on the diving boats until he healed, and a couple of other crew members had opened up a new section that they thought might be the sterncastle.

Gina had found a silver filigreed object among the stone ballast that Trey believed was a pomander, a device for holding spices to be sniffed to mask disagreeable odors.

"Interesting that it was in the hold," he said. "It's definitely not a sailor's personal property. It would have belonged to a higher ranking officer or well-to-do passenger, and they didn't frequent the hold. But a pomander is certainly something they would take with them when they did."

Jeff grinned with pleasure, an expression Lindsay hadn't seen in him before, as Trey told about him finding a helmet and sword lying next to each other. Other finds included more rope and part of a lift-block for supporting the ends of a yardarm, and what was thought at first to be beads from a necklace, but turned out to be sections of a parrel, a kind of bearing used where the yardarm joins the mast.

Every small piece they found was another piece to a three-dimensional puzzle. Slowly, bit by bit, they were resurrecting a ship from the mud at the bottom of the sea. This was the fun of archaeology, reconstructing the whole and finding the story.

Both Lewis and Trey were satisfied with the rate of excavation. Some of the best news, however, was that there had been no new incidents like the one that happened to Nate, no unexpected visitors, no concerns except what is normal for a dig. It was a good day.

Trey didn't mention the letter from Evangeline Jones's lawyer or the letter of protest from King-Smith-Falcon. Of course, he wouldn't have in a debriefing. Lindsay imagined those matters were in Lewis's hands, and she didn't doubt Lewis's ability to take care of them.

After they heard from the survey team and discussed all the problems and issues relevant to the excavation, Lewis rose and gave a brief summary about the television crew.

"They left very impressed with all of us," he said.

"Like that was hard," Gina whispered to those around her.

⚓

Lewis arranged for dinner on the barge that evening—boiled shrimp, grilled hamburgers, roasted corn, and a keg of beer. Lindsay, Bobbie, Sarah, Gina, Juliana, and Harper sat together, shelling shrimp and eating it like popcorn. The sun had not yet set, but hung red against the wall of a gold and orange sky.

"This is really good," Harper said, raising her voice over the rock music.

"It's fresh, today's catch," said Sarah. "Lewis got it from one of the shrimpers."

"I could get used to living like this." Bobbie sat cross-legged in cutoff overalls and a sleeveless T-shirt, stripping the shell off her shrimp.

"So could I," Harper agreed.

"How's the translation coming?" Nate sat down beside them with two plates of food, one loaded with shrimp, another with corn.

"No archaeology talk allowed. This is a night for sensuous pleasures." Juliana stuck a shrimp in her mouth and chased it with a swallow of beer.

"Did I pick the right group, or what?" said Nate.

The corn had been roasted in its husk. Lindsay stripped off the shucks and bit into the yellow kernels. She thought it was about the best thing she had ever tasted.

"How's the arm?" Gina asked Nate.

He raised it slightly, looking at the white bandage. "Fine. Doc here did a pretty good job." Lindsay rolled her eyes. "Trey won't let me dive or drive a boat until the doctor okays it. Until then, I gotta work in the mud with you guys. I'm not quite sure of the logic there."

"What kind of necklace is that, Sarah?" Harper leaned over and picked up what looked to be a coin on a silver chain around Sarah's neck.

"It's a quarter with a hole in it," Sarah said. "I found it on the beach when we got here. It was tied to a fishing line and tangled up in driftwood."

"Someone fishing for sand dollars?" Harper said, returning her attention to shucking her corn.

"I found one of those, too," said Lindsay. "I wonder what they're for."

"Well, I don't think it looks good for you to be wearing artifacts," Nate said.

Sarah frowned at him. "What artifacts? It's a 1974 United States quarter I found on the beach. They're still in circulation."

Trey came and sat down beside Harper. "You guys look like you're enjoying yourselves."

"The food's great," said Lindsay. "Can we do it again tomorrow?"

"Yeah," said Nate. "How about for lunch? It'd be better than those sandwiches. I know, you could have shrimp boiling constantly and we could hop over to the barge anytime we were hungry."

"How 'bout it, Chamberlain?" asked Trey. "Are you up to trying out some of your new diving equipment tomorrow?"

"Sure. When?"

"I'm taking Harper out, I thought you might like to go. Bobbie, you want to be her partner?"

"Sure. Where are we diving?"

"Gray's Reef. The water's clear, and it's a good place to get a little diving time in. We'll go early in the morning."

Lindsay stood and made her way across the barge and dumped her trash into a large barrel. The sun was setting and the darkness was coming quickly. The music had grown louder. A group of archaeologists were in one corner arguing with some of West's people about the disposition of the Kennewick Man. That was an argument she didn't want to get into. She turned and watched some couples dancing.

"Care to dance? I heard you're good." It was Francisco Lewis.

There weren't many division heads who could pull off dancing rock-and-roll without looking ridiculous, but Lewis was one of them. He was a good dancer. After a minute or two, more couples joined in, including Harper and Trey. She and Lewis danced one more, then walked over to the side of the boat.

"Trey tells me you found out some interesting things about our skeleton." Lewis leaned with his forearms on the side of the boat and his hands clasped, staring out at the waves lapping at the barge.

"Yes. I'll finish it up tomorrow afternoon. I'm going diving in the morning."

"I'm glad you're enjoying this dig. I wanted you here rather than teaching."

"Why?" Lindsay leaned against the railing with her back to the ocean and looked at the lights of the cofferdam.

"Because of your broad range of experience with skeletal remains, and because of your imagination. This is the kind of site that requires imagination as well as knowledge."

Lindsay wasn't sure she agreed with that, but she was glad to be here. "I am grateful to have been asked to come."

Lewis was quiet for a moment, seeming to stare out at the horizon. As Lindsay started to leave, he turned around and spoke again. "I know you thought that Gerri Chapman was being brought in to replace you in the department, but that was never the case. If you had known me, you would have realized that. You see, most people think I'm only after the spotlight—and power. They're wrong. I also love good research, and I'm as curious about things as you are. I like to have people of ability—stars, if you will—around me."

Lindsay looked over at him and laughed. The lights on the barge reflected in Lewis's dark eyes as he spoke about himself.

"I admit that I like to be the brightest star, but it's no good being one if there aren't other bright stars in your constellation."

"I'm not going to call you Cisco."

When Lewis smiled, she fully expected to see the lights of the dam twinkle off his teeth.

"No, I don't expect you would," he said and left to join the discussion about whether Kennewick Man was Indian or Caucasoid.

Lindsay turned toward the ocean and looked out at the water. Out of the corner of her eye she caught sight of John West standing against the wall watching her. She walked over to him.

"Care to dance?" she asked.

"I don't dance," he said.

"I can teach you." She held out her arms and he came forward. "Put your arm around my waist like this."

He did and pulled her close. "Like this?"

"That's it."

"I can do this part well. It's the movement where I have trouble."

"Then let me lead." Lindsay led a few steps and West followed. "See, that wasn't so bad."

"It would be much better just to stand here like this."

"No, I think once you get used to the movement, you'll like it better."

"You may be right."

They danced several more steps until the music stopped.

"There's still some shrimp left. Have you eaten?" she asked.

"I'm not hungry. I'd rather just relax here with you."

The argument in the corner of who should be the rightful receiver of the ancient bones, the Native Americans or the archaeologists, grew louder. John and Lindsay looked over at them. She thought she heard Steven Nemo's voice saying something like, "That was nine thousand years ago. How do you know he wouldn't have been offended by their ceremonies as much as our analysis?" The response was lost to the sound of a wave.

"Maybe we should go to the other end of the boat?" West said.

"I think that would be a good idea."

They walked along the port side of the barge to the aft where the noise of the party became an indistinct mixture of sounds. The cofferdam stood beside them like an island, only nine feet above the water. The barge was anchored close so that a gangplank stretched across to the dock of the dam. They were so close that Lindsay could hear the pumps running.

"Do the pumps always run?"

The breeze from the land was chilly and Lindsay shivered.

"Yes." From behind, John wrapped his arms around her.

"What would happen if they stopped?"

"The dam would fill back up with water. The ocean is very persistent. We have to maintain a constant expenditure of energy to keep it at bay. Don't worry. The dam is constantly guarded, and I have backup pumps."

Lindsay shivered again, but this time from her thoughts.

"The ocean wouldn't come gushing in, would it?"

She felt his chest vibrate with a laugh.

"No, even if the pumps stopped, it would fill very slowly. The only way the ocean would rush in is if there was a serious breach in both the inner and outer bulkheads, and we would discover any problem long before it got to that point. You have to trust the physics."

"The whole thing is really quite magnificent. You should be very proud of it."

"I am. The success of this dam is my future."

John's body was a welcome warmth in the cool night air and she felt content just to let the moment last. She knew that something good was happening between her and John. She made a conscious effort not to think about how it would all end if they had a confrontation about Indian burials. That issue was a gulf between them that both of them ignored—but how long could that last, considering what she did for a living?

It was two o'clock in the morning and most of the party had broken up when Lindsay made her way down the hallway to her cabin. Somewhere she had made a wrong turn, for when she opened the door to what she thought was her room and flipped the light switch, the glow illuminated a room filled with computer equipment, wallpapered with maps, and cluttered with data-filled notebooks. She turned to go and met Nate coming through the door.

"Well, this is a nice surprise."

"I appear to be lost," she said.

"Well, damn. I thought maybe you came to change my bandage."

"This looks like a command center." She gestured to the trappings.

"My dissertation. Want a Cook's tour?" He grinned like a kid.

"Sure."

Nate stepped in and turned on his computer. "I'm developing a computer simulation of ocean wind and currents. Look." He pointed to a map. "This is a map of the major ocean currents and wind directions—the blue lines are the currents, the red is wind." The map had several others hanging behind it, which he flipped through. "There are seasonal differences and drifts over decades." He turned his head as if to see if she was paying attention. "We've collected oceanographic data for the past hundred years. The Spanish archives have quite a bit of data from the past and I've recorded those as well."

"What are you doing with it?"

"Right now, developing a model to predict where to find ship-wrecks. Watch." He sat down at the computer and punched keys on his computer and started putting in data. "Say it was reported that a ship went down in 1770 off the coast of Georgia, and we find some artifacts but not the ship. Knowing what the ocean conditions were at that time and what they are now, I can come up with several possibilities of where to find her. Or"—he raised a hand before she spoke—"if we have some idea where she sank, I can use the same variables to figure where she may have drifted to."

"That's an awful lot of variables," said Lindsay.

"Yes, that's what makes it so difficult. And I don't have complete data. I received a lot from the archives of seafaring countries, a bunch more from sea floor core drilling that's really good."

Lindsay picked up an open notebook filled with what looked like map data points. "And you put all those numbers into the computer?"

"Yes, and a lot of other data about the relative energy of a particular spot on the ocean floor."

"I'm not good with computers, but doesn't that take a lot of memory?"

"You bet it does. It's another reason that the biology people are pissed at us. You know Easterall, the biologist?"

"Sure do. The would-be Nobel Prize winner whom UGA got by building him a new research facility and buying a state-of-the-art supercomputer."

Nate grinned wickedly. "Don't you just love celebrity faculty? The supercomputer was supposed to be for all research faculty to use, of course," he said.

"Yeah, sure," said Lindsay. "If you can get time on it."

"Precisely. Easterall hogged all the time, filling it up with his rain forest data—which I have to admit, is a worthwhile project."

True, thought Lindsay, but in the meantime, all the other faculty who had massive amounts of data to analyze had to take a back seat. Lindsay knew part of Easterall's work was here on St. Magdalena, but she really didn't know what his people did here.

"What did you do to make him mad?" Lindsay asked.

"Not me"—Nate looked at her innocently—"Cisco. Here have a seat." He pulled out a chair.

Lindsay sat down, a hint of a smile playing around her lips. Having been indefinitely put on hold herself for only a few hours of computer time she had requested a couple of years ago, she was interested to hear what Lewis had been up to since he arrived at UGA.

"Cisco," continued Nate, "turns out to be a better politician. He really is good. Have you ever seen him work?"

Lindsay shook her head.

"He gets everything done before he even meets formally with the university bigwigs. He starts with politicians, businessmen, and alumni. He shows them numbers—how many people he's going to put to work, and how he can make it pay, and how we are doing something no other state but Texas has done. When he has their support, he meets with university officials. By then, it's almost a done deal." Nate's grin broadened. "All he needs is some initial financial support to go along with the private money he's already raised, and a whole lot of computer time. The upshot of it is, I get to plug my data into the supercomputer and Easterall has to wait."

Lindsay laughed out loud. "I'll bet he hated that."

"He's still fuming. He's got those guys over at St. Magdalena spying for him. The fax machine gets so much use, I'm surprised it hasn't gone up in smoke. We kind of like to feed them rumors to keep 'em going."

"I see. That's where the story came from that Lewis is going to make St. Magdalena a theme park."

"You got it. That was my idea. Carolyn had a friend slip the idea to one of the graduate students in Botany, and she faxed it to Tessa."

Lindsay closed her eyes and shook her head. At least they weren't putting whipped cream in one another's shoes. "You know, you might make the poor woman stroke out."

"No, we're just aiming for them to look like fools."

"Is there that much animosity?"

Nate sobered for a moment and nodded his head. "What do you think? We needed a lot of space and had to build the ware-house for the ship timbers. Cisco arranged to have the biology people moved into less than half the building space they had before we came, and shack up at the ranger station so Harper and some of the other crew could have their apartments. He especially wanted Harper to work at the site, so he arranged to get the largest suite for her."

"I can see why Tessa was so upset by the thought that I might be moving in." Lindsay stood up and yawned. "I need to find my way back. This has been an interesting conversation. Your work is fascinating. I'll look forward to reading your dissertation."

"I'm pretty excited about it. There's a lot of applications it can be put to besides archaeology." He got up, closed the door and pointed to a schematic of the ship. "That's the barge. We are here." He pointed to a room. "You are here, with Bobbie, right?" Lindsay nodded. "Always become familiar with a ship you're in, especially if you plan to do any wreck diving. Always know how the wreck is oriented. You'll find one of these maps behind your door as well."

Lindsay didn't plan to do any wreck diving, but she thanked him for the advice. As she walked down the narrow hallways, she realized that the silver galleon was the wreck Nate was going to find with his program. All he needed was the sea floor location of some artifacts from the galleon or some idea where she sank. And that's why Lewis got so much support for the project. You show anyone credible evidence that you can find a billion dollars' worth of treasure and you have their attention. What's the rain forest or the Nobel Prize compared to that? For the first time ever, Lindsay felt sympathy for Easterall and his students. They had reason to be angry. Further, there's no way a secret can be kept about a sunken galleon loaded with that much gold, silver, and jewels. Someone had to have told Eva Jones. Lindsay knew it.

Bobbie was already asleep when Lindsay climbed in her bunk and pulled the covers over her. She drifted off to sleep, then abruptly awoke and sat up. She realized that Hardy Denton purposefully bid too low because he wanted to be sure to win. He was to have been Jones's spy at the dig, to keep her informed about what the archaeologists found and what they knew. No wonder he was so angry. Lindsay lay back down with an uneasy feeling in the pit of her stomach.

Chapter 12

THE FINAL RESTING place of the *Estrella de España* was under five feet of sand and silt, deep in the middle of a vast sandy desert on the ocean floor in part of the featureless plain that makes up most of the sea bottom along the coast of Georgia. Rising out of the floor of this ocean desert is a seventeen-square-mile limestone oasis known as Gray's Reef. The flat troughs and rugged over-hangs carved in the rock of the reef are home to a lush and color-ful sea life, including sea fans, yellow colonial anemone, red sponges, loggerhead turtles, sharks, whales, and an amazing vari-ety of fish.

But twelve thousand years ago, when glaciers tied up signifi-cantly more water than today, the coastline extended almost sixty miles farther out to sea from where it is now, and Gray's Reef was dry land. Instead of the ocean forest, this place was a terrestrial home to Paleo-Indians, the Indians who fashioned chert Clovis points for their spears and hunted megafauna.

So far in the excavation of the sea bottom around the ship, none of the seventeen bone fragments and fossils found could be linked directly back to Paleo-Indians. The fragments were small, but sometimes small remains tell big stories.

Gray's Reef would be Lindsay's deepest dive—seventy feet, nothing to an experienced diver, but a deep dive for her. She went off the boat backward into the water. It was cool and refreshing, but not cold. She liked the water, but she was a surface swimmer. Diving still made her heart race. Once in the water, she oriented herself facing Trey, Harper, and John West. Lindsay was pleased that John had talked Bobbie and Gina into staying with the boat and letting him be Lindsay's buddy for the dive.

They set a reference on their compass so they could find their way back to the boat and zeroed their timers and gauges. Trey set his global position indicator. Lindsay changed the snorkel for her regulator and moved her jaw back and forth to pressurize her ears. Trey pointed to her buoyancy compensator deflator valve, and she took it in her hand. Everyone was ready.

Trey signaled the descent. Lindsay exhaled and vented her vest. She and the others started down, feetfirst, every few feet equalizing the pressure in their ears. The descent was Lindsay's least favorite part of a dive. In a way, it was like falling in slow motion, but not quite falling. Here buoyancy was a stronger force than gravity. It was hard to get down and stay down without help. It was like being in a place with new physical laws to cope with. After all, people were not made for the water. They cannot breathe it. They cannot withstand the pressure. They cannot stay submerged without help. It seemed forever before Trey gave the signal to level off just above the bottom.

It was another world, a fantasy. This was the payoff for the long descent. Lindsay was a strong swimmer, and during her diving lessons she had discovered a talent for maneuvering underwater with fins. Here, balanced with the weights on her belt and the vest-like buoyancy compensator, she was suspended, free of gravity, free of drifting upward. Must be like flying, she thought.

Lindsay swam through a school of fish that looked like shiny silver coins. An angelfish darted behind a vase sponge. Ahead, Trey pointed to a loggerhead sea turtle. Lindsay dived to take a closer look, wondering how old the huge reptile was. She and John hovered over its back. She touched the shell with the tips of her fingers, awed that any of its kind survived the ordeal of hatching in the sandy beach, running a gauntlet of birds to the water, and avoiding predator fish for the years it took to grow big enough to stop being prey.

They investigated nooks and crannies, pointing out anything beautiful or interesting. Harper was startled by an eel languishing in a deep recess. A tiger fish brushed Lindsay's arm. She would have liked to see a whale, but they came to these waters only in the winter.

She checked her watch. They had been down fifteen minutes already. The time went so fast. They came upon an expanse of sand, like a valley carved in the limestone. Lindsay signaled to John that she was going to look inside an overhang. He nodded and motioned that he was going to swim overhead and look at the top of the overhang. Lindsay examined the sandy floor, brushed it with her fingers, letting loose a fog of sediment. She swam to the other side, resolving to look and not muddy the waters.

Ahead of her, she thought she saw something—a curve in the pattern of rocky sediment. She swam to it, brushed away the sand, clouding the water again. She reached and found the object but was unable to see it in the sediment-filled water. She slipped it into a zippered pocket, then glanced up and realized she couldn't see in any direction through the clouded water that had enveloped her, and didn't know which way to swim. She panicked and grabbed at her belt for her flashlight. Unable to see or to think clearly what she was doing, she mistakenly tugged at the buckle, loosening the belt, and her weights slipped from her waist, into the murky water. Suddenly and quickly, as if having pushed a button in an elevator, she was moving upward.

Don't panic. She let out her breath slowly and stretched out her arms and legs—flaring to slow her ascent. Then she felt an arm around her waist. John was pulling her down. Harper met them with Lindsay's weight belt and helped reattach it around her. Trey watched her closely, motioning, asking if she was all right. She nodded and indicated that she wanted him to take a global positioning reading at the place where she had been.

Lindsay's heart was still pounding and she had to concentrate on breathing normally as they swam down the channel. Out of the corner of her eye she saw John watching her, and she signaled to him that she was fine. Trey led them upward to the top of the limestone rocks. Looking back down at the trough they had been in, Lindsay wondered if it had been a riverbed. What would a riverbed look like after being submerged for several thousand years? Trey pointed to his watch. Time to head back to the place where they had descended.

Halfway back, off to the side, Lindsay saw two other divers swimming just above the bottom, looking only at the sea floor. With the carpet of color and abundance of aquatic life, she wondered at their being so focused. They must be surveying, she thought. For what? She looked at Trey and saw that he had noticed them, too.

"Have a good time?" asked Bobbie when they were in the boat stripping off their gear.

"It's really beautiful down there," said Lindsay and Harper together.

"It's a different experience every time I go," Trey said.

Then the question that Lindsay dreaded. He asked if she was all right. She hoped the redness that she felt creeping into her cheeks didn't show.

"I'm fine. Sorry I scared everybody."

Trey shook his head. "Probably scared you worse than it did us. You didn't ascend that far."

"How'd you lose your weights?" asked Harper.

"I was, uh, grabbing for a flashlight."

"A flashlight?" asked Harper.

Trey looked puzzled. Even in the overhangs the visibility had been exceptionally good.

"Lindsay was lost in a cave once," John offered. "I expect she had a flashback when the water got murky."

Lindsay nodded. "Really, I'm fine. Sometimes I just have this absurd need to know that I have a light."

"Well, you did right to control your ascent," said Trey.

Ever the teacher, he explained what she would have had to do next had a partner not been there.

Harper grinned. "You aren't used to being out of control, are you?"

Lindsay looked at her ruefully. "No," she said.

"What was it you found?" asked Trey.

Lindsay fished the two-inch mineralized object out of her pocket and examined it before handing it to Trey.

"I can't believe it," he said. "Do you know how few fossils have been found here? I haven't found any, and this is your first trip."

"I have an eye for bones, what can I say?"

Bobbie reached for the bone. "What is it, can you tell?"

"It's mammal. I believe a rib fragment. The tightness of the curve makes me suspect it might be human."

As soon as she said it, she thought of John. The phrase "bone of contention" entered her mind, and she changed the subject.

"Did you see those other divers?"

They all had. "Lots of people dive at Gray's Reef," Trey said, but Lindsay knew that he, like she, thought they might be Eva Jones's divers.

Lindsay's long hair was still damp when she settled in the lab to finish analyzing the bones of HSkR1. She yawned and rubbed her ears to get the pressure back into balance. Carolyn had cleaned the bones of fabric and placed a wet cloth over them. Lindsay laid out the long bones and measured them one by one on an osteometric board. She gave each bone a thorough examination, first by gently running her fingers over its surface. It probably looked to others as if she were caressing them, but Lindsay believed in using her tactile senses as well as her eyes.

Once when she was taking a human osteology course, she had been blindfolded and required to lay out a box of skeletal remains in anatomical position, then write an analysis of the individual without ever having seen the bones. She got so good at it that it became a challenge to the other archaeology students to find something that she couldn't identify. Sometimes they would try without success to fool her with animal bones. Though her skills impressed the archaeology students, Lindsay knew that any halfway good osteologist could do the same thing. Her friends swore that if she ever lost her eyesight, she could do her job just as well. She learned some valuable lessons from that experience that she now tried to pass on to her own students, and she made the blindfold test a part of the final examination in her osteology courses.

Lindsay completed examination of each bone of HSkR1 with a detailed visual inspection of every centimeter of its surface, using both her naked eye and magnification. It was a time-consuming process, but its payoff was the story the bones could paint for the discerning eye.

HSkR1 was about five feet, ten inches tall, above average for the men of his time. His muscle attachments were no bigger than average, indicating he was not of muscular build and therefore probably was not one of the sailors, whose hard work showed markedly in their bones. The right lateral attachments were slightly larger than their left counterparts, indicating right-handedness. She found no healed breaks, pits, unevenness, or swelling in the bones that would be evidence of disease. Nor did she find any malformation of the long bones. The individual appeared to have had good nutrition from the time he was a child until he died.

She returned the long bones to Carolyn and took the scapulas. Compared with the left, the beveling on the margin of the glenoid cavity of the right shoulder blade, the cup where the head of the humerus rests, also indicated that he was right-handed.

Lindsay took the skull, set it on the donut ring, and went to the trays of soaking artifacts, looking for one thing in particular.

"Can I borrow this a minute?" she asked Carolyn, pointing to a wooden caulker's mallet.

"Why?"

"I'd like to take some measurements."

Carolyn took the artifact and wrapped it in a damp cotton cloth, warning Lindsay that it was very fragile. She and Korey watched as Lindsay measured and examined the head of the mallet. They came closer, hovering over her shoulder as she placed the head of the hammer against the indentations of the skull and measured the angle of the mallet to the skull.

"Is that it?" asked Korey. "Is that the murder weapon?"

"It was something like this. I'm sure they had many of these on board."

The crew from the cofferdam were arriving, and the noise level in the lab increased. Lewis came over carrying a carton.

"She's found the murder weapon," whispered Carolyn.

Lewis looked dumbfounded for a moment. "You're kidding!"

"I've found a possibility," Lindsay mumbled as she fit the head of the mallet into the indentations at several angles.

"What are you doing now?" asked Lewis.

"The wound isn't even—the side of the weapon where the most force was focused left a deeper impression. By measuring the angle of the depression and the angle of the hammer in the wound, I can figure out the handedness and the height of the perp. Add this information to the hierarchy of the skull fractures, and I can determine the sequence of blows during the attack."

The three of them stood staring at her a moment, and Lindsay realized that she was accustomed to working with people like medical examiners, or her students, who were familiar with the forensic part of her work. She suppressed a smile.

"Well, damn," said Korey at last. "We'll be able to make an arrest by the end of the day."

"This is great," Lewis said, his eyes glistening with ideas. "This is the kind of personal drama we need to get everyone's interest in the project." He set the box he was holding down on the table. "Here's another skeleton. When can you finish with it?"

"Another one already? Is this the one you discovered?"

He nodded, and Lindsay bit her tongue to keep from saying

anything about the excavation being done way too fast.

Lewis apparently was a mind reader. "I put several people on it. Unfortunately, a dig like this one has to be done as quickly as possible. We can't hold back the ocean forever."

"So?" asked Carolyn.

"So what?" Lindsay asked her.

"How tall was the perp and which hand wielded the weapon?"

"Right now, I can tell you that he was shorter than HSkR1 and he was left-handed."

"Couldn't he just have used his left hand?" Korey asked.

"When someone is committing an act as serious and consequential as bludgeoning a person to death, they typically use the hand they have the most facility with."

"You said something about the sequence of blows?" said Lewis.

"Whoever it was came up from behind and struck him on the left side of the head with great force. When the victim fell forward, he hit him twice more."

"Wow," said Carolyn. "You do this all the time?"

"Not all the time, but I've seen wounds like these before."

"What? With a caulker's mallet?" asked Korey.

"With a hammer, a tire iron, a baseball bat. Different wounds, but there are similarities."

"You certainly have a nice life," said Carolyn.

Lindsay smiled at her. "I usually don't get any bodies that are fleshed out. That makes it easier."

That evening, Trey turned the debriefing over to Steven Nemo. Steven had created a giant cross-section schematic of the ship with each deck labeled. The hold was easy to identify with its piles of stone ballast. Above the hold were the orlop deck, main gun deck, weather deck, and the forecastle and sterncastle decks. He had mapped the location inside the ship of the artifacts discovered so far.

HSkR1 had been found in what was described as the sailmaker's cabin because a cache of sailcloth and a leather palm thimble were found there. That made sense. HSkR1 would have been taken there to be sewn into the sailcloth. The mallet, she noted, came from the carpenter's cabin, where they had also discovered part of a saw and a cache of chisels.

Lindsay wondered where the body had been discovered at the time of the murder. Would the journal tell what happened? Surely, something as dramatic as a murder would be worth mentioning. Lindsay bet that Lewis was pressuring Harper to hurry with the translation, just as he was pressing her to finish the skeletons.

HSkR2, Lewis's skeleton, was in a section that Steven said was probably an officer's or an important passenger's cabin. The huge trunk with the bird crest was the first artifact uncovered there; the chess pieces and the skeleton were found next. All appeared to have been jumbled on top of one another.

"I think HSkR2 is a passenger rather than an officer," Steven said. "An officer probably would have been somewhere else in the ship during a storm of such severity that it eventually sank the ship. If the chess set did belong to the passenger Valerian, there's a good chance this was Valerian's cabin. It would be interesting if the skeleton were Valerian, but we have no way at this time of knowing if they are his remains."

"No," said Gina, "I don't want it to be Valerian."

Steven looked at her a moment before setting aside the cross section and displaying a map of the sea floor.

"It's all right, Gina," said Nate. "Valerian's probably having a drink with Elvis as we speak."

"And here back on earth we found another cannon today," Steven Nemo continued, pointing to a series of small drawings. "If you notice, all of them are on a line, more or less. It's the pattern we would expect if they were throwing the cannons overboard to lighten the ship as part of their efforts to prevent it from sinking. When we finish the excavation, I think we'll be able to tell all the steps they went through to try to save the ship. Unfortunately, of course, they were ultimately not successful. That's why we have a ship to excavate."

"Lindsay has finished analysis of the first skeleton," said Trey. "Would you like to tell us about it, Lindsay?"

Lindsay stood and matter-of-factly gave her findings, including the head wounds and her suspicions about the murder weapon. For a moment they were silent.

"So," said Nate, "we need to keep on the lookout for a guy about five-five and left-handed. Do you know hair color, or any distinguishing marks we can look for?"

Lindsay grinned at him.

"You expect us to believe that?" Jeff stood, glowering at Lindsay. "The guy probably got his head bashed in by a yardarm.

It happened all the time on those ships. Or he fell from the mast. Come on. You're trying to tell us it was a murder? It was probably the guy described in the diary who fell and hit the deck."

"Well, Korey and I saw the mallet fit into the wounds," Carolyn responded. "Besides, I think they would have buried the guy who fell to the deck fairly quickly. He died pretty early on. They didn't keep ripe bodies around very long."

"Well, I don't believe it," said Jeff.

"It's not a matter of belief," said Lindsay. "It's a matter of empirical evidence. That's what happened." She felt like adding, And it's not my fault.

"Well, I think it's cool," Juliana said.

"So do I," said Lewis. At that, Jeff sat down. "Lindsay, would you mind making a sketch of what the guy looked like in life by tomorrow morning?"

"Sure." I don't need to sleep, she thought.

⚓

Lindsay and John ate pizza on the screened-in back porch of the lab, looking out over the jungle of flora.

"Good pizza," Lindsay said. "And thanks for saving my life today."

John laughed out loud. "I didn't save your life. You would have done all right if I hadn't been there."

"You know that I believe the bone fragment I found today is human."

"But you don't know for sure?"

"No. It's small, weathered, and heavily mineralized. But I think it's a piece of rib."

"I pick my battles. I don't want to argue with you over such a small piece of bone that may belong to a deer. Is that your concern?"

"I suppose."

John looked out over the wild landscape for several moments before he spoke. "Besides, you have a state of grace for a while."

"And why's that?"

"Because of the kindness you showed my father last year. He's grateful for the gift you sent him—the scale of the Uktena."

"I'm pleased that he liked it, but it was only a quartz crystal."

John smiled. "A crystal used by our ancestors, something we

knew about from legend. He tells me it's very powerful."

"What power does he say it has?"

John shook his head. "I don't know. My father and I are very different. He's more"—John shrugged—"Indian, I suppose. I've compromised."

Lindsay found John to be very Indian, but she didn't say so. "How does he feel about you?"

"I suppose he sees the two of us as different folds in the same garment."

"Did he actually say that?"

"No. That *Kung Fu* guy said it on TV the other night."

Lindsay laughed, and John joined her after a moment.

"You staying on the island tonight?" he asked.

Lindsay nodded. "I'm staying with Harper. Lewis wants a drawing of the murdered sailor by morning."

"Can't the artist, what's his name, Korey, do it?"

Lindsay shook her head. "He hasn't had experience creating likeness from a skull. You have to draw the image with the skull behind it. I usually use a light table. You also have to have a knowledge of the facial features of the ethnic group you're drawing."

"What's Lewis going to do with it?"

"I think he's going to put an article in the newspapers. Maybe send a press release to the TV stations, too."

"What does that do for the site?"

"Public awareness and support often translate into money."

"Then I suppose, since he still owes my company money for construction of the dam, that's a good thing."

Lindsay saw the shadow of a large dark bird fly over and perch atop a tall tree. She leaned forward and squinted her eyes. "Is that an eagle?"

"Yes. I've seen several here."

"You're kidding. This is the first one I've ever seen in the wild."

"He's young. His head is still black. Maybe we can go walking over the island sometime," said John. "There are lots of things to see."

"Yes, I'd like that. Wow, I've never seen an eagle like that before."

The eagle flew away, and Lindsay watched him soar out of sight. She rose and John stood with her.

"Rabbit?"

"Yes?"

"I enjoy being with you."

"Me, too."

"I'm glad I was here with you when you saw the eagle."

⚓

It was eleven o'clock when Lindsay finished the sketch and put it away in her desk drawer. Before locking up and climbing the stairs to Harper's apartment, she went to take a peek at the new set of bones, HSkR2. She wanted to scold Lewis for getting them out of the ground so fast.

The brown-yellow bones were in a tub of water. The skull was upside down in its own tank. Even upside down, Lindsay easily noticed the classic Asian features. Indian? Indians had been taken to Europe—and returned. Distinguishing between American Indian and non-Indian Asian was not always easy. She took the skull, made several mid-facial measurements, and plugged the data into the computer. "I'm going to get too used to this program," she whispered to herself as the map appeared on the screen and placed the skull on the coast near the East China Sea. Lindsay had more trust in calculations she did herself than those computed by a machine. But she couldn't complain about the speed. She studied the map, still distrusting something that fast and easy, so she did the calculations by hand. The skull was probably not Native American.

"Of course," she said aloud. "Valerian's servant." She grinned to herself. She wanted to call Trey, wake up Harper. A human connection. She loved it.

The sound of a door opening at the far end of the lab brought her head up. She expected to see one of the archaeology crew and was surprised to see Mike Altman, one of the biologists and Tessa's husband. His blond hair was disheveled, and she couldn't help noticing that his T-shirt was on inside out.

"I saw the light on," he said without a greeting. "You all keep the place locked up like Fort Knox; we have to get in when we have the chance." He walked to a cabinet and unlocked it. "We do have some supplies in here." He sat on his haunches and rummaged through the cabinet, pulling out what looked like graph paper.

"It's open all day. I'm sure no one would mind if you came to get your supplies."

Mike straightened up to face her. "Right. You haven't been here long, have you?"

"No. But as Bobbie pointed out to Tessa, the dig won't be here forever. You'll get your island back, and things will be back to normal for you."

"After you all build your museum and theme—whatever, this place will be destroyed."

"Come on. Does it really make sense to you that we would build a theme park on this island?"

"It makes as much sense as building a five-million-dollar structure out in the ocean to dig up a bunch of dead, waterlogged wood, then tear it down. There are more than thirty protected species of animals on this island. Yes, a few of them are small and not well known. I get so tired of your kind. You haven't heard of a species of fish or tree frog, so you use your ignorance as a measure of its worth."

"Isn't that what you are doing?"

He looked puzzled, then narrowed his eyes at her. "What do you mean?"

"You don't know what we do or what the value is, yet you judge it to be worthless."

"That's not the same thing."

"I don't want to argue with you. We are here and so are you. We won't be here long, and there isn't going to be a museum or a theme park built on the island."

"Do you know that for sure?"

"This is a national park, for heaven's sake. And we don't build theme parks. It's stupid, and you and your colleagues should know better."

He stared at her wide-eyed for a moment. She thought perhaps it dawned on him that they had been had. He turned on his heel and left. Lindsay watched him go out the door with his graph paper. He was staying at the ranger's station. He had dressed hurriedly and hiked all the way there down the trail to get graph paper? She doubted it. Surely, they wouldn't destroy any of the artifacts. But they were so angry.

Lindsay walked out and made sure that Mike had locked the outside door behind him and watched the play of his flashlight through the thicket. As she passed the main office on her way back, she heard a humming of machinery running. She tried the door. It was locked, and she hadn't brought her keys with her. Probably nothing, she thought and went back to her work.

Before going up to Harper's apartment, Lindsay gave the post-cranial bones a quick glance. Something caught her eye. She donned gloves and took out the left femur and pelvis. The left acetabulum showed a marked flattening, as did the head of the femur, along with spur formation. She checked all the long bones and found similar characteristics, but with disparity in severity. She also found that the neck of the humerus was broken and showed signs of uneven surface healing.

Lindsay put the bones back in their tub of saline solution and sat back on the stool, peeling off her gloves, turning the bones over in her mind. She hunted around the lab for a telephone book and looked up orthopedics in the Yellow Pages.

Chapter 13

Dr. Rosen leaned out the door and called to his nurse. "The patient in exam room three is quite beyond my help."

This elicited fits of laughter from his staff as Lindsay came out of the restroom.

"Who did he come in with?" he asked.

"Me, Dr. Rosen. Your nurse was good enough to allow me to lay him out. I'm Dr. Lindsay Chamberlain." She held out her hand.

He greeted her with a broad smile, flashing bright white teeth set against a neatly trimmed and very dark mustache and beard.

"Yes, you're a forensic osteologist, aren't you?" He shook her hand vigorously. Dr. Rosen was a compact, square-built man a good six inches shorter than Lindsay.

"I just read a paper of yours not long ago . . ." He put the tips of the fingers of his left hand to his forehead. "I have it. Implications of disease in the postcranial skeleton with respect to sex determination. I found it fascinating."

"Yes, I'm flattered that you remember it. I'm also . . ."

He bounded to the table and picked up a femur. "I have an interest in forensics myself. Let's see." He paused. "The bones are wet."

"We have to keep them that way for now."

"Hmm. Been in the water a while, I suppose?"

"A while."

"And this man has been murdered?" he said almost absently, turning the bone in his hand, examining its surface.

"That's the other one. I haven't . . ."

"The other one? You have more than one?"

"Yes. The reason I brought him here is this." Lindsay showed him the remodeled parts of the bones.

111

"Well, yes. The flattening of the head of the femur and the acetabulum. Notice the uneven healing around the broken humerus. I see fractures in the femur with attempted healing." He pointed to the anomalies in the bone. "I suspect if you take a thin-section you'll see microscopic indications, as well. I did a hip replacement on a man last year who looked about like this. You don't see it often—most divers pay attention to their tables."

"Then, you think . . ."

"Dysbaric osteonecrosis. Yes, the man's a scuba diver, in all probability. That should aid in the identification."

"That's what it looked like to me, but I've seen the condition only in photographs and x-rays. However—"

He looked up from the bone. "However?"

"The age of the bones is a problem."

"How old are they?"

"Around four hundred and forty years old."

He stared at her a moment. "I've clearly missed something."

Lindsay grinned. "I'm also an archaeologist, working off the coast of St. Magdalena at the cofferdam site."

"Ah . . . Yes. I've wanted to take one of the weekend tours out there. Fascinating. Then, I'd say it must be disease that caused the bone necrosis, however much it looks otherwise."

"Wouldn't most of the diseases that produce this effect have killed him before it got to this stage in the bones?"

"Yes, many would." He puzzled over the bone.

"What causes dysbaric osteonecrosis?" asked Lindsay.

"Good question. Short answer, nitrogen embolization of the blood vessels. The exact process isn't truly understood."

"And that is from. . . ?"

"Breathing compressed air. Also, there's a relationship with diving at extreme depths." He grinned. "You have an interesting problem."

"I do indeed."

"This fellow—it is a fellow, isn't it?"

Lindsay nodded. "I haven't completed my examination, but I'd say he's Asian and between the ages of twenty-five and forty."

"He's from that ship you all are excavating, then?"

"Yes. He's the second skeleton we've found. Lucky for us. Had they not become buried quickly and deeply, the sea water would have disintegrated the bones by this time."

"And you say the other one was murdered? On board ship?"

"Apparently. I think in the next couple of days there will be a write-up in the newspaper about it."

"I'll keep a lookout." Dr. Rosen took a pad of paper from his pocket and began scribbling. "Here's a list of diseases that result in avascular and aseptic necrosis. Like you say, in that era many of the diseases would have killed him before they were manifested in the bones. I'll leave those off. The fellow could have been an alcoholic or he could have had serious problems with gout." He smiled. "There are many alternatives, but look at the bones that are not involved. Dysbaric osteonecrosis doesn't usually involve the wrists, ankles, or elbows." He threw up his hands. "It can't be dysbaric, I don't know why I'm even considering it." Then he grinned. "But it's fascinating."

She tucked the list in her notebook. "Thank you for your consultation. If you decide to visit the site, I'll give you a guided tour."

On her way out, Lindsay told the receptionist where to send the bill. Bobbie Lacayo sat reading a magazine in the waiting room.

"The grocery store was close by and I picked up the stuff I needed. Want to have lunch on River Street before we head back?"

Lindsay and Bobbie sat in a café eating hamburgers and looking out at the distant big ships.

"This has been a nice break," Bobbie said. "I was starting to feel like an extra in *Waterworld*. So tell me, how are you and John getting along?"

"Actually, we are getting along, which is surprising. We are such opposites. Tell me, what do you know about the history of compressed air?"

"Nothing. How did we get there from here?"

Lindsay told her about the dubious condition of the skeleton. "How about the history of scuba diving?"

"I used to know a little about that. I've dived all my life and I've done a lot of school papers on the topic. But that was in high school." She frowned in concentration, trying to remember. "Alexander the Great had a diving bell named *Columbine*, or maybe that was Harlequin's girlfriend. Something like that anyway. That's all I remember."

"But where would they get compressed air?"

Bobbie made like she was holding something in her fists and

moved her hands back and forth. "Bellows. But, surely, you don't think . . ."

Lindsay waved her hand. "No, it's probably one of the diseases Rosen listed, or alcohol or gout or arthritis even. It's just that what I see in the bones is identical to dysbaric osteonecrosis. When Rosen first looked at the bones, he thought so, too."

"Odd. Lewis will like it."

"Not you, too? Why is it that Lewis's likes and dislikes form everyone's standard of measurement?"

"He writes the checks. Big checks."

"Good point."

After buying a grocery sack full of homemade candy on River Street, Bobbie said she was ready to head for home, and they walked down the cobblestone street to the university's SUV. It was seventy miles to the ferry that took them to St. Magdalena. They were the only passengers on the ferry and sat in the SUV on the short ride to the island.

"Since we have our supplies to carry, we can take the service road to the lab," said Bobbie. "If we're lucky, Tessa or one of her cronies won't be out there to tell us how we're polluting the island."

"Is it really that bad with the biology people?"

"Not really. It's just annoying, and I can't say that we're blameless. I mean, not counting the fact that we took over the place, we do tweak their noses at times."

"Nate told me."

"Yeah, he and Carolyn are the worst."

"Why are they so hostile?"

Bobbie shrugged. "Mike and Tessa are the main ones that are so angry. The others are okay. Mike and Tessa had to give up their suite to Harper. That was a big deal to Tessa. She had her computer equipment set up in her apartment. They all ended up moving to the ranger station. Besides that, apparently Mike had been having a problem with Boote—you know, the old man—and his son, Keith, poaching on the island, selling some of the rare plants and messing up Mike's research. Mike had just got them to stay off, and along comes our advance party, and Nate uses Keith and Boote as informants, inviting them to the island. Mike was furious. I can't blame him. The island is the only place some of the plants they're studying grow."

"What did Nate and the others learn from Keith and his father?"

"Nate and Trey got a look at the junk they picked up on the shore. Boote has searched the beach with a metal detector for years and has jars of coins, I understand."

"Did they find anything from the wreck?"

"Not much. Some metal concretions. Some driftwood that may have been part of a wooden ship that Trey said probably wasn't the *Estrella*. About three years ago Keith found part of a schooner that sank in 1910 near Florida. Not much left of it but a few lamps, brass fittings, and a compass, I think. There was some controversy about it. He kind of looted it without telling anybody. He had an attitude much like Eva Jones—if he found it, it was his. Since the stuff he found wasn't valuable, it all blew over. I think he found a couple of other ships, too. One was fairly modern—some sunken yacht a few miles out from Savannah. I don't know what the other one was. None had anything of real value in it, I don't think. He said he made a few bucks off the salvage."

"And yet he got along with Nate?"

"Trey thought that if they made friends with Keith and Boote, he could teach them why it's important to leave wrecks to be excavated professionally. Trey was in teaching mode at that time."

"And did it work?"

"For a while. This was all before the dam was built. Keith went diving with us a couple of times. I was here at that time doing survey work. Keith got into a fight with Steven Nemo about salvaging wrecks. You heard Steven at the party talking about Kennewick Man. He's really single-minded about archaeological sovereignty."

"Archaeological sovereignty?"

Bobbie screwed up her face. "That's John's phrase. I guess you know, he can get going, too." Lindsay nodded. "Keith stayed away after that, until we had a storm that wrecked some of our boats. Keith helped out. Some kind of code of the sea. Anyway, he and Nate were friends for a while. Nate's pretty easy to get along with. He was trying to stay on good terms in case Boote or Keith found anything. I think Keith and Boote both got tired of us. We work all the time and, to tell the truth, Keith is kind of a beach bum who never grew up."

"What about you? You going to switch to marine archaeology?"

Bobbie shook her head. "I love to scuba dive and this is a lot of fun. Easy 'A.'" She grinned. "But I don't want to do it forever."

115

They arrived at the lab amid a swarm of people with "FBI" written on their jackets.

"What in the world?" said Bobbie.

"Something has happened," said Lindsay.

They left the groceries in the vehicle and hurried through the lab. Lindsay caught sight of Trey standing with Harper just inside the front door. Harper had her arms folded, looking at the floor. Trey stared out the door where several FBI men were gathered. Francisco Lewis was with them. He looked grim.

"Trey?"

"Chamberlain, I'm glad you're back."

"What's going on?"

"They've found a body in the alligator pool."

Chapter 14

"A BODY? WHOSE?" Lindsay looked through the glass doors to see if she could get a glimpse of something, but all she saw was people standing in the way.

"We don't know yet," answered Trey. "This being hot weather, and it being in the alligator pond, and alligators being carrion eaters—well."

Bobbie groaned.

"So, Chamberlain. I got your note." Trey seemed eager to change the subject. "You went to see a Dr. Rosen in Savannah this morning?"

"Yes. He's an orthopedist. I had a question about the new skeleton."

"Well, this must be a first." Trey attempted a smile.

"The skeleton shows signs of bone necrosis—some of his bones looked like they had been dying."

"So, he had some disease, I suppose?" Trey looked out the windows at the authorities. Lewis caught his eye and came walking up the wooden walkway toward them.

"I'll have to thin-section the bone—"

Lewis entered, and they all waited for an answer to the question that was on their minds. But he only shook his head.

"I don't know what they're doing. Lindsay, I'm glad you're back. Perhaps you could find out. Maybe you know some of those agents. I don't understand why the rangers called the FBI."

"That's because this is a national park. The FBI has jurisdiction."

For all Lewis's political knowledge, she was surprised he didn't know that. His face brightened.

"Oh. Is that it? I thought it was, well, something serious." He paused. "Not that this isn't, but more serious, if you know what I mean."

Lindsay hadn't seen him flustered before. She doubted many people had.

"Lindsay, I want you to look into this."

"What? I have no authority. The FBI knows what they're doing."

"I want us to have some control—" he began. Nate, Steven, Carolyn and some of the others began drifting over to them, and he stopped talking.

"Who found the body?" Lindsay asked.

"Tessa," said Trey. "She and Mike were coming up the walkway, and she looked over the side and saw what she thought was a boot caught in the fork of a log."

"Do you know who it is?"

"No. The park rangers and FBI were already here when we got here," Trey replied. "Naturally, Tessa and Mike won't say anything. They probably think we did it to irritate them."

"They can ease their minds about that. If we were the culprits, one of them would be the victim," said Carolyn. They all laughed uneasily.

A Hispanic man in an FBI jacket opened the door and leaned in, asking for Lewis and Trey to come out. Lewis grabbed Lindsay's arm as he passed and pulled her along. The others followed, but stopped just outside the doorway.

"They had a fight." Everyone's head turned toward Mike.

"Who?" asked the FBI agent.

"Nate and Keith," Mike said with a sneer. "Then nobody ever saw Keith again after that."

"Now, wait just a minute!" Nate started for Mike, but one of the rangers stepped in front of him.

"Let's just calm down and let the FBI sort things out."

"You bloody bastard," Nate swore through his teeth. "Who was it that got him and his father thrown off the island for messing up your experiments?"

So it's Keith, thought Lindsay as she followed Lewis through the parting crowd of onlookers. How curious, she thought. Bobbie and she had just been talking about him. The smell of death drifted up from the covered body. Lewis and Trey put a hand to their noses.

"We need an identification," said the man, introducing himself as Agent A. C. Ramirez. "I understand, Dr. Marcus, that you have been here from the beginning. Maybe you know him?"

Lindsay saw Trey and Lewis tense as Agent Ramirez reached down for the black plastic that covered the body, girding themselves for the image they were about to see. He lifted the sheet. It wasn't Keith. Lindsay had been here only a few days, but she could identify the body herself, and he looked as troublesome in death as he had been in life.

Both Lewis and Trey gasped in surprise.

"It's Hardy Denton," said Trey.

Lewis put his hands to his face and let them slide down his cheeks. Lindsay knew what he was thinking.

"He . . ." Trey tried to find the words. "He was a contractor, one of the bidders on the cofferdam project."

"Not the winning bidder, I presume?" asked Ramirez.

"No," answered Lewis. "He was not the winner."

As they spoke, Lindsay scrutinized the body as well as she could from a distance, trying to see if the cause of death was evident. His face, a greenish mask with large purple marks looking like port-wine birthmarks, showed signs of having been nibbled on by aquatic life. Lindsay thought there might have been a bruise on the side of his cheek, but she couldn't be sure, because of the other markings. What most interested her was a slight pink tinge on his nostrils and in the corners of his mouth. Pretending to move back from the body, she let her foot touch his legs covered by the black plastic. They seemed stiff.

"Have we met?"

Uh-oh, caught, she thought. But when she looked at Ramirez, he did not appear to be about to scold her for touching the body.

"We may have. I'm Lindsay Chamberlain. I've given talks at various law enforcement seminars and conferences about forensic anthropology."

"Ah, that's it. I saw you speak last year on locating buried human remains. I learned a lot. So what are you doing here?"

"I'm also an archaeologist. I'm part of the crew at the cofferdam site."

"Dr. Chamberlain is in charge of all skeletal remains we find," put in Lewis, smiling. Lindsay could see that he was delighted that Lindsay had some rapport with the investigators.

"I've read about this in the papers. It's a big deal. Must have meant a lot of money lost for poor Mr. Denton here."

Lewis started to speak, but Lindsay answered first. "We don't really know about his business."

Ramirez's black eyes sparkled as he gave Lindsay a broad-toothed grin and put a hand on her arm.

"Dr. Chamberlain, you are very charming, but I fear you know our methods too well, being in the business yourself, so to speak. You let your bosses answer those questions that they would know about."

Lindsay returned his grin. "Of course."

"By the way, did you know this man?"

"I met him once."

Lindsay could see that surprised Lewis and Trey. Ramirez noticed it, too.

"We'll be moving the body shortly. You may go back inside and be comfortable." He turned to Lewis. "I'll need a list of everyone who works here. We'll have to question everyone. From the looks of it, it will be a long process."

"I'll get you a list," Lewis said. "But not everyone here works on the cofferdam project. There are also biologists who work on the island year-round."

"And is this division of staff the cause of the animosity I just witnessed?"

"I'm afraid so. The biologists were here first and feel displaced."

"I would appreciate it if you would give me their names, too. They seemed to think this was a fellow named Keith."

"Yes," said Trey. "Keith lives on a neighboring island, and his father says he is missing."

"Thank you for your identification. And very nice to meet you, Dr. Chamberlain. Thanks to you, I'll never dig up a grave with a shovel again. Please stay close by. I'd like to talk with each of you later today."

This was a dismissal. Lindsay retreated, wishing he had uncovered more of the body than just the face. She would like to see, for example, the clothes he was wearing. She wondered if they were the same ones he wore when she saw him last.

They went back into the lab, followed by Bobbie, Harper, and the others.

"Denton?" said Steven. "I thought it was Keith."

"That, apparently, was a presumption on the part of Mike. Which, I might add, was not missed by our good FBI agent. I imagine he'll be looking around here for another body," Lewis declared.

"Do you really think Keith is dead?" asked Carolyn.

"No, I don't. I'm sorry, I was simply being sarcastic."

"What do you think, Lindsay?" Trey asked.

"They will ask around about Keith, see if he and Denton were connected in some way. These are not people who believe in coincidences. A disappearance, if it is that, and a suspicious death in the same place at the same time look doubly suspicious."

"Don't you mean murder?" asked Korey.

"No. It could be natural, accidental, or suicide. They'll know more about the manner of death when they find the cause."

Lindsay was deep in thought, working out different time of death scenarios, based on the stiffness of Denton's legs when she noticed them staring at her. Of course, they were all completely unfamiliar with the terms and culture of death investigations. Odd, really. Lindsay had always considered archaeology and crime investigation to be very similar.

"Agent Ramirez will want to talk with all of you," Lewis told them. "Just answer his questions straightforwardly. I'm sure all this will be cleared up soon."

"Well, Doc," said Nate, turning to Lindsay, "Ol' Jeff's going to love this."

Lindsay groaned and the others laughed. She was surprised that even Lewis knew about the Angel of Death thing.

Harper kissed Trey on the cheek and went up to her apartment to work on the translation. After Lewis sent the others off to the lab, he led Lindsay and Trey to his office tucked away beyond the weather room, which was empty of personnel. Presumably, they were outside watching the drama.

"Have a seat," said Lewis, pointing to a table in the corner. He took three soft drinks from the refrigerator before sitting across from Lindsay. Lindsay sat and waited for what she knew was coming. After the sound of three tabs pulled from the soft drinks, Lewis spoke.

"Lindsay, what's going to happen now? Are we all suspects?" he asked. "What's this 'stay close' business?"

"If they find murder, yes, we are all suspects. But that's not as serious as it sounds. It's simply logical. He was discovered here. We are here. He had business with us."

"What do you mean, if they find murder?"

Lewis, Lindsay realized, was a man who, when confronted with unfamiliar situations, worked to find out all the information he could. Make the strange familiar—every anthropologist's credo—at least half of it.

Lindsay folded her hands around her drink in front of her. It was ice cold and made her shiver. She took a sip before she spoke.

"A crime scene forensic team will come and examine the body here. They will also examine the place he was found. They'll take the body to a medical examiner's office, and he'll perform an autopsy to discover the cause of death. When they find out how he died, then they'll try to determine if it was natural, accidental, suicide, or homicide." She took another sip. "They don't necessarily suspect murder. In fact, they probably don't right now."

"Why do you say that?" asked Lewis.

"Unless there was some wound I didn't see, I think he drowned. Most drownings are accidental. It's not a common method of homicide. Denton was a drunk. Most accidental drownings involve alcohol."

"Why do you think he drowned?" Lewis asked.

"The pink foam around his nose and mouth indicates that he may have been alive when he went into the water."

Lewis and Trey made a face.

"He looked like he was beat up," said Trey. "Surely that suggests murder."

Lindsay shook her head. "What looked like bruises was lividity. Blood settling in the face is common in drowning. The body is always facedown in the water."

Trey nodded as if that made sense to him.

Lewis was quiet a moment and appeared to be reading the label on his drink.

"This is very unpleasant," he said. "You said he was a drunk. Do you know Denton?"

"No, but I met him once." Lindsay told them about the scene at the restaurant.

"So he was bearing a grudge. That looks bad for us, and the letters he sent look bad for us. Do you think we should keep them from Ramirez?"

"No. It's not necessary. The university's decision on the coffer-dam bid is very defensible. Don't sweat it."

"Do you know when he died?" asked Lewis.

"I managed to move his legs with my foot, and he appeared to still be in rigor."

Trey and Lewis both registered surprise.

"I wanted some data." She hadn't meant to sound so defensive. "Rigor is not a good indicator of time of death. Too many variables. However, because of the lividity and the fact that he appears to be in full rigor and this is hot weather, I suspect he died sometime early this morning. Between four and five o'clock maybe?"

"What do you think he was doing here?" asked Trey.

"No telling," said Lewis. He turned back to Lindsay. "So you think it was an accident?"

"That's the most likely scenario. But I didn't see the whole body. He may have been stabbed, shot, or held under. Murder is really not that common. It seems like it is, because it makes the news so often, but how much firsthand experience have either of you had with it?"

"None. But you seem to have had a lot," noted Lewis.

"Yes, well, I'm also in forensics."

"I didn't realize forensic anthropologists know so much about"—Trey waved a hand—". . . this stuff."

"You pick up stuff when you hang around medical examiners."

But he was right. She had picked up quite a bit of knowledge that didn't have direct bearing on her speciality. It's the puzzle that pulls her to it, she thought to herself. The challenge of the puzzle.

"Why did you answer the question about Denton's business?" asked Lewis.

"Investigators like to engage people around a crime scene in casual conversation. It's a low-key method of investigation. It can be disarming to witnesses or suspects who will sometimes reveal important information without realizing it. I was just trying to separate Denton from us. No use inviting speculation."

"What a life you have, Chamberlain. I had no idea," said Trey.

"Ah, here you are."

They looked up to see Ramirez standing in the doorway. Lindsay wondered how long he had been there.

"Come to grill us?" she asked with a smile.

"Yes. You first. Can we use this room?"

Trey and Lewis rose and left, looking a trifle peaked.

"Your bosses don't look too good."

"They just I.D.'d a body, a possible drowning victim at that. That's not a pleasant task."

"No, it isn't. This looks like a big operation. How many people are on this project?"

"Let's see." Lindsay ticked off the categories on her fingers. "There are sixteen divers in the survey crew. They look for artifacts that aren't within the dam site. The day excavation crew has fifteen members, and ten night crew, and six crew are in charge of handling the ship's timber. We have two on-site conservators—they're handling the artifacts. One person analyzing skeletal remains— that's me. One translator of archaic Spanish. Three people doing flotation from the site, and one person doing chemical flotation. Two people monitoring the weather. That doesn't count the night watchmen or John West's crew. I don't know how many people he has, but they monitor the dam. Nor does it count the custodial staff that come every other day to take care of the building. There used to be a nurse, but I understand she went back to Atlanta. Didn't like the water."

"So that's what? At least fifty-seven people?"

"Fifty-nine, counting Dr. Marcus and Dr. Lewis."

"That's a lot of people."

"This is a big project. Plus, there are all the biology people. That's another four, I believe."

Ramirez seemed to mull those numbers over in his head a moment. Lindsay wondered if he was going to interview all of them. She doubted it.

"Now," he said, "I would like you to tell me what you know about this Denton fellow."

"I met him once. He was drunk." Lindsay again related the story about the run-in with Denton at the restaurant.

"He made you angry?"

"Yes. He was interfering with my dinner, and he was insulting."

"What did you do?"

"I went to Eva Jones and told her to rein him in."

"And you thought that would work? A macho fellow like Denton who called you a squaw would be reined in by a woman?"

"Yes, I thought it would work and it did."

"And your date. It made him angry?"

"I don't think so. Just annoyed."

"Annoyed. The man is the object of racist remarks, his date is insulted, and he is only annoyed?"

"That was my take on it. I've seen John angry, and he didn't look angry."

"At whom was he angry and why?"

"At me, for digging up his ancestors."

Ramirez looked puzzled for a moment. "He doesn't like archaeologists?"

"I didn't say that. He works for archaeologists, and he dates me."

"If you dig up his ancestors, as you put it, why does he now have such warm feelings for you?"

"Because I'm not now digging up his ancestors, I'm digging up yours."

Ramirez was taken completely aback, and a smile played around Lindsay's lips as she watched his surprised expression.

"Mine?"

"You're Cuban-American, aren't you?"

"Yes."

"Well, the guys out there in the ocean settled Havana."

Ramirez, of course, knew how Cuba was settled, Lindsay guessed, but he had not connected it with what they were doing in the ocean.

"They were Spaniards heading for Havana before they somehow wound up here off the coast of Georgia." She had caught him off guard, and she had interested him in their work. Lindsay was pleased with herself.

"Do you know anything else about Denton?"

"No, but I suspect Evangeline Jones knows him well."

"Tell me about this Evangeline Jones. Who is she?"

"Depending on who you talk to, she is either an international collector or a looter of antiquities."

"Is that what she's doing here?"

"You'll have to ask her. We spend long hours wondering what she's doing here. Whatever it is, she's spending a lot of money doing it."

"And Denton's bid, was his the low bid? Was he justified in his anger?"

"Yes, and no, but Drs. Marcus and Lewis can tell you more about that."

"I would like to talk with John West, too."

"He's out at the dam. We need to go back out there to check on the crew. If it would be convenient, you could come with us and talk to him there."

He would, Lindsay knew. She had him hooked.

Chapter 15

"THIS IS AS big as a football stadium," said Ramirez as they descended into the middle of the cofferdam.

"One hundred fifty feet by eighty feet on the inside," remarked Trey.

Lindsay led Ramirez over to an area near a pump. Trey and Lewis followed, content to let Lindsay handle the FBI agent.

"John's diving right now," said Lindsay. She knew this to be true, because she had told Bobbie to call and ask John to be unavailable for about ten minutes after she arrived.

Ramirez looked up the high walls damp with sea water. Lindsay saw the tension around his mouth and the widening of the eyes—subtle signs of anxiety everyone showed when they first arrived down in the well of the dam. She put her hand on the wet wall as she spoke over the sound of the pump and the crashing of the ocean waves.

"Agent Ramirez, the university is not bound to give a contract to the lowest bidder. It must be the lowest bid that best fulfills specific requirements. People work in here—from UGA and from other universities. They have to be safe. The university has to know that the ocean will not come rushing in and drown everyone."

Warming to the situation, Lewis continued the explanation. "Denton's bid was so low that he couldn't meet the safety requirements. In order to make any money, he would have had to use inferior materials and take shortcuts. Structurally, his design was more suited for bridge construction in a river environment than here in the ocean. John West, who had the middle bid of the three, not only met OSHA requirements, but added safety features of his own that he felt necessary for this ocean environment. West Construction's bid was reasonable and John's design was safe."

Lindsay saw John descending the stairway into the dam. He walked over and held out his hand to Agent Ramirez. His jeans were damp where he had pulled them over his diving trunks and his wet hair was slicked back and tied at the nape of his neck.

"John West," he said, introducing himself. "How do you like my dam?"

"I'm, uh, overwhelmed. I can't quite grasp that we are on the ocean floor."

"We are. I was just checking the seams. We have to keep constant watch."

As if Lindsay had been in collusion with the ocean, just then a wave splashed over the dam, sending a spray of water down on them like a light rain. Ramirez looked up at the top of the dam, startled.

"It's a little windy out there today," John said.

"Is there somewhere we can talk?" He brushed the water from his face and the sleeves of his coat.

John pointed to the field desk. "Over here."

While John and Ramirez went to have their conversation, Lindsay, Trey, and Lewis walked over to the excavation. She looked at her watch. Past time to change shifts. Lewis must have talked them into working longer hours, which probably was not difficult. Most archaeologists she knew would work until they dropped.

"You're a good psychologist, Lindsay," said Lewis. "Bringing him here was smart."

"It's one thing to tell him while he is safe on land that the proposal must meet safety requirements. It's quite another for him to experience the truth of it firsthand. I didn't want him to dwell on the contract, trying to unearth some dishonesty on the part of the department, the university, or West Construction."

"I think he got the point," said Trey. "The spray of water was a nice touch."

The crew had heard about Denton's death and looked up expectantly for news as they approached. Trey shook his head. Jeff followed Lindsay with his eyes.

"We found a couple more skeletons," said Juliana.

"You're kidding. They're going to start stacking up on me," Lindsay said.

"Looks like we might get the whole crew," said Lewis, grinning.

So far, Gina and Juliana's skeleton was an arm and a hand. "It looks to be in as good a condition as the others," commented Lindsay.

"Might be better," said Gina. "These are deeper in the mud. Look at what Jeff found."

At Jeff's excavation unit, several crew were working on different parts of a skeleton that lay in a fetal position. Jeff held a brush in his hand, gently whisking dirt from what looked like iron. Lindsay and the others squatted to get a closer look. It was iron in contact with bones. Lindsay saw a talus and a jumble of tarsals.

"He's in irons," exclaimed Trey.

"That's what it seems," agreed Jeff. "Maybe he's the perp." He looked up and grinned at Lindsay. She was surprised at his sense of humor.

"Poor guy," said Trey.

"This ship has quite a few stories to tell," said Lewis. "I'll have to nudge Harper about the translation."

Trey and Lindsay made eye contact. Lewis, it seems, was "nudging" everyone.

"By the way, Lindsay. I got your drawing. I like it. The *Atlanta Journal and Constitution* is anxious to do a story."

"I just hope Denton's death doesn't overshadow the drama of the wreck."

"I'll try to see that it doesn't. That reminds me, I need to find a sculptor to do the faces."

Lindsay was amazed that the discovery of a body virtually on their doorstep hadn't slowed Lewis down. Actually, she was glad of it.

"Somebody said the police want to talk to all of us?" Jeff asked.

"Just routine," Lewis told him.

"We don't know anything."

"Just tell them that," Trey said.

"I was told this would happen," Jeff said glumly.

"By whom?" asked Lindsay.

"Do you know Gerri Chapman?"

"Yes," said Lindsay, "I know her. Is that where the Angel of Death thing came from?"

"We were at a meeting three months ago. She told us about your proclivity for finding dead bodies."

"I don't think we can blame Lindsay for somebody getting drunk and drowning himself," responded Lewis.

"Is that what happened?"

"We think."

Lindsay was anxious to change the subject. She stood. Trey and Lewis stood with her.

"I meant to tell you," she said. "When I was doing the drawing last night, Mike Altman, one of the biology people, came to the lab. Said he saw the light on, and it was the only time he could get supplies. But I don't know how he could have seen the light. He's staying at the ranger station and you can't see the light from the lab from over there. Anyway, he left with some graph paper. It looked suspicious. I thought you might want to ask the guard to be sure to watch the lab closely."

"That is odd," said Trey. "What do you think he was up to?"

"I couldn't tell. But some of the biology people are very hostile."

"That's my fault," said Lewis. "I suppose I sort of bulldozed them. Do you think he was up to something?"

Lindsay shrugged. "I don't believe he made his way from the ranger's station through the woods in the dark to get graph paper."

John brought Ramirez over to the excavation and Lindsay showed him the bones that Gina and Juliana had uncovered.

"So he was a Spaniard heading for Havana?" Ramirez asked.

Lewis nodded. "Most likely."

"Poor fellow, never made it. Wonder what he was doing way up here?"

"That's one of our research questions," said Trey.

Ramirez scanned the site, looking at the excavation as a whole and moved his head back and forth. "This was a ship." He said it as if he couldn't believe it. "It was big. You have found other remains?"

"Two more. The first one was a Spaniard," said Lindsay. "Perhaps an officer or an official. He was in good health, and his bones don't show evidence of hard work."

"No, we officials don't work very hard," said Ramirez.

"Manual labor," said Lindsay with a smile.

"Ah. And the poor fellow drowned. Possibly like our fellow in the alligator pond?"

"Well, uh, actually," answered Lewis. "He appears to have been murdered."

Ramirez looked up at him, then at Lindsay.

"Blunt instrument to the head," she said. "Three blows."

"But don't worry," Jeff called over to them. "We got the guy in irons."

Jeff seemed in a very good mood. Lindsay was glad of it, for him as well as for the rest of the crew.

"You know who did it?" Ramirez asked.

They led the FBI agent to Jeff's find.

"No," answered Trey. "There were many reasons sailors got put in irons, but it's certainly suggestive."

After the tour, Lindsay, John, Trey, and Lewis walked Agent Ramirez to the top of the dam, explaining that John would give him a lift back to the island and they would wait and go later with the barge.

"Thank you, this has been most educational. My wife's been reading about the project. She'll be thrilled when I tell her I've been here." He turned to Lindsay. "You probably thought your skeleton fellow was drowned, until you got a good look at him and discovered he was murdered. Wouldn't it be interesting if we had a parallel?"

No, thought Lindsay, that wouldn't be interesting at all. It would be darned awkward.

The first half of debriefing that evening was taken up by the body found in the alligator pond and what it meant for the site. Lewis told everyone not to concern themselves with it.

"The authorities will sort it out, and it has nothing to do with us," he said.

Lindsay doubted that it was true. Accident or foul play, Hardy Denton had been at the research station for some reason.

To break up the talk of Denton, Lewis showed the picture Lindsay had drawn of the HSkR1. That spurred discussion of the day's skeletal remains, especially the one that appeared to be in leg irons.

"We may get the answers in the journal," said Trey.

"What exactly was this journal guy doing on the ship?" asked Steven Nemo. "I mean, he seems to be some kind of spy. Do we know his name?"

"No," said Trey. "So far we don't know who he is on the manifest. Nor have we found any mention in the Spanish archives about whatever mission he was on. Unfortunately, his name does not appear on the journal. One thing we do know. He mentions several people by name in the journal and they do appear on the ship's manifest, so we can now say with assurance that we were correct in assuming that the journal matches the archival information. As to how the journal came to be boxed up and bricked in a closet in a house in St. Augustine, we haven't a clue. We assume that the writer of the journal, after surviving the shipwreck, made his way down the coast and eventually took up with the Spaniards who founded St. Augustine."

"What about the second skeleton? The one you found, Dr. Lewis?" asked Sarah.

"What about it, Lindsay?" asked Lewis. "Trey tells me you took it to Savannah. What was that about?"

Lindsay stood, leaning with her back against one of the support columns. "This guy's Asian," she said.

"Indian?" several people asked.

"No. From the eastern coast of China, apparently—" She hesitated. "He may be Valerian's servant. The journal mentions that Valerian had an Asian servant when the ship picked them up in the Canary Islands. And he was found with the chess set, which indicates that the location of the remains may have been Valerian's cabin. Maybe as we read on, there'll be something in the journal to verify the identity."

"Really—the skeleton I found?" Lewis looked like a pleased kid. "That's the first possible match we've been able to make between the journal and skeletal remains."

"It's a good possibility," Lindsay said. "I was excited."

"What did you do with him in Savannah?" asked Steven.

"His bones show some rather severe pathology. I took them to an orthopedist to see what he thought."

"And?" asked Trey.

"Well, it was funny really. It looks identical to other conditions I've seen in photographs and X-rays, but never firsthand. Dr. Rosen, who at first didn't understand that these weren't modern bones, thought the same thing."

"Which was? Are we going to have to pull this out of you, Chamberlain?" Trey asked.

"Dysbaric osteonecrosis." All the divers in the room looked at her wide-eyed.

"Well, that can't be," said Nate.

"Why?" asked Gina. Lindsay explained what dysbaric osteonecrosis is.

"Oh. How odd."

"There are many diseases that can cause bone necrosis," said Lindsay. "I'll have to make some thin-sections of the bone for microscopic examination."

"But it is strange that it looks like it's from scuba diving," said Juliana.

"Well, that can't be," repeated one of the other divers.

"No, it would appear to be impossible," agreed Lindsay, and continued her description. "At the time of his death, his condition was such that he must have been confined to bed during the storm. Was there any indication of that during the excavation?"

Lewis shook his head. "There was a lot of wood, some fabric, though not much, and some rope. He was a bit of a jumble. I believe the sea chest that was found earlier was basically on top of him."

Lindsay couldn't help but wonder if he was excavated too quickly and some good data were lost. However, she didn't say anything.

Two other crew had found the capstan. They pointed it out on Steve's cross section. It was exactly where it should have been. They were quite proud of their find. Slowly, the ship and its story were being exposed and mapped. Lindsay thought it would be instructive to have a model of the ship and add on things as they found them. Like we all don't have enough to do, she thought. The debriefing ended on an upbeat note—the body found in the alligator pond temporarily forgotten.

"You know," whispered Bobbie as she and Lindsay were leaving the lab, "the journal would make a good movie. You think Lewis is talking to Hollywood?"

"It would not surprise me at all if Steven Spielberg showed up at the site next week." Lindsay grinned at her. She fervently hoped Denton's death would turn out to be an accident. This was such a wonderful site, with all the finds and that journal. She didn't want it spoiled by murder.

They caught up with Harper, who stood waiting with her arms folded.

"You're doing an amazing job of translating the journal," Bobbie told her. "We all love it."

"I'm going to publish the translation after the dig is over. Lewis has already talked to the UGA press, and they're enthusiastic. It'd be nice to know who to give credit to for the original."

"I didn't get a chance to thank you for letting me stay in your apartment," said Lindsay. "I was late getting to bed and had to be up early."

"Maybe we can do it again. I was looking forward to some wine and girl talk. Did you have any trouble getting in?"

"No, not at all."

"I was concerned that you might, because we changed the locks on the doors. Sometimes mine sticks. I usually have it bolted. I may be getting paranoid, but a couple of times about two weeks ago I thought someone was trying to break in. I could have sworn I heard the knob rattle. The security guard said he hadn't seen anything suspicious. The second time, it was two o'clock in the morning. I called Trey and the poor guy motored over here from the barge."

"That's strange." Lindsay related the visit by Mike the previous evening.

"That guy gives me the creeps," said Bobbie. "He and Tessa really hate us. The others are all right. They're even interested in what we are doing."

"Well, some of the archaeology crew are egging them on," said Lindsay. She told them about the planting of false rumors.

"That letter she had the other day when Boote fell in the water," said Bobbie. "That was from Carolyn and Nate?"

"Apparently."

"Well, they shouldn't have believed such a stupid story anyway," said Bobbie.

"Well, no," agreed Lindsay, "but we need to lay off. It will be easier on us in the long run if they don't think we're going to lay waste to the barrier islands."

"What are you guys doing for dinner?" asked Harper.

Lindsay shrugged. "I haven't heard from John. What about Trey?"

"He and Lewis are having a meeting. Why don't we go to the mainland, or maybe St. Simons, and have dinner?"

"Sure, I'd like that," said Lindsay.

John entered the lab and pulled Lindsay aside. "How was the interview with Ramirez?" she asked.

"Routine. Thanks for the warning. Look, I've got a meeting with Lewis and Marcus—"

"That's fine, I'm going out with Harper and Bobbie. We're going to St. Simons."

"Want me to get one of the guys to take you?"

"One of the guys?"

"One of my crew."

"I think Bobbie and Harper probably have it covered."

"Call me when you get back."

"Sure, if it's not too late. Everything all right? I mean with the FBI agent?"

"As far as I know. He was interested in the confrontation the other night. I told him there was nothing to it, that you got the pirate lady to kick his butt."

"Yeah, I wonder how Evangeline Jones is fairing with Ramirez."

"She's probably spinning him a yarn." John kissed her cheek and went to Lewis's office.

"Nice-looking guy, that John West," said Harper as they left the building and headed for the dock.

"Yes, he is." Lindsay smiled to herself. John was the first guy other than Derrick in a long time that she was truly interested in.

⚓

Harper was piloting the boat. Like Bobbie, Harper was a long-time scuba diver and boater.

"Ever go sailing?" Harper asked, yelling above the sounds of the motor. "That's what I love. It's like flying over the water."

That's what it felt as if they were doing now. Lindsay's hair was pulled back in a ponytail, but it still whipped back and forth, hitting her face. She couldn't keep the stray tendrils out of her eyes.

"I love this job," continued Harper. "I usually work in libraries and archives. This is the first job I've had where I get to combine everything I enjoy. It's great."

It was about the same distance to St. Simons as it was to Fernandina Beach where she and John had eaten a few nights earlier. But Harper was a faster driver, and they arrived at their destination quickly. She slowed considerably as she piloted to a dock and cut the engine. Bobbie and Lindsay jumped out and tied the boat.

"OK," said Harper. "We have several choices. We've got seafood—which I confess I'm getting a little tired of—Chinese, Italian, French, and probably some others."

"How about Chinese?" Lindsay suggested.

"I love Chinese food," Bobbie agreed.

They walked past the marina for a few hundred yards to the Chinese restaurant. They were seated in a booth—Harper and Bobbie across from Lindsay. They ordered egg rolls, garlic chicken, Mongolian beef, sweet-and-sour pork, and rice.

"This is a feast," said Harper, filling her plate. "Bobbie, I'll bet you need to eat a lot, doing so much diving and swimming."

"I need to eat a lot whatever I do. My mother tells me to enjoy my metabolism while I'm young, because it'll leave me when I get older."

"So, Harper," said Lindsay, "any previews on the upcoming journal entries?"

"Nope, you have to wait along with everyone else. So far I haven't run across any mention of another Asian. Poor man. You said he was ill?"

"Very."

"What about the first one? He was murdered?"

"Seems so."

"I haven't run across anything like that, either. So far, everything's like a happy outing."

"What I want to know is, what's the author up to?" Bobbie asked.

Harper shook her head. "Lindsay, you going to do drawings of all the remains?"

"If there aren't too many. Lewis wants to use them for newspaper articles."

"I thought they might be nice illustrations for the book."

"Lewis is going to hire a sculptor to do the faces from the skulls. You might want to use photographs."

"Or both."

They talked their way through all the Mongolian beef and garlic chicken, three quarters of the sweet-and-sour pork, and two plates of rice. Bobbie explained what a Lumbee Indian was to Harper, and Harper told them what it was like growing up in Singapore. Lindsay told Harper and Bobbie about her archaeologist grandfather and some of the early trips she went on with him.

"I'm stuffed," said Harper at last. "This has been fun."

It was dark when they walked back to the dock. Bobbie and Lindsay untied the boat as Harper started the motor and turned on the running lights. She piloted the boat easily out to the ocean and took off. The ocean air was cool and Lindsay put on her jacket. Bobbie and Harper both seemed to enjoy the wind in their faces.

They were twelve miles from their dock at St. Magdalena and two miles from the shore on the opposite end of the island when the motor began smoking and stopped.

"What in the. . . ?" exclaimed Harper over the whine of the engine as she tried to restart it.

"Well, damn."

She reached for the radio. The cable had been yanked out.

Chapter 16

A Passenger's Diary: Part III

From a voyage on the Spanish Galleon
Estrella de España, c. 1558
—Translated by Harper Latham

AFTER THE STORM we did not immediately set sail. We first buried the poor sailor, which amounted to Father Hernando saying a few words over the body, then throwing it overboard with a cannon-ball sewn inside the shroud. After that, the ship required a few minor repairs, which consisted of caulkers pounding oakum into the separated seams, carpenters nailing lead sheets over gashed places in the hull, and sailmakers repairing torn sails, or hoisting new ones.

The ship's hull below the waterline had to be examined by sailors who cannot only swim, but can hold their breath for an extended period of time. They dived into the water, looking for damage and making necessary repairs. Valerian's servant, Jen, helped in this task. It turns out that he was a pearl diver in his land. The men were glad for his assistance. This is not a favored task, and Jen can stay underwater for a long time.

Three days after the storm, I stood by the grate on the weather deck, hoping to overhear something else, but there was only the steam and aroma of salted pork. The crew around me went about their incessant tasks, as though there had been no fatal storm days before. The page had turned the sand clock and said the third prayer of the morning, when I saw the three of them—Valerian, López, and Captain Acosta—pass me going toward the captain's cabin. I waited until they disappeared, then casually strolled from

139

my post through the arched doorway past the large brass cannons tended by soldiers intent on their own conversation. The few sailors scrubbing the floor ignored me as I passed. They were dressed in ragged clothes and most had bare feet, such a contrast to me in my fine robes and shoes. Some of the crew bid on the clothes of the fallen man, so poor are they that an extra set of rags is considered a fine thing. The money, I understand, will go to the unfortunate man's widow. Such a paltry sum would hardly be worth it to Luisa, but will be a good sum to the poor woman and her children. Such is the disparity between them and me. I am a fortunate man.

I diverge from this journal entry, perhaps because I am ashamed at my failure. I passed the helmsman, who stood at the whipstaff toward the rear of the deck listening for any instructions shouted to him from above. Beyond him was Valerian's servant, Jen, sitting in front of the door to the captain's cabin, cradling his harp in his arms, serenading the crew.

"I saw Valerian come this way," I stammered. I thought that boldly admitting to following them would look less suspicious. "I fancy a game of chess."

Jen grinned at me, and I felt he was not fooled in the least by my ruse. "I tell him," he said, and I nodded, turned, and went to my cabin, feeling foolish and incompetent.

Are they up to something? Of course, men like that are always up to something. But are they smugglers? Smuggling gold and silver has long been a problem for the House of Trade, and they have all but ignored it. Perez, the new governor of the House, thinks he can bring it under control, if he has the right information. I wonder. Smuggling is as established as the Church itself. He thinks that if he can make an example of a few, the rest will follow. But where there is such great wealth for the taking . . . I think it is a hopeless venture. Perhaps when I get to Havana I will talk to my brother about how to proceed. Undoubtedly, he will be a good counsel, and he is as honorable as the good Perez.

I listen, but my discoveries are of little importance. I hear only the common things from the rumblings of the crew. The man Sancho who was salvaged from the ocean after the storm was accused of stealing from another sailor. These men have so little, I couldn't conceive what he could have stolen. I discovered that what he stole was a space to sleep. Imagine. Such are the conditions of the sailor. It ended with the boatswain deciding in favor of the man making the complaint, and Sancho had to find another place. I would not have found this very serious, but I do not live their lives. It was apparently very serious with the crew. Another of the crew accused Sancho of stealing his knife, but upon producing it, it had Sancho's name scratched on it. Sancho, allowing that he could neither read nor write, had had it done in Seville, he said. He got to keep the knife. But it is my understanding that none of the crew believe him, including the steward. I heard the steward complain to the boatswain that Sancho is a clever sneak and to watch out for him.

I spend much time with Valerian. I like him, but I don't know if he seeks out my company because he favors it, or because he is watching me. At any rate, it looks as if the only way I will discover any useful information will be from him. Valerian is a puzzle. He is quite different from the garrulous López and the rather dense captain. What could they have in common?

We are lucky with the weather. Good weather makes for a less quarrelsome crew. However, it seems to me that dissension among the crew has increased with Sancho's arrival.

Valerian conversed with Bellisaro about the sails. I stood and listened, amused. Valerian was suggesting a different arrangement of the sails for faster sailing. I know Bellisaro and how he holds the captain's suggestions in contempt, so I was surprised when he gave Valerian a slight smile and ordered the crew to the ropes to change the tension and angle of the sails. Then he yelled something down to the helmsman. Having thus done (which was not a small task), Bellisaro took his sandglass, threw his log-line into the ocean, then counted and timed the knots as the line reeled. He looked sideways at Valerian and smiled. We were indeed going faster.

That evening, over chess, Valerian explained that it has something to do with the way the wind rushes through the sails. I did not understand. He went on to explain that the sails are like the wings of a bird, and it might be possible to design a contrivance with sails that could seat a man and he could sail from a cliff and fly with the birds. I told him he needs to spend less time in the sun. He went on to assure me that he is not the first to think of this, other great men have designed such things. He said this as if he assumed that I thought wanting to fly was the mark of an intelligent and sane man. "Keeping the motion forward would be a problem," he said, and I told him that no, I didn't think forward motion was the problem. We were sitting cross-legged on the floor, the chessboard between us. He leaned forward, his eyes shining, warming to his topic. "A little over five hundred years ago Eilmer of Malmesbury made a short flight from his abbey. And you are familiar with the ideas of da Vinci?" I wasn't, nor did I know who Eilmer was or where Malmesbury was. But if it was an abbey, he was a man of God and that reassured me and I listened. Actually, I enjoy listening to Valerian. He has a way of opening up the world and looking at its wonders that often holds me spellbound.

"You see," he said, "I believe the failure is in their analogy." I nodded. "Men like da Vinci see birds fly and design their devices so, like Icarus." (I knew who Icarus was and I nodded more vigorously.) "But men are not like birds," he said. On this point, I could agree and said so. "It is like a ship and a rock. A ship floats on water, a rock sinks, even though the ship is much heavier. The two are different," he said.

"True," I agreed, but I did not know why, nor did I ask, so ashamed was I of my ignorance. And so eager was I not to disappoint Valerian. He chose to talk to me because he believes me to be an intellectual equal, at least more of one than anyone else on the ship.

"So it is with a man and a bird," he continued. "However, you can put a rock on a ship and it will float. Don't you see?"

"A ship that flies?" I asked.

"Yes," he said, putting his hands on my shoulders, shaking me. "Exactly. I knew you would understand."

I had to make a bold move if I was ever to discover anything. That is what I decided while lying on my cot listening to the snores of Bellisaro and trying to think of a way to accomplish what Perez has asked of me. Wisps of half-heard conversations, and unsupported and perhaps unfounded suspicions whirled in my brain. I hated the idea of returning to the House of Trade and telling them that, after a month and a half in a confined space, I had failed to discover anything. Then I remembered the crates of Valerian's that were loaded when we stopped at the islands. As I am convinced that Valerian has something to do with whatever intrigue the captain and López are engaged in, examining his cargo seemed a sensible idea. I did not, however, look forward to descending into the dark hold of the ship. Perhaps I should have attended to such a deed during the day when at least some light could drift down to the depths, but I was eager for my activities to remain concealed. I am sure that López and the captain have only vague suspicions. (How could they know anything? I've been so discreet as not to have discovered anything of import.) However, I don't know how either might react to my spying, and I confess that my hands shook with fear as I groped through my travel chest in the darkness for the things I needed for this adventure. I hurriedly put on clothes that I least minded getting soiled, then felt through the chest for a candle and my flint striker. My bowels quickened anew as I slipped the two into my pouch. Order of Santiago or not, if the captain caught me with a lighted candle, I'd certainly be keel-hauled—such is the gravity of starting a fire aboard ship. My hand touched the pomander that Luisa had given me, and I had the odd sensation of missing her. I also recollected the unpleasant aromas rising from below the decks, so I slipped it into my pouch.

Thus armed, I stole from my cabin. I made a furtive glance around me and made my way through the dark corridor to the hatchway. There were two lanterns hanging nearby. Only one was lit. I took the other. If caught, it would be far better if I had a lantern than a lighted candle. I climbed down to the main gun deck, where I tried to be particularly quiet, for many of the crew as well as the soldiers sleep there. However, there were none in the immediate vicinity and I continued down to the orlop deck. Here I stopped and lit my lantern. Some of the ship's stores were on this deck, so I looked around, peeking in adjoining rooms. Valerian's crates had been heavy. I saw that as they were loading them, so I reasoned they would probably be stored in the hold. For this reason, and the fact that the stewards and other officers' cabins were on this deck, I did not tarry.

Upon descending into the hold, I discovered one thing immediately—I prefer the deck of the ship, with all its hazards, to the innards. Surely the depths of hell must be like the belly of a ship, inhabited by the vilest of vermin and saturated with a putrid stench that even the most pungent burning of sulfur cannot expurgate. I feel for the unfortunate men, blessed by neither God nor king, who must attend to the bilge. I reached for my pomander and put the silver metal to my nose and inhaled the fragrant spice. Would that I had some method to tie the thing there. I hung the pomander on my finger and held my sleeve over my nose. It helped, but I had to use all my will to not choke on the smell. To think they store the food and drinking water down there. Meals will never be the same for me.

The hold was not exactly as I had thought, a vast cavern piled with barrels and crates. It was vast, but it was divided into stalls and walkways. I squatted and held my lantern and peered down at the very bottom of the ship between the planks of the walkway where I stood. Undoubtedly the origin of the stench. With the rocking of the ship a greenish putrid fluid flowed back and forth among tightly stacked gray rocks. A partially decomposed rat lay on one of the rocks. I said a silent prayer for the continued good repair of the bilge pump, lest the fouled water reach the stored food and drinking water. The storm, I thought. The pumps had been continuously running. Let's hope the water level in the hold didn't rise too high. It did, however, seem damp down there.

I stood and looked for Valerian's crates. They were the last loaded, so they should be near, I reasoned. The hold was not as full as I would have thought. It seems that most of the supplies are ours. We are supposed to be taking supplies to St. Sebastian. I fear the colonists will be disappointed at the paltry show of provisions; however, we have ample room for contraband. But why not take the supplies over? For surely, after their unloading, there would be ample room for any cargo for the return voyage. It seems almost as if we aren't actually going to St. Sebastian.

The hull was quiet except for the constant creaking of the wood rubbing against itself as the ship wafted. It reminded me that I shouldn't miss the opportunity to look for the crates while there was no one there to observe me. I walked along the walkways, peeking into the various stalls. There are many barrels stored on their side and kept from rolling by wooden wedges jammed between them. Extra rope lies in coiled piles on top. Across in another area, stacked neatly are the staves and bands of barrels that have been emptied. For all the foul smell, the hold is neatly organized. Adjacent to the kegs are sacks of grain and foodstuffs.

I continued searching down the length of the ship toward the bow. The hold is a maze of recesses and alcoves. I feared I would be there all night. I reached the magazine and started back toward the stern, when I spied the crates in a recess. As I examined them,

I noticed that someone had been down before me, for the lids had been pried open and hurriedly fastened back. Not Valerian or his servant, for surely as carefully as they oversaw the loading, they would not have been so careless in the checking of them. I stepped on top of one, raised my lantern, and peeked in the tallest first. I don't know what I expected, but I was surprised at what I found. It was a large bell. For all my suspicions of Valerian, is he actually on some holy pilgrimage to St. Sebastian? Perhaps I have misjudged the poor fellow. I closed and fastened the lid, wondering if the curious fellow before me had been disappointed. I felt relieved. I pried open the other crate, which was actually as large as the first; it was simply on its side. Inside was, at first glance, a coil of rope. However, it is not hemp, but leather sewn into a hollow shaft. I have no idea what such a thing is used for. Beneath the leather coil were other objects, the purpose of which I cannot guess. I closed the lid and quickly blew the light from my lantern just as I heard someone coming. In my haste to secret myself, I dropped my Luisa's pomander and it fell through the space between the planks and into the bilge.

There were two of them. I could barely make out the shadowy figures of two crew members as they moved away from the ladder toward my hiding place. One was the man Sancho, whom we rescued from the ill-starred *Orgullo de España*. The other was a man I have seen but do not know.

"Why did you want to meet down here?" asked the man in a loud, hissing whisper. "This is the worst place on the ship."

"Which is why it is a good meeting place, especially at night," Sancho answered. "So no one will hear us."

"Say what you have to say, so we can leave."

Sancho began relating a plot for his own smuggling. On much less a measure than captains and generals, but illegal, nonetheless. "They will store the gold and silver in the hold, or on the orlop deck. The treasure they do not wish to declare will be offloaded before they take it into port. In a ship this size, they don't go all the way to the port at Seville. Sometimes they load it in small boats and row it to a friendly port."

"So what does that have to do with us?" asked the sailor.

"We can get some of the booty," said Sancho.

"Just how do we do that?" the man asked. I was interested to know myself.

"Easy—we take a few bars of gold and silver and hide them on the ship. When we get off, it goes with us."

"And just how do we get our hands on a few bars of gold?"

"That's where you come in," Sancho answered him.

"I wondered when we were getting to that."

"You work with the cargo. It would be easy to just take a little extra."

"No," the sailor said. "It won't work. We'll get caught and hanged."

"No. I've done this before. It's easy," Sancho told him.

"If it's so easy, then why are you here dressed in rags like the rest of us?"

"If I were here dressed in fine clothes, they'd find me out, wouldn't they? Look. We don't take much. Men like us don't need as much as the rich. You don't get greedy, you don't get caught. I've got a blacksmith friend who can turn a bar of gold into coins. Just a few extra coins a year, and nobody notices but us what's living better. They steal it among themselves, but it's us what does all the work."

A long silence followed. So interested was I in listening to the conversation that I almost forgot about the terrible stench, but it came upon me in the silence, and I had to hold my mouth to keep from retching and making a noise.

"We can't just walk off the ship with gold," said the sailor. "It's heavy and they search our chests. If you've done this before, then you know that."

"We hide it in something that's going off the ship. Once me and a mate hid silver in the ballast, carried it off when we were changing it out. There's more ways than I have fingers and toes. That's not the problem, but I need a mate I can trust." Sancho was very persuasive—I could almost feel the man changing his mind.

"We only take a small amount," the sailor said. I heard Sancho slap him on the back.

"Not enough that they'd notice."

"Let's get out of this place," said the sailor. "We can talk more when we stop in Havana. It's a long way to Cartagena. Time enough, I suppose, to make a good plan."

Mercifully, they left soon after. I waited, holding my sleeve over my nose, hoping to keep out some of the odor. Finally, I could take it no more. I made my way in the dark and climbed up to the top deck. I stood on the bow, breathing in the fresh air.

"Can't sleep?" It was Valerian. He came up beside me so quietly, I jumped. The bow's lantern and the full moon lit his features enough so that I could see his nose twitch. "Been in the hold, have we?"

I smiled. What could I say? I had forgotten that the aroma clings to the clothes.

"Next time you feel like a walk around the bottom of the ship, let me know. I enjoy a good midnight stroll."

Chapter 17

"SOMEONE DESTROYED THE radio." Harper held up the dangling cord.

"I don't believe this." Bobbie threw her hands in the air.

"What are we going to do?" Lindsay asked.

Bobby dug in a box and came up with a flag. "We'll put this distress flag on our antenna, . . . but it's so dark, I doubt anyone will see it unless they shine a light on us. I don't see any boats around anyway."

"Do we have more options?" Lindsay asked, looking out at the choppy ocean and the distant shore in the moonlight.

"Sure," said Harper. "The flare guns are still here." She dug in the boat's locker. "Well, no they aren't. We do have the rubber raft and oars, and we all have our purses."

"Our purses? Oh, but I don't have my cell phone with me," replied Lindsay.

"I don't have one," Bobbie said.

Harper smiled and dug in her purse. "I'm never without mine." She pushed the power button. "However, I do appear to be without a close enough tower. We'll drift in with the tide, so we don't have to worry about that. We can just stay here a while."

They drifted in the boat for what seemed to Lindsay like an eternity.

"Can't we jury-rig a sail?" she asked at last. Harper and Bobbie looked at each other, then at Lindsay. "Maybe we can use an oar for a mast."

"I'll tell you what," said Harper. "You can stand in the middle of the boat with your arms stretched out for yardarms and hold a blanket. We'll tell you which way to turn."

"I take it that's a 'no' on the jury-rigging."

"I vote for the raft," said Bobbie, pulling it out of the locker.

"What about the boat?" Lindsay asked.

"We tow it," said Harper.

Bobbie put the raft over the side and pulled the plug. Within seconds it had inflated itself like some sped-up animated cartoon and sat bobbing next to their boat. They all laughed at the effect, then piled in the raft, and Harper tied the boat to the back.

"Who wants to row first?" Bobbie asked. Lindsay volunteered. "When you get tired, we'll switch out."

"I must say," Lindsay said as she began rowing, "the two of you don't seem too upset about this."

"When you're raised around boats, you learn how to deal with emergencies," said Harper. "Besides, there are usually so many fishing boats about, someone would find us, eventually. The important thing is not to panic."

"Couldn't we signal a boat with a mirror?" asked Lindsay.

"It's nighttime, Lindsay," Harper replied.

"I have a flashlight. We could signal someone with that," Lindsay said. Bobbie and Harper laughed. She hadn't meant to be funny.

Lindsay had a lot of lower body strength—she rode her horse and jogged for exercise, but she was sorely lacking in upper body strength. Perhaps I should get a rowing machine, she thought. She rowed until her shoulders ached, but the shore seemed no closer.

"How about if I take over for a while?" Harper offered.

Lindsay changed places with her. With three of them to switch out, Lindsay thought they should make it to the shore fine. When Bobbie spelled Harper at the oars, the shore did look closer. They all had a turn at the oars again before Bobbie rowed the raft up on the narrow beach.

"Land at last!" Bobbie exclaimed.

They pulled the boat onto the sand as far as they could, and Harper tied it to a tree.

"But where are we?" asked Lindsay.

"The motor died a couple of miles out from St. Magdalena," Harper said.

"So we must be on the north end of the island," Bobbie added.

"Great," said Harper. "We can walk to the lab. About how far is it?"

"The research station is at the southern end of the island, and the island is about twelve miles long," said Lindsay. "I'd say about ten miles."

"Ten miles. Ten miles!" exclaimed Harper. "We have to walk ten miles?"

"It won't be bad. We can always walk on the beach and end up at our dock," Lindsay said.

"Nope," said Bobbie and Harper together. "The tide is coming in. It'll cover the beach."

"Okay," said Lindsay. "We'll have to walk overland."

"How about the shoreline on the other side of the island?" Harper clearly didn't want to hike ten miles through the forest.

"When Bobbie and I took the ferry," said Lindsay, "that side of the island looked like swampland. We'll have to travel inland, but we can't make the trip in the dark. We'll have to stay the night here." She began collecting things from the boat. "You guys have your purses and jackets?"

"What do you mean stay the night here? This is the wilderness," Harper complained, following the beam of Lindsay's flashlight as they walked toward the woods.

"We can't go through unknown woods at night. Walking in the morning will be much safer and faster," Lindsay explained.

Bobbie and Harper went over all the reasons they couldn't stay the night before they noticed that they were no longer near the shore and that Lindsay was busy constructing something.

"What are you doing?" asked Bobbie.

"Building us a shelter."

"I must say," said Harper, "you don't seem too upset over *this* turn of events."

"You guys were raised on the water. I was raised in the woods. The trick is not to panic, as someone once said. Why don't you guys collect some wood for a fire?" She handed them the flashlight from the boat. "Stay together and don't go far from this clearing. Watch for snakes and other nocturnal creatures."

Harper and Bobbie delivered several armloads of firewood. Apparently, a recent storm had freed up all the dead wood in the trees. Probably the storm Bobbie had mentioned. When the two of them returned for the last time, each with an armload of wood, Lindsay had finished a lean-to constructed with limbs and a tarp from the boat.

"Well, that's cute," said Harper.

Lindsay threw her a bottle of insect repellant she found in the first-aid kit. "Rub this on yourselves. There are lots of insects about, especially mosquitoes and ticks."

"I've felt them already," said Bobbie.

Lindsay used her Swiss army knife to whittle off a pile of shavings from a piece of wood. She placed the shavings over a pile of pine needles, then began stacking wood over the tinder and kindling.

"That looks like a Mayan temple," Harper observed.

"It's a good design that will last most of the night. The fire will keep the chill off the night air and help with some of the mosquitoes. After stuffing ourselves with that Chinese meal, we shouldn't have to eat again for another week. We have bottled water, a first-aid kit, and some blankets from the boat. I'd say we are pretty well off."

Bobbie put one of the blankets on the ground under the shelter, and she and Harper sat down. Lindsay lit a long sliver of wood with a match and used it to light the tinder. She gently fanned and blew between the logs until she got a stable flame. She joined them after she was confident the fire was going well.

"We need some marshmallows," said Harper, "and a bottle of wine."

They sat watching the fire, listening to the sounds of the night—a cacophonous mixture of ocean waves, tree frogs, crickets, night birds, and wind in the trees. Off in the distance there was a scream.

"What was that?" asked Harper.

"A bobcat," answered Lindsay.

"Bobcat—as in wildcat?"

"Yes."

"Oh, Lord."

"He'll probably stay away from us—" said Bobbie. "Won't he, Lindsay?"

"Yes . . . unless it's a rogue male, and then he may pick up our scent and come to drive us out of his territory."

"Really? Really?" replied Bobbie and Harper together, their eyes wide.

Lindsay laughed. "Haven't you ever heard ghost stories around a campfire? No, he won't bother us. I don't think—I mean, they hardly ever do."

"Oh, you," said Bobbie, laughing uneasily.

"What other animals are on the island?" asked Harper.

"Well," said Lindsay, "you know about the alligators. You live with one next to your house."

"You mean they aren't confined to the pond?"

"Think about it," Lindsay said. "It's really a pool, and it isn't a closed system. The alligator has relatives somewhere on the island. There're also raccoons. They will probably come around and try to steal stuff from our campsite. I think there are also some feral cows. Deer, lots of birds. I saw an eagle the other evening."

"I saw one, too, last week," said Bobbie.

"I've never seen an eagle," Harper said wistfully.

"Maybe we'll see one on the way back tomorrow," said Bobbie.

"If we ever get back," Harper said. "These woods are like a jungle. How will we ever find our way through them?"

"There are trails made by the larger animals, and the biologists survey the island all the time. I'm sure we'll find the trails they use." Lindsay tried to reassure them. "It'll be a beautiful hike through the woods."

"So, while Bobbie and I were growing up in the water, you were out in the woods?"

"My dad loves the woods and is pretty good at woodcraft. When I was growing up, he took me with him a lot when I wasn't off with my grandfather surveying for archaeological sites. We'd camp a lot, too. When my brother, Sinjin, was home, he, Dad, and I would go fishing. We knew how to rough it pretty good."

"Your mother didn't go?" asked Bobbie.

"She didn't like to leave the horses." Lindsay told Harper about her mother's Arabians.

"Sailing was my dad's thing," said Harper. "Mom didn't like it much. I took after him. I love the sea."

"My whole family scuba dives," said Bobbie. "I don't remember any vacation where we didn't go somewhere to dive."

Harper grabbed a blanket and pulled it around her, squinting into the woods. "What kind of trees are those? I'd like to have one in my yard at home."

"Live oaks. Picturesque, aren't they?" said Lindsay. "They look like the jungle."

"What about that one, the one that looks like it's blooming?"

"I'm not sure what kind of tree it is, but those are probably orchids."

"Orchids?"

"This is a subtropical island. You get quite a few flora here that are also found in the tropics," answered Lindsay. "In fact, there's a program to place a lot of endangered tropical species of animals here to increase their numbers."

Harper started to laugh.

"What?" asked Bobbie.

"I'm shipwrecked on a tropical island. I somehow thought it would be different."

Lindsay and Bobbie laughed with her.

"Too bad Trey isn't here. I might like to be shipwrecked with him." Harper gave Lindsay a little shove. "So, how about it, Lindsay, wouldn't you like to be here with John?"

Lindsay thought about John and what it would be like if it were just him and her here in the shelter. She smiled.

"What about you, Bobbie? Who would you like to be ship-wrecked with?" Lindsay asked.

"Adrian Paul."

"Who?" Lindsay asked.

"That guy with the sword," said Harper.

"Yeah, that guy with the sword." Bobbie smiled.

"He'd do," agreed Harper. "How about somebody here at the site? Met anyone?"

Bobbie shook her head. "No, nobody I'd like to be shipwrecked with."

"Some of the guys guarding the dam look really good," Harper replied.

"They're mostly Indians from tribes different from mine," said Bobbie. "We always get into arguments."

"Well, from what I understand, Lindsay and John started by getting into arguments."

"How do you manage that?" asked Bobbie. "John's not ever going to change his attitude about Native American burials, and I can't see you changing, either."

"Right now we just don't discuss it."

"That won't last forever," said Harper.

"I know, but I'll think about that tomorrow."

"Where do you stand on the issue?" Harper asked Bobbie.

"I can see both sides. But I'd like to check the DNA of Native American burials and compare them with my people. I'm a

Lumbee, you know. Nobody knows where we came from. The truth is out there somewhere." She grinned.

"You mean there's no knowledge whatsoever of where your tribe came from?" asked Harper.

"Not really. My ancestors were living like Europeans when they were first discovered, so to speak. Their Indian culture was completely lost. We do have many of the names of the lost Roanoke settlers. I believe my ancestors absorbed them into their community."

"Lacayo is Spanish," said Harper. "Have you traced that? You're probably related to some of these guys in the wreck."

"I've done some research, but Lacayo is a common Spanish name. There were lots of them that came over during the expeditions." Bobbie sighed. "Maybe we should try to get some sleep."

"You're right," Harper agreed. "We have a long way to go tomorrow."

"It won't take that long," Lindsay said, rising to put a blanket over the opening of the shelter. "I do a ten-mile run at least once a week."

"Great," said Harper. "Bobbie and I'll stay here while you go get help."

Just then, like a sudden explosion nearby, another cry of a bobcat split through the calm.

"OK," said Lindsay. "You two can stay here."

"Never mind," said Harper. The three of them settled back in the shelter that Lindsay had constructed and pulled the blankets over themselves.

Lindsay awoke first. She slipped out of the makeshift bed and made her way into the woods to go to the bathroom. When she finished, she walked to the shore where the waterline was up to the vegetation. Sure enough, there was no beach. The sun was just above the horizon, giving the ocean a golden sparkle. Lindsay slapped at her arm. The mosquitoes never rested. She made her way back to camp just as Bobbie and Harper were waking up.

"Oh, good," said Harper. "We are still alive." She sat up. "God, I'm stiff. And bitten."

Lindsay put out the smoldering fire and gathered up the supplies they would take.

"We'll put the rest in the boat."

They folded the tarp, gathered the extra blankets, and walked to the boat.

"The boat's gone!" cried Bobbie, as the three of them stood on the bank where Harper had tied it to a tree.

"That's impossible. It couldn't have pulled loose."

"Did you use a quick-release knot?" asked Lindsay.

"Yes, but the boat wouldn't have pulled it loose."

"It was probably a raccoon," said Lindsay. "I've had them unzip my tent and come in and steal food."

"You're kidding. So—what, it was looking for food and when it didn't find any it untied the boat for spite?"

"Quick-release knots are often used to tie up sacks of food in a tree. It probably learned how to release it while stealing food. They're smart little guys with humanlike hands. The boat can't have gone far. The tide was coming in. It probably drifted down the shore. Trey can send someone to look for it and tow it back."

They decided to take a bottle of water for each of them, the insect repellent, the first-aid kit, and one blanket, but left the rest of the supplies under a tree to retrieve later. Then they headed south. Lindsay looked at her watch. It was just past seven A.M.

"We don't have a compass," she said, "so we have to try and keep the sun to our left . . . and stay on the trail."

"I'll bet you can find your direction looking at the shadow of a stick in the ground, can't you?" said Harper.

"As a matter of fact, I can," said Lindsay.

"I thought so. Okay, Daniel Boone, lead the way."

Finding a good trail wasn't that easy. They passed through areas under stands of live oaks with no visible trails. Lindsay constantly checked the rising sun to make sure they were going straight. When she did find an animal trail, it was narrow and overhung with brush and thick with sharp palmettos.

"Okay, B'wana," said Harper. "I'm getting scratched up and eaten alive by insects. When's the trail going to widen some? Aren't there any big animals on the island?"

Lindsay passed down a bottle of insect repellant. "They may be inland. I was trying to go more parallel to the shore so we don't get lost."

"Not that I'm complaining," said Harper. "This is the most adventure I've had in years."

The trail widened into a clearing, and they stopped to rub themselves down with repellant. "This place has lots of ticks," said Lindsay. "Rub yourselves down good."

"I'll bet insecticide is illegal on this island," said Bobbie. "You know, toxins in the environment."

"I won't tell the biologists if you won't," Harper replied. "Don't you get some kind of dispensation for emergencies?"

A bird flew over, landed in a nearby tree, and called out in a loud screech. "That's a parrot!" Harper exclaimed.

"Yes," said Lindsay. "I told you this is a subtropical island."

"I know. But, well, you just don't expect to be lost in the jungle in Georgia. We won't run across any lions or anything will we?"

"No," said Bobbie. "But if we're lucky, we might spot a manatee in one of the rivers. I understand there are several who live near here."

"Really?" said Harper. "They're endangered, right?"

"Yes," said Lindsay. "It's illegal to approach them, but we can look if one swims by."

"Aren't manatees where the legend of mermaids came from?" Bobbie asked. She handed Lindsay the repellant, and Lindsay stuffed it into the sack with the blanket and first-aid kit, and they set out again.

Lindsay nodded. "Sailors saw them and thought they were women with fish tails. Presumably, the sailors had been out to sea for a while." They giggled.

"I understand that Darien, Georgia, has a sea monster," said Bobbie.

"A sea monster? Like Loch Ness?" asked Harper.

"That's what I hear," Bobbie answered. "Gina was out with Rick, and she said it nudged their boat. There have been lots of sightings over the years."

"What do you suppose it is?" asked Harper.

"People seeing what they want to see," Lindsay replied. "Some of the descriptions I've heard describe a large snake-looking creature with two humps. I think they might have seen a pod of dolphins. A couple of dolphins, one behind the other, jumping out of the water and back could give the impression of a serpent, kind of like an optical illusion."

"Maybe," Bobbie replied thoughtfully, "but they described the head and everything."

"It's thought that the whole idea of sea serpents started with people finding the bones of beached whales," Lindsay said. "You take away the flesh and collapse the ribs, and you have a head and a very long vertebral column. It would look like the skeleton of a sea serpent. They described what they thought the head would look like if it were fleshed out, and the descriptions were handed down."

"That's not as romantic," said Harper.

"But it makes sense," said Bobbie.

"A lot of legends are rooted in some real observation like that. The cyclops, for example," said Lindsay.

"You mean Odysseus' cyclops? The big guy with one eye in the middle of his head?" asked Harper.

"Yeah, that one," said Lindsay.

"Don't tell me you have a logical explanation for that?"

"The fossil bones of pygmy elephants. Elephants have their eyes on the side of their head, and their orbits are open. They don't look like orbits when you see them in a skull. But the nasal passage—for the trunk—is quite large and does look like an eye socket. You find one of those skulls, you think you've found a giant guy with one large eye in the middle of his forehead."

"That makes sense, too," said Bobbie.

"Well, dang. Lindsay just burst another bubble."

They marched through another thick forest of hickory, birch, and live oaks hanging with Spanish moss. After about a mile the terrain began to slope downward dramatically, and they found their way blocked by a seemingly endless field of reeds and cordgrass populated by egrets looking for food in the shallow marsh water. Lindsay stopped and walked the length of the edge of the marshland looking for a trail. Harper and Bobbie waited, taking several sips of water from their bottles.

"Here," Lindsay called. "I believe I see a wooden bridge ahead. This must be one of the trails used by the biologists. It skirts the woods."

Lindsay led them down the trail and over the footbridge, all the while followed by a swarm of small black flies.

Harper swatted at her face. "Are we going to get malaria?"

"No. These are just gnats," Lindsay replied. "Pesky, aren't they?" Lindsay brushed her legs.

"Too bad we didn't have the foresight to wear something more suitable for being marooned in," said Bobbie, waving her hands. "Yuck, they flew in my mouth." She stopped and spit. "Ugh. I thought these things were confined to the beach."

Lindsay looked at her watch. They had been hiking for an hour and a half. Though not high, the sun had long since knocked the chill off the air, and she was perspiring.

"There's another footbridge up ahead," said Harper. "Let's stop and rest."

This bridge, like the last, spanned several feet across a wide, slow-moving stream. They stopped on the bridge and took several long drinks of water.

"Oh, look, look, look!" shouted Bobbie, pointing at the stream.

"What? What?" yelled Harper, jumping away from the railing of the bridge.

"In the water. It's a manatee."

"It's beautiful," said Lindsay, watching the huge gray walrus-like creature glide under the water.

"Oh, perhaps the sailors weren't so crazy, after all," said Harper. "They look so gentle. This is certainly worth all the trouble we've been through."

Before continuing their trek, they watched the manatee swim under the bridge and out of sight. After another fifteen minutes of walking, they saw another large expanse of woods ahead where the terrain again sloped upward.

"Are we about there yet?" Harper asked.

"I think we only have about four miles to go."

"Four miles!" exclaimed Harper. "I think rowing would have been easier."

"No," said Lindsay, "rowing would not have been easier."

"You say that because you're good at walking. I'm better at rowing. Oh, look . . ." Harper pointed at a herd of gazelles in the distance. "I don't believe it!" She rushed ahead to watch them bound out of sight.

"Don't get off the trail," Lindsay warned.

"We're almost to the woods, surely—" Harper screamed.

"Oh, God, quicksand!" Bobbie exclaimed.

"Harper, don't panic. You'll be fine. Grab my hand."

"It's sucking me down," Harper cried.

"No, it isn't," Lindsay calmly replied. "You are sinking, but you'll probably hit bottom in just a second. You'll be able to float. It won't suck you down, I promise. Most of what people think about quicksand is a myth. Now stay still and grab my hand."

Harper was up to her chest in the sand. Lindsay tested for the edge, lay down, and reached for Harper's hand.

159

"I think I've hit bottom," Harper said, making an effort to breathe slowly.

"Good, now we're going to pull you out. Don't try to pull against us. Just let us pull. Bobbie, take her other hand."

"Wait, my shoe came off," Harper protested.

"Don't worry about your shoe," said Lindsay.

Bobbie reached in to grab Harper's other hand, but as she pulled her arm out of the quicksand, she screamed and shook her hands back and forth, and something flew into the bushes.

"I've pulled her arm off! Oh, God, I've pulled her arm off. Oh, God! Oh, God! Oh, God!" Bobbie jumped up and down screaming.

Harper looked at her own mud covered hand, startled. Lindsay let go of the hand she held and stood up. "Bobbie, you probably grabbed a branch . . ."

Harper shifted, trying to get out. "Hey, help, I'm falling," she yelled.

Lindsay turned to her. "You'll float. Just lean back."

As she did so, Lindsay's eyes widened in surprise. Bobbie screamed anew in horror. Harper saw their faces and turned her head. Her scream cut through the air, drowning out all other sounds.

Chapter 18

As HARPER LEANED back, a head rose from the mud behind her, and a muddy arm reached around her shoulder. She screamed, panicked, and fell forward, trying to scramble out of the quicksand pit. Lindsay grabbed for her hand and pulled.

"Bobbie, help me," Lindsay yelled.

Bobbie kept screaming.

"Bobbie, now! I need help."

Bobbie grasped the arm that Lindsay held, and they both pulled as hard as they could. Lindsay managed to turn herself to use the ground for leverage. Harper grabbed Lindsay's arm with her other hand, and finally, she scrambled onto firm ground, crawled several feet, turned over, and scooted backward.

"Oh, my God! Jesus, Mary, and Joseph!" she shrieked. "What was that? I thought you said no one gets . . . Oh, God, I think I'm going to throw up."

"Me, too!" Bobbie exclaimed. She ran to the edge of the grassland and plunged her hands into the brackish water, scrubbing them against the sandy bank.

"What was that?" asked Harper.

Whatever it was had settled back into the quicksand and now looked like a lump of sandy mud, vaguely in the shape of the upper torso of a man.

Lindsay examined the thing that Bobbie had tossed into the bushes. It was indeed an arm. A decayed arm.

"What was that?" repeated Harper. "Someone get trapped before me?"

After she said it, the two of them looked at each other. "You don't think—"

"It's a good possibility," said Lindsay. "Keith Teal."

Harper started to put her head on her arms. Seeing the mud, she stopped and looked down at herself.

"If I live to be a hundred, I will never have a worse experience. Oh, no."

"What?" asked Lindsay and Bobbie.

"My purse. It's in the quicksand pit."

"It'll be retrieved. Along with anything else down there," said Lindsay.

Harper stood on shaky legs and walked to where Bobbie was washing her hands as if she were Lady Macbeth.

"I touched that thing," said Bobbie. "I touched it." She dipped her hands into the water again.

Harper looked around for a place to climb into the water.

"Don't," said Lindsay. "You don't want to get stuck in the mud in the water. Besides, there are live creatures in there."

"I don't care. Nothing could be worse than that thing, and I'm going to wash this stuff off me." She sat on the bank beside a pooled-up part of the marsh and tested the bottom. "It's muddy, but I'm going to get in just long enough to rinse off."

"Well, scream if you need help. I know you can," said Lindsay.

While Harper washed off, Lindsay cut some of the marsh grass, found a couple of rocks and pounded it flat, folded it over and pounded it again until she had two more or less rectangular shapes. She then cut the blanket into four strips.

Harper got out of the water, rinsed of the quicksand, but soaking wet. Lindsay tossed her the remainder of the blanket to dry off and came over to her with her creations.

"What's that?" asked Harper.

Bobbie, deciding her hands were as clean as she could get them, sat back and watched.

"You lost your shoes and you are going to need something."

"Is that the something you have there?"

"Yes. We'll wrap your feet in these two strips of blanket. I've made some soles out of marsh grass. It won't be the first time the grass has been put to the same use. It's usually woven, but I don't have time. Anyway, we'll put the soles on and hold them in place with these other strips."

"You're kidding, right?"

"We have about four miles to go through the woods, and these woods are full of briers, thorns, and other sharp and sticky things.

Unless you're accustomed to going barefoot and your feet are well calloused, you'll have to wear these—unless you have a better idea."

Harper stood, her feet wrapped in Lindsay's makeshift boots, standing first on one foot then the other, testing them out.

"Okay," Harper said, "this is the plan. Lindsay, you'll take point like you've been doing. Bobbie, you'll walk in the middle, and I'll bring up the rear. You see anybody coming or we reach civilization, give me a warning and keep everyone at bay until I can get these things off. No one—but no one—is going to see me in these. Is that straight?"

"I wish I had a camera." Bobbie laughed.

"If we had a camera," Harper replied, "we certainly could have documented the trek of the century."

"All right," said Lindsay. "Let's go. And keep in line and on the trail. No side trips."

"You've got it," Harper agreed. "From here on out, it's walk like an Egyptian."

The way was mostly sand, as most of the trip had been so far, and not too hard on the feet, but they stopped frequently to allow Harper to rest hers.

"How you doing?" Lindsay asked.

"Not too bad," Harper answered. "I'll make it."

"It won't be much farther."

"I'm going to run a hot bath and stay there the rest of the day and into the night. Maybe I'll get Trey to massage my feet."

The path narrowed into a thin animal trail bordered by sharp palmetto leaves.

"I used to love this stuff. Now I hate it." Bobbie rubbed her arms and legs as they finally emerged into a wider trail.

"Look," Lindsay yelled, "I see the roof of the lab."

"Okay. Let's stop and let me take these things off my feet."

"We still have a ways to go," said Lindsay.

"I'll manage. Not that I don't appreciate your effort . . ."

Harper pulled off her primitive footwear, tossed the reeds aside, rolled up the strips of blanket, and stuffed them in the sack Lindsay carried. She wiggled her toes in the sand.

"Okay, I'm ready."

They didn't get far before one of the crew spotted them and went to get help. Before they knew it, they were surrounded by

163

Trey, Lewis, and Agent Ramirez. Trey hugged Harper. Lewis radioed John, who was searching with the Coast Guard in the ocean.

"Harper, your feet. Where are your shoes? You didn't . . ."

"Long story," she said.

"What happened?" asked Lewis. "Are you all right, Bobbie, Lindsay? An hour ago we found your boat drifting along the shore. We were worried sick when you didn't return last night."

"Someone sabotaged the boat and yanked out the radio while we were in the restaurant," said Harper. "The motor quit on us in the middle of nowhere. We had to row ashore and spend the night on the other end of the island."

"My God," Trey exclaimed.

"It wasn't too bad," said Harper. "We walked straight across the island. Only made one side trip, hardly worth mentioning. Lindsay's a great trailblazer."

⚓

Lindsay, Bobbie, and Harper sat around a table in the lab and related the story to Trey, Lewis, John, Agent Ramirez, and Lieutenant Damon of the Coast Guard, who listened to the narrative with the proper gaping-mouth expressions.

"Are you sure it was a body?" asked Damon. "From your description, you all were pretty hysterical."

Harper leaned forward with her elbows on the table and stared at him, unblinking.

"It's true I was sinking in quicksand at the time, and Bobbie had a rotting arm in her hand, and the two of us may have been excited to the point we couldn't recognize the shape of a man. However, let me tell you, Lindsay takes both quicksand and dead bodies with a great deal of aplomb, and if she says it was a dead body, then that's good enough for me."

Ramirez cleared his throat. "We do have a missing person— Keith Teal."

"It's easy enough to check, Lieutenant Damon," added Lindsay. "Go look. He isn't going anywhere, and he's in no condition for anyone to try to hide the body."

"Well, that is more Agent Ramirez's jurisdiction. I've had two cutters out looking for the three of you. When you are lost, the best course of action is to stay where you are until someone finds you."

"We weren't lost," Lindsay corrected him. "You didn't know where we were, and we couldn't communicate with anyone. But we knew where we were and knew how to get back to Magdalena House."

"Still . . ."

"Have you checked the north end of the island?"

"No . . ."

"Then we'd still be sitting there swatting mosquitoes."

"I think time would be better spent trying to find out who sabotaged the boat," said Lewis, intervening in the argument. "We are grateful that the Coast Guard responded so quickly. We are also grateful to have our colleagues back safe. We've had one diver shot, and now this. We need to discover who's behind it."

"We looked at the boat," Damon said. "It looks like vandals. The oil line was cut, but not through. That's why they got as far as St. Magdalena. The radio cables were jerked out haphazardly. Did you see anyone you recognized in the restaurant or on the docks?"

The three of them shook their heads. "Not a soul," said Bobbie.

"A familiar boat at the dock?"

"No, but we didn't look at the boats that were docked," Harper replied. "We had no reason to at the time. Look, I'm going to take a long, hot bath. If you have any more questions, I'll be glad to answer them when I'm finished."

Lindsay stood. "I like that idea. Thanks, all of you, for looking for us. We truly are grateful. It's good to know someone knew we were missing and was trying to find us, but we are all tired and in need of a bath." She turned to Ramirez. "I'm sure one of the biologists can show you where the quicksand pit is located. Tell them it's about four miles from here on the edge of the marsh."

John took Lindsay and Bobbie to the archaeology barge docked at the cofferdam. Bobbie disembarked, but John held Lindsay back.

"I was worried about you," he said.

"I'm sorry you were worried. We had a few anxious moments ourselves."

Lindsay's words sounded sharp to her own ears, but she didn't know how to soften them. They were being treated like teenagers who had stayed out all night. No, that wasn't fair. It was really only Lieutenant Damon, and he was also skeptical of Nate and Sarah. Obviously, he didn't trust anyone.

"It must have been bad for you. I just wanted you to know that, well, I worried."

"I'm sorry if I seemed sharp. I'm worried, too. Damon seems to think someone sabotaged our boat as a prank. I don't believe it. Not with the other things that have been going on." She took his hand between her two.

"How about a nice quiet dinner on my barge after you've rested up?" he asked. "Maybe we could watch some television. I understand you like old movies."

"Who told you that?"

"Bobbie."

"You know, Bobbie's very nice," Lindsay told him.

"I know."

"You know she's an Indian."

"Yes, I know that, too. Where's this going?" asked John.

"I think she feels a little like some of you don't think she is, because of the mystery surrounding her tribal affiliation."

"She had an argument with Luke. He's the only one who holds an opinion. Apparently, she gives his opinion a lot of weight," said John.

"She must," agreed Lindsay.

"Luke went out looking with the rest of us. He was very worried, too."

"That's good to know."

"So how about dinner and some television?"

"I'd like that."

Chapter 19

RAMIREZ STOOD LOOKING at the bones Lindsay was examining. They were alone in the big lab.

"And who is this?" he asked, touching the skull sitting on the donut ring.

"He's the sailor with the leg irons. He was between thirty and fifty, probably around thirty-five. Spanish. He had rickets at some time in his life. He was left-handed. His bones show a lot of stress, like he worked hard at manual labor. He had back problems and syphilis. His teeth were decayed. And sometime before he died, he had a wound in his left hand, like something driven through it."

"You mean like a crucifixion?"

"Perhaps he was in a fight, held up his hand in front of him and someone stabbed him, but not with a knife, more like a nail." Lindsay put her left hand in front of her face to illustrate. "I don't see any evidence of other defensive wounds, but there may not be any. Or," she continued, "it was a common practice to nail a sailor's hand to the mast for various infractions. That may be what happened."

"What a hard time these men had," said Ramirez, patting the skull as he would a sick child.

"Some of them. The first skeleton, the one who was murdered, looked as if he had quite an easy life, relatively speaking. But it wasn't a particularly easy life for any of them." Lindsay placed a wet cloth over the bones.

"You can tell a lot from bones?" he asked.

"Quite a bit."

"We think the body in the quicksand is Keith Teal."

Lindsay grimaced. "That's what I had guessed. His father's going to be devastated."

"He is. He thinks someone here killed his son."

Lindsay frowned. "Does he suspect someone in particular?"

"He's confused about who to blame. Sometimes he blames you archaeologists, sometimes he blames the biologists who ran him and his son off the island. I think he may have been the one who sabotaged your boat."

"Boote? No. Why?"

"I'm not sure. But I suspect he saw it docked and saw the University of Georgia name on the side and got angry. By all reports, he's quite often drunk and doesn't think clearly. He probably thought you would not be able to start the boat. I don't think he intended to strand you in the ocean."

"Why do you think it was him?"

"Something he said . . . and his reaction to the news that the three of you were stranded. He likes Harper and Bobbie, they've been very nice to him."

"Well, that actually makes me feel better. I was afraid it was someone with more purpose. What about Hardy Denton?"

"What about him?"

"Have you determined the cause and manner of his death?"

"We're not sure. There are some peculiarities."

"Can you tell me what they are?"

"You know better than that."

Lindsay began putting the bones back in their tanks. Ramirez had come to her for a reason. She would wait. "We have to keep the bones in water until we rinse all the salt from them. It's sometimes a slow process."

"I read about that. Artifacts that have spent a long time in the ocean can't live outside. The salt water becomes their amniotic fluid." He studied the bones through the clear glass tank. "Perhaps there is something you can help us with. It's very puzzling."

Lindsay placed the skull in another tank. "We've been disappointed not to find any remnants of brain tissue," she said. "It would have been a long shot, but not unheard of."

"Really, after over four hundred years?"

"Yes. You can get some amazing preservation in an anaerobic environment."

"I'm learning a lot on this case. Even if I don't solve it, I will have become better educated."

Lindsay stripped off her gloves and washed her hands. "What is it that's puzzling you?"

"Hardy Denton was moved. We know that from the bruising." He paused, but Lindsay was silent, waiting. "You know about forensics. In drowning cases you get wet or dry drownings."

"He was drowned, then?"

"Oh, yes. He was drowned, but someplace other than where he was found. The medical examiner tells me that in drowning situations, it's a matter of ruling out everything else. Not very precise, to my thinking, but"—he shrugged—"what can you do? Anyway, in a dry drowning the laryngeal airway closes, water doesn't enter the lungs, and the victim suffocates."

Lindsay nodded.

"In a wet drowning the victim gets liquid in the lungs and he suffocates. Hardy Denton's was a wet drowning. And I thought, now that will be helpful. Salt water, he drowned in the ocean— brackish water, he drowned in the marsh—fresh water, he drowned in a stream. It's a small island, that will narrow it down. I feel good. So you can imagine my surprise and puzzlement when the medical examiner told me he had sugar water in his lungs."

Agent Ramirez threw up his hands. "I don't know where to look for a river of sucrose. So I thought we could brainstorm together."

Lindsay had dried her hands and was rubbing lotion into them, still silent.

"You have an idea," Ramirez said. "I can see it in your face."

"And he had carbonized plant remains in his mouth," Lindsay said. It was a statement and not a question.

"That was one of the things we were holding back."

Lindsay sighed. "Come with me." She led him down to the dock warehouse. Isaac wasn't there. It was probably his day off. The sink was empty and clean.

"This is where we do chemical flotation," she said. "It's how we separate carbon material from other heavier fractions in dirt samples taken from the site. In the past we have used Calgon; it breaks up the mud and allows the lightweight particles to float to the surface. Here on the island we are using sugar to change the specific gravity of the water." She pointed to the trash barrel containing empty sugar bags.

Ramirez put a hand close to the thin edge of the sink, almost touching it. "Yes," he said. "This is where he died. I thank you. You have taken what for me was a confounding puzzle and solved it. Dare I ask who has access to this place?"

"Everybody." She explained how the barge came every day to store the heavier artifacts here. "Isaac Jones does the chemical flotation. He may be close by, or he may be taking a day off. We also have a night watchman. I don't know who he is."

"Is it locked at night?"

"Yes."

"Who has a key?"

"Most of us. A lot of us, anyway." Ramirez frowned. "That's how a university works," said Lindsay. "We lock everything up and give everybody a key."

"Why," asked Lewis, "did you tell him about the chemical flotation?"

He sat behind his desk with his elbows on the polished wood. They had the door closed this time, in case Ramirez was lurking outside. Trey and Lindsay sat at the table in the corner.

"Because he would have discovered it on his own after a while and it would look suspicious to keep it from him," said Lindsay.

"Look," said Trey, "he obviously was killed here. This makes no difference."

Lewis rubbed his fingers through his hair, unmollified. "You should have come to me first."

Lindsay shook her head. "No. That's information that directly connects to the case he's working. We can't keep that kind of information from the FBI."

"How are you coming on the case?" asked Lewis.

"Me?"

"I asked you to look into it for us."

"I've been doing other things. I can't just barge in on their case. I suspect there is bruising on his neck or chest from the edge of the sink where his head was held in the water," Lindsay replied. Lewis made a face.

"The bruising is why they suspected he was moved. Then the sugar in his lungs confused them."

"You should have allowed them to stay confused."

"No, he asked me something that I knew. He would have found

out I knew it. If I hadn't told him, he could have charged me with obstruction in a federal investigation. Besides, it's not a good thing at all to have a killer running loose."

"What else do you know?"

"Mostly, what I told you before. Denton was moved shortly after he was killed. We know that because livor mortis set in while he was in the pond."

"Livor mortis?"

"Lividity."

Lewis nodded his head. "I'm glad you know these terms."

"What the FBI doesn't have a clue about is motive. What I did not tell him is that there is a great big motive somewhere on the bottom of the ocean."

"You think that's involved?" asked Lewis.

"That'd be my guess. I can't think of a more compelling reason for murder." She told them about her theory that Hardy Denton's bid was so low because he wanted to get inside the dig to find out about the other galleon.

Lewis and Trey both looked at her wide-eyed. "I hadn't thought of that," said Lewis. "I should have. It makes perfect sense."

"That's why he was so mad," said Trey. "I couldn't really figure out why he should be so angry. He has other projects. But, of course, he's been hanging around Eva Jones instead of tending to his business."

"So, it's safe to say the Jones woman knows about the galleon. Damn!" Lewis pounded his fist on the desk.

"It was hopeless to think a secret like that could be kept," said Lindsay.

"Why didn't you tell Ramirez?" Lewis asked. "You are right, that provides a big motive."

"Several reasons. I don't know if the silver galleon is related to Denton's murder. However, I am certain there is only one place he could have drowned in sugar water and gotten charcoal in his mouth." Lewis gestured his head toward Lindsay, conceding that point. "I don't want to give away company secrets and I don't want to have the dam circled by even more pirates. And as far as I know, the silver galleon is a rumor at this point. We aren't looking for it to my knowledge : . . . are we?"

Both Trey and Lewis kept silent.

"Are we?"

Silence.

"Great, stealth archaeology."

Lewis gave her a rueful smile. "Nate's team is looking. His divers don't know it, but their surveying is for that purpose."

That's why his team doesn't find many artifacts, thought Lindsay. They aren't looking for *Estrella* artifacts. "Is Nate the only person who knows?"

"Sarah," said Trey. "She and Nate have worked together a long time."

"Is Nate using his computer program to search for it?" asked Lindsay.

"You know about that?" asked Lewis. "Yes, he is. But the problem is, we don't know where the ship went down exactly. We only know it was somewhere off the coast of Georgia, or Florida, or even South Carolina. We're hoping Georgia, but that covers a lot of acres of ocean."

"You don't have any clues?" asked Lindsay.

"A few minor clues," answered Trey. "And Nate has plugged those into the program. But we have no confidence in them. He's mainly using this site to test his software."

"They've found nothing in the survey?" Lindsay asked. Trey shook his head. "Where do Boote and Keith Teal fit into this?"

"Who says they do?" asked Lewis.

"Keith was murdered also. It would be quite a coincidence for the two murders not to be related. Some of the crew knew both of them. Did they know each other?"

"Did Ramirez say Keith was murdered?" asked Lewis. "Couldn't he have gotten drunk and fallen in the quicksand and drowned, or whatever it is you do in quicksand?"

"Quicksand has a bad rap. It's not like it is in the movies. Harper is what, about five-five? She sank up to her chest and said she could feel the bottom."

Trey made a painful grimace.

"How tall was Keith?" asked Lindsay.

"Six feet, I'd say."

"Okay, then. Normally the pits aren't deep. In any case, they don't suck you in. Getting out is not impossible. Besides, what would he be doing drinking in the middle of St. Magdalena? It's not exactly a social spot."

"Great, another murder," said Lewis.

"I don't know if Keith knew Denton or Jones," said Trey.

"Both Jones and Keith Teal were treasure hunters. I'll bet they knew each other," said Lindsay.

Trey shook his head. "Jones is what you might call world-class. She's got the fancy equipment." Lewis laughed and Trey joined him. Lindsay just shook her head. "Keith was just a beach bum who got lucky with a couple of ships he found."

"Did he find anything that could be linked to the silver galleon?"

"No," said Trey. "Nate and I looked at everything he and his father had collected."

"He might not have shown you everything. Especially if it had significant value or he thought it might lead to something of value."

"Maybe. But . . . I don't know," said Trey.

"What is it you know about the galleon?" asked Lindsay. "When did she sink?"

"In 1556 or 1566. We don't know for sure. The source we looked at was not in good condition. Not that much evidence really," said Lewis. "The archives said she went way off course and was lost in a storm. The records make mention of them being chased by pirates."

"But, surely, you could connect her to a fleet? The House of Trade was nothing if not merciless bureaucrats. Wouldn't they have had meticulous records? And, at that time, wasn't there a law against lone galleons traveling with gold?"

"Yes, to both of those observations," said Trey. "But we couldn't find the fleet she sailed with. What we found was in a letter to one of the members of the House of Trade. The letter didn't mention the fleet. And we didn't find a reference in any of the silver galleon fleets that sailed during that time."

"Could she have been a Pacific Manila galleon?" asked Lindsay. "Did you look in those records?"

"The Manila route wasn't discovered until about 1565," said Trey, "right on the edge of the last date we have. We looked, but didn't find anything. The only real clue was a fleet sailing from Havana in 1556, the first date. The records show a fleet of seven ships leaving Havana for Spain. All of them made it, but it looks like the original number was eight, and that was marked out. There was no mention of a shipwreck. Like you said—the House of Trade loved paperwork. If there was a wreck, it should have been mentioned. It may be a mistake, or that may be the missing ship."

"That's not much. I wonder what Jones has?"

"You think she has something?" asked Lewis.

"I don't think she's working only on a leak from us. She must have other information. Maybe she heard the rumor and did some research herself and found something," said Lindsay.

"Perhaps," said Trey. "But I don't know what that could be."

"Could there be any link between our ship and the silver galleon?" asked Lindsay.

"There's no indication of that," said Trey.

"I tend to think that Jones is after artifacts from the *Estrella*," said Lewis. "I just don't see how she could know anything about the silver galleon. Now, what I'd like you to do, Lindsay, is find out who killed Denton. We don't need the kind of publicity his murder is bringing. So far, we've been lucky. Have you seen the papers?" He retrieved several from his desk, laid them on the table, and sat down with Lindsay and Trey.

Lindsay picked up a copy of the *Savannah Morning News* containing a feature section about the dig, complete with a drawing of a galleon. It also had Lindsay's drawing of HSkR1 and a description of its injuries, with the lurid title of "Murder on the High Seas." The *Atlanta Journal and Constitution* had the drawings of three of the four skeletons Lindsay had done and the story she had told from their bones. Steven Nemo had drawn a cross section of the ship and placed some of the artifacts they had discovered, along with photographs of them. Again the murder victim was the star with top billing—"Murder in the Hold" was the title. It didn't matter that he was found two decks up.

"The people love murder when it's in the past," said Trey. "They hate modern murder. I don't want these deaths to take anything away from the wonder of this dig."

"Lewis, I'll do what I can. But the FBI isn't going to give me information just because I ask. They won't like me being a private detective. And you've not thought of one important point."

"What's that?"

"What if one of our crew is guilty?"

"Do you believe that?"

"In my heart of hearts? No. But it's a possibility."

"We'll cross that bridge when we come to it."

"I'll have to tell you right now straight. I won't withhold a murderer from the FBI."

"That wasn't what I meant. I just mean we'll figure out something."

Lindsay wasn't comforted.

"I've got another skeleton to analyze and a murderer to find, so I'd better get busy."

Lewis grabbed her hand as she got up to leave. "I'm sorry I came down so hard about the Denton thing. You did the right thing, of course."

Of course, thought Lindsay. She just hoped nothing would come up in the future that he wanted kept from the authorities.

Carolyn wasn't finished with the fourth skeleton, so Lindsay gathered up her drawing tools.

"I'd like to make some extra copies of these skull photographs—"

"There's a copy machine in the main office," said Carolyn. "Be careful of the other guys."

Lindsay took the digital photographs to what was referred to as the main office. A woman was there that Lindsay had seen, but not met. As she started to speak, Lindsay braced herself.

"Hi, I'm Gretchen."

"Lindsay Chamberlain. I came to use the copy machine." She held up her photographs.

"Skulls?"

"These are two of the human remains we've found. I use photographs of the skulls to draw a picture of what they may have looked like in the flesh."

"Oh, how interesting. I saw the first one in the newspaper. You actually use the skull?"

"Yes, I like being able to put a face on the remains. When they've been skeletonized, it's sometimes easy to forget that they were people." As Lindsay spoke, she listened to the hum of the copier. It was the same sound she had heard coming from the room the evening she encountered Mike Altman in the lab.

"What are you doing here?" The voice was so sudden and harsh, it was almost as though Lindsay had conjured him up from her thoughts.

"She's using the copier, Mike. Chill out."

"It won't take long." Lindsay tried to sound cheerful. "It was locked up the other night," she said, "and I didn't have a key. I thought I'd use it in the daytime." She smiled sweetly at him before turning to make her copies.

"I'll be glad when you people are gone. The lot of you are mean-spirited, disruptive, ill-adapted for this environment, and inclined toward hysteria. The sooner—"

Lindsay whirled around at Mike with such vigor, he was startled.

"You were there. You heard us yelling when Harper fell in the quicksand and you didn't come to help."

Mike recovered quickly. "You didn't need it. Like you said. Quicksand isn't like the stories written about it."

"You didn't know that she wasn't hurt and you had to know we were missing. You didn't think you should tell someone where we were?"

"Mike," said Gretchen, "you knew where they were, all that time?"

"Not all the time. Look, I'm not their keeper. If they can't take care of themselves, they should get off the island."

"And you call us mean-spirited." Lindsay took her copies. "Nice meeting you, Gretchen. Thanks for your help." She walked out the door, down the hallway, and downstairs to the lab.

"You had a run-in with one of them, didn't you?" Carolyn stood staring at Lindsay as she took her seat at her desk.

"Does it show?"

"Yeah. We've all had experience with them—Mike and Tessa, anyway."

"It's getting out of hand. That Mike guy is so bitter."

She took out some paper, went to the light table, and began drawing. After an hour she looked at her watch. It was about time for the crew to come in. Maybe she could get John to take her to visit Boote.

Chapter 20

"No," said John, "I won't allow it. Boote sabotaged your boat. I'll not risk you going there."

Lindsay stared at John for a long moment. The wind-driven ocean waves sprayed fine mist on her bare legs as she stood at the edge of the dock.

"I understand. I'll get someone else to take me over." She turned to go, but he held her arm and turned her to face him.

"Why are you doing this?" he asked.

"Lewis asked me to."

"Maybe I need to talk to Lewis."

"Maybe you don't."

"Lindsay, Boote blamed us for the disappearance of his son even before he knew he was dead. What do you think he'll be like now?"

"Boote's a grieving old man. He's no danger. Ramirez isn't even sure he's the one who cut the oil line. And if he did, he thinks he only meant to inconvenience someone from the university—not to strand anyone in the ocean."

"You're going anyway, aren't you?"

"Yes."

"And if I asked you not to, for me?"

"I'd fold my arms and tell you I don't play emotional games with men I'm involved with."

John sighed and looked over at the other dock where the barge was anchored. The timber crew was offloading the artifacts of the day and storing them in the warehouse. His face was set in a grim frown. Lindsay was sure he was trying to think of words he could say that would stop her.

"What was it you called me when you first met me—a high-maintenance girlfriend?"

His frown melted a little. "Yeah, and I was right. You worry a man to death."

⚓

Boote lived on the mainland across from St. Magdalena on the edge of a brine marsh. His house was a little dingy yellow shack amid a row of similar shacks that looked like they should have blown away a long time ago. As Lindsay and John approached the paint-worn door, it burst open and a man in a ski mask came running at them, pushing John backward and knocking Lindsay to the ground before either of them could react.

"What the . . . Lindsay, are you all right?" He helped her to her feet.

"I'm fine."

John turned to give chase, but the man was already in his car and speeding down the one-lane road.

"Boote!" Lindsay exclaimed. She raced into the house.

The front room had been trashed. It had a strong smell of cinnamon, or peaches, or flowers; she couldn't tell. Lindsay called out for Boote. They heard crashing about and grumbling in the kitchen. Boote was in the middle of the kitchen floor next to an overturned chair.

"Crazy son of a . . . who're you?"

"I'm John West, old man. You remember me?"

"The Indian. Yeah, I know you. What are you doing here?"

"Are you all right, Mr. Teal?" Lindsay asked.

"Mr. Teal? Who the hell are you?" With John's help, he stood on shaky legs, squinting at Lindsay. He smelled like alcohol and had about five days' worth of beard on his wrinkled face.

"Do we need to take you to a doctor? Did that man hurt you?"

"Pissed me off. Kept asking me where it is. Wouldn't tell me what he's looking for. What kind of stupid thing is that? How'm I gonna tell 'im where *it's* at if I don't know what *it* is? Stupid bastard."

"We need to call the police," said John.

"No, we don't. Don't want no police around. They can't do

nothin'. That's what they've been telling me for days now. I reckon I believe 'em."

"Do you know who he was?" asked Lindsay.

"No, he had his face covered. Didn't ya' see 'im?"

"Did you recognize his voice?"

"No, I didn't, and who are you anyway, lady?"

"This is Dr. Chamberlain," said John. "She was with Bobbie and Harper when they got stranded in the ocean after their motorboat quit working."

"Oh. You here about that?" Boote lowered his head. "Look, I didn't mean—"

"I'm not here about that, Mr. Teal."

"Call me Boote, missy."

"Boote, I wanted to say I'm very sorry about your son."

"Why? You didn't do it, did you?"

"No, Boote, I was expressing my sympathy. But I'd like to find out who did do it."

"I'll tell you who. One of them people you work with on the island, or that man-made island in the ocean."

"Why do you say that?" Lindsay asked.

"Let's go out on the porch. That damn woman next door thinks smells cure everything. You know, she sneaks over here when I'm gone and leaves bowls with smelly wood shavings and dried plants." He nodded. "She does. Says it has healing powers. Calls it roaming therapy. She wants me to marry her and thinks that'll work. Crazy, ain't she?"

"I'd say so," said John.

They went out on the concrete porch, etched with years of cracks that looked like drawings of dead trees. Boote sat on the steps made from cement blocks. Lindsay and John stood on the sandy walkway.

Lindsay saw a few pieces of mail scattered on the lawn and she picked them up.

"I'd like to find out what happened to your son," she said, handing the papers to Boote. She glanced at a post card. There was something familiar about it.

"Keith sent that to me last year," said Boote.

Lindsay turned it over and looked at the picture of Daytona Beach. What, she wondered, was it? "Can I keep this a while?" she asked. "I'll give it back."

"Go ahead, if you think it'll help." Boote put his head in his hands. "I know what happened to him. Somebody killed him."

"Did the police tell you how he died?"

"No. Police don't know nothin'. They can't go to the island anyway. Said I have to talk to the FBI. Some foreign fellow. I didn't know they had foreigners in the FBI."

"Agent Ramirez."

"Yes. That's the one. Ramirez."

"Did he tell you anything?"

"Said somebody stabbed my boy Keith and dumped him in quicksand. They weighted him down with a chain. Hey, you one of the girls that found him, ain't you?"

"Yes," Lindsay replied.

"Least I can bury him. He won't be coming over on Sundays no more. I always looked forward to that."

"Do you know if he knew Hardy Denton?" asked Lindsay.

"Who? Hardy Denton? No. Never heard of him."

"How about Eva Jones?" Lindsay asked.

"Now that sounds familiar. Eva Jones. He said something about her once. Talked about her and her expensive equipment. He said you don't need expensive equipment."

"Equipment for what?" asked Lindsay.

"I don't remember. I don't think he ever said."

"Do you know if your son was ever threatened?"

"Keith? Who'd threaten him? He got along with everybody."

Not everybody, thought Lindsay. "Did he ever talk about anyone who was mad at him?"

"No. He didn't tell me his business much."

"Did Keith have a best friend? Or someone he dated a lot?"

"Keith stayed in Savannah a lot. He knew a lot of guys at the bars there. He liked to talk to the sailors from different countries."

"Do you know which bars he liked?" asked Lindsay.

Boote shook his head. "I'm not much of a social drinker myself."

"How about a girlfriend?"

"There's a girl in Atlanta he liked a lot. I don't know her name."

"Did he have any friends here?"

"Sure, everybody liked Keith, I told you."

"Do you have a name?"

"Sure, missy, I told you my name is Boote."

Lindsay took a deep breath. "Can you name one of Keith's friends?"

"No. He didn't bring his friends around much."

"Do you have any idea what that man was looking for?"

"No. I ain't got nothin' much."

Lindsay couldn't think of anything else to ask. The trip was probably a waste of time.

"Are you sure we can't take you to the doctor?" she asked.

"He just shoved me around and made me mad. I'm okay. He ran when he looked out the kitchen window and saw you two coming."

"You need to call the police. He might be back," said John.

"He comes back, I'll be ready for him."

Boote rose to go inside. When he opened the door, Lindsay noticed something she hadn't seen when they first went in. A mason jar filled with quarters had spilled out onto the floor. She went in with Boote and picked up several. All of them had holes drilled in the middle.

"Boote, what are these?" Lindsay asked.

"Those? They belonged to Keith."

"Why did he put holes in them?"

"I don't know. He's been punching holes in quarters since he was in his twenties and working on a fishing boat. He says that some fish like shiny things. But—" He shrugged his thin shoulders.

"He used them for bait?" asked John.

"I reckon. I ain't never heard of it, but then I'm not much of a fisherman, neither."

Lindsay put the coins in the jar and said goodbye to Boote.

Lindsay climbed in the boat and put on her life jacket. "Well, I suppose that was a waste of time," she said, sticking the postcard in her notebook next to Dr. Rosen's list of bone diseases. She tucked the notebook in the backpack she had stored in the boat locker. "I hardly learned a thing."

John waited to start the engine. "Lindsay, you aren't going to canvass the bars on Savannah's waterfront. The kind of places Keith would frequent are not the kind of places for you to be asking questions. I'm sure this is not what Lewis had in mind for you to do. He meant for you to just use your brain. I'll go to Lewis; I'll lock you up in my barge if I have to."

"Are you finished?"

"Yes."

"I have no intention of going to bars or interrogating sailors, as romantic as that sounds."

"Good. You want to go get something to eat?"

"Sure. You pick the restaurant," said Lindsay.

He took her to a small, quiet restaurant with French cuisine on St. Simons Island. Lindsay had a cheese soufflé and John a bacheofe, and they both had a glass of a cabernet sauvignon.

"Nice," said Lindsay. "I like this."

John nodded. "I've eaten pretty well on this job since you got here." He took a sip of wine. "Why did Lewis ask you to investigate Keith?"

"He didn't. He asked me to investigate Hardy Denton."

"Then what were we doing at Boote's?"

"I believe the two deaths are related. And if I can discover how they're related, I'll have made some significant progress."

"What makes you think one has something to do with the other? There's nothing that connects them."

"Yes, there is. Both were found dead on St. Magdalena. Just what do you think the murder rate is on that island?"

John made a face and shrugged. "I imagine it used to be zero."

"I assume so. And we have two bodies found just days apart. I don't believe in coincidences of that kind." John was silent. Lindsay took that to mean that he'd like to disagree, but couldn't. "Another thing. Hardy Denton was working with Eva Jones—she's a treasure hunter. We know that Keith had more than a passing interest in finding shipwrecks—he found at least three several years ago."

"And you think they are both interested in your ship?" This time Lindsay was silent.

"Is there something you aren't telling me?" he asked.

"Yes, and I can't tell you now. But I think you should know since you provide security for the dam, and I'm going to ask Trey to tell you when we return."

"Am I going to like this?"

"Probably not."

"Does it involve you?"

"Not in the least. No more so than anyone else on the dig."

John smiled. "Thank heaven for that. This place has a great caramel custard for dessert."

⚓

Lindsay lay in her bunk trying to think of where she could get information about Hardy Denton. Ramirez would interview all the pertinent people. What she needed was for Ramirez to confide in her. She'd have to work on that. There was Isaac. She could ask him if he found anything unusual around his work area. There's the security guard that guarded both the lab and the warehouse—she could speak with him. She knew Ramirez was asking questions of the people staying at the lab. She could find out what questions he was asking—she might find a clue there.

Lindsay turned over on her stomach, hypnotized by the wafting of the barge. Her eyelids grew heavy as sleep approached. What she really needed to do was the work she was hired for: analyze the skeletal remains and excavate the ship. Lewis could solve his own mystery. John would like that. John liked her a lot. How did she feel about that? Good. She felt very good about John. That was her last thought before she succumbed to sleep.

Lindsay worked at the dam in the morning, helping Gina and Juliana finish their burial. She had missed getting down in the sandy mud, even missed the sound of the waves against the bulkhead. Darn Lewis and his political machinations. Agent Ramirez was perfectly capable of solving this without her help.

She had lunch on top of the dam with Gina and Juliana. The catered brown bag held a banana, a package of peanuts, an apple turnover, and the two sandwiches of the day—egg salad. She hated egg salad. Lewis could provide a little extra for at least two choices for sandwiches, she thought. She took a few bites and folded it back up in the plastic wrap. She peeled the paper off an apple turnover and took a bite.

"Who do you think killed that guy?" asked Gina.

"Which guy?" asked Juliana. "The Spanish sailor or that Denton person?"

"Denton. What about it, Lindsay?" asked Gina. "Scuttlebutt has it that you're investigating."

"By the way, the night crew found it last night," said Juliana.

"Found what?" asked Lindsay and Gina together.

"The scuttlebutt. It was in the same section as the brass bell discovered yesterday."

"And that is what?" asked Lindsay. They looked at her over

their sandwiches. "Sorry. I don't know all the parts of a ship yet."

"It's a water barrel where the sailors got a drink when they were thirsty."

"Ah," said Lindsay, "that makes sense."

"What?"

"Watercooler, scuttlebutt, gossip . . ."

"Oh, yeah," said Gina. "Interesting. Some things don't change."

"I'm surprised it wasn't lost in the storm," said Juliana. "Wasn't it on the top deck usually?"

Gina nodded. "Forecastle, I think. Maybe it got wedged between something, like the belfry. But getting back to the topic— are you investigating?"

"I'm asking some questions. Lewis naturally wants to know what's going on."

"Well, what is going on?"

"I really don't know. I haven't been able to find out much."

"Well, I heard that the guy was killed in the warehouse," Juliana commented.

"It doesn't look like you guys need any information from me," Lindsay said. "By the way, has Ramirez talked to you?"

"Just asked us if we knew the guy," said Gina. Juliana nodded.

"Did you?"

"Is this an interrogation?" Gina grinned over her apple turnover.

"Sure," said Lindsay.

"I didn't know him," said Gina.

"Me neither," agreed Juliana. "But I think Sarah's avoiding Ramirez. I saw her about to come into the lab yesterday and duck out when she saw Ramirez in there."

"Why would she do that?" asked Lindsay.

"I assume it's because she didn't want to talk to him," Juliana answered, stuffing her food wrappings back into the paper sack and taking a bite out of her apple.

"How about you and West?" asked Gina.

"He was really upset when you and the others went missing," Juliana said.

"We're doing okay. John's a good guy."

"Tell me," asked Gina. "What's Harper like? She has Trey's head turned."

"She's funny," said Lindsay, "and very smart."

"She'd have to be, to do those translations," said Juliana.

"You know, I've been on a lot of digs," Gina said. "But I've never had something like this diary. It's strange to read about this ship, then come work on it, creepy sometimes. Like that pomander I found. When I read that in the diary, it sent chills up my spine. It was his, and he was the last person to touch it and I held it in my hand, the next person to touch it."

"Why don't you do a paper on just that artifact?" asked Lindsay. "What it is, how it was made, who used them. You can connect the spices in the pomander with their role in exploration. Then you can add the personal vignette—like a short case study of its use."

"That's a great idea," Gina said.

"I'll bet you can get it published, too," Juliana said. "Lewis is going to see to it that everything out of this site gets published."

"I'm as impressed as the next person with Lewis's ability to get things done, but he can't do everything. Journals are juried by people not unlike Lewis. He won't be able to control what is accepted for publication. But if you write a good article, it will likely get published."

"What if you get Lewis or somebody to be coauthor?" Juliana asked.

Lindsay had to concede that point. She could see that the number of articles Lewis would get from this dig would be what her aunt called a gracious plenty.

"Do you think the diarist . . . you know, we need to give him a name. I don't know why he couldn't have just signed the thing," said Gina. "Anyway, do you think he will mention the murder?"

"I would think so," Lindsay replied. "It probably was a pretty big deal. Then again, it happened right around the time of the storm. The diary may just end abruptly."

"Oh, I hope not," said Juliana. She peeled the banana. "You know, Jeff complains about these lunches, but I think they're pretty good."

After lunch, Lindsay got a ride from one of John's crew over to St. Magdalena. He was the young man who checked her in when she arrived.

"Thanks for the ride—Luke, isn't it?"

"Luke Youngdeer."

He had a heartbreaker smile, and the way his shoulder-length black hair blew in the breeze of the speeding boat, Lindsay guessed he had several of the female crew charmed.

"Luke, I understand you helped search for us. I thank you for it."

"Glad to do it."

"How do you like it out here in the water?" she asked.

"I love it. I wish this job would last forever. Is Bobbie working at the dam today, do you know?"

"No. She's diving today," Lindsay told him.

Luke Youngdeer maneuvered the boat into a slot at the dock. "Here you are, safe and sound."

"Thanks." Lindsay climbed out and tied the boat to the dock. Luke hopped out after her to secure the aft end.

"If you need to come back before the barge comes for the day, here's my beeper number." He searched all of his pockets before he found a dog-eared business card with his name and number on it.

"Thank you, Luke. I appreciate it."

They walked down the dock together. "Do you know where Bobbie's crew is diving today? How deep they planned to go?"

"No, sorry," said Lindsay, wondering why he wanted to know the depth. Then she realized. Luke was probably a diver, too. Knowing the depth, he could get an idea of how long they'd stay down, and how long they'd have to wait between dives. In other words, how long Bobbie would be gone.

Luke waved as he disappeared toward the lab. Lindsay stopped at the warehouse. Isaac was at his post sorting the carbon fraction from dirt samples. Lindsay hadn't seen him at the dam. She wondered if he got to do anything else. Briefly, almost in passing, she wondered if he could have killed Denton. But why? What motive would he have had? She realized that, although she had been telling everyone that the murderer was probably no one at the site, she really didn't know. She didn't know very many people here. She really didn't know them at all.

Chapter 21

Isaac Jones stood at the sink dressed in cutoffs and a rubber apron. He reminded Lindsay of a grandaddy longlegs—all skinny arms, legs, elbows, and knees.

"Hi," she greeted him, looking over the racks of bits of drying pieces of carbon.

Isaac stepped away from the sink, wiping some sweat from his brow. He grabbed a Coke he had sitting on a table and took a long swallow.

"Hi. Gets hot in here."

"I can imagine. Did Ramirez come talk to you?"

"Yeah. Jeeze. I felt like a suspect."

"I'm afraid all of us are suspects, simply because we're here. But they'll rule us out quickly."

Isaac sat down on his stool and stretched his long legs. "I know, but he was killed here—in my sink. Creepy." He shivered.

"Isaac, why were there water and flotation debris in the sink that night?"

He hung his head a moment. "The one time I don't clean everything up, I get caught. I always finish whatever bag I'm working on before I shut down and clean up. Always. Except last Tuesday. I was working late. Some of the guys asked me if I wanted to go to Florida to have dinner and mess around. I wanted to go, but I had to hurry and shower to get ready. I didn't think it would matter if I left this just once."

"That's the way it always happens," said Lindsay. "Did you notice anything different when you returned?"

"That's what that FBI agent wanted to know. You know, my parents wanted me to be a lawyer or some kind of corporate something or other. They didn't like archaeology at all. Now I'm a sus-

187

pect in a murder investigation because I shirked my duties. That's going to be a double whammy for my dad."

Lindsay decided she was going to have to let Isaac get this off his chest before she could get any information from him. She listened to his anxieties and sympathized.

"What does your dad do?"

"He's a U.S. marshal."

"Really? That's interesting."

"I thought it was great when I was a kid. While all the other kids played *Star Wars* characters, I was always a cowboy—a little retro-kid. But you can see my problem. He's a very straight kind of guy. The thought that I'm mixed up in this, well—"

"You aren't really mixed up in it. Ramirez talked to everybody. Me, Lewis, John, Trey—I don't think any of us had anything to do with his death. Anyway, did you notice anything different?"

"Not really. Some water splashed on the floor, but we use a lot of water in this place. I didn't think anything of it."

"No overturned chairs or anything?"

"No. Nothing like that."

"Did you find anything on the floor, in the sink, or with the carbon fraction?"

Isaac shook his head. "No."

"Do you know the security guard here?"

"Dale Delosier. He's a retired cop."

"What's he like?"

Isaac shrugged. "All right, I guess. I don't know him very well. He comes on duty after I leave. I've just met him in passing when I've been working late."

"Anything out of the ordinary about him?"

"No. Just that he shows no interest in what we do here. That's kind of strange to me. Everyone else who visits here is really interested in the excavation—ship's timbers, everything. But that's hardly anything against him. This just isn't his thing."

"Does he stay on the island?"

"No. He comes on the six o'clock ferry."

"Do you know if there are any docks on the island other than the ones we use or the ferry uses?"

"No. But you'd better ask the bio people."

"If I can get them to speak to me."

"They aren't so bad. It's mainly Mike and Tessa. The others are pretty nice and like to know what's going on with the dig. Besides, you really can't blame them. We did kind of push them out."

"That's true. Thanks for talking with me. If you think of anything, let me know."

"Sure—you and Agent Ramirez."

Lindsay walked to the lab. Carolyn and Korey were bent over their work. Carolyn was working on a ceramic jar the size of a fist. Korey was busy with an encrusted piece of iron.

"Hi, you guys look absorbed," said Lindsay.

"Cisco is going to have to get some more people in here if he wants all these artifacts processed," said Carolyn. "Right now, all we can do is stabilize them as they come in."

"Two of you don't seem to be enough," agreed Lindsay.

"The problem is, he doesn't want to bring any more people to stay on the island. We're maxed out right now. And he doesn't want to send the artifacts off."

"What about ferrying some more workers in?" asked Lindsay.

"I'm going to have to ask him to do that if he keeps pushing like he's been doing."

Lindsay sat down at her station and worked on her bone analysis reports. After the bones were through the desalinization process and dried, she would make another, more thorough, examination. But right now, preliminary reports to the funding agencies were coming due.

When she grew tired of the reports, she called up the Web and searched for the history of diving. She was surprised at how far back diving for wrecks and the use of compressed air went. A drawing of a bellows adorned the tomb wall of the governor of Thebes. Jeremiah 6:29 mentions the use of bellows. Aristotle, in the fourth century B.C., wrote about "instruments for drawing air from above the water and thus [men] were able to remain a long time under the sea." Bobbie was right—Alexander the Great, a student of Aristotle, descended into the sea in a contraption called a Colimpha. In the first century A.D., Hero wrote a manuscript called *Pneumatica* about the use of air pressure and vacuum. In 1240, Roger Bacon invented a machine for breathing underwater. The bends was actually recognized as far back as the seventeenth century when it was called "a bubble in the viper's eye."

Lindsay searched for the term "dysbaric osteonecrosis" and found more hits than she could look at. Ultimately, she'd have to go to the library and search the medical journals, but for now she scanned a few of the entries. One source said the condition was rarely seen in recreational divers, and most often in saturation divers—whatever they were.

"Do either of you guys know what a saturation diver is?"

Korey and Carolyn both looked up and shrugged.

"That's a diver who has to stay at a great depth a long time."

Lindsay looked up at John coming toward her desk. "Hi," she greeted.

He pulled up a chair and sat down beside her. "You become saturated when your tissues absorb as much nitrogen as they can hold at your depth." He leaned against her and looked at her computer.

"You planning on doing some deep diving?"

"No, I'm certainly not. Why would anyone stay down that long?"

"You got to do a job, it takes a while. After you're saturated, decompression time doesn't increase the longer you stay. So you get the job done, decompress at the end."

"How do you use the bathroom?" asked Carolyn.

John looked over at her and laughed. "You usually work out of some kind of pressurized underwater habitat or diving bell."

"How do you know so much about it?" asked Lindsay.

"I've done some of it in the navy and working on oil rigs."

Lindsay took a long look at John. "Did you suffer any damage from it?"

"No. You mix the gases right and decompress according to the tables, and it's safe. Relatively speaking." He tapped the computer screen. "You worried I might get this?"

"The whole thing seems very dangerous to me."

"Dangerous, yes. But like I said. You do it right. Besides, who are you to worry about dangerous?"

She grinned at him. He looked good—tan skin and white T-shirt. Instead of having his hair tied back, he wore it long and parted in the middle. Every feature of his face was well defined. Even the slight crow's-feet around his eyes looked good on him. The two of them held their eyes locked in an intimate stare for several moments.

"I try to stay out of danger," she said at last.

"You don't try very hard." He took her hand. "How about it? It's Saturday night. Want to go someplace?"

Lindsay glanced at her watch. It was only three o'clock. The security guard wouldn't get here for another three hours. At least on Saturdays they didn't debrief.

"Let me talk to the security guard first. He doesn't get here until six."

"Sure."

Lindsay closed out her computer and cleared off her desk. "You going back to the dam?"

"Not for a while," he said.

"Want to walk on the beach?" she asked.

"Sure."

The breeze was refreshing after the stuffiness of the lab. Lindsay took her shoes off and walked on the wet sand in her bare feet. John put his arm around her waist.

"Have you met with Trey?" Lindsay asked him.

He nodded. "I met with him and Lewis on my barge this morning early. I have to say I was surprised. A sunken treasure ship is the biggest motive for a lot of things that I've seen. I'm amazed we haven't had more trouble."

"You know, I had forgotten about Nate's attack. I thought that probably had something to do with drugs. Nate said it was pirates. I'll bet they were surveying, searching for signs of the ship."

"It seems likely."

"John."

"Lindsay, I don't like the way you said that."

"It's your name."

"I know it is, and you are about to ask me something that I'm not going to want to do."

"You know me so well."

"In so short a time. What is it?" He released her waist and walked backward in front of her. "I'm so grateful you aren't prowling bars in Savannah, I might agree."

"I want to visit Evangeline Jones on her ship."

"I obviously don't know you well enough, or I wouldn't have made a rash agreement like that."

"I don't think she's dangerous. We'll tell Lewis and Trey where we're going."

John stopped and put his hands on her shoulders.

"Lindsay, someone, maybe several someones, killed Hardy Denton and Keith Teal. You keep going to visit people, you are

191

eventually going to hit the ones who committed the murder."

"That's the idea. However, I don't think she'll do anything. I just want to talk with her."

"All right. Let's get an okay from Lewis and Trey first. Will you do that?"

Lindsay nodded. "How about dinner and a movie tonight?"

"Sounds good."

"And tomorrow we visit Jones."

"If Trey and Lewis okay it."

They walked about a mile up the narrow beach. The smooth sand and lapping waves felt good on Lindsay's bare feet. She especially liked the feel of the sand rushing from under her feet with each retreating wave.

"You know," she said as they turned around and headed back, "I would have enjoyed being marooned out here with you."

"I can arrange that."

"We'd have to get rid of the bugs."

"Now, that might be a problem."

Lindsay wondered if their romance could live only here on this island in the absence of everyday anxieties, with no Native Americans for her to excavate and John to protest against, no arguments about the sacrilege she committed against his people, no choices or compromises to make about either of their beliefs in order to make their relationship work. The island was sort of an anaerobic environment for the heart, preserving fragile feelings that would otherwise erode over time. She felt like Luke Youngdeer. She wanted this job to last forever.

John held her hand tightly as they walked and watched the waves come up around their feet. Lindsay wondered if he was thinking the same thing she was. She brought his hand up to her lips.

"What are you thinking about, watching those waves?" she asked.

"From Here to Eternity," answered John.

Lindsay started laughing, let go of his hand, and backed away. He ran after her and grabbed her around the waist.

"No. Deborah Kerr had on a bathing suit, and I've got to meet with the security guard."

"I've seen you archaeologists when you're working—you're covered in sand. He'll just think you've been working." He picked her up. "You know, for a slim woman, you sure are heavy. I'm going to have to start working out."

She cuffed his shoulder. "I'll have you know, I'm all muscle and I'm tall. If I'm so heavy, you can put me down."

"You want me to put you down, I will." His eyes twinkled as he grinned at her.

"No."

"Are you sure? If you want me to put you down in the sand, I will."

"Don't you dare."

She kissed him, and he gently let his arm slip from the back of her knees so she stood on the ground.

"This doesn't have to end," he said.

"What do you mean?"

"I mean, when we leave here, we can find a way to work things out."

So he was sharing her thoughts. She liked that—liked that he wanted something beyond this island.

"I hope so."

As they walked silently up the beach, Lindsay watched the ground, as was her habit. Having gone on so many surveys with her grandfather and worked on so many sites, it was her nature to scrutinize the ground for interesting things wherever she went. Just ahead, she saw three objects brought up by the surf. She dropped John's hand and ran over to pick them up.

"What is it?" asked John.

Lindsay held the irregular rounded objects in her palm. She rubbed her fingers over them.

"What?" asked John again.

"Gold coins. Spanish gold coins."

"You're joking."

She held them out to him.

"They're shiny," he said.

"Gold doesn't tarnish."

John took the coins and rubbed them with his fingers. "Which ship?" he asked.

"I don't know. I assume the officers on our ship could have their own personal money, so it could be from the *Estrella*."

"But it could be from the other one, the one Trey called the silver galleon."

"Yes, I assume so. But . . ."

"But what?"

"I've never given that story much credibility. Mainly because I don't know what it could have been doing here. Cuba was the place where they did all their commerce. There was nothing up here but St. Augustine in 1565, Santa Elena in 1566, and a few failing missions. I don't know why a silver galleon would come to a colony."

"So you think it belongs to the *Estrella*?" said John.

"If I had to bet, that's what I would bet on. We're almost directly across from the site."

"They're pretty, aren't they?" asked John.

He weighed the three coins in his hand and jingled them together before dropping them back into Lindsay's palm.

"I can see why men get treasure fever. There is something powerful about gold. It has a magic that grabs you," he said.

Lindsay could imagine running her hand through a chest full of these. The coins weighed heavy in her pocket as she walked to the lab to talk with Dale Delosier. John was right. They had a power.

She found the security guard entering the back of the laboratory building. She had expected him to be an older man, and he was, but he was also straight and lean and walked with a spring in his step. His security guard uniform was crisp and pressed, his nails manicured, and his steel gray hair neatly held in place—all taken together, the look of a man who took pride in his appearance.

"Mr. Delosier, I'm Lindsay Chamberlain." She held out her hand to him and he shook it.

"Dr. Lewis told me you might want to talk with me about that night."

"Why don't we sit down at a corner table in the break room," suggested Lindsay. "I don't think anyone is using it."

She was right. Most everyone had escaped for dinner. The small coffee shop was empty. Dale Delosier sat down, shaking his head.

"In all the time I've been doing security work, nothing like this has ever happened. When I took this job, I thought I would be basically a night watchman. Not that I don't take it seriously, I do. But this is an island. I looked at the two buildings and decided that the majority of my watch would be spent here. Nothing in the warehouse could be moved without a crane. Here is where the people sleep, here is where the valuable equipment is stored—"

"That sounds like a good plan to me," said Lindsay. "No one expected that you could be two places at once."

"If you don't mind . . . Lewis asked me to speak to you, but he only told me that you're one of the archaeologists. I don't understand. . . ."

"I'm a forensic anthropologist also, and I've worked with law enforcement. I think Dr. Lewis believes that I might bring another point of view to the investigation."

He nodded his head. "I see." He shifted in his chair uneasily. Lindsay couldn't tell if he was anxious to get to work and avoid another incident, or if he was guilty of something, or if he felt uncomfortable being interrogated by a woman almost young enough to be his granddaughter.

"I won't keep you long," she said.

"I don't actually start until eight o'clock. I'm here early because that's when the last ferry gets here."

"What do you do between six and eight?"

"I read." He reached in his briefcase and brought out a copy of *American Locomotives: An Engineering History, 1830–1880.* "I collect trains. That's why I took this job. I have a good retirement program that keeps me and my wife comfortable, but I like a little extra income to buy my trains. Here, I'll show you."

He pulled out a magazine from his briefcase and laid it on the table in front of Lindsay. It was actually a model train catalog and was folded back to a specific page. He pointed to a locomotive that could pass for a photograph of a real train.

"It's called a Big Boy. I'm interested in the digital system. It gives you a lot of control over speed and acceleration."

He looked at the picture longingly. Lindsay looked at the price. It wasn't so expensive that one needed an extra job to buy it.

"Two hundred and thirty dollars. That's not too bad," said Lindsay.

Delosier looked pleased. "That's what I told my wife. The problem is, you don't just get the locomotive, there's all the cars."

"They don't come with it?"

"Oh, no. See that's part of it, constructing the whole train, choosing the cars. And, of course, they have to have a place to run. You can't have trains like this riding around in a circle. They've got to have a station, trees, houses, water towers, tunnels. . . ." He gestured with his hands. "I've got the entire basement for my collection. You should see it."

"I can imagine, and I guess you have to have tools and paint and all that?"

"You understand. Millie and the girls don't. I have four grown daughters, and they think I should spend my retirement traveling to foreign countries with Millie. Why would anybody want to do that?"

Lindsay flipped through the catalog. It wasn't all of model trains. It had airplanes and ships, too. She stopped and looked at a picture and pointed it out to Delosier. "That's our ship—or one like it."

"What?"

"The one we are excavating. All the timbers we are hauling into the warehouse belong to a ship that looked like this."

He picked up the catalog and looked at the photograph of the model galleon. "Well, what about that. It's a pretty thing. If you want, I'll copy this page and an order form."

"Thanks. That would be nice. What time do you get off?"

"What? Oh, six in the morning. I take the ferry back. I live in Darien."

"Did you hear anything strange that evening?"

He smiled. "I've been hearing strange things ever since I set foot on this island. It sometimes sounds like a jungle out there. But in answer to your question, I didn't hear anything out of the ordinary. If I had, I would have checked on it."

"Can you give me the times you were here and the times you checked the warehouse?"

He nodded and pulled a piece of paper from his pocket. "I gave this information to the FBI agent."

Lindsay unfolded the paper. It was his schedule. She noted the times he said he was away from the warehouse. She had no doubt that this was the schedule he made for himself and a schedule he planned to follow, and probably thought he did. But this wasn't a demanding job. He probably made a few rounds and settled down to read. She believed that someone as absorbed in a hobby as he appeared to be probably became so engrossed in reading and planning his model railroad landscape that he frequently lost track of time. She doubted this was a reliable schedule of his movements on the evening Hardy Denton died.

"Do you know everyone who works here by sight?"

"Pretty much. Not many folks come around at night."

"Who does?"

"Let's see." He put a hand to his chin. "A meteorologist is always working in the weather room. I reckon they have to watch it twenty-four hours a day. Dr. Marcus is sometimes here. There's a woman who lives upstairs who called him a couple of times. Said she thought someone was trying to break into her apartment, but I didn't see anyone on the premises. I think she just wanted Dr. Marcus's company."

Lindsay looked down at the sheet Delosier had given her. "It says here on your schedule that you're at the warehouse at two in the morning."

He looked puzzled.

"That's when Dr. Latham reported an intruder," Lindsay explained.

"Dr. Latham? I thought it was Dr. Marcus . . ."

"Dr. Harper Latham is the woman who reported someone trying to get into her apartment. She called Dr. Marcus. Since you were at the warehouse at the time, is it possible you didn't see or hear anyone at the house on the second floor trying to get into Dr. Latham's room?"

A deep wrinkle appeared in the center of Delosier's forehead. "Of course, that's a possibility."

"Besides Dr. Marcus, who else have you seen coming around at night?"

He thought a minute. "I'm usually pretty good with names and make it a point to know everyone. Let's see. Mike Altman, he's one of the biologists. I've seen him there occasionally. Nate Hampton, he's a diver. He comes over sometimes. The guy that works with metals, Korey, and the woman he works with are often down in the basement late. They both have apartments upstairs. And I've seen some woman with red hair occasionally. I believe she's one of the biology people, or maybe a diver. There's a boy, Isaac Jones, who works past six sometimes in the warehouse, but he's never around late. And I've seen this guy, John West, I believe his name is, at the warehouse. He looks a lot like an Indian."

"He is an Indian."

"Really? You don't say. What does he do here?"

"He owns the construction company that built the cofferdam.

He and his crew maintain it. Were any of the people you just named here the night Hardy Denton was killed?"

"No, it was a quiet night."

"Think back. Are you sure?"

Delosier thought a moment. "No, I don't remember anyone here then."

Lindsay decided that, however well-meaning Dale Delosier was as a person, as a witness and perhaps as a security guard he was useless. Both she and Mike Altman were in the lab that evening.

"These people you mentioned. Why were they here in the middle of the night?"

"Most of them were working. Dr. Lewis and Dr. Marcus gave me a list of people who work here. If they are supposed to be here, I don't bother with them too much. The West fellow was here picking up a package that came over on the ferry with me. Dr. Marcus told me to put it in the warehouse, and he'd tell West to pick it up."

"Have you seen anyone you don't know?" asked Lindsay.

"No."

"I'm sure Agent Ramirez showed you photographs of Hardy Denton and Keith Teal. Have you seen either of them anywhere?"

"No, never have."

"Have you heard any strange or unusual rumors?"

He shook his head. "I don't talk to people much when I'm working. Usually there's nobody around to talk to, except the weathermen. Sometimes we have a cup of coffee together."

"Thank you for talking with me, Mr. Delosier."

"I can't imagine who killed that fellow—or the other one. No one I've met here seems like they'd do something like that. I think it was someone who came by boat to the other side of the island. I would have noticed any strange boats at the dock."

Lindsay left him with his reading, and she went to the weather room. William Kuzniak was there poring over a satellite map. Lindsay could only see the top of his bald head.

"I hope the good weather's holding out," Lindsay said.

He looked up and smiled. "Hi. So far it is, but we're in hurricane season."

"I guess you weather people have to be here around the clock?"

"Pretty much. It wouldn't do to have a storm sneak up on you guys."

"Who was on duty last Tuesday evening and early Wednesday morning?" Lindsay looked at the printout of the map. It looked Greek to her.

"Ah, the night of the murder. I can't believe it. I feel like I'm in a bad film noir. I was on duty. Ramirez talked to me. Suspicious fellow."

"It's his job to be suspicious. What were you able to tell him?" William looked at her over his glasses.

"Lewis asked me to follow up on things," said Lindsay.

"I have a hard time believing that something like that was going on while I was here. This room is fairly soundproof, being in the middle of the building the way it is. I didn't hear a thing. I had coffee with the old guy—the security guard, if you can call him that. As near as I can figure, he reads about trains while he's here and goes off to check the other building when he feels like he has to stretch his legs." Kuzniak stopped to look at something on his computer. "Ramirez asked me my whereabouts between three and four o'clock that morning, if that gives you any information."

"It does." Lindsay had guessed between four and five. "And I suppose you gave him an alibi?"

William laughed. "At least I can die now knowing that in my lifetime I had to have an alibi. Actually, yes and no. I was here most of the time. I had coffee with Dale at 3:00 A.M. I didn't stay long. He gets to talking about model trains and he'll go on all night. I talked to my girlfriend on the phone at four-thirty. She's in Atlanta. She gets up at that time to get ready for work. Anyone who works in Atlanta is out of their mind. But I had plenty of time in between to go down to the warehouse, off the guy, and return without anyone being the wiser."

"Did you hear anything when you were on break?"

"Nothing but the wonders of a digital train system."

"Harper thought she had a prowler a couple of nights . . . actually I don't know when, but it was before I got here . . ."

"Yeah, Terry told me about it. Trey came over. We told Harper she could call on us. Her suite is in the back of the house here and is kind of isolated. It's separated by a hallway from the rest of us, and we didn't know one another as well then."

"Have any ideas?"

"I personally think it was one of the bio people trying to scare her. They come over here at night to work some. Can't blame them.

They were here first, but some of them act like big babies sometimes."

"How many biologists are there? I've sort of met four."

"That's all. Mike and Tessa Altman. They're the worst. The other two, Gretchen Wheeler and James Choi, are both very nice but have to walk a fine line with Mike and Tessa. There were more working here, but they left. I assume they'll be back when we leave."

"And you, Terry, Korey, Isaac, Carolyn, and Harper are the ones staying here at the lab?"

"That's right. We stay in the rooms upstairs. Terry and I room together. Carolyn has her own room and Korey and Isaac share the other suite. It's pretty nice really."

"Have you heard any strange or interesting rumors while you've been here?"

"About what?"

"Anything."

"The sea monster at Darien."

"Thanks for the info."

"Sure. You know, I'd like Lewis to hire some more security around here. Nate said he was going to seriously suggest to Lewis that he get at least two—one to watch this place and one to watch the warehouse. It is rather unsettling to be working here at night thinking one of us might be a murderer, or worse yet, a victim."

"I'll mention it to him. By the way, I hardly ever see the rangers. How many of them are there?"

"There are usually about three, I think. They're all staying at Cumberland Island now that the biology people are staying at the ranger station. They come once a day and check on the place."

"Do you know if Lewis is on the barge or in his office?"

"I believe he's in there." William motioned with his head toward the door.

Lindsay walked to the back of the room, knocked, and entered when she heard his muffled "come in." He was hanging up the phone when she opened the door.

"Hi, Lindsay. Making progress on the Denton investigation?"

"No one saw or heard anything. I need to find out why Denton was on the island. I have a plan for that. I would like—"

A knock on the door stopped Lindsay in mid-sentence.

"It's West, Lewis. Is Lindsay here?"

"Come on in, West. We need to talk." John came in and pulled up a chair beside Lindsay.

"I'm hiring two extra security guards," Lewis said. "I'm going to ask Korey and Isaac to live on the barge and give them their room. Have you found more divers?"

John nodded. "They'll be here in a couple of days. I have room on my barge for them."

"Good. That should take care of the security. You were about to say something, Lindsay?"

"I'd like to talk with Evangeline Jones on her ship."

"You think that's wise?"

"No," John answered before Lindsay could say anything. "But I was thinking, if we take a few boats out and have a presence in the water, it should be safe."

Lindsay looked over at John, pleased that he agreed to the point of making a plan.

"That sounds fine then. I have no problem. You think you can get her to tell you anything?"

"I think that she'll want information from me as much as I want some from her. I may learn something from the questions she asks."

"Go for it then. I hope you find that she is the murderer. That'll get rid of two problems at once."

Lindsay stood and put her hand in her pocket. "Don't expect her to confess anything tomorrow. Now, I have something for you. Hold out your hand."

Lewis raised his eyebrows and did what he was told. Lindsay took out the coins and dropped them into his palm. Lewis sat up straight, as if his chair had an electric charge.

"Where did you find these?"

"On the beach."

"Do you know which ship they're from?"

Lindsay sat down again and gave him a how-would-I-know-that look. "I believe they're from the *Estrella*, simply because it's directly across from the island at the point I found them, but—" She shrugged.

Lewis rubbed the coins and weighed them in his hands just as John had done. He looked up and caught Lindsay smiling at him and looked sheepish.

"Powerful, aren't they?" she said.

"Sure are. Can you imagine a shipful?"

"Barely."

"Did you mark the spot where you found them?"

"Sure. I drew an arrow in the sand and put an *X* on the spot." For a moment she thought Lewis believed her. "I paced out the distance in a straight line to the vegetation and built a carne."

"Has Trey seen them?"

"No, I just found them."

"Don't mention them to anyone," said Lewis.

"I won't."

"I'll have to tell Trey, of course, and Nate. He can plug the information into his program."

"How's that coming?" asked Lindsay.

Lewis's gesture was between a nod and a shrug. "He's fine-tuning the variables. It could be an amazing program. It has possibilities far beyond finding shipwrecks. I can see him taking it to the level of simulating parts of the ocean if he can get enough good data, but there are big gaps at the moment. He's tried some test runs with the *Estrella*'s artifacts that were strewn about during the wreck. Since we know where the *Estrella* is, it was a good test, and he has had a fair amount of success. I've got him transferring to Georgia next fall."

"So if he plugs in the location where I discovered the coins and it leads back to the *Estrella*, then we can be virtually certain that these came from our ship."

"The *Estrella*, yes."

"Do you really have hopes of finding the other ship?" asked Lindsay.

"Of course. I'm already planning the museum that will house the two of them on campus."

"You're kidding."

"No. I'm already having people look at property on River Road."

"Lewis, you're scary."

Lindsay could hear Lewis laugh even after she shut the door to his office.

"How about seafood on St. Simons?" John asked. "It's a little late for dinner and a movie, so I thought we could cruise on the ocean—if you aren't spooked."

"Suits me. I'd love it."

"I hope you don't mind, but Luke and Bobbie are going with us."

"No, I don't mind. How did that come about?"

"Luke asked me. I think rather than coming out and asking Bobbie for a date, he's going to present it to her as a group outing."

Chapter 22

Twenty shot glasses with oysters, a plate of lemon wedges, and a pitcher of beer sat in front of the four of them. Luke, it seemed, had never had raw oysters.

"You take a bite of lemon, then take the shot glass and let the oyster slide down your throat and chase it with a swallow of beer, like this," said Bobbie, illustrating the technique.

Luke gave it a try, nodded his approval and tried another. John chased his with water since he was piloting the boat. "I think it loses something without the beer," he said.

"I tried it with root beer once in high school. It was awful," Lindsay said.

"Yuck, why would you do that?" Bobbie wrinkled her nose and downed an oyster.

By the time all the shot glasses were empty, a feast of seafood arrived on a giant platter set in the middle of the table.

"This looks decadent," said Bobbie, reaching for a crab leg.

"It looks great," said Luke.

"This is the way the sailors on the *Estrella* ate," Lindsay commented. "Off a communal plate. Only, not so well."

They ate, more than talked, about half the platter's worth. A plate of oysters on the half shell hoisted on the arm of a waitress sailed past and headed for a booth in the far corner. Lindsay followed the tray with her gaze.

"Pearls," she said. "Wasn't Valerian's servant a pearl diver?"

"Who's Valerian?" asked Luke.

Bobbie gave him a short summary of the journal so far.

"Yes, he was," said Bobbie. "What about it?"

"There's a possibility that HSkR2 is Valerian's servant, plus his condition has the look of dysbaric osteonecrosis."

"Ouch," said Luke. "But how. . . ?"

"That's the question," said Lindsay. "But what if he was a pearl diver? Would free diving cause bone necrosis, I wonder?"

"Is this the saturation diving question you asked about earlier?" John asked, and Lindsay nodded. "I wouldn't think he could possibly go deep enough or hold his breath long enough—besides, don't you have to be breathing compressed air at deep pressures to contract that?"

"I believe so," Lindsay said. "It just all seems an interesting coincidence."

"The diary gives no indication that the servant was ill," said Bobbie.

"I know. I'm just speculating."

"I wish Harper would hurry and finish the translation," Bobbie said. "I want to find out what happens."

"The ship sinks," Luke replied.

Bobbie turned to him, brows knitted together and eyes narrowed. "You had to ruin it for me."

"Why don't we get dessert to go and eat out on the ocean?" Luke asked.

"Good idea." John picked up the tab the waitress left at the table. "We can pick up a couple of six-packs of drinks to take along with us."

The four of them, a six-pack each of Coke and Dr. Pepper, two cheesecakes, one chocolate cake, and one pecan pie loaded into the boat.

"Check the engine and the radio," Lindsay ordered.

"I did. They're fine." John kissed her cheek. "We won't get stranded." John piloted the boat out into the silvery moonlit ocean where he stopped and let it drift while they ate their dessert.

In the distance, Lindsay watched the lights of the boats on the water and thought about the men who sailed the *Estrella* across the water—the men whose bones she had touched. What a thing it was to sail all the way across the ocean with no telephones or radios, nothing but the things they were finding in the wreck. And what a disappointment to have wrecked so close to land. Some had to have survived—the diarist, of course. Who else? Lindsay found herself hoping that Valerian made it. How hard it must have been to be different in a time when differences were little tolerated.

"What do you see out there?" John asked.

"I suppose I was trying to see the *Estrella*—wondering who survived."

"I think about that, too," Bobbie said. She turned to Luke. "Would you like to read my copy of the journal?"

"Yeah, sure. It sounds like something they could make a movie out of."

"It wouldn't surprise me a bit if Lewis was trying to work it out right now. What's that?" asked Lindsay.

They all followed the direction she pointed. A diffuse glow under the water was traveling slowly toward their starboard side.

"It's a reflection—the moon," said Luke.

"No," said John. "It's not the moon." The glow passed behind them and John hurriedly started the engine and began flipping switches on the panel in front of him.

"What. . . ?" asked Lindsay.

"Sonar."

"You're kidding." Lindsay looked incredulously at John.

He grinned at her. "This is a fishing boat."

He slowly followed the glow. The small green screen on the panel made dull pings as what looked like a glowing second hand of a watch made a revolution. When he was over the light a blip appeared on the screen. "What you think, Luke?" John asked.

Luke rose and looked at the screen. "Can't be."

"What?" asked Lindsay.

"A sub."

"As in submarine? You're joking." The blip disappeared off the screen as they spoke.

"No. I believe it's a minisub."

"Doing what?" asked Bobbie.

"I'd say looking for . . ." he hesitated, "artifacts."

"You mean, it's our pirate lady?" Bobbie asked.

"Don't know for sure," John replied, "but what else is there to survey this close to shore in the dead of night?"

"Should we call someone?" asked Bobbie.

"They aren't breaking the law . . . I don't think," John answered. "However, I'm going in and report it to Lewis." He turned the boat and sped toward the cofferdam.

⚓

"Damn," said Lewis, throwing down his pen. He sat in his cabin behind a desk with an array of paperwork spread in front of him. Lindsay sat on his bunk and John in a chair in front of the desk.

"You're sure that's what it was?"

"No," said John, "but what else?"

There was a knock on the door and Trey entered.

"It has to be her," said Lewis. He frowned and explained to Trey what Lindsay and John had seen.

"Then they know," said Trey. "That sub's just too expensive to be used on a mere hunch."

"Is there anything we can do?" asked Lindsay.

"Find the ship before she does," Lewis replied. He rose. "I'm going to Nate's cabin to tell him to do nothing but try to find this ship. Sarah can lead his diving team."

"You think he can find it with just the location of the coins I found?" asked Lindsay.

"He has to," Lewis declared. Lindsay felt a pang of sympathy for Nate.

"The two murders are related to this. I know it," she said. "Gold is a compelling motive. I once worked on a skeleton that had all the teeth removed. I thought it was a feeble attempt at hiding the identity. It turned out the killer was after the gold caps on the teeth." Everyone in the room winced.

"It doesn't have to be related," said Lewis. "Keith Teal led a suspect life. Anyone could have killed him. And Hardy Denton was a man who made enemies."

"Both their bodies were found on the island where neither of them should have been. It's related." Lindsay was certain.

Later, as Lindsay lay in her bunk, it occurred to her that Lewis might have a strong motive for murder if he thought Teal or Denton were trying to find a ship he claimed as his own. Lewis was not a man who liked to have things taken from under his nose. She did not like that scenario, but the last thing he had asked her when she left his cabin was to try and find out what Ramirez knew.

⚓

Evangeline Jones's schooner, *Painted Lady*, was beautiful. The sails were furled, and she was anchored ten miles out from the cofferdam. Eva, dressed in white slacks and blouse, greeted Lindsay and

John as they boarded the ship and led them to a table near the bow, where the man Lindsay had seen at the restaurant was seated. He was pouring wine into four glasses.

"So nice of you to visit," Eva Jones said. "I was surprised when you called my ship. But you really didn't need to bring your fleet. You're quite safe here."

"Thank you for having us." Lindsay introduced John West.

Eva Jones gestured to a chair. "Please, I've had the cook bake bread and slice some fresh fruit. It really is nice to have visitors, isn't it, Carson?"

The man had an amused expression on his face. "Yes, it is."

He was, thought Lindsay, Eva's lawyer. He looked like a lawyer, from the cut of his wavy hair to his Rolex watch, to his smug countenance. Eva confirmed it.

"By the way, this is Carson MacMillan, my attorney."

Lindsay took the glass of wine he handed her. John declined. "I'm driving the boat," he said.

"This is the man who escorted me down into the cofferdam, Carson. I didn't know at the time that you built it," she said to John. "It's quite wonderful." Eva passed John and Lindsay a plate of fruit, cheese, and bread.

"Thank you. We think so," he said and took the gold-rimmed, bone china plate from her hand.

"I'm very sorry about your friend Hardy Denton," said Lindsay.

"We didn't know him well. Odd, his dying virtually on your doorstep."

"Yes, it is. Do you know if he had any enemies?"

Eva looked amused for a moment. She took a bite of bread and a drink of wine. "You people are the only ones I know of."

Lindsay laughed. "If we counted as enemies everyone who lost a bid at UGA, well—we let many bids, and there's only one winner each."

"I think he felt it was rigged against him," said the lawyer. "He was planning on suing."

"He would have wasted his money," said Lindsay.

The lawyer shrugged. "That's a matter of opinion. In court, anything can happen."

"It was both a matter of physics and the laws of economics. Not only would he have lost, but his reputation would have been ruined, as his proposal would have received close public scrutiny. I really don't think he was planning on suing. I'm sure it was only bluster."

Lindsay pointed to a large canvas-covered object near the stern of the ship. "We saw your little minisub last night. I'll bet that's fun. Do you drive it?"

Evangeline Jones and her lawyer sat silently for a moment, stunned. A surprise hit between the eyes. Lindsay concentrated on keeping an innocent smile on her face. Eva recovered first.

"I, uh, it belongs to my half sister, Marcella. A little project of hers. You remember she was with us at the restaurant? She's sort of a—what can I call her? Anyway, nautical engineering is her hobby."

"What does she do for a living?" asked John.

"What? Oh, I get it, that's funny." Eva laughed. "Marcella is one of those fortunate people born rich and smart. She's sleeping right now, or she'd be here with us. Where'd you see her?"

"Cruising the bottom of the sea," said Lindsay.

"Where were you?" asked Carson.

"We were cruising, too." Lindsay didn't mention that they were above the water.

"Really? I don't think she mentioned seeing anyone, did she, Carson?"

"Probably didn't see us," said John. "What with the stealth and black light."

Eva and her lawyer glanced at each other, wide-eyed. "Well," began Eva. "That-what—"

"They're putting you on."

A woman came from behind Lindsay, apparently up from the living area, wearing a bathing suit covered by a thin white gauzy shell. Her small valentine face and short dark hair gave her a pixy look, very different from Eva. She picked up an apple off the tray, sat down, and bit into it.

"There's no such thing. They were above me. I felt you ping me." She smiled at John.

Eva threw back her head and laughed. "Tell me, why didn't Lewis or Marcus come with you? Are they out there circling my ship?"

"No. They're probably at the dam," said Lindsay. "I really only came to see if you can tell me anything about Hardy Denton. We are naturally concerned about his getting killed, as you say, on our doorstep."

"We really don't know anything about him," said Carson MacMillan.

"What was your association with him?"

Eva shrugged. "Just acquaintances. He had a boat out here sailing around. You know, it becomes like a small community here on the water. We went out to dinner a few times. That's the extent of it. He wasn't very pleasant, really. Got drunk one too many times at the restaurant. We had decided to decline the next time he asked us to go out."

"Did you know Keith Teal?" asked Lindsay.

"Why are you asking us all these questions?" Carson asked, leaning forward, putting his forearms on the table.

"Like Eva said, we are a community out here, and a couple of members have been murdered." Lindsay turned back to Eva. "Did you or Denton know him?"

Eva patted Carson's hand. "She's right. Carson never stops being an attorney." She gave him an indulgent smile. "I didn't know him," said Eva. "I really don't know if Hardy did or not."

"What about you and Marcella?" asked Lindsay. Marcella shook her head.

"The reason I ask is that Keith's father said he mentioned you often. Talked about your expensive equipment."

"We didn't know him," said Eva.

"Had Hardy ever mentioned the name of Keith or Boote Teal?"

"No," said Eva. "Not to me." She turned to Carson and Marcella. "Did he say anything to you?"

They shook their heads.

"We only read about you girls getting hysterical and screaming over him." Carson grinned broadly and popped a slice of pineapple in his mouth. "I assume, even in death, he had a way about him."

"Do you ever use a twelve-inch airlift?" asked Lindsay.

"You don't mind broadsiding a person, do you?" said Eva. "The Coast Guard showed me the piece of airlift that was discovered near where your two divers were attacked. I don't hide the fact that I deal in antiquities, but I do it legally. As you know, a twelve-inch airlift smashes fragile artifacts. Last month I sold a teacup and saucer for $2,000. Six months before that I sold a whole set of eigh-

211

teenth-century Dutch porcelain for $230,000. Had I used an airlift that large when I recovered those finds, I'd have destroyed them. Broken antiquities are as useless to me as unprovenanced artifacts are to you. That airlift wasn't mine."

"Surely you know that the University of Georgia has a claim on the *Estrella*, and anything you find of hers belongs with her. We know that her crew was tossing her cannons and cargo overboard before she sank. You can't salvage her cargo."

A smile spread across Eva Jones's face. "If I find anything that belongs to the *Estrella*, I'll surrender it, of course—provided you can prove it. However, we are only here vacationing. Marcella is trying out her toy and I'm indulging her."

"At night?"

"What's night down there?" said Marcella.

"What exactly is your toy?" asked Lindsay.

"Small subs are used most often for very deep work. I'm using this for shallower work and improving the visibility for visual scanning. I can scrutinize the ocean floor with it and send back clear pictures faster than scuba divers can survey the same area." Marcella rose and threw her apple core in the ocean.

"Why not use scooters?" asked John.

"No place to carry equipment."

Lindsay turned to Eva. "If you think of who Denton may have been visiting on the island, please contact us—or Agent Ramirez of the FBI."

"I will. I'll ask my crew. Perhaps Hardy said something to them."

"We'd appreciate it."

Lindsay stood and held out her hand. "Thanks for your hospitality."

Eva took her hand and shook it. "My pleasure. Please come again, and I'll show you my ship."

Lindsay and John climbed down the ladder to their waiting launch and John piloted them back toward the dam. Lindsay watched Eva's ship. Suddenly the sails began to unfurl. Lindsay motioned for John to slow down. He stopped and cut the engines, and they watched the *Painted Lady* get under way. They could hear the capstan raise the anchors and see the sailors managing the sails. Although they were vastly different kinds of ships, this must be a glimpse of what it look liked when a galleon set sail. It was rather magnificent.

"It looks difficult," said Lindsay.

"What?"

"Maneuvering the sails and all of it."

"It just a matter of learning the ropes. If you'd like to go sailing, I understand Harper's a pro, and I've had some experience. So has Trey."

"I think I'd like to sail on one of those large sailing ships once. Just to see what it feels like."

"Did you learn anything?" asked Lewis. He and Trey were both at the cofferdam. Rotating shifts the way they did, letting the crew members choose any two days a week off, they kept a good size crew working every day. John went to check on his crew. Lindsay, Trey, and Lewis sat atop the dam at one of the tables.

"I think so. They know about the galleon and are looking for it."

Lewis leaned forward. "She said that?"

"Not specifically, but they have a minisub surveying the bottom. One of the things she wants to know is if we know she is looking for it. I believe I convinced her that we don't. She seemed very pleased."

"So that sub you saw was definitely hers?"

"Yes, they admitted that. They said it's a toy they're playing with."

"Expensive toy," Trey said.

"What else?" asked Lewis.

"There's a good chance that wasn't her airlift found around the artificial reefs."

"Why do you say that?" asked Trey.

"Because she says she prefers selling artifacts to breaking them."

"Maybe, depending on what the cargo is," said Trey. "But if we're talking about gold, silver, and jewels, then you can afford some breakage."

Lindsay conceded the point.

"They denied knowing very much about Hardy Denton, including why he was on the island. They also denied knowing Keith Teal. Keith, however, according to his father, was familiar with Jones, or at least her equipment resources."

"So," said Lewis, "they are making an all-out effort to locate the ship—including surveying at night."

"I would say so, yes."

"How did they find out about it?"

"I don't know. But I would think they have some precise information. Just to know something exists is one thing. Finding it is something else. The ocean is big. And I think they have known for a long time. If I'm right, that's why Denton made the bid for the dam."

They heard someone coming up the ladder to the dam and turned in time to see Agent Ramirez's head appear above the bulkhead.

"Hello," he said.

"Did you bring your family?" asked Lewis.

"My family? Oh, no. This, I'm afraid, is business."

Chapter 23

AFTER GETTING RAMIREZ a chair to join them, Trey took his seat again next to Lindsay. Agent Ramirez looked around at the sand, trailers, scaffolding, the barges, then out at the ocean.

"Did you see *Waterworld*?" he asked.

Trey smiled and replied, "I visited an undersea oil rig once. It's a rather unique environment, too."

"The reason I came by is to tell you that the Camden County sheriff called. Boote Teal was attacked in his home last evening."

"Oh, no," said Lindsay. "I was out there just yesterday."

"Yes, Dr. Chamberlain. That's what I wanted to talk to you about. Why didn't you call the police?"

"Boote asked us not to."

"You should have reported it anyway."

"Yes, I should have. I got absorbed in other things. I'm sorry. How is he?"

"In and out of consciousness. The perpetrator hit him over the head and tied him up. He then searched his entire house. He even broke the toilet tank."

"Since you got a look at the earlier perp, Dr. Chamberlain, I told the sheriff I would talk to you." He pulled out a pen and paper.

"He wore a ski mask over his face."

"Boote was able to tell the sheriff that."

"When John and I approached Boote's house, he came rushing out the door, pushing me down and John backward. He ran to a car; it looked like a dark blue Pinto."

"Can you give me any kind of description of him?"

"He wore black leather gloves and boots, blue jeans, and a green and black plaid long-sleeve shirt. He was about six feet, and I would guess somewhere around 190 pounds. Muscular, right handed, brown or dark hazel eyes. He had been eating food with garlic. It all happened very fast."

"That's a pretty good description for a fast look."

"He was breathing hard, so the odor was fairly obvious, and I make estimations about height and weight of skeletal material fairly routinely. Do you know what he was looking for?"

"He stole a box that had been mailed to Boote from the owner of a bar that Keith Teal frequented. Neither Boote nor the bar owner know what was in the box. After some questioning, Boote finally revealed that he had something secreted in the toilet tank."

"What was it?" asked Lindsay.

"A gold cross about seven inches long encrusted with what Boote thought were emeralds."

The three of them sat speechless. Lindsay was the first to recover. "Did he say where he got it?"

"He didn't know about it until a neighbor was defrosting his freezer and found it embedded in the ice that adhered to the back of the compartment. Boote taped it to the bottom of the toilet tank lid. He said he knew Keith had found something because he had hinted several times during his Sunday visits that things would be changing for them. I don't suppose you know anything about it?"

"There were Spanish clerics on board the *Estrella*," said Lewis. "They often had gold religious symbols for the mission churches."

"You think it belongs to your ship, then?" Ramirez asked.

"I don't know."

"Is Boote going to be all right?" Lindsay asked.

"The doctors think so, but they aren't sure. He is an old man and not in good health."

One of the crew called up for Trey. Lewis went with him. Lindsay guessed it was because he wanted her to stay with Ramirez and pump him for information.

"I'm sorry about Boote," Lindsay began.

"You think this is related to our murders?" Ramirez asked.

Lindsay nodded. "His son is murdered on an island where the offshore excavation of a Spanish galleon is in progress. Boote is attacked, and one of the things stolen from him is something that sounds to be a Spanish artifact. Yes, I think the events are related. I have already said that I think the deaths of Hardy Denton and Keith Teal are related and why. If they are, then logically, the death of Denton and the attack on Boote are connected."

"Ah, a simple syllogism?"

"If my propositions are correct. Look, Agent Ramirez, my boss would like to get to the bottom of this. We don't want a murderer on the loose for many reasons, some altruistic and some self-serving. I have already interviewed several people to that end. I will share with you what I learned from those interviews, no strings attached. I would like you to share with me. I am sometimes able to put clues together in effective ways."

"And modest, too. You didn't happen to get a look at the teeth of the man in the ski mask did you?"

Lindsay grinned. "You've been talking to the D.A. back home."

"He told me about your courtroom testimony in a murder case he prosecuted. He said the murderer was wearing a ski mask, and you were able to identify him based on a five-second look at his teeth."

"That was a lucky break. Teeth are something I analyze. I was unfortunate enough to witness a horrible crime, but the perp showed me a mouth full of teeth having a number of peculiarly distinctive features that allowed me to match him up with some corroborating evidence. I don't do that kind of thing every day."

"It certainly enhances your credibility," Ramirez said. "Tell me what you have found out about this case."

They were interrupted by a spray of water showering up from the ocean. Ramirez shifted uneasily.

"Would you prefer to go back to the island?" Lindsay asked.

"Yes, I would. I don't see how you can work here, fascinating as it is. It doesn't feel safe to me."

Lindsay went to Lewis and borrowed the key to his office.

"Do you think he'll share information with you?" asked Lewis.

"Possibly. Look, I called someone I know at the FBI the other day and sort of asked him about Ramirez."

Lewis smiled as if he appreciated Lindsay's methods.

"Ramirez is a good guy. Conscientious and honest. I think he needs to know about the ship."

Lewis shook his head. "I don't know."

"I'll tell him the importance of keeping it quiet—that it will give the Coast Guard a real headache if word gets out. But I think the possible existence of the ship has a direct bearing on these cases."

"Possible existence? Do you not believe there is a ship?"

"I don't know. What was it doing way up here?"

"Chased by pirates. We know firsthand how relentless they can be."

Lindsay smiled. "How about it? I won't without your say-so."

"Go ahead. I trust your judgment. But we need this resolved. I'm getting inquiries."

Back on the island, Lindsay led Ramirez into Lewis's office where they sat at the corner table. She brought them both coffee from the break room. As he put cream and sugar in his, she told him about her talk with Boote.

"I didn't learn much from him," she said.

"He doesn't trust you university types." He put down his spoon and took a sip of coffee.

"I talked to Isaac Jones." Lindsay related that conversation.

Ramirez confirmed Isaac's alibi. "Isaac was out that evening with Jeff and a couple of guys on the scuba teams. They stayed the night in Savannah and started back to St. Maggie at six o'clock."

"After Isaac, I interviewed the security guard," said Lindsay.

"And did you discover anything important?" asked Ramirez.

"That he is probably a well-meaning, decent man, and probably believes he has been guarding the two buildings well, but, in fact, has done very little. He prides himself on remembering names of people, but in my talk with him, although he knew most of the men's names, he knew none of the women. Both Gretchen from biology and Sarah on our scuba team have red hair. He appears to not be able to tell them apart, even though the red hair is their only common characteristic. He lives with a wife and has four daughters; even so, or perhaps because of it, I suspect that women are alien to him. He considers them frivolous, as I suspect they do him and his love of model trains."

"I think you have sized him up accurately. He seems to have seen nothing."

"I asked him if anyone was here the evening that Denton was murdered; he said no. But I was here until about 11:30, before I went up to Harper's apartment. While I was working that night, Mike Altman came into the lab."

"What were you working on?"

"I was doing a drawing of one of the skeletons and analyzing bones."

"And what was Altman doing?"

Lindsay related the conversation with the biologist.

"So you don't believe he came for graph paper?"

"No."

"What, then?"

"I don't know. At first I was afraid he might destroy some artifacts for spite."

"But?" Ramirez leaned forward encouragingly.

"I don't know."

"You know that places you on the scene at the time of the murder?"

"Yes, and I have no alibi whatsoever. Harper was asleep by the time I got to her apartment—"

"You're sure she was there?" asked Ramirez.

"Yes. She had made up the couch for me in the living room. Her bedroom is off the living room, and the door was open."

"Did you have any reason to kill Denton, other than that he interfered with your dinner?"

"No."

"How about John West?" asked Ramirez.

"What are you asking?"

"Did he have a reason to kill Denton?"

"No."

"Denton was angry at not getting the contract."

"That would be a reason for him to kill John, not the other way around," said Lindsay.

"Denton was making trouble, I understand. Threatening to sue, writing letters to the other bidder about abnormalities in the process. He said that West made dangerous changes in the normal design of the dam."

"Yes, he was making trouble, but in the long run, more for himself. The plans for the dam and proposals for all the bidders are on file. The plans for the cofferdam structure itself were reviewed by independent engineers. The only changes that West made were to add safety features. He didn't change the basic cofferdam design. The changes were in the internal rings that keep the dam from collapsing on itself. The pressures on this dam were going to be— are—massive. In addition to the normal rings, he designed extra triangular braces. Things like that. He can tell you more about it. In no way did he make the dam less safe. And anyone, including the other bidder, would be able to see that."

"You and West see each other, don't you?"

"Yes. But that doesn't change the facts of the dam design," Lindsay replied.

"Do you know he was arrested for attacking a man?"

"Yes. His sister told me about it. I was working on a dig with her. She was there to observe our handling of the skeletal remains. This was a couple of years ago. It was the first time I met John, by the way. Their clan had just won a lawsuit to regain land the clan had purchased back in 1834 but that was taken from them a short time later. The clan had mistakenly thought back then that if they went the white man's route by purchasing the land and getting a deed, at least some of the Cherokee land would be protected from seizure. They were wrong. When gold was found in the area, Andrew Jackson took away all the land of the Cherokee in north Georgia and gave it to the State of Georgia, even though the U.S. Supreme Court ruled that the land belonged to the Cherokee. Neither Andrew Jackson nor the State of Georgia honored the deeds held by John's clan."

"Was this part of the Trail of Tears incident?"

"Yes. That happened in 1838."

Lindsay sipped her coffee. It was lukewarm. She pushed it aside.

"Five years ago, John's clan went to court to gain their land back. Because of their original deed and more sympathetic modern attitudes, they won their case. John's sister, Emily, was dating one of the brothers whose family held title to the land prior to the lawsuit and who were being bought out and displaced as a result of the settlement. Another of the brothers, who thought she had used her relationship to spy on them, attacked her, and John came to her rescue. As would have my brother, and as I'm sure you would if you had a sister being attacked. The charges were dismissed, as I'm sure you know."

"But he can get angry enough to attack someone."

Lindsay shook her head. "He didn't attack the man out of the blue. The man was attacking his sister. He'll defend the people he loves. I imagine he doesn't even have to get angry to do that."

"He said he was asleep on his barge all that evening," Ramirez said.

"I'm sure he was. Most of us here were asleep and therefore have no alibi. I know John. He wouldn't do anything like this."

Skepticism slid across Ramirez's face like a mask.

"I know. You hear that all the time. Sometimes it is true. When you mainly deal with the worst of people, it's easy to forget that good and honest people are legion." Lindsay could see she hadn't convinced him.

"He may be perfectly innocent. He probably is, but you, my dear, are in love with him and are biased."

"Consider, then, that I might be the kind of person who falls in love with someone for their goodness. If he were capable of murder, it would show in his behavior, even if subtly," Lindsay replied.

Ramirez grinned broadly. "Dr. Chamberlain, I see a handsome man, a man whom you would admire for his culture as well as his good looks. And I see a beautiful young woman. The kind of love and trust you speak of takes years to nurture. At this time in your life, it is all hormones. Trust me, I was young once."

Lindsay tried not to laugh. "I can't disagree that there is that aspect, but I trust my judgment also."

"And I trust my experience. Now tell me about Lewis. I understand he has run over a lot of people in his career."

"He has that reputation. He also has the reputation of making a lot of people's careers. I don't know him well, but I believe he is a very pragmatic person."

"Do you think he would kill if he deemed it practical?"

Lindsay had wondered the same thing the evening before. Having Ramirez say it aloud made it different from her only thinking about it—harsher, more unthinkable.

"No. I don't believe that everyone is capable of cold-blooded murder. Most of us may be capable of defending ourselves and our family, but to murder someone for gain or convenience, no."

"How about to protect a livelihood? A reputation? Do you believe everyone could be capable of murder for those reasons?" asked Ramirez.

"No. For one thing, I think most people are moral. Beyond that, I think for most people the payoff has to be greater than the consequences of the act. If you are protecting someone you love from being killed, the payoff is big, worth the risk. If, however, you are protecting a job or reputation, there is a good chance the act itself will bring about the consequences you are trying to avoid. Murder is forever. You can't take it back. I believe Lewis is a person who leaves his options open. If for no other reason, I don't think he would do something that couldn't be reversed."

"Interesting theory. How do you analyze those who do resort to murder?"

"Most murderers are people who can't control their temper or who have been socialized so poorly that they have no conscience or judgment. Some lack the ability to see past the short-term solution, and allow themselves to believe that they won't get caught."

"I'm not sure I agree, but—" He shrugged. "You may be right. What about Trey Marcus? What do you call him, the principal investigator?"

"I've worked with Trey before. I can't imagine his killing anyone. Again, there is no reason."

"Going back to your theory again. What if instead of protecting a loved one, you are protecting something you value very highly, like irreplaceable fragments of history or a protected species of plant or animal? Then would the payoff be worth the risk?"

Lindsay was silent for several moments. "You have me there. I suppose we would have to rely on the morality of the person who was tested. But the threat would have to be clear and present," she replied.

"Yes. You see, the problem with motive is that it varies with the individual. People will kill for an inheritance of $10,000 because for them that is a fortune. Others would not kill for less than several million. And there are those who would kill for tennis shoes." He threw up his hands. "Motive is always difficult. It is easier to rely on method, opportunity, and physical evidence, and worry about motive later."

Lindsay took a deep breath. "You won't feel that way when I tell you what I think the motive for these murders and the attack on Boote is connected to."

"Ah, you have something?"

"Yes, and please, it must be kept secret. If it isn't, not only us, but the Coast Guard will have their hands full."

Ramirez raised his eyebrows.

"There is rumor of another galleon—a silver galleon that sank in this area with hundreds of millions of dollars worth of treasure."

Ramirez set his cup down with a splash. "How long have you known this?"

"I don't know it for sure. It's a possibility, one that I have a tendency not to believe. I heard about it shortly after I got here."

"When I talked to Lewis, he knew the cross may have come from that ship?"

"Possibly from that ship, and possibly from the ship we're excavating. He didn't see the cross. As suggestive as it is, we don't know it is even an artifact. If it is, it's unprovenanced. That's a big deal to an archaeologist."

"Lewis could have told me."

"I'm telling you now, only thirty minutes later in this room with the door closed. Look, we really don't want this to get out. It would be like a gold rush. This part of the ocean is accessible even to people without the sophisticated equipment that we have or Evangeline Jones has. I can't even begin to imagine what it would be like out here and how dangerous it would be for everyone if word got out that there may be a fortune in Spanish bullion here waiting to be found."

"Is that what the Jones woman is looking for?"

"I'm sure. She's using a minisub. We saw it the other evening."

Lindsay told him about the visit she and John had made to the *Painted Lady*. She also told Ramirez she believed that Denton wanted to win the bid because he and Jones probably thought the *Estrella* was the silver galleon they were looking for and they wanted an inside man.

"That's why Denton was so angry," she said. "It had nothing to do with his losing the bid for the dam construction. It was something much bigger."

"Well, this puts a different spin on it altogether. What was it you said—the payoff has to be big? This is the kind of motive worth the risk."

"When was Denton killed?" asked Lindsay.

"Between three and four in the morning."

"He had a bruise across his midsection from the rim of the sink?"

"Yes."

"Boote said Keith was stabbed."

"Yes, we think he was in water, perhaps diving, when he was stabbed."

"When do you think he was killed?"

"Boote first missed him fifteen days ago. We figure a few days before that."

"Was he moved sometime after death?"

"Yes, why do you say that?"

"Having been buried in quicksand, it seems like he should have decayed much more slowly. He was coming apart when we met him. If he had been dead only fifteen days or so, it suggests that the body must have been in an environment that promotes decay before he ended up in the quicksand."

"We think he was weighted down with chains and dumped in the quicksand perhaps a week or more after death."

"How did he end up on St. Maggie?" Lindsay asked.

"That's a good question, isn't it? Perhaps he washed up," Ramirez suggested.

"And to save Boote funeral expenses, someone put him in the pit?"

Ramirez shrugged. "If we knew that, we might know who did it."

"Who do you think attacked Boote? Could it have been one of the same individuals who attacked Nate?" Lindsay asked.

"I don't know the answers to those questions," Ramirez replied.

"Were these people killed because they knew where the galleon is, or to keep them from finding it, or for some other reason entirely?"

"I don't know the answers to those questions, either. Is there anything else you know?" Ramirez asked.

"I interviewed William Kuzniak, one of the meteorologists. He was on duty that evening. He didn't hear or see anything, either."

"I talked to him, too. Whoever killed Denton was quiet and invisible." Ramirez rose to go. "If you discover anything else, let me know."

"Wait."

"Already?" he said.

"Keith had the peculiar habit of punching holes in quarters."

"He did? Why?"

"I don't know. But the first day I arrived on St. Magdalena, just after Keith disappeared, Boote came here drunk, looking for Keith, and fell into the alligator pond. Apparently, one of the railings was loose. After he was fished out and taken home, I found one of those quarters with a hole in it wedged in between the wood slats in the walkway. What if Keith was killed there and he dropped the coin? He could have gotten in a fight with someone and one of them fell against the railing, loosening it. Then, Boote came along drunk, leaned on it, and fell into the alligator pond?"

Ramirez nodded his head. "I like that. Yes. I like that. Then what?"

"They took him out to the ocean and dumped his body," said Lindsay.

"Yes, and—" Ramirez gestured his hands in encouragement.

Lindsay stood for a moment thinking. "Okay, they hauled him out to the ocean and dumped him, but he washed back up on-shore, and—who found him and put him in the pit?" she asked.

"Maybe whoever it was thought they had gotten rid of him, so they tried an alternate method," Ramirez suggested.

"It was a lucky break for the killer to be the one to discover the body when it washed up."

"Maybe someone else—someone who didn't want the body found."

Lindsay wrinkled up her face. "Why would someone else not want the body found?"

"It had to be someone who knew the quicksand pit was there," Ramirez said. "Who knew?"

"The biologists . . . or one of us who had become familiar with the island . . . I'm sure Boote and Keith knew; they practically lived on the island before they were run off, I'm told. They could have told any number of people about it. For all I know, it may be on a map of St. Magdalena. That scenario kind of fits Denton, too," Lindsay said.

"How?"

"Well, suppose it is the same person. I'd like to think we have one murderer instead of two." Ramirez nodded in agreement. Lindsay continued. "Denton is killed in the warehouse and the killer decides to—" She stopped.

"You have another idea?" asked Ramirez.

"Denton was a strong man. Holding his head under water was a difficult way to kill him. Why didn't the killer use some other method?" Lindsay asked.

"The killer didn't want the sound of a gunshot or the blood of a knife wound. Poison was too slow, the roof was too high to hang him, and he couldn't get behind Denton to hit him on the head," Ramirez answered.

Lindsay suppressed a laugh and coughed instead. She took a

drink of her cold coffee. "Torture. The killer wanted to know something, so he held Denton's head under water. Maybe he didn't even mean for him to drown."

"That's not bad. I could hang my hat on that. What was it they wanted? The cross? The location of the ship?"

"Maybe to know why Denton was lurking around the island," Lindsay suggested.

Ramirez nodded. "What was the other thing? The thing you said fit with Keith's death?"

"Oh. The murderer killed Denton. I'm assuming it was a man. It would be hard for a woman to hold a man's head under water. After Denton died, the killer had the problem many killers end up with—getting rid of the body. He hauled it to the deck on that side of the warehouse. Got a rowboat so as not to make noise. We have lots of boats of all kinds around this place. He towed him behind the boat because that was easy, and was going to leave him in the waterway or take him out to the ocean. But the killer lost Denton's body in the alligator pond," finished Lindsay.

"That's good, too. The M.O. kind of fits. I like that. This has been a good conversation. Please let me know if anything else occurs to you."

Ramirez had brought someone from his office with him to pilot the boat to the dam. The young man was waiting in the break room with several of the scuba crew in from their dives. Lindsay looked at her watch. Time had passed quickly. Ramirez shook her hand and thanked her again.

"You have been a big help. I think you have this half solved. Good luck with your excavation."

"Thanks."

Lindsay went back to Lewis's office to clean up the coffee cups. As she passed through the weather room, she noticed that they seemed busier than usual.

"How are things?" she asked.

"William looked up from a readout and smiled. "Oh, we're getting some weather. Nothing to worry about. It's far away from here."

"Good, keep it far away."

She emptied the mugs and washed them out in the small kitchen off the break room.

"Was that the FBI man?"

Lindsay looked up to see Sarah, coffee cup in hand to wash. "Hi. Yes, that was him."

"How're things going? Are they going to find the person who's doing this? I mean, some of us are kind of afraid."

"Yes, they are making progress. I don't think you need to worry. Lewis is putting on extra security."

"That's a relief."

"How's the diving going? Any more cannons?"

"As a matter of fact, yes. One of the other teams found another cannon and a cask."

"How do you retrieve the barrels and cannons? Don't they weigh a lot?"

"We call for the barge, tie several balloons to it, and raise it to the surface, to be hoisted onto the barge."

Seeing Sarah reminded Lindsay: "Are you going to be in this evening? I need to talk to you and Nate about Keith Teal."

"Lewis has you detecting, I heard." Sarah made a face. "Sure, I'll tell you what, we'll have dinner on the barge tomorrow evening. I'll bring Nate."

"Thanks. I'm sorry about doing this, but—"

"I know. We all work with Lewis. What he wants, he gets."

"Thanks." Lindsay took her coffee cup. "It's the least I can do."

Lewis was in the break room when Lindsay came out of the kitchen, drying her hands on a paper towel. He took her arm. "We took up Gina's skeleton today. Thought you might like to get on it."

Lindsay looked at Lewis and smiled. "When would you like it done? By tomorrow morning?"

Lewis smiled back. "If you can do that, I'd love it."

"No problem."

He pulled her outside the break room and into a corner. "How did it go with Ramirez?"

"Fine. He's going to keep our secret. He was a little miffed at not being told in the beginning, but I explained that it isn't something we actually know is there."

"Good, he bought that?"

"Yes, because I believed it to be true."

"Great. I knew I did right in bringing you here. You have great connections, ones that I don't have."

"I'm glad to fill in a gap in your associations."

"You have a great sense of humor, too." He squeezed her shoulder and went to meet Trey coming through the door. "The skeleton's downstairs. Carolyn put it in a tub of water before she left," he yelled back at her.

Chapter 24

LINDSAY WAS RUNNING her fingers over the right humerus of the new set of bones when John came into the lab. Carolyn and Korey had the evening off, and she worked alone at one of the artifact tables. Lindsay didn't see him until she lifted her head.

"Hello," he said and walked over. He stood for a moment. "You love bones, don't you?"

"Yes, why?"

"Oh, just watching you with them. What is it you feel?"

"From the bones? Their story. Every one is different."

"What's his story?" asked John.

"I don't know yet. It'll gradually unfold as I examine the bones."

"I was not unmoved by the story you told of my ancestors buried on Royce's land when we met."

Lindsay could see this was going to lead to a conversation she was not yet prepared to have, but she didn't quite know how to stop it.

"I know we will always differ about"—he hesitated, searching for words—"about what you do. Not even members of my own tribe agree, nor do all the members of our nation agree, but you didn't use that as an argument against me, and I appreciate that."

Lindsay remained silent, not certain of what to say, not wanting to break the spell of the island, hoping John wouldn't. He came closer.

"It makes no sense," he said, not without some vehemence, "that I should be falling in love with an archaeologist."

Lindsay's gaze lingered on John for a moment, then searched the room as if the words she wanted could be found close by. "I want there to be a solution that doesn't require either of us to compromise what we believe. Wanting the impossible is, well—"she shrugged.

"You and Derrick were close." This was a conversation Lindsay didn't want to have, either. She took a breath.

"We were. Derrick and I were in graduate school together. He was—still is in some ways—my best friend. I loved him, and it meant something. It's hard to let go of some of it. I don't mean I yearn to have him back, I mean—the friendship, the memories . . ."

"I understand. I wouldn't mind your being friends with him, just don't be with him, if you understand what I mean."

"Yes, I do. Are you still close to your ex-wife? You have kids together."

"Sometimes we are close. We didn't end as amicably. But yes, there are memories. Good memories. You worry about my ex-wife?"

"No. I worry that one day we're going to fight over the matter of what I do for a living that puts us at opposite ends of a pole, and we won't be able to find our way back together." Lindsay put the humerus away.

"I've got to run some errands. I was going to offer to bring you something for dinner from the mainland if you're staying here."

"Yes, I think I'll ask Harper to put me up for the night. I feel like I'm behind, and this will give me a chance to catch up. How about another of those pizzas—mushrooms, sausage, and pepperoni?"

"You got it."

"Thanks for thinking about me."

"I think about you all the time," he said and waved as he left.

The lab filled up and emptied as everyone came in and then read that there would be no debriefing this evening. Lindsay was alone in the lab as she took the skull measurements of HSkR4. Steven Nemo entered and began flipping through his charts, filling in finds on the cross section of the ship, matching a map he brought with him with the one on the chart. Lindsay put the skull back in the saline solution and walked over to him.

"Is it my turn?" he asked.

"Yes."

"What does Lewis hope to accomplish by having you do this?" Steven's black hair, neatly trimmed black beard, and the scowl on his face gave him a devilish appearance.

"Control, I think."

Steven nodded. "I can see that. From what others have told me, the crime happened between 3:00 and 4:00 A.M. Well, I was asleep on the barge between 11:30 and 5:30, so I guess I have no alibi."

"Most of us don't. I was asleep on the island during those times, and I had a confrontation with Denton only days earlier."

"Does Ramirez really suspect us? He's got Isaac scared to death. Isaac wouldn't hurt a fly."

"I don't think Isaac is a serious contender. It was his bad luck Denton was drowned in his sink. Did you ever meet Denton?"

"No. I don't think any of us did. West's men had a run-in with him once. I'm not trying to get them in trouble. It's just that his beef was about the dam."

"How about Keith Teal? Did you know him?"

"We went diving together a few times. He showed me some of the things he retrieved from a wreck he found a few years ago. He was a pothunter, but he knew the area."

"Do you have any idea what he was doing here when he was killed?"

"I don't know. We weren't using him as an informant anymore. Mike Altman, the biologist, had more of a reason to do him in. Keith apparently decided to try his hand at horticulture. He stole some of the rare plants on the island and sold them to collectors. Pissed Mike off good, and I can't say as I blame him."

"You think if Keith came around again trying to do the same thing, Mike might do something?"

"I don't want to blame anyone, not even the bio people." He sighed. "It's possible that he and Keith would get in a fight. I suppose if I were to stretch things, I could see that Mike might have killed him accidently, but he wouldn't have hidden the body."

"When was the last time you saw Keith around here?"

"Not for about a couple of months."

Lindsay couldn't think of anything else to ask. She actually felt silly interrogating the crew and turned her attention to Steven's cross section. "A site like this deserves our undivided attention."

His mouth widened into a big grin. That, and the dimples in his cheeks, made him look almost angelic. "I agree. This is just the best site I've worked on. I pore over those diary pages every night looking for descriptions of the ship, matching them with our finds. You know Lewis wants to build a museum."

"I heard."

"I went to Athens a couple of weeks ago, and we looked at some land. If everything goes well, there's this spot on the Oconee River that would be perfect. Lewis wants the museum near campus and near water. We're going to reconstruct the *Estrella* inside. It will be great. Can you imagine"—he gestured to the cross section, then made a wide arc with his arms—"that huge ship reconstructed? It will be magnificent. In a few months he and I are going to England to look at the *Mary Rose* and the museum there."

"I like the idea of a museum."

"Odd thing, however; when we talked about the space, I got the feeling he was planning for two ships. Do you know anything about that?" He gave Lindsay a hard stare and she said nothing. "Oh, God, I knew it. I've heard—"

"What have you heard?" she asked.

"Whispers about a second ship from some of the scuba divers."

"Can you tell me who?"

"Bobbie for one. Her team's searches take them out of the grid and she doesn't understand why. Nate just tells her he's running experiments with that program of his. I got the feeling that she doesn't like working on his dissertation and not on the main part of the excavation."

"What do you think of his computer program?"

"I don't know much about it. Great thing, if it works. Awful lot of variables."

"Don't pass on any rumors that you hear," Lindsay warned.

"No. I keep pretty much to myself. Damn! Another ship."

"Don't say it out loud, either."

"What? Why? No . . . oh, shit, you're not saying . . . that's impossible."

"Just keep all your thoughts in your head."

"Oh, God, what a nightmare that would be."

"Thank you for talking to me. I know it's a nuisance."

"Not really. This murder business is the nuisance, and just so odd. Jeff says this happens to you all the time."

"Not all the time."

"Still, more than once is amazing. Was HSkR1 really murdered?"

"If the authorities brought me a modern skeleton with those same wounds, I would call it murder. He was hit from behind and sustained repeated blows. The really strange anomaly is HSkR2— the Asian skeleton."

"I've been thinking about what you said during debriefing. You know Valerian's servant, Jen, was a pearl diver. Could that account for his condition?"

"I thought about that, too, and I don't know. It's one of the things I'm going to have to research. So far, everything I've learned suggests that kind of bone necrosis to be a problem only for very deep divers. There's a depth limit to free diving."

"You're right. This site deserves to be the main show. I'd like to strangle whoever it was who killed those two—so to speak." He grinned.

Lindsay went back to her desk and keyed in the measurements to the computer program. She looked at the map and was shocked. She did the whole procedure over, hoping for another outcome. It was the same.

"Oh, no," she said, loud enough for Steven to hear.

"What?" he asked.

"HSkR4—Gina and Juliana's skeleton—his skull measurements suggest he is from North Africa, particularly Morocco."

Steven came over to her desk and looked at the numbers, wrinkling his brow. "Morocco, you mean—not Valerian? Wasn't he Portuguese and Moroccan? Like Gina, I'd kind of hoped he survived. Maybe it was one of the crew."

"Maybe, but I'm not sure a Spanish ship would have had a crew member from a Muslim country," Lindsay said. "Spain was a place where blasphemy against Christianity was a worse offense than stealing. The Spaniards had just driven the Moors from their country. Philip II was persecuting the Moriscos in Spain."

"Who were they?" Steven asked, scrutinizing the skull, as if looking for Valerian in the bony features.

"Converts—Christian Muslims."

"But the Muslims occupied Spain for centuries. There was bound to be intermarriage. How accurate is the program?"

"Mixed offspring is the weak point in the attempt to apply ethnic origin to skeletal remains. The program doesn't write its conclusions in stone. But it is suggestive."

"I hope it's not Valerian. Are there other ways you might be able to tell?"

"I'll read the diary again, and maybe the untranslated parts we don't have yet will have clues. Lewis all but ordered me to match the remains. I think I've caught his desire to match the bones with people in the diary, and I'm jumping to conclusions every time I look at a skeleton. There were over two hundred people on the ship, after all."

"I know what you mean about Lewis. You should be talking to him about the ship. I expect any day now he'll come to me with the idea of reconstructing it so it'll sail again." He laid a hand on Lindsay's shoulder. "It's easy to get caught up in his enthusiasm— or his orders." Steven went back to his maps.

Steven was right. What business did she have questioning the crew? The murders were bad enough without having one of their colleagues pulling them aside and giving them the third degree. She wasn't going to do it anymore. Ramirez was more than competent. She was an archaeologist, not a detective. She'd talk to Nate and Sarah, and that'd be it. She wasn't making any progress anyway. Everyone said the same things.

Lindsay went up to Harper's apartment and knocked.

"Hey, come in. I thought you were Trey." Harper was dressed in a yellow sundress and leather sandals.

"I was wondering if I could borrow your couch tonight?"

"Sure, that'd be great. We aren't going to be out long. Trey's got to get back to the dam." Harper reached in her purse and handed Lindsay a key. "Want us to bring you something?"

"John's bringing me a pizza."

"I'll take the evening off. I need it. Lewis acts like this translation is easy. I'd rather have some good girl talk this evening. I swear, if there's another murder on this island, it'll be Lewis and I'll be the perpetrator."

"I think you'll have to take a number."

When Lindsay returned, she had the lab to herself. She hesitated to do too much to the new set of bones. Fabric adhered to them in places, and she preferred to let Carolyn take care of it. In fact, she imagined that Carolyn wouldn't like it much if Lindsay decided to clean the bones herself. She did take up again the humerus that she was examining when John had interrupted her. She thought she had noticed a break. She was right. It had been broken near the distal end, set, and healed well. She made note of it. The measurement of the humerus indicated that he was between five-three and five-six. The measurements of the other long bones would give a more accurate estimation. She put the arm bone back in its solution and looked at some of the other bones. Many of them had bits and pieces of fabric, so she left them alone. It wasn't good methodology to pick and choose bones to examine. It needed to be done systematically.

She turned on her computer to record the information. After Windows came up, a pop-up window opened.

"What in the—"

A morgue photograph appeared. Lindsay stared in shock. It was a picture of the Black Dahlia, a famous Hollywood murder victim of the '40s who was cut in half and left in a field. Except that it was Lindsay's face on the corpse, and large, flashing red letters sent her a warning. "Is the snooping worth it? She was a bitch. You are, too."

Lindsay's hands shook as she reached for the computer keys. She pulled them back before they touched the keyboard. She had to show someone. Who? Not the guard, Dale Delosier. One of the meteorologists. She stood up. The message changed—"Time Out, Goodbye"—and it was gone. Lindsay took a deep breath. Fingerprints. She turned it off and gently closed the lid. She put her hands over her mouth. It was so quiet down here.

She placed the computer in its case, snatched up the photographs of the skulls, drawing pencils, paper, and her overnight case, and hurried out of the lab for the safety of Harper's apartment. Terry Lyons was on duty in the weather room. Lindsay stopped in, more out of the need for company than anything else.

"Hi. How are things?" she said, trying not to sound terrified.

"We have some storms far to the south of here. But so far we're fine."

"Do you know when we're going to get the new security guards?" Lindsay asked.

"Tomorrow, I think. William and I will be relieved. You staying here tonight?"

Lindsay nodded. "See you later."

She hurried up the stairs and into Harper's room, sat down on the couch, and put her head in her hands. If the person meant to scare her, it worked. She was scared. But she was also alerted to the fact that the culprit was someone here, and he had panicked. She searched her purse for Ramirez's card and dialed his number from the phone on Harper's desk. Voice mail. She started to call his home, but stopped. No use ruining everyone's day. She left him a message. She wished John would get here with the pizza.

Lindsay leaned back on the sofa and concentrated on breathing evenly. Stay in control. Don't let them see they got to you. She wished she had taken up transcendental meditation.

Why were they panicked, she asked herself. She hadn't discovered anything—had she? She put the tips of her fingers to her eyes and rubbed. Think. It has to be a person who knows computers. Not just software packages, but someone who can create programs and make them come up on her computer. It has to be someone who has access to the lab where her computer is kept. It probably isn't Lewis. He has the power to simply tell her to stop. Unless he's a maniac, he wouldn't ask her to find out what happened and then secretly threaten her to stop. The thought gave her comfort. Lewis seemed so obsessed with finding the ship. She realized she had actually been worried that he might be getting rid of the competition. But Keith wasn't much competition. Jones, and by extension Denton, are the competition. Unless Keith had accidently stumbled upon the site of the wreck, he didn't have the resources for a real search. But he had found the cross. No, he had in his possession a cross of unknown provenance. The cross could have been a trinket he found in a yard sale. But he wouldn't have gone to the trouble of freezing it into the ice of his freezer if that's all it was. He could have stolen the cross from Denton and Jones and they killed him, and now Jones has her men looking for it. That made sense. But who killed Denton?

Lindsay stood up and began pacing the room. It didn't have to be related to the ship. What if it was related to the island? What if it was Mike Altman? What if he caught Keith stealing plants again and killed him and Denton saw him and he had to kill Denton, too? She sat back down on the sofa. They were killed weeks apart. Maybe Denton decided to blackmail Mike. That was why he was on the island, and Mike killed him. Mike's wife is a computer expert. Lindsay really wanted it to be Mike. The door burst open. Lindsay jumped up and picked up a lamp, ready to hurl it.

Chapter 25

"I'M GOING TO have to get a new key. That one keeps sticking—whoa, Lindsay?" Harper, Trey, and John stood in the doorway staring at Lindsay.

She put the lamp back on the table. "Sorry, I was afraid it was someone else."

"Who?" asked Harper.

John set the pizza down on the small table next to the door, came over and sat Lindsay down on the sofa. "What's happened?"

For the first time, tears started to form in her eyes. She told them what had happened with her computer.

"Oh, God," said Trey.

John pulled her over to him and cradled her head in his hands for several seconds before she pulled away and sat up.

"You say it popped up when you booted up your computer?" Trey asked.

"Yes."

"They put it in your startup file."

"Would it take a lot of computer sophistication to create a message like that?" she asked.

"Not a lot, really. More than most have, I suppose. Is this your computer here?" He reached for the computer case.

"Yes, but I hoped that Ramirez might find fingerprints."

"I'll hook it up to Harper's computer. I'll be careful." Trey took the computer out, touching as little of it as possible. He connected it to Harper's and turned it on, using her keyboard and monitor. Lindsay made herself watch as the photograph came up.

"Oh, my God!" Harper exclaimed, putting her hand to her mouth. "My God."

John's face hardened. He grabbed Lindsay's hand and held tight.

"Sick," Trey said. He found the program and copied it to a disk and deleted it from her computer. "Look, Chamberlain, you have to stop investigating. The hell with what Lewis wants. This is sick."

"I won't let whoever this is control what I do."

"Lindsay—" Harper began.

"Do you have any idea who could have done this?" John asked.

"I was trying to go over in my head who knows about computers, but I don't know the amount of knowledge one would need. I know Mike Altman's wife, Tessa, knows about computers."

"Yes, she does," Trey agreed. "She's an expert. Why do you suspect her and Mike?"

"Several reasons. One, I found out he heard Bobbie and Harper scream when we found the body of Keith Teal. He was in the area and he knew we were missing and he did nothing."

"What?" said Harper. "That son of a—he knew?"

"Are you sure?" Trey asked.

"He admitted it to me himself."

"That does it. I'll have Lewis get them off the island until we're finished."

"Not all of the biology people are as hostile and angry as he is," Lindsay cautioned. "They do have legitimate research interests."

"Who else knows about computers?" John asked.

Trey shook his head. "Who has the ability to do this? Me and Nate. The weathermen, William and Terry. Bobbie, Juliana, and several of the divers. I'm sure some of your people, John. There're probably more. I believe we can rule out the people we know."

"And I'll bet some of Evangeline Jones's people are good with computers," Harper said.

"Could they get on the island without being seen?" Trey asked.

"Evidently Denton and Keith did," Lindsay said. "I put in a call to Ramirez, but I doubt he'll call back tonight."

"Why don't you and John have the pizza before it's ice cold? I'll get us some beer," Harper said, as she headed toward the refrigerator.

"Sure," said Lindsay. "I'll not let some maniac ruin my appetite."

Harper had a breakfast table under a window. She and John sat and ate pizza while Harper and Trey lounged on the couch and sipped beer. Lindsay gave them a rundown of her thoughts on the murders.

"You know," Trey said, when she finished, "I hadn't thought about the murders being related to Mike and his project. "It makes sense. It might not have anything to do with us at all."

"I'm going to stay the night here," John said. "I'll stay in the hallway. Lewis said the new security comes tomorrow."

"You can't sleep out in the hall," said Lindsay.

"I don't intend to sleep."

"Well, you don't have to stay in the hall," Harper said.

"You've had someone try to break into your room. If someone tries again, I'd like to see who it is."

"Why do you think they'll come tonight?" asked Lindsay.

"It's the last night before the extra security comes. I think it would be a good idea just to keep watch."

"I agree," Trey said. "I'll stay on the island tonight, too. If John is staying up here, I'll stay in the lab and see if anyone tries anything else."

"I was saying to Steven tonight that this site deserves our undivided attention," Lindsay said, looking out the window at the alligator pond in the moonlight. "I'd like to find out who's behind this so we can get back to doing what we do." She looked at the three of them in turn. "I must be close. Why else would someone do this?"

"Close?" said John. "What have you discovered for certain?"

"Nothing much that I can see, but someone feels threatened. I might have discovered something that hasn't dawned on me yet."

"Could it be a joke?" Harper asked. "Maybe one of the crew here doesn't like you asking questions."

"Sick joke," Trey said, "but you have a point."

"This seems awfully wicked for a joke," said Lindsay.

"Where did they get that ghastly picture?" Harper asked.

"The Web, most likely," Trey answered. "You can get the most sublime and the most depraved our society has to offer on the Web."

When he finished his beer, Trey armed himself with blankets and a pillow and headed for the laboratory downstairs. Carrying one of Harper's chairs, John took up a post amid shadows in a corner of the hallway.

Lindsay, in a nightshirt, with legs tucked under her, sat on the sofa with a mug of hot chocolate that Harper had made. Harper sat on the other end sipping hers.

"How you feeling?" Harper asked.

"I'm fine, really. It was probably only a sick joke, just as you said. So tell me about you and Trey."

"I like Trey. He wants me to come to UGA. They have an opening in Romance languages."

"You're at Chicago now?"

Harper nodded. "It's a temporary teaching position."

"It sounds serious between you two."

Harper took a sip of cocoa and smiled into the cup, dipped her finger into the chocolate and put it in her mouth. "Well, I suppose so." She looked up at Lindsay. "If it weren't for the murder and mayhem, this place would be paradise. So tell me about you and John. He seems very fond of you, and this archaeology thing doesn't seem to be getting in the way."

"I think that's because our relationship—romance—is new. When the newness wears off, the archaeology will become very important."

"Do you analyze everything? Seize the moment."

Harper's apartment was over the reception area of the research lab. The breakfast table window was exactly over the front door. When they suddenly heard the door slam and running footfalls on the wooden walkway, Lindsay and Harper jumped up and looked out the window in time to see someone disappear into the wooded area bordering the alligator pond, with Trey in pursuit and Dale Delosier, the security guard, bringing up the rear. They ran to the hallway to tell John, but he apparently had heard the commotion and was running down the stairs three at a time.

Lindsay slipped on her jeans and sandals, and Harper threw on a robe. The two of them ran down the stairs to the front door. John, Dale, and Trey were back by that time.

"What happened?" Lindsay asked.

Trey was breathing hard.

"I slept in the corner on one of the couches, and I heard someone brush by a chair near the artifact table. I jumped up and yelled and they switched off their flashlight and sprinted for the door. I lost them in the bush out there. It was pitch black."

"They can't get far out there," Dale said.

"If it's someone who knows the island, they can," Trey said.

"Did you see anyone come in?" Lindsay asked Delosier.

"No. Whoever it was was real quiet."

More likely you were real absorbed in your model trains, thought Lindsay.

"Did you get any kind of look at them?" John asked Trey.

"No. I should have had a light on in the lab. He, or she, was dressed head to foot in black. I'm going to make a trek to the ranger station and have it out," Trey said.

"Let me go," John said. He reached and took a flashlight from the security guard's belt. "I'll bring it back."

He was gone before Trey could protest. Lindsay thought it was probably a good idea. The mood Trey was in, he might make things worse.

Trey turned to Dale Delosier. "You didn't hear or see anyone?"

"Not until you all came running out the door."

A retort teetered on Trey's lips—Lindsay could see it on his face, but he only turned to her and Harper. "Let's wait inside for John."

They sat in the break room, Trey with a mug of coffee he wasn't drinking. Delosier went to check the warehouse.

"You think it was one of the biology people?" Lindsay asked Trey.

"Yes, I do. I don't know what they were up to, but who else?"

"It could've been Jones's people. It could've been someone from the barge, as much as we don't want to think that it was. Or, it could be some friend of Keith Teal who knows the island."

"I suppose you're right. I guess it was a good idea for John to go. I'd have accused them point-blank, and that would've made things much worse, I'm sure."

John came through the door and sat down beside Lindsay. "I went to the ranger station and told them we had a prowler. I asked them if they were all right and if they had heard anything. I don't think they were fooled by my concern for their safety, but they didn't get mad, either."

"What did they say?" Trey asked.

"That they heard nothing, nor saw anything."

"Who did you talk with?"

"James Choi came to the door first. He was up working. He said Gretchen was in bed. Tessa and Mike came to the door when they heard us talking. None of them were breathing hard, or showed any indication they had been out. I thought it best not to accuse anyone."

Harper stood. "Well, I'm going back to my apartment and to bed."

"Me, too," Lindsay agreed. "I don't think they will be back. Why don't you two get some sleep?"

"No," Trey said, "that's what they may think and try again."

"I think this is silly," Harper said. "Get what's-his-name, the security guard, to stay in the lab and keep an eye out."

"Right," said Trey.

"Good night, everyone." Harper and Lindsay went upstairs. John yelled that he'd be up later.

"What were you saying about this being a paradise if it weren't for all the murder and mayhem?" Lindsay asked, stripping off her jeans.

"What do you reckon is going on?" Harper asked.

Lindsay gathered the cups off the breakfast table where she and Harper had set them down. She thought she caught a fleeting glimpse of someone in the distance going into the woods. She looked around the room. "Harper, check and see if you have anything missing."

Harper eyed her. "Why? What's wrong?"

"I thought I saw someone outside. The lab thing could have been a diversion."

"They couldn't know that we'd go downstairs."

"No, but maybe they were waiting for you to go to sleep, or—I don't know."

Harper checked her drawers and closet. "I don't have any valuables missing."

"What about the translation?"

"I keep that in a safe. I thought it was silly of Lewis, but he bought one of those safes that looks like a nightstand. I checked it. It doesn't look like it was even discovered."

"The computer?" asked Lindsay.

"It has a lock on the keyboard that requires my password to get into it. Trey is the only one who knows it besides me."

"Does it look like anyone was in here?"

"No."

"Do you keep the original journal here?"

Harper shook her head. "No, it's at the University of Georgia. I have photocopies. Why would anyone want the journal anyway?"

"Treasure hunters might want to have a look at it." As soon as

Lindsay said it, she realized that Harper might not know about the silver galleon. She decided not to ask. "I'll go down and tell them what I saw."

She opened the door just as John was raising his hand to knock.

"I was just going to tell you I'll be outside the door."

Lindsay told him about the figure she saw.

"Could it have been the same person?"

"I have no idea. I only got a fleeting glimpse."

"I'll go warn Trey and come back."

"Did either of you ask in the weather room?"

"Trey did. They had the door closed and locked and didn't see or hear anything."

The morning brought another small calamity. Someone had broken into the warehouse and opened the chest that was soaking in the brine tank.

Chapter 26

ISAAC HAD FOUND the desecration when he entered the warehouse. Lindsay, Lewis, and Trey were in the lab discussing the previous evening's events when Isaac burst in, breathless with the news.

"They drained the tank, broke open the trunk, and spread the contents out on the floor. It's a mess."

"They what? They what?!" Carolyn had overheard. "Tell me I didn't hear right."

"I'm sorry," Isaac said.

"What is going on here?" Lewis slammed his notebook down on the floor.

"We'd better take a look," Trey said.

They met Ramirez on the way out of the building. Lindsay filled him in on their way down to the warehouse.

Steven Nemo had arrived in the meantime and stood looking over the disorder. "Do you know what's happened?" His dark eyes were as angry-looking as Carolyn's blue ones.

"That's what we're here to find out," Lewis replied.

The chest sat open inside the empty tank. The water that had drained from the opened plug at the base of the tank had made a dark stain where it had run toward the center of the floor to the drain. Scattered on the floor were those things the chest was made to hold: a pile of fabric, a silver goblet and plate, a spoon and knife, an ivory comb, a filigreed pomander, clay jars, a silver manicure set, a compass, an astrolabe, a sandglass, brass dividers, and a large wooden box. Inside it sat an exquisite Chinese lacquered box. The Chinese box was open, revealing jars, a mortar and pestle, a knife with an ivory handle, and a pile of gold coins.

"Does it belong to the navigator?" whispered Steven, looking at the astrolabe.

"Look at this!" Carolyn turned to Korey. "Go get me some containers."

"And get your camera," Lindsay told him. "Not the digital one."

Korey trotted off at a fast pace to the lab. Carolyn started toward the objects, but Lindsay put a hand on her arm.

"Look, there's a long, slender damp spot on the floor and several rectangular ones. Some artifacts were stolen. Let's get a photograph of the floor."

Carolyn turned to Ramirez. "If you find who did this and he's dead, I'll save you some time. I will have been the murderer. I'm going to rip their heart out when I find them."

Lindsay surveyed the floor, hoping to find a damp footprint. She thought maybe she saw the toe of a shoe near the edge of the water stain, but it looked like whoever it was stayed mostly clear of the water. Lindsay looked at the chest in the tank. An exclamation must have escaped her lips, for they all looked at her.

"You see something else?" Trey asked.

"Look inside the lid of the chest. Doesn't that say 'Valerian'? These are Valerian's possessions."

"Valerian's?" Lewis asked.

"Yes, that makes sense," Steven agreed, lowering himself to his haunches to get a better look at the artifacts. "The chest was found in the same grid that Lewis found the chess pieces and the skeleton that Lindsay thinks was Valerian's servant."

Trey joined Steven near the floor. "You're right. It fits."

"Who is this Valerian?" Ramirez asked.

"He was a passenger on the *Estrella*. We've all grown rather fond of him. He apparently was a free thinker," Lindsay replied.

"Lindsay thinks she may have found him," Steven said.

"What? No," Lewis said. "Are you sure?"

"Don't tell me he died in the wreck," Carolyn said.

"I don't know for sure, at all," Lindsay answered. "It was just that the skull Gina and Juliana found appears to be North African."

"That's right. Valerian was Moroccan," Lewis said.

"Moroccan and Portuguese," Lindsay corrected him.

Korey arrived carrying armloads of trays and buckets and a camera. He began snapping pictures at Lindsay's instructions.

"Get me some water out of those tanks." Carolyn pointed to where the timbers were stored.

"We need to try and get fingerprints before you—" Ramirez began.

"No," Carolyn disagreed, "these are going into the water before they deteriorate."

"Look—" he began again.

Lewis stepped in. "Right now the mishandling of artifacts is the only crime."

"These are irreplaceable," said Lindsay. "We can try and get fingerprints from the outside of the tank, but all these things must remain wet."

"I'll have to call someone at the Smithsonian and find out how to conserve the lacquered box," Carolyn said. "I've never dealt with one before. I can't believe this. So help me—" She placed the items in the trays and poured salt water over them.

Something nudged the back of Lindsay's mind about the Chinese box, but she couldn't put her finger on it. That was the trouble. Everything seemed to be in the back of her mind these days. Maybe it was something from the diary. She'd have go back and do some rereading.

Ramirez pulled Lindsay aside. "Can I speak with you about your call?"

"Yes. A lot of things happened last night. Let's go back up to Lewis's office."

Trey used Lewis's computer to show Agent Ramirez and Lewis the surprise message Lindsay had received the evening before. Sitting at the table, Lindsay could see the screen out of the corner of her eye, but she couldn't bring herself to look at it again.

"It's very adolescent," Ramirez said.

"It's very sick," Lewis responded.

"And this is the machine?" asked Ramirez, indicating Lindsay's computer.

Trey nodded.

"I'll have it checked for prints."

"And how are you this morning?" Ramirez asked Lindsay as he and the others sat down.

"I'm fine. I was shaken and scared last night, but I'm fine now."

"I shouldn't have asked Lindsay to look into things," Lewis said.

"Perhaps it would be best left to us," Ramirez replied, not taking his eyes off Lindsay.

"I don't like being controlled by murderers," Lindsay objected.

"How about by me?" Ramirez said to her. "Stop investigating!"

"I'm not doing all that much. But I must have gotten close."

"Not necessarily. Sometimes murderers just don't want you asking questions," Ramirez said. "Who here has computer skills?" Trey handed him a list of everyone he knew who possessed the skills needed to have created the message and put it on Lindsay's computer. Ramirez looked at the list. "You said you have extra security coming?"

"They're here now, looking around the place," Lewis said. "I asked John to show them around. I think they're making a plan."

"Good. Now, you said other things happened?"

Trey gave Ramirez a description of how he and John had spent the past evening.

"What do you think they were after?" Ramirez asked.

"I don't know," Trey replied.

"Do you have any idea who they were?"

"No. We thought it might be the biology people, causing trouble, but with this latest thing, I—"

"I don't believe it. It isn't enough that you take over the place, but you are now accusing my people of criminal activity. I won't have it, Lewis. I'm taking it to the Board of Regents."

They all turned their heads to the door. A man in his late thirties, with frizzy brown receding hair, a mustache, and wearing a khaki shirt and chinos, stood in the doorway. Lindsay had seen him and his photograph many times. Evan Easterall—one of UGA's so-called celebrity faculty. This ought to be interesting, she thought. Mike Altman stood behind Easterall.

"Don't bother knocking," Lewis said. "Come in and meet Agent Ramirez."

Lindsay had heard people's description of Lewis when he was angry. They said you had to know him. It's all in his eyes. She thought she saw what they were talking about.

"Things are going to change around here," Easterall said. "My staff need room to do their research, and I'm going to see that they get it."

"You can have it all back when we're finished," Lewis responded.

"If everyone here lives that long. People are being found murdered; members of your staff are running hysterically around the island. This whole project is out of control."

Lindsay wasn't thinking of the nasty surprise she got on her computer last evening, nor was she thinking about Lewis, the murders, or the site. She was thinking about how two years ago she had submitted a request for time on the supercomputer for analysis of her research data—an analysis that was of critical importance to her, her students, and the future of the archaeology lab. She remembered Easterall picking up the request she handed to the people who were supposed to be in charge, taking a glance at it, and throwing it back in front of them, saying that he couldn't interrupt his work for inconsequential trivia. He had never looked at her, even though he knew she was standing there. He had dismissed her and her work as easily as if he were brushing away a fly.

"You're jumping to conclusions—" Lewis began, but Easterall cut him off.

"This whole project and the way it is being run is a disgrace and a danger to the lives of my people as well as yours. I'm going to—"

It must have been the heat of anger stimulating the synapses in her brain, Lindsay thought later. Small facts and bits of conversation were shifting into place. She stood and faced Easterall. "You'll do nothing. It's one of your staff who is behaving disgracefully."

Easterall's look of annoyance at her made Lindsay more angry. Not just a fly, a pesky fly, but he did look at her. "And you are Miss . . . ?"

"Dr. Chamberlain. I'm a tenured faculty member at UGA. Your man Altman has been feeding confidential information to Evangeline Jones regarding the archaeology site."

Mike opened his mouth to protest, but Lindsay pressed on.

"Eva Jones is a pothunter, a looter of antiquities. That would be like me going to the people who cut down and abuse the rainforests and helping them do a better job of it, simply because I got mad at you."

"You're lying." The words came from Mike Altman in a hoarse whisper.

"I visited Jones on her ship. They don't think they are doing anything wrong, so they didn't mind letting things slip."

Easterall turned to Mike. "Is what she is saying true?"

"I, it was nothing. It wasn't secret, they talked about it, I just—"

"Just what?" asked Easterall.

"Copied diary pages stolen from Carolyn's desk and gave them to Eva Jones through Hardy Denton," Lindsay replied before Mike could answer. "That's why Denton was here that night. He was probably here other nights before that, receiving information stolen by Mike from the archaeology project."

Lindsay turned to Mike. "Which one of you tried to break into Harper's room to get the whole diary? You? It used to be your apartment before we came. You didn't realize that Lewis had changed all the locks. It must have been frustrating. Now, Easterall, you wait in the break room, and Lewis will get to you when he's finished. We have important business."

Easterall stood for a moment, clearly not wanting to back down. Ramirez broke the silence.

"Mr. Altman. Please do not leave the building. I want to speak with you."

That got both of them moving.

Lindsay closed the door behind them and sat down. Trey and Lewis looked at Lindsay, speechless. Slowly a smile spread across Lewis's face.

"He denied you computer time, didn't he?"

"It was the way he did it."

"Well, tell me how he did it, so if I have to deny you anything I won't do it that way."

"When did you arrive at all those conclusions?" Ramirez asked.

"Just now. They just materialized in my head. I knew Mike had heard us when Harper fell into the quicksand. He used the term *hysterical* to describe us, and I guessed that he had witnessed the whole thing. When I confronted him later, he confirmed my suspicion. Jones's lawyer used the word *hysterical* to describe me, then Easterall used it again. Mike showed up at the lab the same evening that Denton was here, and I later heard the copy machine running behind a locked door. I just made a leap."

"So, it was a bluff?"

"I had a lot of information."

"It was a bluff. A good bluff." Ramirez rose. "I need to talk to Altman, in case he decides to get lost on the island. I'll finish my discussion with all of you later."

"So, does this solve everything?" Lewis asked. "It seems to me that all the facts point to Mike Altman."

"I don't know. Maybe," Lindsay replied. "I don't know why

Mike would kill Denton, unless perhaps he also killed Keith Teal, and Denton witnessed it and was blackmailing him."

"I like the way you make these paths from words to small events to a larger picture," said Trey.

Lindsay shrugged. "I may be wrong."

"You weren't wrong about his copying the diary translations," Lewis said.

"I can't see Mike opening that chest and stealing artifacts," Lindsay said.

"But you were afraid he might destroy artifacts in the lab," Trey reminded her.

"Yes, but none of the artifacts in the warehouse were destroyed. A select few were taken."

"Jones, you think?" asked Lewis.

"I can't see her leaving some of that stuff, not the gold coins, the silver, or the Chinese box or—or none of it," Lindsay said. "That has me puzzled."

"I feel like most of the puzzle is solved," Lewis responded. He started to rise when someone knocked on the door. It was the two new security guards. The two of them were dressed in suits and looked as if they worked for the Secret Service. Lindsay hoped they had brought a change of clothes. They came in followed by John.

Lewis made introductions. Trey pulled more chairs from the weather room so that everyone fit around the table while Lewis filled Tom Bowers and Robert Eberhardt in on the latest information.

"Did Mike put the message on Lindsay's computer?" John asked.

"We don't know that," Lewis replied.

"That would be the message you told us about?" Bowers asked John. John nodded. "So, at least some of the break-ins have been solved."

"It seems so," said Trey.

Bowers, the apparent spokesman of the two, laced his hands in front of him and addressed Lewis. "I know you mentioned letting the current security guard go, but I think if we put a desk in the lobby area facing the front door and let him man it, his proclivity for reading on the job won't matter. He'll see whoever might try to come in. I'll stay in the Magdalena House here, and Robert in the warehouse. We'll make rounds outside around the buildings and docks at random times. I think that will prevent anyone from trying anything else."

Lindsay liked the plan, particularly the part about keeping Dale Delosier. Not that she especially wanted him to keep his job, but she admired people who could use available resources effectively. She felt safe.

"I'm going to get to work," she told Lewis. "Do you want a drawing of the latest skeleton?"

"The one you think is Valerian?" Lewis asked. "Definitely."

Lindsay went through the weather room where both of the meteorologists were at work. "How's the weather?" she asked.

"We have a tropical storm in the Carribean. It doesn't look like it will come this way, but you guys may get some heavy winds out at the dam." William smiled at her. "That should make for a little excitement."

"We told John," Terry said, frowning at William. "He's going to install extra pumps in case the waves get high. But everything looks fine."

"I'm glad you guys are here," Lindsay told them.

"We won't let a storm sneak up on you," Terry said.

Lindsay waved at them as she went past the door where the emergency evacuation plan was posted. She realized she hadn't read it and didn't really know what to do if a bad storm hit. She made a mental note to look over the emergency procedures.

She was thinking about that when she ran into Tessa Altman on the stairway leading down to the lab. Tessa's blonde hair stood out in perfect corkscrew curls around her face. She was very pretty and usually wore makeup, which wasn't common for people doing fieldwork. The crow's feet around her eyes and slight lines in her forehead suggested she was older than her husband Mike.

"I was looking for you," she said, her face suddenly angry. "Do you know what you've done? Do you?"

"Apparently not," Lindsay replied.

"It's important for Mike to work with Easterall. You've put that in jeopardy."

"Not I," Lindsay protested. "His behavior may have something to do with it."

"You bitch—"

"What did you call me?" Lindsay stepped toward Tessa and

backed her against the wall. "Did you happen to write those sentiments in a message on my computer?"

"What are you talking about? Back away from me."

"Answer my question. If things are getting out of hand around
here, you and your husband share the blame. Did you send me an
obscene message?"

"No! Why are you blaming me?"

"Because the author used that word."

"It's not like I'm the only one who uses it. You probably
deserved it."

"You think so? You think I deserve to be cut in half and left on
a morgue table?"

Tessa's eyes widened. Lindsay backed away from her.

"I didn't send you any message. I was referring to your cal-
lousness toward Mike. This island is our research project. You may
not appreciate it, but we do important things here."

"I do appreciate it. Most archaeologists are conservationists.
Like I told Easterall, what Mike did with Jones is the same thing as
my offering to help polluters because I don't like you. Do you see
how reprehensible that would be? Jones doesn't care about history.
She wants to loot valuable artifacts, and Mike has been helping
her."

"Eva Jones came to him. He didn't think it was a big deal,
because Carolyn let Gretchen read part of the diary one day."

"What about trying to break into the apartment? It frightened
Harper, and she's done nothing to you. She was assigned by Lewis
to stay there."

"That was our home. We still had a key. Okay, I'm sorry. We
weren't going to steal anything, just borrow a page or two to copy.
That's all Jones said she needed—just a page or two."

"So she wanted a Rosetta Stone," Lindsay said, almost to herself. "What does she have that needs translating?"

"I have no idea."

"Why didn't Mike come to help us when we were lost?"

"He heard you telling the person who fell into the pit that she
would be all right. You seemed to know quicksand, and you
weren't that far away from home. Just four miles. He was busy
with his work, recording some observations. And he didn't know
you had found a body. He only heard screaming. Good God, nothing like this happened here before all of you got here."

"Are the pits marked on a map?"

"Yes, of course. There's one hanging in the lobby behind the elephant ears."

"Did you know Keith Teal?"

"Don't try to pin this on me or Mike. He came home that night after seeing you were in the lab and didn't meet Denton. We had nothing to do with the murders."

"I'm not saying you did. I was just asking a question."

"Well, I don't want to answer any of your questions. I want you to leave us alone. It's bad enough that you've made problems with Easterall. Now you've got the FBI talking to him."

"It was Mike and Easterall who came barging into Lewis's office threatening to run us off. Easterall brought the FBI attention to himself. If you think of anything suspicious you know or saw and feel like telling me, let me know."

Carolyn was still fuming over the artifacts when Lindsay made it down to the lab. "How badly were they damaged?" Lindsay asked.

"I don't know. They were still damp. I think I got to them in time. Did you see Tessa? She was down here looking for you."

"I saw her."

"She looked mad," Carolyn said.

"She was. I wish all of these hostilities would stop."

"They started it. If you want something to take your mind off it, you can look at HSkR4 if you like."

"Thanks," Lindsay said. First, however, she took another look at HSkR2, the Asian skeleton Lewis had found. The one who had a good chance of being Valerian's servant, Jen.

She examined the specific points on the skeleton that Dr. Rosen suggested would not be involved if the bone necrosis were from deep-sea diving. The only bones that showed pathological remodeling were the proximal ends of the humerus and femur and their respective sockets. The evidence was still suggestive of deep-sea diving, but it was only suggestive. She took out her notebook where she had stuck the list of diseases Rosen had given her. She thought she would ask a graduate student to fax her photographs of X-rays or other information on the diseases that might be contained in medical journals at the UGA library.

She started to put her notebook back when she noticed that the post card she had borrowed from Boote was missing. She remembered sticking it next to Rosen's list. She searched her desk and around the floor. Nothing. Perhaps it was in the university's SUV. She'd make a note to look. She hated losing something that she said she would return.

Lindsay replaced the Asian bones and took out HSkR4, the skeleton she thought might be Valerian. Odd if it were, with Carolyn conserving his possessions and she analyzing his remains. Unwilling to consign Valerian to an early death, Lindsay thought of the remains simply as skeleton 4. He was about five-six and left-handed. His left humerus and left tibia had been broken and healed, but probably didn't give him much trouble. Other than the breaks, his bones were healthy, as were his teeth, with the exception of one molar that had abscessed and healed after it was pulled. It must have been painful. His muscle attachments suggested that he was muscular.

She was glad to be back working with bones and wished many more would be found. But it would mean they went down with the ship—a sad thought. Lindsay put the bones back in the tub.

"I have something for you." Korey came from the darkroom waving some eight-by-tens in his hand.

"These are the photos from the warehouse?" Lindsay took them out of his hand. "I appreciate this."

"Anything to help you find whoever did this," he said.

Lindsay put the photographs on her desk and examined them. They showed what she had seen with her own eyes and nothing else, no pattern or clue jumped out at her. The stain she thought might be the toe print of a shoe still looked like one, but it would be impossible to—she took out a magnifying glass and looked at the mark. She went to Carolyn and asked to see the manicure set.

"It's metal. It will be all right won't it?" Lindsay asked.

"Will this somehow help you catch the bastard who did this?"

"Perhaps," Lindsay responded. Carolyn handed her the folding set of grooming tools. "This is beautiful." Lindsay gently caressed them with her fingertips.

"Silver often gets a nice patina like that."

Lindsay placed the silver artifact on the bone board, measured it, and gave it back to Carolyn. Next she measured the same artifact in the picture and figured out the ratio of the two.

Korey looked over her shoulder. "You know, this is like working in a crime lab. I might put it on my résumé."

Lindsay took a ruler and measured the toe print from the tip to the side where it began a slight curve before disappearing into the whole of the damp area. She multiplied her ratio by the measurement and looked at the stain under the glass again. It looked bulky like a running shoe. She subtracted for the shoe and did the math for the whole foot.

"Oh, I see what you're doing. That's clever." Korey bobbed his head up and down in appreciation.

"Just standard stuff," Lindsay said.

"What?" said Carolyn, coming to look over her shoulder.

"She's finding out how big his feet are," Korey said.

"What size shoe do you wear?" Lindsay asked Korey, grinning up at him.

"Who, me? Ten."

"I believe this is a guy because the feet are fairly large for a female, and he wears a size eleven to twelve shoe. I'd say he is probably between five-nine and six feet. But that is a very rough estimation, so don't go around measuring people."

"What'd I tell you? Just like a crime lab."

"Lindsay." She looked up at Lewis, who had just walked into the lab. "I wanted to say I appreciated your quick thinking this morning. It short-circuited anything Easterall was thinking about trying."

"I was thinking I behaved rather badly," she said.

"Badly? No, you were great."

Lindsay shrugged. "Can I talk to you?"

"Sure, shoot."

"Privately?"

"Let's go to my office."

The corner table was becoming too familiar, and evocative of less than pleasant feelings. It was the place where all serious conversations were held.

"Can I get you anything to drink?" asked Lewis.

"If you have something cold, I'd like that."

He got the two of them cold Coca-Colas in bottles. Lindsay took a long drink.

"While I'm in your good graces, I'd like to ask you some questions," she said.

Chapter 27

"MAYBE I SHOULD have gotten us a stiffer drink," Lewis joked.

"I spoke with Tessa. From what she told me, it appears that Eva Jones wanted copies of a few pages of the original diary to compare with the pages she obtained from Harper's translation."

"Indeed. Then she was trying to construct a key. She has something she's trying to translate, do you think?"

"Yes, I think so, but the stolen diary pages could serve as a key to translating her pages only if whatever she has was written by our diarist. Or—"

"Or what?" asked Lewis.

"Or she saw the articles in the paper that suggested that the diary is written in a kind of code that Harper had to translate. Perhaps to Eva Jones a code is a code is a code. If that's what she thought, then she believed that the key to breaking our code would also break her code."

"Then too bad she didn't get a copy of some original pages. The futile attempt to find the code would have proved very frustrating to her." Lewis stood up and walked over to his desk.

"You know, I quit smoking a year ago, but I'd sure like to have a cigarette." Lewis let out a breath. "So, she must be looking for the silver galleon. I had hoped she was simply in search of the antiquities from the *Estrella*. Did Eva Jones tell Tessa or Mike about the silver galleon?"

"I don't think so. I think she is as anxious as we are to keep it a secret." Lindsay hesitated a moment. "Who knows about the second ship?"

He turned to her. "What do you mean?"

"Whom did you tell?"

Lewis sat back down and took a long drink of his Coke. "The

president of the university, the chancellor, and a couple of businessmen." Lindsay closed her eyes. "I impressed upon them the importance of secrecy," he added.

"Why did you tell the businessmen?"

"I wanted funding."

Lindsay leaned forward."What do they hope to get out of it?"

"I told them that the contents of the ship are to remain intact. That they are artifacts."

"But you were counting on them thinking about the dollar value and forgetting about the prohibition."

"Of course."

"Whatever items may be found on the galleon, even bars of gold, are artifacts."

"Lindsay, once it's found, the state, the U.S. government—everyone is going to want their cut." Lindsay laughed. Lewis frowned at her. "What?"

"*Cut.* When the Spanish captains took the gold and silver ingots to the House of Trade, the assayer would take a knife and cut a slice off the bar to test for purity. They would keep the slice. That was their 'cut.'"

"Ah, interesting—and fitting."

"They're artifacts," Lindsay said again.

Lewis took another drink and looked at the bottle for a long moment, then at Lindsay. "My father was a salesman. He sold a lot of things throughout his career—vacuum cleaners, encyclopedias, cookware, farm equipment. He liked it and was good at it. We had a nice house, he bought me and my brothers all the sports uniforms and equipment we needed for school, we had piano lessons and he sent my sister, me, and two brothers to college on the commissions he made from selling things. He had this maroon notebook in which he wrote down all his appointments, numbers, and contacts. When he came home from a trip, or a day's calls, he'd come in the kitchen and put his billfold, that notebook, his watch, and comb in a tray he kept there for that purpose. Then he'd hang his coat on the back of the kitchen chair and sit down at the table with Mother and they would tell each other about their day. Sometimes we kids would join them. He did this all the time I knew him. I was in college when he died. He came home one day and while he was talking with Mother, he had a stroke and died."

Lewis looked at a painting of an orchid hanging on the wall, his eyes out of focus, as if looking into the past. "I came home that day and went into the kitchen. My aunt had put a linen napkin over the tray. I lifted it to look at my father's things, and what struck me was how most of those things went out of use with his death. His billfold had his driver's licence, his social security card, his emergency information, and his maroon notebook had his appointments. No one could use them like they were. They could be keepsakes, but that's all. But not the watch."

Lewis looked back at Lindsay. "Those items were like a Mississippian ceramic bowl. It will never be used to hold corn or acorns or whatever again. Its use died with the people who made it, and now it's studied, or sits in a museum. That's what an artifact is." He held up a hand before Lindsay could protest. "'Any object or observable phenomenon whose properties are the result of human activity.' I know. But there is this quality about artifacts that has to do with their functionality being stuck in the time from whence they came. An ancient carved African face mask can never be a ceremonial object again, but is a work of art to be looked at."

"And gold?"

Lewis took out his pocket watch. "This is my father's watch. I can still use it to tell time. I can use it the same way he did. The gold is the watch."

"You don't think you are rationalizing?"

"I'm sure I am. But I'm not sure I'm wrong to do so. I'm not talking about taking the jewels out of the gold ornaments, I'm talking about the gold and silver ingots. Their use has not timed out."

"Lewis—I don't know what to say."

"Say you disagree. That's fine. But you can't stand against all the officials who are going to want some of the gold for some purpose other than sitting in a museum. Besides, do you know what kind of security would be required to keep a treasure like that together? The university couldn't afford it."

"Nevertheless, I'll work to keep it together—provided we find it—provided it's out there in the first place."

"Fair enough. I'm feeling very kindly toward you at the moment. You gave me enough information to halt Easterall in his tracks. Do you still need time on the supercomputer?"

"No. I got a friend to run my data at her university."

"See, more ammunition. It's not right that our faculty should have to go to another university to analyze their data because

Easterall is hogging all the time." Lindsay shook her head. She had a sudden vision of Lewis and her fighting off invaders, him shooting and her reloading his pistols. "What were you doing just before I came up?" he asked. "It looked interesting. It had Korey and Carolyn excited."

"Oh, I found what looks like a toe print of a shoe in the photographs Korey took in the warehouse this morning. I think the thief is a male about"—she shrugged—"five-seven to six feet tall with a size eleven or twelve shoe."

"You're joking. You can do that?"

"There is a regularity of size in bones, that is why we can make stature tables. But, before you get excited—the print may not be from a shoe; small people can have big feet and big people can have small feet. This is a guess, it may be a complete fantasy."

"Still—it's a possibility."

"Yes."

Lindsay showed him a photograph of the lab floor. "Look at these marks here. I think the rectangular one may have been a book. This one"—she pointed to a stain that appeared to be about a foot long and a couple of inches wide—"could be a scroll of some kind—a map maybe. I'm wondering if this is some attempt to—I don't know—"

"Someone is still looking for information about the galleon, and for some reason thought they would find it in this chest?"

"Far-fetched, I know."

"Not as far-fetched as everything else that's been going on around here. You don't think Jones did this because she would have taken the silver and other items of value, but could someone have done it for her? Mike maybe, or Tessa, or one of the other biologists?"

"Maybe. I didn't confront Tessa with this, but I imagine Ramirez will."

"Do you think that Mike is the murderer?" Lewis asked.

"I don't know."

"Do you think Tessa sent you the warning message?"

"I confronted her, and her surprise seemed genuine. So I don't know that, either," she said.

"I think Ramirez will be focusing on them. I'm glad we have a rapport with him." Lindsay shook her head. "We don't?"

"Don't let his friendliness fool you. He's not our friend. He's not our enemy, either. There's been a murder—two murders, and he has no idea who committed them. Murderers can be as charming as FBI agents. Ramirez is good at his job. He makes you feel like confiding in him, telling him things."

Lewis looked as if his feelings had been hurt. Lindsay almost laughed. "And people call me cynical," he said.

"If it were social, he would be a friend. But this isn't. He suspects everyone."

"Even you?"

"I'm sure it crossed his mind that I may have sent myself that note to throw him off guard. It happens. I don't think he seriously thinks I did, because it doesn't fit the facts as a whole. For one thing, Teal was dead before I arrived on the scene, and I'm sure he tracked my movements before I arrived."

"Mine, too?"

"Yes. I'm sorry, Lewis, yours, too."

"I thought he was on our side."

Lindsay did laugh this time. "Don't tell me that you never operate that way?"

"Does this mean you don't trust me?"

"I never trust anyone who always gets what they want."

Lewis grinned at her.

Debriefing was short and focused on the excavation. Neither Trey, Lewis, nor Steven mentioned the break-in at the warehouse. It was not the finds that got everyone's attention. It was Terry Lyons, the meteorologist.

"It looks like Tropical Storm Harriette has turned into Hurricane Harriette—a category one hurricane. Category one means wind speeds of no more than ninety-five miles an hour. It's heading northward. That's typical. The steering winds are not strong; that means tracking it is difficult. Right now it's far to the south, but we will get some high wind and waves."

"If you can't track it, what are we paying you for?" called Jeff from the back of the room.

"So we can warn you in time to get your butts out of the way."

When John spoke, he had everyone's attention.

"You've all heard us test the alarm a few times. We will be testing once a day from now on at eleven in the morning. The test will be two long signals. The real thing will be the same signal over and over. It won't stop. When you hear the signal, it will be because the waves are getting too high. It doesn't mean the hurricane is upon us. You will have plenty of time."

"If the alarm sounds for real," said Trey, "the evacuation plan will go into effect. You should have had a copy of the evacuation plan in your original packet of materials. I'm handing out additional copies in case you can't find yours. Read it over. The general procedures are as follows: Everyone but the skeleton crew—you know who you are—will leave the dam immediately. The skeleton crew who remain behind will stake screening material over the wreck. Hopefully the screen will hold it in place. And we will flood the site at the last minute. Being drowned in water again won't harm it and the covering of water will protect the excavation from the force of any storm waters. John's crew will be the last to leave. They will remove the roof so that the wind doesn't uproot it and damage the dam. We are very optimistic about the survivability of the dam in high winds. The important thing is not to worry. We have plenty of time. If evacuation of the dam is necessary, you will not go to the island. The boats will take you straight to the mainland, and from there to an inland shelter we have arranged. Now, go have dinner and don't worry. The storm is a long way off, and there's no indication it's coming here."

"Yeah, right," someone muttered. "That makes me feel great. If it's not murders, it's hurricanes."

"And all diving is suspended until further notice. Is that understood? No diving for any purpose—except John's crew," Trey ordered. "The dive teams will either help Carolyn and Korey in the lab, or work on the excavation."

"We got a third choice?" asked one of the divers.

"Yeah," said another. "How about we do a little anthropological research on River Street in Savannah."

"Yes, there's a third choice," said Trey. "You can write reports."

The divers groaned.

John made his way to Lindsay. "You going to have dinner with Nate and Sarah on the barge?" he asked.

"Yes, want to join me?"

"Sure, but I can't stay long. There's a lot to do at the dam."

"I can imagine."

Lindsay put her arm through his and walked out with him. Everything will be all right, she said to herself. The hurricane will stay out in the ocean and John's dam will be fine and the ship will be fine. She searched his profile to see what he was feeling, but he wasn't showing any emotion.

"Are you all right?" she asked.

He took her hand and squeezed it. "Fine. This is one of the dangers of building in the open ocean. Hurricanes come with the territory. My dam will hold."

"Hey, Lindsay." Bobbie came up behind her. "You staying on the barge or at Harper's tonight?"

"The barge. We're going there to eat. Want to join us?"

"I heard it was macaroni and cheese." She wrinkled her nose. "Luke's taking me to a little restaurant on the mainland."

"You tell Luke to watch the weather," John said.

"We will. Lindsay, I found this diving today." She gave her a long, slender spike tied with fishing line to a quarter with a hole in it. "The rod or whatever was stuck in the sea floor. It looked like a trap of some sort for something. I know you said you found a quarter like this. Thought you'd like to have it."

"How odd. Thanks. Have a good time and watch the weather."

Bobbie trotted off toward the dock.

"You know, after you raise them, they're on their own," John said.

"And who said that, *Father Knows Best*?"

"My aunt. Let's go eat."

Lindsay sat down with a plate of food across from Sarah and Nate. The galley was not as big as she had supposed for the number of crew the barge held. She wondered if the designers meant for the sailors to eat in shifts. The tables were plain metal with matching hard metal chairs. Nothing fancy on a barge. John sat down next to her. It would have been a good night to go out to eat on the mainland. The barge bobbed up and down and Lindsay felt a little queasy.

"We don't have an alibi, neither of us," Sarah said.

"Join the club," Lindsay replied, opening a carton of milk. "No one does. You expect everyone to be in bed at night."

"But what surprises me," Nate said, "is that everyone appeared to be sleeping alone. What does that say about us?"

Lindsay laughed at him. "Look, I'm sorry about this." She looked down at her plate. Macaroni and cheese, green beans, and applesauce. She felt as though she were back in junior high. But then again, macaroni and cheese was always soothing to her when her stomach was unsettled.

"It sticks to your ribs," said Nate, as if reading her mind.

"How's your arm?" Lindsay asked.

"Fine. You did a good job, Doc." Nate took a drink of milk out of the carton.

"What happened to your hands?" asked Lindsay.

Nate looked at the rash and his Calamine lotion–covered hands. "I think it's poison ivy, but I'll be damned if I know how I got it out here on the water. But it's just on my hands, thank heavens. I was in misery with it every summer as a kid. All I had to do to get infected was walk past the stuff."

Lindsay couldn't help but think about the other evening and the person fleeing into the woods. Had Mike Altman not confessed, she would have suspected Nate.

"Tell me anything you know about Denton or Teal," Lindsay said.

"Didn't know Denton," Nate replied, "except from the correspondence Trey let me read. He was raising all kinds of ruckus over John here winning the contract. We're all lucky the university didn't go with the low bid. We'd all be drowned rats by now."

"I didn't know him, either," Sarah said. "I'm glad I didn't. He seemed thoroughly disagreeable, from what I've heard."

"How about Keith Teal?" Lindsay asked.

"Yes, we both knew him. Trey had us trying to socialize him in the ways of archaeologists. I'm afraid we failed."

"When was the last time you saw him?" Lindsay asked.

Nate looked at Sarah. "I don't know. Sometime after the big storm a few months ago—sometime in May. I guess that'd be about two months. He helped us with some boat repairs."

"Did you ever hear from the Coast Guard about who attacked you?"

Nate shook his head. "I haven't. I think they told Trey that the Jones woman denied any connection. But we know that. I suppose without more to go on there's nothing they can do. If the biology people scuba dived, I'd think it was them. I heard that the FBI's talking to Mike about stealing diary pages."

"Who told you?"

"Trey, just a while ago. I tell you, if I run into Mike—"

"You'll let the FBI handle it," Sarah interrupted. "I don't suppose we can talk about something more pleasant?"

"Do either of you fish?" Lindsay asked. Neither Sara nor Nate did. Lindsay looked at John. He didn't either.

"Did you say fish?" Steven Nemo sat down with them. "I love it."

Lindsay tried to remember back when she went with her father and brother. "You know those spinning blades?"

"Spinner blades. What about them?"

"How much do they cost?"

"You want to go fishing? I have a bunch I can give you."

"I was just wondering. Are they more than twenty-five cents each?"

"No, that'd be kind of high. I get them by the tens. They come to about fifteen cents apiece, I would guess."

"What do you catch with them?"

"Well, bass, trout, crappie—a bunch of different fish."

"Do you ever stake them out on the bottom and let the fish come to them, then go pick the fish up?" Lindsay had never heard of that kind of fishing before, but she wasn't a fisherman.

"What?" Steven laughed until tears formed in his eyes. "Who told you that? They taking you snipe hunting?"

"Hello, guys." Lewis pulled up a chair on the corner between Nate and Sarah. "What's so funny?"

"Don't ever take Lindsay fishing with you," Steven replied. "She's got some funny notions about how to do it." Steven took a bite of food, still laughing. The others joined in, including Lindsay, mainly because he was laughing so hard.

"Nate," Lewis said, "how's the computer program coming?"

"Great. I recalculated the *Estrella* finds. Out of seven items, two came within twenty yards of the *Estrella*, two within fifty yards, one within a hundred, and two within a half-mile."

Lewis slapped him on the back. "That's great, Nate, great. That's much closer, that's significant."

Nate didn't seem to enjoy praise from Lewis. Lindsay knew how he felt. Praise from Lewis meant more work at a faster pace. Steven was thinking the same thing, apparently, from the eye contact he made with Lindsay.

"I've put in a lot of new data that I'm getting from different places," said Nate.

265

"Have you tried the other?" asked Lewis.

Lindsay understood the 'other' meant the gold coins she had found.

"You know," Nate said, "the last time I tried to get computer time, there was a problem, and I've got more variables now."

"I had a long talk with Easterall today. I don't think there will be a problem. You can get on it this evening."

"I have a lot more data I'd like to plug in. The more data, the closer to the target, and the less time we spend on the diving end of it."

"Do you need help keying in the data? I can hire—"

Nate was shaking his head. "I'd just have to double-check their work. I'd rather do it myself. I have to have confidence it's right. Accuracy is essential."

"I'm glad it's going so well." Lewis turned to Lindsay. "Do you have a drawing of the last sailor yet?"

"No, but I have a plan. I can draw with my feet and one eye and examine bones with my hands and the other eye."

Lewis stood up, flashing his white teeth. "If you can do that, it'd be great." Lindsay and Steven made eye contact again.

When Lewis left, Steven asked John if Lewis had been that pushy with him when he was building the dam.

"Once," John said.

"What did you say to him?"

"I told him he could have quick or he could have dead."

They laughed.

"I suppose that had a lot more impact coming from an Indian than it would from us palefaces," Steven said.

John grinned. "I think it probably did."

"I think I've had my fill of macaroni and cheese." Lindsay picked up her dishes and took them to the kitchen, followed by John.

"I have to go soon. How about we take a walk on the deck?" he said.

"I'd love to." Lindsay thanked Nate and Sarah as she left.

"You know, Lindsay, I have this fish whistle you can call them with. I'll sell it to you," Steven yelled as they were leaving.

The sun was near the horizon, bright orange against a sky that had all the shades of blue. Dark clouds were moving across the face of it, and the wind blew so hard it whipped their long hair. In the opposite direction, seaward, the sky was a navy blue and dark with more clouds. Lindsay looked over at the cofferdam, shining like a jewel in the crown. John stood behind Lindsay and put his arms around her, shielding her from the biting wind.

"We had more wind than this when we were building her. I designed her for the ocean." His breath was warm in her ear. "She will protect your Spanish ship."

John made the cofferdam sound like a goddess rising from the sea floor guarding one of the ocean's mysteries. Lindsay turned around in his arms and faced him. He put his hands on her shoulders.

"Lindsay."

"What?"

"Take care of yourself."

"Is that what you were going to say?"

"No. You are going to do what you will do. Just be careful doing it."

Lindsay kissed him. "You better go take care of your mistress over there so she won't get cranky and drown us."

⚓

Lindsay was in bed reading when Bobbie came in.

"The sea is rough out there. I think Luke and I traveled as far vertically as we did horizontally." Bobbie changed into a night-shirt, brushed her teeth, and crawled into bed.

"You have a nice time with Luke?" Lindsay asked.

"Yes, I did. We didn't get along at first, but we do now. Did you figure out what that thing is?"

"The quarter? No."

"Maybe it was marking something."

"Maybe," Lindsay agreed.

"You know, we have a map that shows a trail of artifacts, and we have grids we search. But my team hardly ever searches within the parameters of the expected area of recovery. I've been think-ing—I mean, it's almost like Nate is looking for another ship."

"Don't think about it."

"Why?" Lindsay didn't say anything. "Lindsay?" Bobbie jumped out of bed and came over and sat on the foot of her bed. "You know something, don't you?"

"Bobbie. I can't say anything, and I won't lie to you. But please, don't voice your thoughts on this subject out loud."

"Oh, my. Wouldn't that be fun? But why would it be a secret? I guess you wouldn't want the Jones woman to loot it. What kind of ship is it?"

"Bobbie, go to bed."

Bobbie crossed her legs and got comfortable. "I heard you cleaned Easterall's clock today. Mike's, too."

Lindsay put down her reading and told Bobbie about the conversations.

"I'll bet that was satisfying," Bobbie said.

"Well, I confess it was."

"Interesting stuff in the chest. I like it that it's Valerian's. Do you think Mike broke into it?"

"I don't know."

"Well, you've got to hurry and solve all this. What are you reading?"

"Harper finished the translation. Yours is on your bed if you're interested."

Bobbie jumped off Lindsay's bed and settled into hers with the diary.

Chapter 28

A Passenger's Diary: Part IV

From a voyage on the Spanish Galleon
Estrella de España, c. 1558
—Translated by Harper Latham

A MAN WAS accused of stealing food today. The steward, I understand, is swift in his punishments for thefts. I do not know all the particulars, but the steward's food storage area was broken into and some biscuits were found wrapped in a cloak in the man's sea chest. Valerian and I stood together on the deck to watch the punishment. We didn't have to, but we did. The crew had to watch, and I was listening to their grumblings as they assembled. I discovered that the man was the same one whom the boatswain had favored over the rescued sailor, Sancho, in the matter of sleeping space. This made me suspicious and I searched the crew's faces for Sancho and found him near the front, a smirk on his face.

The sailor had his head bowed as he was taken up to the poop deck by a couple of his mates where he would be tied to the shrouds to receive his lashes. I felt for the sailor and, as at many other times on this voyage, felt fortunate for my station. Because I am of the Order of Santiago, I would be exempt from such punishment, even by the House of Trade. I am thankful for my good service as a soldier, the pure Spanish blood of my ancestors—and my wealth. I noted a serious expression on Valerian's face. Perhaps he was thinking my thoughts, thinking about his own mixed heritage and the fact that it is only his own personal wealth that gives him any protection.

I looked back toward the poop deck in time to see the man

break away and leap down, race across deck, streaking past Valerian and me—the boatswain and steward in pursuit. We were all surprised. His comrades did not try to stop him. However, some of the soldiers on deck did, only to be menaced by the sailors. The man sprinted across the deck to the bow of the ship and leaped down onto the prow, where the pursuit stopped.

I was puzzled. The man was at the end and could go no farther. Why didn't the boatswain and steward take him? "Sanctuary," Valerian whispered to me. I watched, fascinated.

"You were already taken," said the boatswain. "Come back. It will be worse if you don't."

The sailor shook his head vigorously. "I protest. I am innocent."

"We found the biscuits in your chest," said the steward.

The sailor pointed to Sancho. "He put them there. You know that's true," the sailor implored the steward. I saw the steward and the boatswain exchange glances. "Please," he said, "let me take it to the House o' Trade." They looked to the captain and he nodded. "Oh, thank you," said the sailor, kneeling. "You are most generous."

That ended the episode. I discovered that the crewmen are not without some recourse. That is a good thing.

López approached me today. I was at my favorite post on the weather deck looking out at the ocean when he came up behind me. "Why are you on this voyage?" he asked of me. "You are a man of a wealthy family. The captain said that your brother requested the favor that you sail with us, but I think that the favor was for someone more important, eh?"

There are many things I could have said to him. I could have said, "You are acquainted with my wife's cousin. She and my wife were raised together and, though quite different in appearance, they are as alike as twins in temperament." But that would have defamed my Luisa to another (however accurate the portrayal of her). I could have hinted at misjudgment in the management of the meager inheritance left to me, and said that I asked my brother to find me a position in the New World. That would not be true, but it is so common a story that it is credible. I could have said I am adventurous to the point of suicidal, which I am beginning to believe is true, having agreed to come on this journey. However, such explanations would have exposed me as a man with something to hide, so I said to him the only thing that would make him believe all of the above explanations (if they were ever told him). "My dear friend López, you ask things that are not your concern." As a man of honor, I refused to answer his excessively probing questions. But I could not help but wonder if Valerian had told him of my midnight ramblings in the bowels of the ship.

I saw something wondrous today. The ocean has been calm and the air warm. The ships in the fleet are spaced wide apart. Life is good. Valerian and I spend much time on the upper decks watching the sea. It can be hypnotic. As a child, I was told many stories about monsters that lurk in the seas and on distant lands. I see now how such stories come to arise. I heard the thing before I saw it. Valerian was about to explain something to me when I heard the hiss of a serpent. A sailor yelled and pointed and the men scrambled. I looked to see what could cause such a sound and at a distance not more than the *Rosario* was from us, I saw the supple, shimmering neck of a sea serpent. That was my first thought and I think I must have exclaimed, for Valerian gripped my arm and I heard him laugh. I soon discovered that the creature was a column of water, lifted by what, I can't imagine. (Valerian says the wind, but Valerian also thinks he can fly.) It moved across the water as if alive. Bellisaro yelled instructions to the helmsman and we veered away, as did others in our convoy. No ship was hurt by it, but I understand it could have destroyed us had we the misfortune to sail through it. I watched it until it disappeared into the horizon.

The evening last, following the sighting of the monster, Valerian and I played a game of chess. Before going to bed, we had drinks with the captain and López in the captain's cabin. We were jovial (as were the crew). We have not many more days left before we reach Havana. After drinks, I bid him good night and went to bed. I slept soundly during the night. I awoke late, but refreshed. I fancied myself becoming quite a good sailor.

I went to the forecastle deck and found that we are in a very strange place. The waters are clearest blue and the sea is calm. A strange mass of green plants floats in the water and we seem to be entangled in them. The crew, whose moods I am learning to read, are quiet but nervous. Some stare at the sails, for there is little wind. I looked to see if the rest of the fleet are thus quelled. They are gone. I searched the seas in all directions, squinting at the horizon for a familiar silhouette. We are alone in this strange sea.

When I discovered our situation, I felt fear rise in my stomach, then felt a hand on my shoulder. Turning, I faced Valerian. I saw in his eyes a look of intimate knowledge, his lips upturned in a sliver of a smile. "Do not be afraid of adventure, my friend," he said.

The ship moves slowly through the watery forest. Valerian says the slowness is not the floating vines, but the lack of wind, but that is all he will tell me. I realize that whatever it is the three of them are up to, I will find out soon enough. I watch Bellisaro. He does not use his instruments as much, as he has the crew tend the sails and the helmsman tend the tiller. Watching him calms me. He is so engrossed in the progress of the ship, his face so intent on his task, and it came to me how much he loves the sea and the challenge of guiding a ship through its waters, catching whatever wind he can.

The way through the sea is slow, for there has been little wind for three days. Today we were completely becalmed. Bellisaro gave the order for the guardián to lower the ship's boats. Once in the water, the guardián directed the oarsmen and they towed the ship. Progress now is even slower and the crew grumble. They are fearful of such a calm sea and strange plants that hang on the oars as they come out of the water.

We do, however, eat much fresh fish. It is a welcome change, and the steward is not stingy with the crew's food, as he usually is. I am glad the captain saw fit to order extra rations. Whatever mission we are on, the captain realizes the benefit of a satisfied crew.

Today was the second day towing the ship. I was fishing along with Valerian and the cook when a fish jumped out of the water and flew. Flew! Its flight wasn't far, perhaps three codos before it dipped back into the water. I have never before seen a fish fly. I hadn't known they could.

The things that delight me and Valerian make many of the sailors apprehensive. In these dead, calm waters surrounded by the seaweed and sea creatures, traveling less than a knot through the water, oppressed by the wet heat, tempers erupt at the slightest provocation. However, many men take their spirits from Bellisaro. If he does not seem worried, then neither are they. Indeed, he does not seem overly anxious, though I have noticed a growing tenseness in him throughout the voyage. But it may be my imagination. Bellisaro is not an easy man to read.

It was another day of no wind. The crew grows more restless

and short-tempered. Even Bellisaro seems to grow weary of the slow pace. The captain wanted to cut the food ration. I thought that would be a disaster. I overheard López talk him out of it. Sometimes the captain is a fool. He knows nothing about the sea or sailing the ship, which is common among ship's captains. I find that odd. There are a great many rules and allowances in the House of Trade that I question. But then again, here I am, trying to do their bidding. I'm beginning to think that sending me on this errand is yet another example of their folly.

I passed the day in my cabin reading a book that Valerian loaned me—a strange text written by an English Franciscan friar named Bacon. I'm not sure what I think of it.

Tempers are worse. There is still no wind. The captain yells at Bellisaro as if he were controlling the wind and, out of contrariness, forbidding it to blow. The men are afraid we will remain stranded here. At our slow pace, I'm not sure they aren't right. It is hot.

The poisonous Sancho's cleverness turned against him today. I would like to say that I pity him in his present situation. It was my father's opinion that I was not suited for the military—too tenderhearted, he said. My father was wrong. He, like many, confused my sense of justice and compassion toward the least of God's creatures with being faint-of-heart. Sancho did the unthinkable. He struck the boatswain, his superior. Out at sea, as on a military mission, discipline can be the difference between success and failure, life and death. His action required swift and severe punishment. I confess, I was also relieved at Sancho's plight because I had been brooding over not being able to tell the captain about his plotting.

The origin of the argument began with the boatswain reprimanding Sancho for not carrying out his tasks. Sancho answered by striking the boatswain across the face. The boatswain hauled him for lashes, which was a light punishment in my opinion, but I believe the boatswain was allowing for the frustration of our present circumstances. I was on deck and saw them as they came up to the poop deck, the boatswain grasping Sancho tightly so he would not bolt for the prow. The boatswain was relating to the captain Sancho's offenses when Sancho accused the boatswain of blasphemy. The boatswain turned red and sputtered and denied the accusation. The captain scowled at the boatswain, forgetting Sancho and ready to punish the boatswain for this most serious offence. The boatswain did not deny yelling at Sancho but emphatically denied committing blasphemy.

Surprisingly, it was López who came to the boatswain's defense. "I was in the hold, inspecting some supplies," he said, startling everyone with his sudden proclamation. "The boatswain did not blaspheme. The man lies." I saw the sneer disappear from Sancho's face and terror come into his eyes. After López's declaration, the punishment was swift. Now Sancho stands with his left hand nailed to the mast.

Adding to our misfortunes, Valerian's servant, Jen, suffered a strange accident. He broke his arm near the shoulder. He was with the men in the boats rowing when, by the accounts of the men around him as well as his own, he pulled the oars and felt a sharp and sudden pain and couldn't use his arm. They took him to the surgeon who diagnosed the break. Jen confessed to Valerian that he had been having pains in his limbs, and indeed had started to limp, but he thought nothing of it. Valerian related all this to me over a game of chess. "For a bone to break with normal movement is vexing," he said. However, one of the most surprising things about this event is the concern shown by López and the captain to the poor Jen. These are not men who sympathize with men of Jen's station in life, but their concern is genuine.

On two occasions I have heard both López and the captain ask Valerian what they are going to do. An odd question to ask Valerian. It has something to do with Jen's illness, I believe.

This evening Valerian came to me. His eyes flashed with anger, a state in which I have never before seen Valerian. "I have a favor to ask of you, my friend," he said.

"What?" I asked.

"Will you change cabins with López? I want to bring my good servant Jen to our cabin so that he might have a chance of recuperating. López, the swine, is against it. He will not share his quarters with a servant."

"But López seems so sympathetic," I said.

"It is not sympathy, but selfishness," he said. "Look, my friend, you have the protection of your title and your wealth. I have only wealth. Jen has nothing. The two of us are in need of your goodwill and protection. Will you give it?"

"Of course," I said, though I was puzzled. "But will López mind?"

Valerian grinned. "No," he said simply.

So this evening we changed cabins, and Valerian brought Jen and gave him his cot. Valerian is a kind man, more kind than my father accused me of being. Jen has considerable discomfort. Valerian has a red-lacquered ornate box in his chest. I have seen others like it from China. It contains vials with various powders and herbs. He chose one, mixed it with water, and gave it to Jen to drink. It wasn't long before the poor man fell into a deep sleep.

Valerian thanked me for my kindness, sat back, and pulled a flask and glasses from his trunk. He handed me a glass after pouring into it some very strong spirits. When we had settled, I asked, "Now you can do something for me, my friend. Tell me what we are doing out here off course and away from the fleet."

"Of course," he said. "I owe you an explanation." He took a drink and began this story.

"About a year ago, a Terra Firma fleet loaded its cargo at Cartagena as usual. However, a prodigious amount was loaded into the *Espada de Nuestra Señora de la Limpia Concepción.* She was a large ship, sixteen hundred toneladas, and she was overloaded. Early in the voyage during a storm, she disappeared from the fleet. Actually, the pilot took her off course, up the coast of La Florida, heading to Puerto de la Serpiente del Mar."

"I have not heard of this port," I said.

Valerian waved his hand as if dismissing the statement. "It is a secret port. You would not have heard of it. It is an inlet where the ship was to be hidden while unloading its cargo to smaller ships." He told me that these smaller ships are of the type that sail among the islands in search of corsairs who attack the treasure fleets. "No one would suspect these ships to be loaded with treasure. The *Concepción* was to be scuttled. The new ships were to return to Havanah to be offloaded."

"In Havana? But—" I began, but Valerian interrupted me.

"Spain and the House of Trade are not the whole world. Many men are making their empires here in this new one."

I wondered if my brother knew about this. Valerian continued his story, taking my silence to mean that I had no more questions. "The *Concepción* was crippled in a storm and was dangerously overloaded. Although she was almost to her destination, the crew, along with the master and the pilot, allowed her to sink in shallow water instead of trying to save her. The pilot recorded her exact location. They rowed the ship's boats to shore and made their way to the port, from which they were transported back to Havana."

I thought about what he had told me. It seemed to me that he must not have known about my mission, but I was wrong and very surprised at what he told me next.

"My friend, I like you. You have been good to me and my servant and I see that you have compassion for those who do not have your good fortune. This is why I tell you these things."

I felt I had to be honest with him and blurted my mission. "I am bound to tell Perez what you tell me," I said.

Valerian only smiled. "Perez knows. These are his machinations."

I could not believe my ears. "No, he sent me to . . ."

"Dear friend, why do you think Perez sent you—you who know nothing of the sea, nothing of the fleets, nothing of the new world, nothing of politics?"

I was stunned. "Are you saying he wants me to fail?"

"He knows you will fail. The House of Trade has tried many things—sending investigating committees, judges. They might as well have sent cats to ferret out all the rats on all the ships. You see, the problem with so much wealth is that if you do find a way to kill the rats, then you have to contend with all the cats."

"Why send me at all?"

"All this wealth flows through Spain. Spain is a country that has to buy everything it needs, as it produces nothing. In addition to that, your King Philip II is a man who spends much and therefore needs much. Perez was placating the king with the brilliant idea of planting a spy among the smugglers."

"Do López and the captain know what I'm doing here?"

Valerian shook his head. "They suspect," he said.

"How did you know about me?"

"Perez told me."

I felt foolish and angry. I believe him. I remember Bellisaro's surprise at being allowed to leave Spain on time when fleets are notoriously late in departing. Only the House of Trade could have seen to that. Valerian sensed my gloom, for he laid a hand on my shoulder.

"Why are we here?" I asked. "To look for the sunken ship?"

Valerian nodded. "Yes, that is why I am here and why the captain and López are so upset over the illness of Jen. He is—was—to be the diver. He was a pearl diver when I met him. Together we found a small fortune in pearls by diving in deeper waters. So lucky were we with our diving successes that we began diving in old wrecks when we could find their location. I knew the pilot of the *Concepción*. When he penned the location of his ill-fated ship, he did so in a code that only he and I could decipher. That is how I came to be on this mission."

I had a sudden thought. "Was Bellisaro the pilot of the *Concepción*?"

"No. Bellisaro knew nothing of the real purpose of our ship in this fleet. García, my pilot friend, met a mysterious death. I suspect it was in connection with the *Concepción*. But García had passed the document containing the location of the wreck to his captain, who took it to Perez. Tricky missions require good pilots. That's why Bellisaro was chosen. But he was not told about it until we were well under way."

"Why do the captain and López not know about me?" I asked.

"Perez doesn't tell everyone everything."

"And my brother?" I asked. "Does he know?"

"No, but the governor of Havana does."

"How do you know so much?"

Valerian smiled at me. "I have many friends in high, middle, and low places. I make it my business to find things out."

I have grown weary. Despite all the fantastic information Valerian has enlightened me with, I shall retire to bed.

⚓

Today started out worse. Not only were the crew in low spirits, but I as well since Valerian confided in me.

The surgeon wants to cut off Sancho's hand. He says it's getting infected and he will lose it anyway. Sancho will not let him.

We found a breeze. It has lifted all our spirits along with the sails. It did not take long to leave the strange sea behind. Back in the familiar ocean, Bellisaro found a good wind and we made good speed.

I saw a bird. I assume this means we are near land. What a grand thought.

Quite suddenly, Bellisaro ordered the ship stopped and anchored. I assume this means we have come to the location of the *Concepción.* The boatswain gave orders to hoist Valerian's crates out of the hold. I noticed that the captain and López watched eagerly as they were unpacked. The thing I thought was a bell was placed near the railing on the port side of the ship and another contraption with cranks and wheels constructed beside it under Valerian's guidance. That done, Valerian unloaded other mysterious things. I helped him, unenlightened as to what they were. Valerian called them a pneumatic contrivance. I still had no idea what they were, but I have since learned their function.

The captain explained to the crew that he needed a volunteer from among the men who could swim. He said they were looking for something on the bottom of the ocean. He didn't tell them what. I believe he should have. They will know soon enough when it is found, and I think they would be more eager if they knew.

Valerian explained that with the mechanisms he had brought with him, they would be able to breathe underwater. I was not surprised when no one stepped forward. He told them that Jen has done it many times. They murmured among themselves but did not volunteer.

"I will go," I said. They looked at me as though I'd gone mad. The crew stood back, glad that an idiot was on board. I was an idiot, but as Valerian spoke I became aware of an overwhelming desire to know what is on the bottom of the ocean. No, I want not only to know, but to see with my own eyes. Land where the air is water, inhabited by creatures that I have barely glimpsed near the surface. Will there be monsters, cities of lost souls, derelict ships piloted by the bones of the dead? That is why I came, I realized then, not for my king or any sense of justice, but for a burning curiosity I possess and only now acknowledge. Had Valerian said he had a giant crossbow and wanted to strap a man to the bolt and shoot him to the moon, I would have stepped forward. I want to see all those things that God has created and hidden away.

Valerian was as surprised as anyone else. "Do you know how to swim?" he asked. I replied that I do. I was not raised in the city but on my father's estate where my brothers and I swam frequently in the lake. López and the captain nodded their heads in approval. The relieved crew went about their tasks while Valerian explained to me about his pneumatic device.

There are actually two devices. The bell is a small compartment with a glass window whereby a man can sit and be lowered down to the sea floor. A long leather conduit supplies the compartment with air. The other is a device to be worn. It looks like an armor helmet with neck guards and pauldrons of leather and a visor of glass. This, too, has a leather conduit attached to the skull plate. Valerian explained, as he fitted yet another contraption together, that from the deck of the ship at intervals he has worked out and by means of a bellows, he can send air to each of the pneumatic devices, assuring that I will not drown. "Jen has done this many times, as have I," he told me. Valerian is truly an ingenious man.

Valerian himself donned a leather mask with a glass face plate, stripped himself of his outer garments, and jumped over the side of the ship. He disappeared under the water for a short time before surfacing and climbing aboard with the help of some sailors who must have thought him a madman. "The water," he said, "is not as clear as I had hoped. I think the pneumatic helmet would be best. You will have more freedom of movement."

It was to the point that I must either back out or don the regalia. I took a deep breath, removed my outer cloak, and allowed Valerian to fit the device on my person. He told me to put my spittle on the inside of the glass window and rub over it. I had a difficult time obtaining spittle. Having done thus, Valerian began securing the helmet in place. I tried not to shake.

"Breathe slowly," he said. "Remember to breathe slowly. You will be tied to a rope that is attached to the ship, so you will not become lost from us."

Bellisaro had measured the depth—66 codos. That seemed very deep to me, but Valerian assured me that Jen had been deeper— even without the breathing devices.

The time had come. I held on to the rope as they lowered me into the water. The breathing armor is heavy and I descended rapidly. I panicked and thrashed about. My breath came rapidly. I tried to remember the first time I faced the enemy in battle, hoping to quell my fear. My feet touched bottom, causing a cloud of particles to swirl upward. I heard a faraway voice tell me to breathe slowly. Had I gone mad so quickly? Was it God? No, I recognized the voice of Valerian. Apparently he yelled down the leather conduit. I assume he could hear me as well. I concentrated on regulating my breathing. I looked up to try to see the bottom of the ship and my feet drifted out from under me. I floated on my back.

I thrashed, panicked again, but managed to right myself. I had seen a shadow, but I didn't know if it was the ship.

For this first descent, Valerian told me to only turn and look in all directions. He would use a sand clock to time my stay and bring me up in a short while. "You need to get used to being underwater," he said. I took note of my surroundings. The water was not as clear as I would have preferred, but I could see some distance around me as I slowly turned. It was a wavering greenish-blue world—like a dream. And like a dream, my movement was slow. My mask fogged around the edges so that I had a smaller window from which to observe this world. I squinted, trying to see far into a distance that faded into a subtle green emptiness. I looked down. The sea floor looked not different from a sandy soil with scattered rocks and some weeds waving with the movement of the water. I had a tendency to float away from the sea floor, but I found I could move my arms certain ways and manage to stay upright and grounded. I saw fish. They did not appear to be afraid, some swimming past me, brushing my legs and shoulders. Besides fish, another creature, like a clear white cloud, floated past me.

All too soon, it seemed, I felt a tug on the rope. My time underwater had ended. I held on to the rope and was lifted upward.

As I sat on the deck shivering, rubbing my face, Valerian told me that I did fine on my first venture into the deep. López and the captain slapped me on the back. Even Bellisaro graced me with a smile.

"We will wait until tomorrow to go down again," Valerian said. "Go to our cabin and rest. Tell Jen of your adventure."

⚓

I slept soundly last night and dreamed I was a fish. Valerian said that I should not eat before I went down again and I agreed. I could not imagine a worse experience than retching in that situation. I donned the pneumatic contrivance and was again lowered into the ocean. I did not panic as much this time, remembering my ability to swim. I was much better at controlling my position in the water. I reached the sea floor and stood for a moment, waving my arms to keep me steady and on my feet, concentrating on breathing normally. The air was not fresh, but considering I was underwater, it was quite breathable. I released myself from the sea floor and began swimming, quickly reaching the end of my tether.

I wanted to be free to swim where I willed. I began to swim in an arc at the end of the tether. Halfway around the ship I tired and stopped to rest, standing on the sea floor, remembering to breathe slowly. This was a wonderful world and I was overjoyed to see it. I walked in my slow fashion in another direction.

Slowly appearing out of the blue-green watery fog I saw a sight that stopped me cold and left me gasping for air. My heart quickened its beat and my stomach staggered at the ghostly apparition before me. The ship—the *Concepción.* It sat on the bottom, almost upright, and still—a ghostly galleon with tattered sails gently waving from masts and yardarms that looked like giant crosses rising from the deck. The creatures of the deep are now her only crew. It is a glorious thing.

I am awed and blessed that I was the one to see her. It made me feel close to God. I swam toward the magnificent cathedral only to be pulled backward. No, I thought. I have to go to her, to feel the wood of her hull, to walk her decks. I moved forward again, and again I was jerked backward. I righted myself and by happenstance looked down. There was something half covered with sand. I seized it just before I was propelled upward. I heard a voice so muffled and distant I couldn't understand the words. Slowly, not of my own volition, I ascended away from the *Concepción.* I watched it disappear.

My next awareness was on the deck of the *Estrella* with Valerian removing the helmet and shaking me. I started to speak when someone noticed the thing I clutched in my hand. López reached down and took it from me. My inclination was to hold on to it, but his was to take it. I heard gasps and exclamations. The thing I had managed to grab off the sea floor before I was snatched back to the bosom of the world above water was a large gold cross studded with sizable emeralds. The gold glinted in the sun.

The captain and López simultaneously asked me where I had found it. "Where you snatched me from," I said.

That answer wasn't satisfactory to them but Bellisaro interrupted. "It would be the length of the conduit and in the direction from which Valerian pulled him back."

"Yes," I said.

"Did you see the ship?" asked Valerian.

I nodded. "It sits there as if whole and upright. It is a wondrous sight."

281

After Valerian walked me to our cabin and saw me safely onto my cot, he told me that he did not think that he would now have any trouble getting volunteers from among the crew.

In fact, he did not. All the crew who knew how to swim, and several who didn't, volunteered, Valerian told me later when he brought me a cup of hot soup. Bellisaro has figured the depth and the height of the sunken ship. The mainmast should be not that far from the surface. We have the idea that a man can swim down guided by the mast and take a look at the deck and main hatchway. The plan is to send the best swimmers down with the helmet. They will swim into the hold and tie ropes around the chests of treasure and we will hoist them up like cargo.

"It sounds like a good plan," I said, sipping the warm soup.

"So, my friend, how did you like it at the bottom of the sea?" he asked.

"It was quite fantastic," I said. "A world quite unlike this one."

"It is, is it not?" He clapped my shoulder and left to tend to the preparations.

After relating my story to Jen, who took in all my descriptions as eagerly as he did the soup Valerian had brought him, I hurriedly write this entry in my journal. I am anxious to go back on deck. If I am lucky, I might be able to persuade López to let me look at the cross I found.

Our luck seems to have turned against us. The seas have grown rougher. They now sparkle a silver gray, and a brisk breeze has come our way. Bellisaro wants to move the ship, but the captain says no. He is eager to get the treasure, and now he is using the soldiers to back him up. The helmsman must follow his orders.

Worse, when I could not find López in his cabin or on the deck, the boatswain helped me look for him. We did not find him readily, but one of the crew noticed that Sancho had blood smeared on his shirt and held him for the boatswain. The boatswain and I went to where Sancho was held. He looked frightened but said the blood was from his hand, which was swollen and had started bleeding again. As the blood was on his left sleeve, the same one that held his injured hand, we did not believe him. The boatswain searched Sancho's sea chest. We were both thinking, I'm sure, about the cross. He found it wrapped in a shirt. The boatswain slapped Sancho across the face and ordered him to tell where López was. He stood mute.

It did not take long for rumors to spread about the ship, agitating a crew already excited by the prospect of gold. Valerian and I helped in the search. He and an apprentice and I discovered López in a stall stacked with barrels of drinking water near the hull. It was not far from where I stood not many nights ago. His head was caved in and his blood was smeared on the side of the ship.

López was not a man I liked but he was not a bad man, and I felt great pity for him as we stood waiting for the captain and Father Hernando. The ship wafted harder and Valerian looked worried. "The sea grows rough. This is not good," he whispered, looking at poor López. He was the second dead man I have had to deal with on board. I, of course, have seen dead men in battle, have been the one to make them dead, but deliberate murder is beyond my comprehension. Father Hernando and Captain Acosta arrived with the boatswain. As the good father prayed over him, I shook my head at the little halos of his splattered blood. Poor López, for all his desires and aspirations, this was all that was left of him. I prayed for his soul. Valerian and I helped carry him up one deck to the sail master whom I watched for a second time take care of the dead.

Sancho was put in chains below deck. He yelled to all who would listen that he was innocent and he had found López already dead and that is how he got blood on his sleeve. He pleaded not to be put in chains during a storm. His entreaties fell on deaf ears.

Day Unknown

I make these entries from a shelter of canes, straw, and mud. Miraculously, my journal survived—I wonder at that when so many men did not. I was dragged ashore by the people native to this place. They have treated me well.

I cannot be the only survivor, but I am the only one here on this island. I have tried to ask about others, but they do not speak my language and I do not speak theirs.

After regaining some strength, I roamed the island looking for signs of survivors—the young pages, Valerian, Father Hernando, someone. I can't believe they are all dead. Why would I be the only one to survive? Am I blessed or cursed?

On my return from such an outing, I saw a strange sight in one of the rivers. I believe my eyes deceived me, but as my gaze rested on a ripple of water, a quite large, finned snakelike creature emerged and quickly disappeared.

Near the village, I picked up a feather from the ground and fashioned a pen. I managed after much difficulty in discourse to get from the Indians a liquid that I can use for ink. I'm not sure what it is, but I think they use it to draw designs on their bodies. I am glad for the pen and ink, for I feel the need to lay out what happened.

⚓

After seeing to the body of López, Valerian and I went to our cabin. The ship's rocking had increased considerably and I wanted to wait out the rough sea. Valerian tended to Jen. The level of wind and waves did not increase any more over the course of the day or night. I foolishly thought the danger had passed. The captain, for all his bluster, had not been able to send any men down to the *Concepción* because of the bad conditions, yet he would not leave this spot for fear of losing the location. I cursed the captain for being a fool.

Into the next day the wind increased and in the distance like an advancing army came a line of black clouds. Bellisaro told the captain that if he wanted to survive to spend the treasure, we would have to leave. The captain relented, perhaps seeing that the soldiers, who were not good sailors, were uncertain of his judgment.

Bellisaro's idea, I believe, was to sail past the storm and out into the open ocean, staying out of its way. But the sky quickly filled with the approaching dark clouds. It began to rain and the winds grew to such an extent that he could no longer keep up the main sails and ordered them furled. The best he could do was to turn the ship into the wind and to keep her steady.

A wave crashed over the ship and washed three soldiers overboard before they could be helped. Another wave lifted the ship, tossing her so that the yardarm dipped into the ocean. I had been in a doorway and was thrown against the wall. I crawled to my cabin, believing at the time that the fewer people in the way, the better for all of us. I checked Jen, he slept soundly. Valerian had tied him to the cot. I took a piece of leather from my trunk and for what reason I don't know, perhaps I had a premonition, I wrapped my journal in it and, as best I could, bracing myself in a corner, sewed it into the inside of my clothing. Apparently, of all the things in my trunk, I held my journal the most dear.

The pitching of the ship escalated, mostly to and fro, but occasionally side to side. I remembered Valerian's words during the first storm and reckoned that Bellisaro must be having a difficult time in this one. The sound of the waves crashing over the ship, the lightning, the howling wind, and the rain were most horrendous. I left my cabin and met Valerian in the narrow corridor. "We need men to bail. One of the pumps has broken," he yelled, his words almost drowned by the terrible noise. He led me to a place where I stood in a line and passed buckets of water to the man beside me for what seemed like eternity, while Valerian went below to work on the pump. He was successful, yet we bailed for another eternity while the pumps caught up. I thought perhaps everything would be all right. Indeed it seemed to me the rocking had subsided slightly and the fearful noises were not as great as before. I was about to retreat to the cabin when the boatswain, soaked and dripping in water, grabbed my arm and told me to help with hoisting the cannons overboard.

I could not keep track of time. The clouds were so black I could not place the sun anywhere in the sky. I have no idea how long it took, or what part of the day it was when the gray ocean swallowed the last cannon.

I stood under the forecastle deck out of the blinding rain, trying to catch my breath, holding fast to the door frame lest I should fall on the slippery deck. I saw that Valerian's equipment was gone. I imagine it went over the side before the cannons. A steady line of men worked—I know not how they withstood the raging storm—bringing cargo out of the hold and tossing it over the side. I think I realized then that the ship was sinking. The pumps could not keep up with the water crashing in, or she had a leak, or something was not allowing her to stay afloat. I prayed for God to help us.

The sailors had tied ropes across and along the decks to hold on to. Across the way I saw Bellisaro giving directions. I could not hear what he said over the din of the storm, but the men fetched axes and began chopping down the masts. Lord have mercy on us, I prayed, as another wave crashed over the ship. I saw a sailor lying sprawled, his ax by his side. I made my way across the water-washed deck to it and helped with the felling of the mainmast. I have toppled many trees on my father's estate, so this was a contribution I could make. I was thrown to the deck many times by waves hitting me from one side then another and by the lurching of the ship upon the giant seas. I don't know why I was not struck by an ax or how I failed to strike another man, but finally with a loud creak and groan, the mighty mainmast toppled over into the ocean. I went to help with the foremast. Behind me, I heard the mizzenmast fall.

We were a boat adrift and rudderless in an angry ocean, still sinking, more slowly for all our efforts, but still sinking. Waves crashed over the sides more furiously than ever as the ship sat lower in the water. I was exhausted. My ears were exhausted from the incessant noise of the wind, rain, sea, and groaning ship. I tried to shut out the sounds of screaming souls.

Bellisaro stood on the deck near the stump of the mainmast, holding on, his legs spread wide, his face contorted from yelling orders. Sailors were bringing up the anchor rope from the hold. Something else to throw overboard, I supposed, and broke in line to help carry the huge rope. Three sailors had one end of a messenger rope tied to the end of the anchor rope and they jumped in the water with it while others fed the rope over the side. Surely not, I thought. I went to the other side of the ship where men held on to the railing with wet, bleeding hands, watching for the swimmers. They were wrapping the enormous anchor rope around the ship's hull, tying the ship together with it. A desperate act, I thought, as I gave every assistance I could. The best we could hope for now was that the rope would hold the ship together and it would not break apart under the constant battering and tossing of the waves and give us time enough for the storm to pass.

But the storm would not abate, and Bellisaro gave the order to abandon ship. We had only four boats, which would carry ten men full, perhaps sixteen men overloaded, not nearly enough for the close to two hundred men on board. The sailors loosened the boats and they fell into the water. I saw Valerian for the first time in a while. He was helping Bellisaro throw the young pages into the first boat.

The captain rushed to jump over the side and into the boat. Bellisaro tried to stop him, but several soldiers threw the pilot to the deck and jumped into the boat with the captain. I only hoped the craven men would not throw the poor pages over the side. I looked at the poor young fellows huddling in the bottom of the boat as it was tossed about in the waves. I wondered if they would have been better off staying on the ship. The sailors and soldiers fought over the remaining boats.

I saw Valerian go below and I remembered poor Jen. I followed with great difficulty and fear. The servant was still tied in his bed, and sleeping. How, I wondered, could anyone sleep in this storm?

"I don't think I can get him on deck," Valerian yelled to me.

"I don't know how he could survive," I yelled back. "Look what a deep sleep he is in. I believe he is dying. At least he is far from this misery we are in now. Leave him be."

Valerian was anguished. I said a prayer for the unfortunate Jen. I believe he was beyond any of our help and perhaps better off than any of us. I pulled Valerian out of the cabin and onto the deck in time to see Bellisaro fall through the broken grate and down into the ship, followed by a flood of water from a wave that washed over us. The ship was suddenly raised high and turned over, throwing the two of us out into the ocean. I gulped in salt water and was tossed about like a wine cork. I lost sight of Valerian. Something hit me in the back and I choked, almost losing my breath. I was surely going to die, I knew. I grabbed hold of the thing that hit me. It was an overturned boat. I prayed it was not the one with the children. I tried to climb onto it, but couldn't, nor could I find a place on which to cling. I thought I was lost. I swam. I had no idea that I made any progress in the raging sea, but I determined I would try. I hit another piece of debris floating past me and clung to it as if it were gold. It was a sea chest.

My memory after that does not serve me well. I remember being in the ocean, holding and kicking, thinking of nothing but doing those two things. I think I remember washing up on the sand, but I'm not sure. My first clear memory after the storm is of Indians bringing me to this shelter and giving me food. I am grateful. Perhaps they know the way to a Spanish mission.

Chapter 29

THE DAM GROANED louder than Lindsay had ever heard it and waves crashed over the bulkheads, sending sprays of water into the interior. The extra pumps elevated the rhythmic ambient noise inside their well. It was going to be a day that tested her stress threshold, Lindsay thought, as she dug in the wet soil. The back and forth chatter was brief and focused on the excavation. Everyone worked faster and breathed harder. It started to rain and the rapid drops of water on the roof sounded like muffled gunfire. But there was no alarm.

The day reached the eleventh hour of the morning and the sudden loud blast of the siren sent a shock through Lindsay. Two blasts. The test.

"Shit," said Juliana. "That nearly gave me a heart attack."

Trey came down the stairs and stood at the edge of the excavation. "I've talked with the meteorologists. This is just a rain and some wind. The hurricane is stalled far south of here. The seas are rough, but we've had rough seas here before."

Jeff keeled over, landing with his face in the mud. The worker closest to him pulled him over on his back. Lindsay rushed to his side, pulled a bandanna out of the pocket of her cutoffs, and wiped his face. He was breathing in rapid, shallow gasps and his heart beat fast.

"Call the Coast Guard," she yelled. "Tell them we have an emergency."

"What's wrong?" Trey asked. "What happened?"

"I don't know. Did anybody see what happened?" she called out.

"He just fell over," Gina said. "He seemed fine before."

"When help comes, they'll have to get him to the top," Lindsay said. "Can you use the timber hoist?" Trey nodded. Lindsay looked at Juliana, who was kneeling on the opposite side from her. "Go to the field desk and get the asthma spray. Bring back any other medication you find. Is he taking anything else?"

"I don't know," Juliana answered.

"Me neither," Gina and the others replied.

Juliana jumped up and ran to the desk, searching the drawers. She brought a plastic bottle of asthma spray to Lindsay.

"I've noticed that he's been a lot happier lately," Lindsay said. "Is he taking something for stress? Depression?"

"I don't know," Juliana almost shouted.

"They're on their way," Steven yelled.

"Trey, you and Juliana go to the barge and look in Jeff's room for any medication he may be taking. We have to send it with him."

"You think it's some kind of overdose?" Trey asked.

"Possibly. Please hurry."

John came down the stairway to see what was happening. The other crew stopped their work and looked on. Lindsay looked at the anxious faces. They were thinking about murder, she realized.

The paramedics came and put Jeff on a stretcher and started a standard IV. Lindsay gave them the asthma spray. "They've gone to his room to find anything else," she told them. She also explained how he had been very anxious working down inside the dam.

"I can understand that," one of the paramedics commented.

"I think he may have been taking something for it," Lindsay said. "He seemed very happy lately, almost manic sometimes."

"Yeah," Gina agreed. "I just thought he was adjusting."

"Here they come," Lindsay said.

Juliana and Trey hurried over and Trey thrust a pill vial into the hands of the nearest paramedic, who looked at the label. "Prescription. But the doctor may not have known he was an asthmatic."

They strapped a pale Jeff to the stretcher and with the help of Steven, John, and Trey, hoisted him to the top of the dam where they carried him down to the boat. John climbed to the top of the dam to assist.

"Someone should go with Jeff," Gina said.

"If you like, you can get cleaned up and I'll have someone take you to the hospital later," Trey said. "There's nothing you can do now. Lindsay, I need to talk to you."

As Lindsay followed Trey to the field desk, she heard Gina ask Juliana what was wrong.

"Nothing," Juliana snapped. "Let's get back to work." The anxieties of the past several days were getting to all of them.

"What is it?" Lindsay asked, looking at Trey's worried features.

"While Juliana and I were looking for medicine, we found some things."

"What things?"

"A gold and emerald cross and what looks like soggy leather books or something."

It took a moment for what Trey told her to sink in. "No."

"I'm afraid so. Juliana was really upset, of course."

"It doesn't make sense. Why would Jeff do that?"

"Why anybody? If Jeff's been in some altered state of awareness the last few days, he may have thought he had some good reason."

"Not to attack Boote, wearing a ski mask." Lindsay thought back to the incident. Jeff was shorter than she thought the attacker was, and she had a sense that the thief was heavier. But then again, the best view she got of him was when he knocked her down. Jeff's eyes were the right color, but hazel eyes are common. "I don't like this."

"Neither do I, but maybe, you know, the guy just went nuts. Jeff was a little peculiar when he got here."

"Peculiarity doesn't lead to criminal behavior."

"He had the items tucked away in the bottom drawer of his chest."

"Where are they now?" Lindsay asked, then saw a box he had put down on the field desk.

"I've got to call Carolyn and find out what to do with the stuff. I can't believe this." Trey took the box and he and Lindsay went up the ladder to the top of the dam and into one of the trailers.

Lindsay looked in the box at the waterlogged contents. One item appeared to be a book with an embossed leather cover. Another piece of leather or something lay in a pile in the corner. It looked like it was disintegrating. An object wrapped in a rag lay in the end of the box. Lindsay picked it up and unwrapped it. It was startlingly beautiful—a seven-inch shiny gold cross encrusted with huge emeralds. It weighed heavy in her hand as she rubbed her fingers across the stones. She could see how something like this was tempting. The beauty of it had its own vitality. This piece alone was worth a princely sum of money. She couldn't imagine an enormous ship full of objects like this.

"Rather intoxicating, isn't it?" she asked.

"Too much so." Trey called Carolyn and told her about the found artifacts, omitting mention of the cross and Jeff. "She said to put a seawater-soaked cloth on them and get them to her. I fear some of them are already ruined. Look, I'm going to take this myself."

"What are you going to do about the cross?" asked Lindsay.

"Give it to Lewis—" he began.

Lindsay interrupted. "What about Boote? It was stolen from his house."

"It's an artifact," Trey said emphatically.

"His lawyer, and he will get one, will tell you that you don't know for sure where it came from. And you don't. I have to tell you, I think he'll have a good claim on it."

"Damn. I don't want this kind of problem."

"You've got it anyway."

"Jeff has a lot to answer for," Trey said.

"I wonder where Keith found it?" Lindsay commented. "That might help Nate with his program. What do you think of it?"

"The program? I was skeptical at first. What Nate described in his prospectus was virtually a simulation of the ocean, or at least a part of it. Do you know how many variables are involved?" Lindsay said she did. "The ocean is a very intricate ecosystem, and we've only begun to understand how all the parts interact. But he's only dealing with the variables that contribute to motion. That helped me to be more enthusiastic. What do you think?"

"Same thing. But he has a lot of data on currents and he's had some successes with mapping artifacts from the *Estrella* back to her."

Trey stood up. "I'll take the cross to Lewis and we'll figure something out." He grinned at Lindsay. "I'll tell him you're our conscience."

"Thanks, he'll love that."

Later in the day they received word that Jeff was in fair condition. Lindsay was correct, he had overdosed on prescription tranquilizers.

When Lindsay arrived back at the lab, everything was in an uproar. The first thing she witnessed was Lewis and Trey ganging up on Harper in Lewis's office.

"What were you thinking?" Trey was asking.

"I was thinking about doing what I've been doing all along—translating night and day, copying and delivering the translations to the staff. It's what I'm getting paid to do. If you wanted me to use my powers of clairvoyance, I charge a lot extra for that! How was I to know you were keeping some big secret?"

"Surely," said Lewis, "you could have used some judgment."

"Judgment? Judgment? You want to talk about judgment? What about hiring one disinterested retired guy who only cares about model trains to guard the whole island!"

Lindsay stood with her arms folded; Bobbie stood beside her frowning. "Guys," Lindsay interrupted.

"Have you read the diary?" Lewis asked with irritation. "It tells all about the silver galleon—Harper handed out copies and now everyone knows about it."

"Yes. The cat's out of the bag. Why didn't you let Harper in on the secret?"

"How were we to know that there was a connection between the two ships?" Trey asked.

"The same way Harper was to—what did you call it, Lewis—use her judgment?"

"So, you're on her side?" Lewis asked. "Is this a male versus female thing?"

"No, it's an acting like an adult and being reasonable thing. Lewis, Harper has done an outstanding job here. What's wrong with the two of you?"

Trey closed his eyes and rubbed his temples with his fingers. "I know. I'm sorry, Harper," he said. From the look on Harper's face, that wasn't going to be nearly enough.

"Lindsay's right," said Lewis. "You were just a target we had in sight. Everybody else is out of reach."

"Has anything else happened?" asked Lindsay.

"Jeff is going to be arrested for attacking Boote and stealing the cross. Agent Ramirez is coming to take possession of it. Jeff is also being questioned about the murders."

"Arrest him? I don't think they have enough evidence. Are you sure?"

"The cross was found in his possession," Trey said.

"No," said Lindsay. "It was found in his room. There's a difference. They would need to have some corroborative evidence in order for the DA to charge him."

"Maybe they've found something." Trey shrugged.

"I don't believe it," Bobbie said. "I've been working with Jeff, and I just can't see it."

Lewis's phone rang and he picked it up, listened a moment, then cursed. "Can you get hold of the picture?" he said. Pause. "Well try. And fax it to me." He slammed the receiver down. "Son of a bitch. It looks like the diary thing is academic anyway."

"Who was that?" Trey asked.

"A lawyer who's watching things for us. Damn."

"What?" asked Trey.

"It's that Jones woman," Lewis said. "She's recovered a bell and is getting a court order to have it arrested."

"For what?" Harper asked. "Pealing without a license?"

"I guess those bells can be dangerous," muttered Bobbie.

"You are going to have to explain that one," Lindsay said.

Lewis raked his hands through his hair. "She's discovered the wreck of the *Concepción* and is in the process of becoming salvor in possession. In order to lay claim to a wreck, the law requires that you have an artifact from the wreck and put it in the hands of a U.S. marshal who issues an arrest warrant for it. It's one of the peculiarities of treasure salvage."

"Won't it belong to the state?" asked Bobbie.

"Depends on how far out," Lewis answered. "Rights to the *Atocha* were given to the salvor. At any rate, the university will have no claim."

"She still has to meet certain criteria," Trey said. "Look, Harper. I am really sorry for jumping down your throat."

"I'm going to have a cup of coffee," Harper responded. She turned and left the office.

"I think I'll join her," Lindsay said.

Lindsay, Bobbie, and Harper sat at a table in the break room listening to the conversations around them. Everyone was talking about the ghost ship—the golden galleon—the *Concepción*.

"You know," Harper said, "I just think the diary is a great story."

"It is," Lindsay agreed. "Trey and Lewis aren't doing too well under pressure right now."

"So," said Bobbie, "we know the murder victim was López—and the murderer was Sancho. That's really interesting."

"The diary explains the injuries to Valerian's servant, Jen," Lindsay said, "Perhaps it really was dysbaric osteonecrosis."

"You know," Harper said, "even with the murders, getting stranded at sea and on land, the threat of hurricane, I was still having a good time."

Lindsay put a hand over hers. "Harper, you will again. They were wrong and they know it."

"Yeah," Bobbie agreed. "Just tell Trey he was an ass, but you'll forgive him if he doesn't be one again."

Harper smiled at the two of them, then frowned. "Uh-oh. Here they come."

Trey and Lewis came and sat down at their table, still looking glum. "I thought you all would like to see the fax of the artifact Jones has in her possession," Lewis said.

Lindsay took the fax from Lewis's hand and examined it. Her lips twitched. She pushed it across the table.

"What do you think, Harper?"

Harper looked at the picture. Bobbie leaned over her shoulder.

"I think the guys had better go raise some money and bail that bell out of jail," said Harper.

"I agree," said Bobbie.

"What?" Lewis asked, clearly not understanding.

Lindsay looked at him and Trey in turn. "I don't normally use strong language to make a point, but I'm going to make an exception with you guys. Get your heads out of your butts and be a little more observant."

She took the picture from Harper and handed it back to them. They stared at it.

"What?" asked Trey.

"It's Valerian's diving bell. It has his seal on it. It belongs to our ship—the *Estrella*. Chances are, Jones found a collection of artifacts and jumped the gun, thinking she had found the *Concepción*. Now what you have to do is get the digital camera and photograph the insignia on top of Valerian's trunk and the pages out of the translation that describe Valerian's crest on his ring and the ones that describe his diving bell and fax those to your lawyer. Tell him that bell has to be well cared for because it has extremely important historical significance. It is an artifact from the earliest recorded incident of deep-sea diving off the coast of Georgia, perhaps in the Western Hemisphere."

The two of them looked dumbfounded for a moment. "You're right," Trey said. "It is Valerian's crest."

"We've got to get on this right away," Lewis urged. As he and Trey rose to leave, he turned to Harper. "Look, Harper, I talk to everyone like that at one time or another." They went off to thwart Evangeline Jones.

"Was that an apology?" asked Harper.

"I think so," Lindsay replied.

Carolyn came over and sat down with them. She turned to Lindsay. "Do you think Jeff is guilty? I've had classes with him, and he just didn't seem like the kind of person who would do any of this. He's a little odd, but aren't we all?"

"I don't know. People do funny things. What size shoe does he wear?"

"I don't know," Carolyn said. "Maybe we should find out."

"What happened to your hands?" Bobbie asked Carolyn.

"I have no idea. Korey says it looks like poison ivy. It sure itches like the dickens. But I stay either in the lab or in my apartment just about all the time. I sometimes go out to look at the alligator and occasionally go out to dinner, but that's all. I hate the outdoors, so I don't know how I could have gotten this. I hate it."

"You think you could be developing an allergy to the chemicals?" asked Harper. "You've used them for a long time. That sometimes happens."

"God, I hope not."

"Can you salvage the artifacts?" asked Lindsay.

"I'm not sure. One was a leather scroll. It's in bad shape. I'm going to try to flatten it out and get Korey to photograph it. That may be our best representation of what it is. The other two are leather bound books. They are in better shape, but I'm not sure about them, either. That's another thing. Jeff knows better than this. I just can't see him doing it."

"I'll be right back," Lindsay said. Gina, Juliana, and some of the others had just come into the room and Lindsay rose to meet them. "Do any of you know what size shoe Jeff wears?"

"How would we know that?" someone said.

"I'm not sure," Juliana said, "but when we were having lunch one day, I noticed that his feet aren't much bigger than mine. I wear a size seven. I don't know what that translates to in guy sizes."

Certainly not eleven or twelve, thought Lindsay. "That's something in his favor. If my calculations are correct, his feet are too small."

"That'll be good if he has to go to court," Carolyn said.

"No, not really. I couldn't testify for sure that the stain I'm basing the shoe size calculation on was even part of a footprint."

"What?" asked Bobbie and Harper. Lindsay explained her rather tenuous procedure to them.

"It will give Jeff some comfort, anyway," Bobbie said. "I'm sure he must be terrified."

"What's the hurricane doing?" Lindsay asked. "Anyone heard?"

"I went to the weather office to ask," Carolyn said. "William was on duty. He said something about wind vectors or something. I didn't know what he was talking about and decided I didn't want to know."

Debriefing was canceled. Trey and Lewis were busy on the phone trying to counter Eva Jones's sudden move. John was doing double duty at the cofferdam. Lindsay, Bobbie, and Harper decided to visit Jeff in the hospital.

Jeff was awake and already had a visitor. "Hello, Lieutenant Ramirez," Lindsay said.

"Good to see you. I was just talking to your friend here."

"He thinks I did it, all of it," Jeff said. He looked pale and there were dark circles under his eyes. "I don't know how those things got in my room."

"For the record, Agent Ramirez, we believe Jeff," Lindsay said.

"You do?" Jeff responded. He looked more surprised than elated.

"Why is that?" Ramirez asked.

"Many reasons. Several of the crew know him and say this just doesn't fit." Lindsay took out the photograph and her calculations. "I'll tell you up front, this is not the hardest of evidence, but look at this water mark on the floor jutting out from the larger stain where the tank was drained. It looks like the toe of a shoe."

"It does somewhat," conceded Ramirez.

"Bones have a consistent size relationship to one another. The tip of the toe is here, the distal end of the first metatarsal connects with its corresponding phalanges at this curve here on the medial side of the footprint. I measured this, taking into account the size ratio from the photograph to real size. I did this by measuring one of the artifacts and its image in the photograph. If I know this part of the foot measurement, then I know the size of the whole foot. This partial footprint represents about an eleven and a half to size twelve shoe."

"I wear a size nine," Jeff said.

"This person, I believe, was squatting, looking at the artifacts. I think that because the entire toe area of the shoe left a mark, like he had been leaning forward. In running shoes the toe area is elevated slightly when standing and wouldn't leave a print with something so subtle as a water stain. It's important to note that neither Isaac, who found the open chest, nor Steven, who came in after him, walked among the artifacts. It was not their feet."

"Interesting, but as you hinted, not completely convincing."

"Add to that the fact that the thief of the cross ran into me at Boote's house and pushed me down. I'm tall, taller than Jeff. This guy was about the same height as me. And I had a sense he was heavier than Jeff."

"I'll never call you the Angel of Death again," Jeff said.

Ramirez raised his eyebrows.

"Murder on sites I work at is becoming more common than I would like, especially considering that murders hardly ever occur at archaeological sites."

"I see." Ramirez smiled. "I'm willing to take these two bits of evidence into account. Do you have any theory as to how the artifacts got into his room?"

"Someone put them there," Bobbie said.

"Who?" asked Ramirez.

"The person who took them," Bobbie answered.

"A hurricane is coming. We are all under some stress," Lindsay said.

"Last I heard, it was threatening the coast of Florida," said Ramirez.

"Oh, that's great news," Bobbie said. "I mean, not for the people in Florida, but—"

"Agent Ramirez," Lindsay said, "I believe that Jeff was an easy target for whoever set him up. He has been under a lot of strain from working in the dam. That's how he got into trouble here. Besides, he's a classicist. They all act strange."

"Now wait a minute," Jeff protested.

"Do you have any idea who did this?" asked Ramirez.

"Not now, but—"

"But what?"

"Have you ever felt like you know something, but the knowledge keeps eluding your conscious mind? And people mention certain words that tickle your brain but you still can't put your finger on what it knows?"

"And you call us classicists strange," Jeff said.

Ramirez bowed his head and smiled just a little. "Yes, I know what you are talking about."

"That's where I am now. I feel like I know the answer, or part of the answer, but can't quite put my finger on it yet."

"When you think of it, give me a call."

"What's going to happen to the cross?" Lindsay asked.

"The courts will have to decide. It looks to me like it will go to Boote."

Lindsay had mixed feelings about that. Boote could use the money that the cross represented, but it was an artifact and now that the diary was completed, there was evidence that the cross belonged with the *Estrella*. Maybe Boote and the university could come to some agreement.

As Lindsay, Harper, and Bobbie were leaving, they ran into Gina and Juliana coming in.

"Hi. How's Jeff?" Gina asked.

"He's doing well," Harper replied. "I think Sherlock here about convinced Ramirez that Jeff is innocent."

"Great. Was that the shoe thing?"

"That and the fact that I did get a look, albeit briefly, at the person who attacked Boote. And it wasn't Jeff. You guys had dinner?"

"Just a while ago. There's a small shopping center that has a good sandwich shop. It's about a block away. That's about the only place in this town unless you want fast food."

They followed the directions and went into the small café. Mike and Tessa Altman were there having dinner.

Chapter 30

"GET A TABLE, I'm going to speak with Mike and Tessa," Lindsay said. Bobbie and Harper followed her anyway.

"We'd like some peace," said Tessa. Mike stared at the glass of iced tea in front of him. The two of them sat side by side close together in a booth. Tessa had her arm through his.

"Look," said Lindsay. "We're all stuck in the same tar man. I'd like to let go and I imagine you would, too."

"Perhaps we'll get lucky and the hurricane will blow the lot of you away," Mike said without looking up.

"Or maybe it won't, and we'll be here forever," Lindsay responded.

"Will it get rid of you if we talk to you?" Tessa asked.

"Yes, it will. May I sit down?"

Tessa motioned toward the opposite side of the booth. Bobbie slid in first, Lindsay beside her, and Harper dragged a chair and sat at the end.

"Can I get you anything?" asked a waitress.

"No," said the Altmans together.

"We're moving to another table in a minute," said Lindsay.

"Are you two ready to order?"

"Give us a few more minutes, please," Tessa answered. She waited until the waitress was gone. "So, does this take all three of you?"

"Apparently," said Lindsay. She turned to Mike. "First, I'd like to end this feud. Tessa told me that you genuinely didn't think we needed help at the quicksand pit, and I'm willing to accept that. So are Bobbie and Harper." Harper opened her mouth and looked surprised. Lindsay kicked her under the table. Tessa almost smiled.

"If you had been in real trouble, I would have helped," Mike said. The admission seemed to hurt him.

"I accept that. I'll put a stop to all the rumors that have had all of you upset."

"So you've been doing that?" said Tessa.

"Not me personally, or Bobbie or Harper, or most of the staff. But I know where they've come from, and I'll have Lewis put a stop to it."

"So, what about the museum and the theme park?"

"They were just jerking your chain. There is no museum, no theme park. Once we're gone, the warehouse goes. When it can be released, I'd like you to read the diary Harper has been translating. It was written by a man who sailed as a passenger on the ship we're excavating. He was an intelligent and compassionate man and he provided us with incredible insight about the people who came over here to colonize. It will help you understand what we do and why we were so very angry about your association with Jones."

Mike and Tessa were silent. All in all, Lindsay thought that was a good sign. She continued talking.

"I'm not going to ask you for alibis for the night in question. None of us have them, and I don't expect you to have them, either. I'll accept that you were in bed asleep."

"I wasn't," said Tessa. "Mike was. I was doing some research on the Web—if I understand that the time in question is the wee hours of the morning. That's the time Ramirez wanted to know about."

"Did you hear anything when you were up?"

"No. But the ranger's quarters are surrounded by thick flora."

Lindsay looked at Mike. "You said that Nate and Keith fought. When did you see that?"

Mike shrugged and looked at Tessa. "Several weeks ago," he said. "One of the windows in our apartment looks out over the walkway. They were yelling at each other about the wreck. From what I gathered, Keith wanted to have some of your artifacts for all his help." Mike shook his head. "The fool, just like with my plants. He thinks he can just take things. Anyway, it ended with him pushing Nate into the railing—that's how it broke—and stomping off. I don't know what happened after that."

"Did you see him after that?"

"No," said Mike.

"I did, a couple of days later," Tessa said, "down on the beach. He was looking at the surf. Keith was nothing but a beach bum."

"Did you ever witness anyone else arguing with him?"

"That other guy, what's his name?" Mike asked. "Captain Nemo, Keith was always calling him."

"Steven."

"Yeah, that's the guy. He wasn't too bad. Not loud and in your face like Nate."

"Steven Nemo argued with Keith?"

"Several times. You could tell he didn't like him, called him a looter and a pothead—"

"Pothunter?"

"Yeah, that was it. Pothunter. I looked all over the island to make sure Keith wasn't planting any marijuana patches."

"That's a word we use for a person who loots archaeological sites."

"Wish I'd known, I could have saved myself some work. Anyway, Nemo really didn't like Keith. Nemo also fought with Nate and Trey Marcus about using Keith and the old man to help locate whatever it was you guys are trying to find."

"Objects from wrecks often wash up onshore. Keith and his father have been searching the islands for a long time, and Trey wanted access to their collections."

"Did you all ever find anything?" asked Bobbie.

Tessa held out her right hand to Lindsay. She had a beautiful gold ring with a large ruby in it. "Mike and I found the stone in the sand. I stepped on it with my bare feet. Mike had it set for me. I'd like not to have to give it up."

"Keep it," said Lindsay. "Do you remember where on the beach you found it?"

"A couple of miles up the beach from the house."

It sounded like the same spot that Lindsay had found the coins.

"Did anyone else argue with Keith?" Lindsay asked.

"Trey had a big fight with him in the break room a few days after Nate did."

"What was it about?"

"Let's see. Same thing, I think. No, he accused Keith of taking something out of the lab." Tessa thought a moment. "An astro something—"

"Astrolabe?"

"I suppose. Keith thought that, since you all had two of them, he could have one. Trey didn't see it that way. He was very angry."

"I can imagine. Thank you for talking with me. I won't keep you from your dinner any longer."

They moved to another table and ordered soup and sandwiches. When the Altmans finished, Tessa stopped by Lindsay's table.

"Look, someone will probably tell you this sooner or later, so I'd rather you hear it from me. Before we knew what a complete jerk Keith was, Gretchen dated him a couple of times. This was way before all of you got here and it ended before any of you arrived. Gretchen isn't involved in this and her mother is in a nursing home and not doing well. Gretchen has a lot to deal with and she doesn't need to be questioned by you or the police. She is a very nice person. She even likes you guys."

"I'm not official anyway," said Lindsay. "Ramirez may find out on his own, but not from me."

After the Altmans left, Bobbie said, "You sure were easy on them."

"I did lay into Mike and Easterall pretty heavily already. Besides we wouldn't have gotten anything from them if we'd been hostile."

"I know, but you gave her a ruby ring, for heaven's sake. Lewis isn't going to like that," said Harper.

"There was no provenance. There was nothing to dispute that a tourist simply lost the set out of her ring and Tessa found it."

"Well, Trey didn't have anything to do with Keith's death," said Harper.

"I thought you were mad at him." Lindsay teased.

"I am, but I don't want him to go to prison."

"I've known Trey since he got a job in the Archaeology Department. I don't believe he's a murderer. I'm sure if I'd been here and met Keith, I'd have had an argument with him, too. It looks like everybody on the island did at one time or another."

"You ever date him?" Harper had her elbow on the table and her chin resting in the palm of her hand.

"Who? Trey?" Lindsay looked surprised.

"Yes, Trey."

"No. We almost went dancing once, but events were kind of overtaking me at the time. Why?"

"Just wondering. So, Bobbie, how's Luke?"

"He's good. John's got him working a lot now. I don't think he's going to get any time off for a while."

"Are they related?" asked Harper.

"Cousins," said Bobbie.

"So, Harper, you going to come to UGA?" Lindsay asked.

"Maybe. I have indications that the Language Department is interested."

"They certainly ought to be," Bobbie said.

They left the restaurant and drove the SUV to the guarded lot where several of the university vehicles were parked and motored across the intracoastal waterway to the island. It was a short trip and they were grateful because the water was choppy, even between the mainland and the island.

The barge had left St. Magdalena hours ago for the dam and Lindsay and Bobbie didn't want to take a boat in the dark with the water as rough as it was. So they stayed in Harper's apartment.

Harper was greeted with a bowl of orchids sitting on her desk—and a card from Trey.

"You think he picked these on the island?" whispered Bobbie.

"No," Harper said. "The card is from a florist. Isn't this sweet?"

"I suppose he must be really sorry." Lindsay smelled one of the flowers.

"He says he is." Harper grinned.

"What's this?" Bobbie asked, pointing to a large flat box sitting on the breakfast table.

"A candy box," Harper said, "with lots of candy."

"He must be really, really sorry," Bobbie said. Bobbie and Lindsay gathered around her as she opened the card.

"No," said Harper, "Lewis is really sorry."

While they talked about everything from the guys, the diary, to the state of the union, and ate the candy, Lindsay worked on the drawing of the HSkR4, the last skeleton.

"Here he is," she said at last.

"That's him then? Valerian?" asked Harper.

"I don't know. Someone. I've looked at all the bones, but I need to do it again and read the diary again. I'm afraid that the way things are going lately, I might have missed something."

"I somehow pictured Valerian as more handsome," Bobbie said.

"I could work on him some," offered Lindsay.

"You gave López a long nose, and the guy in chains, Sancho . . . do you think he is Sancho?" asked Bobbie.

"Probably. He's the only one the diary said was in chains," Lindsay replied.

"You gave Sancho a short nose. How do you know?"

Lindsay touched the bridge of Bobbie's nose. You can tell by the length of the bridge of the nose and nasal sill. Long noses need support."

"How neat," said Bobbie.

"Yes, it is." Lindsay yawned. "I'm getting tired. How about we get some sleep?"

"You got my vote," agreed Harper.

Harper pulled a rollaway bed out of the closet for Bobbie. "Maybe we'll get lucky and in the morning the hurricane will have just wound down," Bobbie said as she pulled the covers over her.

In the morning Hurricane Harriette was moving northeast. The south Florida coast was the most likely target for landfall. Lindsay went to the dam to work, but her mind was on the murders. Were they about the treasure ship? Had Keith found it? Is that where he got the cross? But if he found it, why didn't he have more of its treasure? Ramirez did tell her that he had found no evidence that Keith had been trying to sell gold or gems on the local market.

What did Hardy Denton have to do with it? Keith didn't have the equipment to go after the wreck himself? Maybe he brought Denton and Jones into it. He'd tell where the wreck was and they would help him bring it to the surface—but they double-crossed him. Then why was Denton killed and why was Jones having the Altmans steal information? Lindsay was getting a headache.

She wondered if she was wrong not to speak with Gretchen. After all, she knew nothing about the woman. This could be a crime of love gone wrong—certainly a more common motive than fighting over Spanish treasure. But then, where did Denton fit in? Did he witness it? But why would he be killed so long after Keith? Maybe he was blackmailing Gretchen? Perhaps that was why Mike and Tessa were stealing information for Denton and Jones. That would mean that the three of them would be in on Keith's murder.

"Lindsay, Lindsay! Are you in there?" It was Trey sitting on his haunches beside her.

Lindsay rose to a sitting position. "Oh, hi. How is everything? Did you get the bell bailed out of jail?"

"We heard from the lawyer this morning. The judge refused to issue a warrant. The lawyer said we should have been there to witness Eva Jones in district court. He said the hurricane was nothing compared to the whirlwind she caused."

"Aren't we lucky that Harper provided me the complete translation, so that I could recognize the bell for what it was?"

"Thanks, Lindsay. I needed you to remind me. Is Harper still mad at me?"

"The flowers helped. So did the candy."

"What candy?"

"Oh, yes, I forgot. The candy was from Lewis."

"You're in a great mood this morning, aren't you?"

"Actually, I have a headache. How's Jeff? Have you heard?"

"He's doing well. I think they're letting him out of the hospital today. The police are holding off on charging him. Seems you convinced Ramirez."

"I doubt it. They just didn't have enough corroborating evidence. At most, the DA probably thought that without other evidence, my testimony would ensure reasonable doubt in a jury's mind. You can bet they still have their eye on him. Is Jeff coming back here?"

"He's going to work with Carolyn in the lab for a while. I'm sending several divers back home until the danger is over. That will be fewer people to evacuate if it comes to that. Lewis is very impressed with you, by the way."

"Good. Do you think this would be a good time to hit him up for a raise? Look, Trey." Lindsay lowered her voice. "I'm not having very good feelings about the disposition of the contents of the treasure ship if we find it."

Trey was silent for a long time, staring at the sandy mud and the wooden form that Lindsay was excavating. "I know. We've had long, hot conversations with him about it."

"What are you going to do?" asked Lindsay.

"I told him I'd fight to keep it together."

"So did I," she said. "He didn't seem to mind."

"No, I imagine not. Lewis is a man very sure of himself."

Lindsay wanted to ask Trey if he thought that Lewis could kill anyone. But she felt as if she were plotting mutiny the way it was, so she kept silent about that. She did ask Trey, "Is Lewis computer literate?"

"You still skeptical about Nate's computer model?"

"Yes." Lindsay was skeptical, but that wasn't the reason she was asking. Lewis had used the phrase "timed out" in talking about artifacts. It was one of the phrases in the threatening computer message to her. It concerned her, yet for the life of her she couldn't figure out why Lewis would be involved in murder. Besides, everybody used that phrase these days. But she was glad Trey misunderstood the intent of her question.

"Lewis doesn't know much about computers at all. But he is into chaos theory, and he liked Nate's description of it in his prospectus. And I've seen a printout of Nate's last couple of runs. I'm impressed."

"Well, at least the two of you set Jones back a few squares."

"You did, really," Trey said.

"What's the weather like?"

"You worried?"

"I think we all are. It's heading this way, isn't it?"

"John has a lot of confidence that the dam will remain standing," Trey replied. "I don't have to tell you that putting it out in the ocean was a very controversial affair. But his design got an okay from all the engineers we submitted it to. At any rate, none of us will be in it when the storm comes. It will fill up with water." Trey smiled, trying to look optimistic. "What are you excavating?"

"Another sea chest. Maybe we can hoist it up by the end of the day."

After work Lindsay wanted nothing but to spend a quiet evening with John. She sat beside him in a sheltered corner of his barge.

"You cold?" he asked.

"Not really. I was just trying to see some stars in the sky, hoping for a clear opening." A white, orange, and black calico cat jumped in her lap. "Who's this?" Lindsay stroked her long fur and rubbed her head as the cat vibrated with a loud purr. "She has a strong motor."

"That's Polly. Stan is here under my chair." Lindsay squinted her eyes, finally seeing the black tuxedo cat curled up beneath John. "They keep the barge free of mice. Very good at it, too."

"I guess you heard about Eva Jones trying to take possession of the ghost ship."

"I heard. I also read the diary pages. Bobbie showed them to Luke and he showed them to me, so I guess the ship is an open secret now. Good thing about the hurricane or we'd start having more boaters out here to deal with."

"Lewis is determined to find it. From the account in the diary, the *Estrella* was almost on top of it when the storm hit."

"But 440 years and thousands of storms later, no telling where it is. They had to move several feet of silt and sediment off the *Estrella*. No telling how deep the other one may be buried." John yawned.

"You must be tired. Why don't I send you to bed?" At the word *bed*, Polly jumped from her lap and ran down the passageway to the cabin area.

"After this is finished and I dismantle the dam in a few months, maybe we could go somewhere, take a trip."

"I'd like that. Someplace calm."

"Rabbit, I don't think you could take calm."

"Do you ride?"

"Ride what?"

"A horse."

"Not since I was a kid."

"There's a trail ride across Iceland I've always wanted to take."

"What? On a horse across Iceland? That's not what I had in mind at all."

"It'd be fun."

"No, it wouldn't." He stood up and pulled her up with him. Stan awoke, meowed, and followed the trail of Polly down into the bowels of the ship. "This is what I had in mind." He kissed her.

"The two are not mutually exclusive."

"They are if we're on frozen tundra or a glacier or whatever's up there."

"Well, where did you have in mind?"

"I've always wanted to go to Aruba."

"You mean with sand and beach and ocean? I think by the time this is over, I'm going to want a change."

"You be thinking about a place. Somewhere that supports life."

John walked Lindsay to her barge and they kissed good night. Over his shoulder Lindsay saw an opening in the clouds and a patch of stars. She hoped that was a good omen.

Bobbie was already in bed when she returned, but not asleep. "Jeff's out of the hospital. He's staying on the island," she said.

"How is he?"

"He looks a little pale, but I think he's all right. He's grateful not to be in jail. Do you think you can solve all this mess?"

"I don't know. It's not really my job."

"Jeff hopes you do. He's really worried."

"I'm just out of ideas and people to interview. The FBI has more resources. I'm sure they will come up with something."

"Well, everyone has faith that you are going to get to the bottom of it. It was impressive the way you described a man by just seeing his toe print."

"That's not exactly what I did."

The morning brought bad news. Hurricane Harriette had been upgraded to category two and was moving. The steering winds had increased in strength; however, the meteorologists were not sure where she would go. She was moving northward, closer to their site, and she had been moving all through the night. The local weather was deceptive. The winds had died down and there were patches of sky among the clouds. But to the south the distant horizon looked dark gray.

Lindsay worked on excavating the sea chest. The night shift had been suspended and the night crew were working with the day crew. Many of the divers were helping with the excavation. It was almost crowded in the well of the dam.

It gave some a sense of security to have all the people in the dam. But it made Lindsay nervous. It radiated a sense of hysteria.

At noon the sky grew darker and the sound of the waves grew louder. No one ate lunch. Lindsay was reminded of the Gordon Lightfoot song "The Wreck of the Edmund Fitzgerald"—"boys, it's too rough to feed you."

Lindsay looked up to see John's silhouette at the top of the dam. She had a bad feeling in the pit of her stomach. He started down the ladder. A wave sent a spray of water over the top, wetting them all.

John came to the center of the site and stood with Trey on the scaffolding. "The hurricane has changed directions. She is heading here," John announced. "And she is now a category three. When the siren goes off, those who are not in the skeleton crew, evacuate. The archaeology barge will take you away to safety. My barge will take those who stay behind."

"I hate this," Gina said. "It's so scary. I wish I'd stayed on the island today. I'll bet they are already evacuating."

"It'll be all right," Juliana assured her. "They won't let us stay longer than is safe. Will they, Dr. Chamberlain?"

"No, they figured everything out ahead of time."

The excavation stopped and everything that could be was taken up and stored on the barge. No one spoke except to give or respond to orders. A few looked as if they might have tears in their eyes. It was hard to tell, because everyone was covered with a fine mist of salt water. Lindsay wanted to comfort John. She couldn't imagine how he must be feeling.

That sea chantey, the sad one, the last one sailors sang while working the pump before they left the ship, played in her mind over and over.

> *The work was hard, the voyage was long,*
> *Leave her, Johnny, leave her!*
> *The seas were high, the gales were strong,*
> *It's time for us to leave her!*

Lindsay felt like crying. But every time she looked at John, up on top of the dam working with his crew, he seemed calm, undisturbed. Maybe he welcomed a test of his dam.

A large, thick screen lay at the end of the dam, along with piles of long spikes. The early afternoon was spent hoisting up the heavy artifacts and packing the smaller ones. Lindsay was so absorbed in work that when the siren came, she jumped. The sound went on and on and on. More waves sent water raining down into the dam.

Lindsay asked Trey if she could stay and help with the skeleton crew. He nodded absently. She assisted in covering the wreck with the screen. Her wet hands slipped on the wire and she almost cut her hand. When the wire was laid out over the wreck, she helped with pounding stakes into the ground using a wooden hammer not unlike the one used on poor López's head.

The sky grew darker. It was then she noticed that there were no lights in the dam and the pumps were not running. They were going to let the dam fill up and simply pump the water out again. It wouldn't matter to the waterlogged ship at all. Most of the exposed wood had been removed anyway. The rest was under a layer of sand and mud. It was all they could do, and it was time to leave her to whatever Harriette had in mind.

Lindsay was wet and exhausted; the salt water chafed her skin. Her sneakers were caked with mud and heavy on her feet as she made her way in the dark to the stairs. Suddenly there was nothing.

Chapter 31

Lᴉɴᴅsᴀʏ ᴀᴡᴏᴋᴇ ᴄʜᴏᴋɪɴɢ on muddy water. Her head hurt. It was black, black like a cave, like THE cave. She panicked, punching with her fists at something hitting her face. Plastic. She was under plastic. She pulled it until she found an edge and gulped in several lungfuls of air. The words leave her, leave her, leave her, kept running through her dulled brain. She pulled herself up on something—a metal bar?

Leave her.

She was in the dam and the water was almost to her knees. She called out, but her voice was lost to her own ears under the rushing sound of the waves and wind and darkness. Lindsay felt around the metal jungle gym–like object. The stairway. Working her way around she found the steps and slowly climbed them to the top of the dam. In the darkness, against a howling wind, with ocean spray stinging her skin, she stepped from the stairway onto the wall of the dam.

The sand, where was the sand? There was nothing but thick rubber stretched over the top of the dam like the head of a drum. The wind pushed her down and she slid on the wet rubber, hitting the bump where the inner bulkhead stood above the sand, slipping half over into the well. Electric panic sparked through her body as she clawed at the rubber, sliding. There was nothing to hold on to. She slipped over the side. By some miracle she caught hold of the tie ropes that threaded around the edge of the rubber like huge stitches holding it in place. She hung from the rope, suspended on the side of the dam. Her wet fingers hurt. Think. The stairs. They were not a yard away. Gripping hard with her left hand, she let go with her right, stretched it over as far as she could, and grasped another part of the rope. She remembered now—they were going to cap the top of the dam so the water would drain into the well or into the ocean and not soak into the sand. John's crew were doing that when she was taking up the artifacts. She held tightly with her right hand and moved her left over. She could reach the scaffolding again. Safety. Don't count your chickens.

Lindsay took hold of the metal scaffolding with her right hand, and before she could chicken out, she let go of the rope with the left and grabbed the metal bar with it, while searching for a foothold. With her feet on a lower bar and her hands on a higher one, she baby-stepped around the metal structure. It shook as if the footing was no longer on solid ground. She ducked under the bar and lay on the stairs, tired and sick. She yelled again. Only a crashing wave answered her. Don't let grass grow under your feet.

She climbed the stairs again to the top, this time staying low. She crawled onto the slippery rubber. She strained trying to see out in the ocean. Off in the distance she saw a fuzzy light—the barge, a ship, the shore? She was alone. They left her. Trey and the others left her. John left her here in the dark. She yelled his name. He wouldn't leave her here. Her head hurt.

In the flash from the lightning she saw the trailers. She crawled on her belly so she wouldn't make a target for the wind. Don't go in a trailer in a hurricane, some voice said in her head. But what if there's something there? Something? What? Take a breath—a deep breath. You have to get your brain back if you want to live. You're alone. You have to have your brain. Air tanks. Maybe they left some diving equipment. That's it. Good thinking. Would that help? It's calm underwater isn't it? Isn't it? Dear God, please let there be diving equipment. She inched her way to the trailer and held on to its side with one hand and turned the doorknob. It wouldn't turn. It was locked. No. No. There's no reason for it to be locked. Locked out. I can't be locked out. Left out and locked out. She held on to the side until she reached the other door. She turned the knob. Please don't be locked. The door flew open in the wind. She climbed into the trailer and stopped a moment, resting.

Don't rest long. Remember what happened when you rested too long in the cave. It was so much calmer in the trailer. No wind to hit her, no rain, just a little rocking. It's deceptive, her inner voice said. It will blow away and you with it. Get on with it. Lindsay headed for the closet where she knew they kept tanks. She passed the bathroom. Aspirin. She felt in her pocket for her key chain and the small flashlight on it. Never, never be without light. Light is life. If people wouldn't think she was nuts, she'd put it on a bumper sticker. She took four aspirin. It will make you bleed. Was she bleeding? She felt her head. Wet, but not sticky. I'm not bleeding. Don't scare me like that, she admonished her inner voice.

Lindsay almost jumped for joy when she found a full air tank and diving gear. She pulled on the buoyancy compensator, tank, and mask. Someone's weight belt. Not hers. The wrong weight. Doesn't matter, any weight is good weight. She grabbed a diving knife from the floor. No flippers. Flippers would have been good. She could go fast in flippers.

She hated to leave the trailer. It felt so much safer. It rocked violently. It's not safe. Go outside. There was a map next to the door. She didn't know what of, but she remembered Nate's advice. Always orient yourself in the right direction. Good advice, she didn't want to swim farther out into the ocean. She recalled a mental image of the dam and where land was and where ocean was. Remember that image. She put the mask over her face and stepped out the door. The wind knocked her into the side of the trailer. Maybe she could crawl under the rubber and wait. And suffocate. Maybe she could hold on to the stairway until the storm passed. John thinks the dam will hold. But, John doesn't have his butt out here testing it, does he? What if it doesn't hold? The alternative is the ocean. Look at it. It was dreadful, choppy, boiling. But people escaped sinking ships in boats. Boats! They always kept a boat at the dam. That was a rule. Never leave the dam without a boat. They had a small one on the land side of the dock, an outboard. You don't know how to drive a boat, her inner voice told her. "I'll learn," she screamed at it. She had two plans—swimming underwater and driving a boat to shore. One of them would work. She'd think about what to do when she got to shore.

Lindsay crawled to the stairs leading down to the dock, grateful to have something to hold on to. Her hands were cold and wet, and she squeezed the bars until they hurt as she descended. The boat was there. It was a small motorboat. A mouse of a boat. Not worth taking along with them—thank heaven.

It was tied to two moorings, fore and aft, and bucked in the water like an unbroken horse. The ties kept it from crashing into the bulkhead. She somehow managed to climb into the rocking boat and fell onto its bottom. It had water in it, but that was all right. It was only five miles to shore. Five miles, short for calm water, a light-year in a hurricane.

How do you start the motor? Like a lawn mower? Does it have a starter button? She tilted it back so the propeller was in the water, trying to remember her father and brother taking her out fishing. Quick—rudder—she felt for the rudder. Clutch—she found the clutch. Start. What if there's not a key? There wasn't. A starter rope. It had a starter rope. She pulled. Nothing. She pulled again. Nothing. Third time wasn't a charm, but the fourth was and the motor rumbled to life and screamed at the sight of the storm waves. She took the knife and cut the ropes, positioned the rudder in a manner that she hoped would take her away from the dam, and gently moved the clutch.

The boat shot away from the dam, bouncing as if it were made of rubber. Each bounce hit the water hard, jarring her head, making her nauseated. It didn't matter. Nothing mattered but getting to the shore. Then what? Doesn't matter. Get to shore, get to shore, get to shore. She'd make it. The wind slammed at her side. Not good. She remembered the diary. Keep the boat into the wind to ride out a storm. I don't want to ride out the storm, I want to get to shore.

A wave slammed into her, almost turning her over. She was sitting in water. Nothing she could do. Pray you get to shore before she sinks. Maybe you should have stayed at the dam. Too late. The dam was behind her. Don't look back, you'll turn to salt. Besides, if she was lucky, the dam was a couple or three miles behind her. She put the clutch in another gear and went faster, bouncing harder. Get to the shore as fast as you can. Haste makes waste— maybe, but sometimes haste makes fast. She couldn't see the shore. What if she was going in the wrong direction? No, she was going in the right direction. Go, go, go. She was lucky—she bounced, but stayed afloat. People did get to safety in storms in lifeboats, she told herself over and over. Was that it ahead? The shore? There was a line of dark something ahead. Maybe it was the shoreline. Maybe it was clouds. Her head throbbed. Why wouldn't the aspirin take effect? Maybe that was the wrong thing to take. Too late now.

Another wave slammed into her, tossing the boat over on top of her in the water. She sank. The water was not calm below the surface. Her inner advice had lied to her. The wind reached down under the water, churning it. It swirled her around like a mixer.

She fought to get her regulator in her mouth and took a breath. She was hopelessly turned around. She'd never find her way to shore, she was going to drown. No. I'm not going to drown. The waves are going ashore. They will take me ashore.

She felt sick, nauseated. Don't throw up, not now. Later— when you're on the shore. Breathe slowly, be calm, try to dive deeper where it's calmer. You'll go to shore, that's where the water's going. You're close, you were almost there, weren't you? Before you turned over, didn't you see the dark line of trees blowing in the wind? Lindsay let out some air in her BC so she would sink deeper. The water was still choppy. A wave must have gone over her, for she suddenly bobbed and tumbled forward. Just breathe until you have no breath. She reduced her BC some more, sunk a little farther. The water was still rough. Another wave went over. She hit the bottom of the ocean hard, the regulator jarred from her mouth, she slammed the side of her face against the bottom of the sea. Don't breathe, don't breathe. She scrambled for her regulator and put it in her mouth and breathed. It still worked.

Bellisaro stood holding the stump of the mast, yelling at her to hold on, telling her he was sorry. She clawed at the bottom of the ocean until her fingers hurt. The water rushed over her like a river, but she moved against it, swept by some magic current. The floor of the ocean was so hard, and it hurt her fingers. She felt a stabbing pain in her arm. She was going to die.

I'm sorry, she whispered in her mind to all those people who would mourn her. Another wave crashed over her, and another, and another, and she was on land. A tree limb blew on top of her. Her left arm hurt, but she wasn't in the water. She pulled the regulator out of her mouth. The bottom of the ocean still hurt her fingers as she dug them into it trying to rise. It's so hard. Where's the sand? She rose to her knees, pulling off her gear with shaking fingers. The wind blew another branch in her face. She wanted to scream at the trees. In the dim light she looked at the vegetation blowing in the wind. Why was she so high? She looked down, then all around her. No. It's impossible. She heard a creak, a groan, and a crash. She stood.

She was standing on the deck of a galleon. The jagged stump of the mainmast was directly in front of her, the railing to her right. The wind pushed her sideways, the deck started groaning and giving way under her feet. She jumped, landing hard in the wet sand, knocking the breath out of her.

On all fours, gasping for breath, she crawled to the trees. Impossible. She looked again. It was there, impossibly damaged, collapsing, majestic. With another groan, the ship keeled over. Lindsay crawled into the woods, looking for a low place, something with protection, anything. She fell into a shallow depression filled with water and laid her head on the sandy bank.

Lindsay awakened with a start, gasping for air. She had slipped into the ditch and her mouth filled with water. But there was no sound. Had it passed? As she slept, unconscious, it had passed, and now it was morning. Was this the eye? Something told her that no, it wasn't. That, as bad as the winds were, they were not near hurricane strength. Her arm throbbed in pain. She remembered the dream. Bellisaro, the ship. She wondered how she had lived.

She walked on aching, throbbing legs, out on the beach. It had to be a dream. But there in the sunlight lay the ship. Its bow plowed into the foliage, the rest in shallow receding water. It was enormous. Even decayed and crumbling, she was grand. Lindsay walked toward it, the water gently lapping around her ankles—as if only the evening before it hadn't treacherously tried to drown her.

The ship had a gaping wound in her side. The shallow water and thin stretch of sand glittered with gold. A chest had broken open, spilling bars out into the surf. Piles of coins lay in the sand. Lindsay knelt and put her hands in them. Some gold, some silver, some stuck together. She looked inside the hold. It was stacked with barrels and chests. She wanted to walk in. Her better sense, returning to her in the daylight, told her not to. She backed away and picked up a gold bar. It was unbelievably heavy for its size.

She looked up at the sun. Late morning. She had slept a long time. Did anyone miss her? It hit her then what had happened. She hadn't even thought about it until that moment. She touched the back of her head. Someone had hit her and left her under the plastic to die. She felt a stabbing pain in her arm. She looked down at it and fell to her knees.

It's all right, it's all right. It's not that bad, she told herself. A splinter about six inches long was imbedded under the blood-caked skin of her forearm just below the elbow. She touched it tenderly. It was sore. She tugged gently to pull it out and was rewarded with enough pain to make her cry. I've got to get home. Surely someone is looking for me.

She walked around the ship through the vegetation to the other side. Most of the hull on that side was missing and the ribs were showing. The decks were collapsing. No one is going to believe this, she thought. She still held the gold bar. She held it close and started walking in the direction of the house. Every step hurt, her face throbbed. The saltwater-soggy sneakers hurt her feet. My teeth, the regulator! She stuck her fingers in her mouth, feeling. They were all there, but two of her upper incisors were loose. They would tighten back up. Just as long as they were there. She felt no jagged edges, either. The side of her face felt swollen. I'll bet I look like the wreck of the *Hesperus*.

She walked despite the pain. If she stopped and rested, she wouldn't be able to get back up. Her side began to throb. Cracked ribs. She stopped walking, dropped the gold bar, and felt her rib cage. Sore, but she didn't think there was a break. Her side was black and blue. She picked up the gold bar and continued up the beach. It was heavy; she should have picked up something else. The thin strip of sand was getting wider. Ahead she heard voices and saw the dock. She was too tired and sore to yell. She walked.

"She was supposed to be on the archaeology barge." It was John.

"She wasn't. I think she stayed to help. I'm not sure." That was Trey.

"We'll, uh, send divers out to the dam, and—" Lewis didn't finish.

"She helped with the screen, I'm sure." That was Steven.

"Well, why the hell wasn't someone counting heads? That's why we had a plan." John again.

Ramirez was standing with them, looking out to sea, as were Bobbie and Harper, and the two new security guards. No one was looking up the beach. She supposed she had better tell them she was alive. She tried to speak and it came out in a squeak. She cleared her throat.

"Guys. Guys."

They hadn't heard. She walked closer to the dock.

"Guys," she shouted.

They all looked at her for a moment as if she were a ghost.

"Lindsay?" said Trey.

My God, she thought. They don't recognize me.

"Yes."

"Lindsay!" John jumped from the dock and ran toward her.

The others followed. He put his arms around her and lifted her off the ground.

"I was afraid, afraid—"

"I'm not," she groaned.

He put her down.

"Lindsay," said Lewis, "you look awful. Your face."

"I feel awful. I've just had the worst night of my life."

"Why did you stay out there?" Lewis insisted. "You've had us worried sick."

"Oh, I don't know, Lewis. I guess I just thought, well, this is a once in a lifetime experience, I think I'll ride out the hurricane in a cofferdam in the middle of the ocean."

"I think we need to get Lindsay to the hospital," said Ramirez.

"One thing," said Lindsay. "Lewis, this is going to make you very happy. Just remember, you owe me big time."

She handed him the gold bar she had been holding to her chest.

"What is this?"

"Just what it looks like. You think you can have it arrested, or whatever?"

"Where did you find it?" asked Trey.

"It was on the ship I rode in on."

"What?" asked Trey.

They all looked at her as if she were crazy. But there was the gold bar. They couldn't argue with that.

"Lindsay," exclaimed Harper, "your arm. We need to get her to the hospital."

John picked her up in his arms.

"It's a splinter from the ship," she said.

"Are you serious? You know where the wreck is?" asked Lewis. "You can find it so we can start excavation?"

"You don't need to. She sort of excavated herself."

"What?"

"It's down the beach a couple of miles. I told you, I rode it ashore. Me and—well, never mind. That's how I got the splinter in my arm. It's part of the deck. You had better get someone out there to guard it. But I'll have to tell you. You will be tested severely. There's treasure spilling out all over the place and there's probably a trail of it from wherever it was to the shore."

"You're not joking?" asked Lewis.

"I don't have that kind of sense of humor. No. I'm not joking. Better get out there before Jones or somebody finds it." Lindsay laid her head on John's shoulder.

"Lindsay," asked Ramirez. "What happened? Just tell me quickly."

"Someone must have hit me on the head and covered me with plastic under the stairway. When I woke up, all the trains had left the station."

"Oh, God," said Bobbie.

"I really don't feel well," Lindsay said.

"You have to save the splinter," said Lindsay. "It's an artifact. Proof, of a sort."

The doctor looked up at John who stood with her as she sat on the examining table in the emergency room.

"She's an archaeologist. They're peculiar."

A nurse shooed John out to the waiting room while the doctor examined Lindsay. They sent her to X-ray before they removed the splinter. It seemed like hours before she found herself tucked safely in bed. Were it not for the mild concussion, she could have left. But she didn't complain. A night without her bed wafting back and forth or worrying about a prowler wasn't so bad.

The mirror brought another horror. She had insisted on showering and washing her hair. When she finished, she looked at herself for the first time. The whole left side of her face was bruised like her side. She did look awful. Both eyes were black. Her arm hurt. She probably shouldn't have gotten it wet, they hadn't bandaged it. Her entire rib cage ached. For that matter, all of her muscles hurt. There was blood in her urine. The doctor told her that her kidneys had taken a hit, but they would heal in a few days. All in all, she was lucky, which John told her before he left to check the dam. Bobbie and Harper came bearing flowers.

"You sure scared everybody," said Bobbie. "John was beside himself."

"Trey was tearing his hair out when it was discovered you were missing. He had forgotten you stayed."

"He was busy and I wasn't assigned to the skeleton crew. I just couldn't leave with the rest."

"Sentimental?" suggested Harper.

"I was worried about John. The dam means so much to him."

"You're an idiot," said Harper.

"Tell me what happened with you guys," Lindsay asked.

"We went inland to a school basement. Not much to it. The others were at another school—that's why no one knew you were missing. They thought you were with us and we thought you were with them. It was this morning before anyone knew you weren't there."

"What happened with the hurricane?"

"Wasn't one. It veered out to sea and headed north where it was downgraded to a tropical storm again. We were lucky. We only got some of the effects of it," said Harper.

"Then the dam should be all right?"

"Would you quit worrying about that damn dam? It's probably better off than you are," said Harper. "We were all worried."

"Someone wasn't," Lindsay said.

"I know," said Harper. "That's scary. Can you tell us what happened?"

"I'd like to know that, too." Agent Ramirez walked into her room carrying a basket of flowers. Lindsay told her story, from waking up under the plastic, to passing out somewhere in the woods.

"That was quite an adventure," said Ramirez. "Do you have any idea who could have done it?"

"No, not a clue."

"I've posted a guard outside your door."

Harper patted her shoulder and Bobbie gave her a hug. "Get some sleep," Harper said. "We'll see you tomorrow."

"I slept for hours last night."

"I know this isn't as luxurious as sleeping in a swamp, but make the best of it," said Harper.

"Tell John he doesn't have to come by this evening. I know he's busy with the dam."

They left and Lindsay drifted into a comfortable sleep, dreaming of sea serpents and buried treasure and her aunt Maggie rolling out pie crust and spouting aphorisms. She awoke to the sight of John sitting in a chair beside her bed.

"Good morning," he said.

"Morning? How's the dam?" she asked.

"The dam's fine. I told you she would stand up to the winds. I'm pumping the water out now and a crew is putting the roof back on."

The doctor released Lindsay, with a prescription for antibiotics, telling her to keep quiet and take aspirin or ibuprofen for pain, drink plenty of water, and keep an eye out for dizzy spells, nausea, and blurred vision. John took her to the island, where she would be staying with Harper.

"We all insist," said John. "The rocking barge is likely to be too uncomfortable."

Harper had made a bed up for Lindsay. "I can't take your bed," Lindsay said.

"Yes, you can. I'm finished translating, and don't need the perks. We'll all be happier if you're comfortable."

"Well then, thanks."

"There's a debriefing in an hour or so to catch everyone up. If you feel like it, you might enjoy it. Bobbie's bringing us dinner to have in my room. Trey, John, and Luke are joining us—that is, if you feel like a dinner party."

"As long as all of you don't mind looking at my face."

"If you're going to have adventures, you need scars to show for it. How's your arm?"

"Very sore. But they gave me all kinds of shots."

Lindsay actually got a hug from Lewis as she walked through the door to the lab.

"You got the ship secured?" she asked.

"The governor sent a detachment of National Guard and asked the Coast Guard to put a boat in the water off the island. Since the ship is on national parkland, claim is easier in some respects. The Guard have offloaded most of the treasure they can safely get to. They are guarding the rest while we dismantle the ship. Most of the treasure spilled out into the water, of course. I brought in the divers to start locating it and the missing timbers."

"How's Jones taking it?"

"Haven't heard from her, or seen her ship, but I think she is still trying to make a claim based on the bell and a few pieces of wood. I don't know if she knows that it's washed up onshore, but I'll bet she does. She may try to say that she found it before the hurricane hit."

"The ship had to be in close to the shore."

"It must have. We were looking farther out all that time. You know, a sunken ship named the *Alatoona* washed ashore after a storm like this thirty or forty years ago on the coast of North Carolina. It came to an ignoble end. The surf eventually pounded it to pieces, campers built fires in what remained of its hull, and now it's gone. This one will have a happier future. It will be displayed next to the *Estrella*." Lewis grinned from ear to ear.

Everyone greeted Lindsay warmly. Nothing was mentioned about an attack, but she was sure everyone had heard by now. She scanned their faces, looking for someone who was disappointed or uncomfortable. But they all seemed happy to see her.

Ramirez was there in the doorway. She wondered why. She looked questioningly at him. "Everything all right?" she asked.

"Just keeping an eye out," he said.

"On what?"

"Things." He smiled and patted her shoulder. "I like it here. Usually I have to travel all over the place looking for the bad guys and witnesses. This is what's nice about an island. Everyone is in the same place. I don't have to travel so much."

Lindsay sat down on the couch between Bobbie and John.

"As you know," Lewis addressed the group, "Lindsay, during her ocean adventure, located what we believe to be the *Espada de Nuestra Señora de la Limpia Concepción*. We have been looking for her all along, but for obvious reasons had to keep it a secret. We didn't know, however, that the *Concepción* was connected in such an interesting way to the *Estrella*, as has been revealed to us by the diary." Lewis gave Harper a nod. "The diary has been a special and unusual addition to the excavation. Not only do we have a ship and part of the crew, but an account of the voyage. We think we may actually have been able to establish the identity of some of the skeletal remains after being lost over 440 years under the sea."

Lindsay hoped he wasn't going to make a long speech. She ached from her toes to the top of her head.

"So," said Korey, "we now know this guy Sancho killed López, and López is our guy with the dented head, and Sancho is our guy in chains."

"He said he didn't do it," Juliana protested.

"They all say that," Sarah replied.

"Well, sometimes they are telling the truth," commented Jeff, not without some emotion.

Neither Lewis nor Trey seemed to mind the debriefing degenerating into a discussion about the diary; in fact, they seemed to welcome it. Someone had tacked up copies of the pictures Lindsay had drawn of the skeletal remains—four of them. She looked at each in turn. The last one, the one she had thought was Valerian, startled her. That face was the one in the dream, or hallucination, that her mind gave to Bellisaro.

"Who else could have killed him?" Steven asked. "Let's not make a mystery where there isn't one. It's pretty straightforward."

"Sancho is innocent," said Lindsay, and everyone turned to her.

"You all right, Doc?" asked Nate. "You look like you've been shot at and missed, and shit at and hit."

When the laughter died, Lindsay smiled at him.

"Thanks for that image of my appearance. I assure you, I feel much worse than I look. Sancho, whatever misdeeds he committed on the ship, did not kill López."

Chapter 32

LEWIS WAS THE first to break the surprised silence. "Okay, who did kill López?"

"Yeah," said Nate, sitting with his feet propped on a chair. "You're going to be hard-pressed to convince us that someone else did it. It happened, after all, about 440 years ago. Are you that good?"

"We'll see. Go ahead, Lindsay. You have our interest." Lewis leaned back on the edge of the table, half sitting, half standing.

"Yes," said Carolyn, "you've got some of the principal characters and evidence sitting over there on the table. Go for it."

"Sancho had blood on him and he had the cross," said Steven, reminding Lindsay of the heavy evidence against him.

"Which, apparently," said Lewis, "is the same cross we have. It has to be handed over to our FBI friend here, but I think we can prove it belongs with the *Estrella*." He held it up. It was stunning.

"Possession of the cross doesn't mean he took it." Lindsay saw Jeff nodding his head in agreement. She had convinced him already. She half expected to hear an "amen" from his corner. "Nor does it mean he killed for it. Blood on his clothes only connects him with the crime scene. Not with the murder." Lindsay noticed that Ramirez eyed her closely, wanting to disagree, but saying nothing.

"But can you prove to us that he didn't do it?" asked Nate.

"I can prove that the evidence doesn't show that he did. Are you asking me to prove a negative?"

"I'd never do that," Nate said, grinning.

"I'm making an assumption that the diary is an accurate account," she said. A big assumption, but she knew they would agree. They all wanted it to be accurate. They were all planning papers around it, and so far it corresponded with what they had found.

Lindsay limped across the room and retrieved López's skull and the mallet. She was having fun and after the previous evening, it was welcome.

"López was killed with an instrument like this. Because of the angle and placement, the killer was probably left-handed." She held the skull up in her right hand, facing the audience. In her left hand she held the head of the mallet and touched it to the skull, illustrating how the first blow occurred.

"What was Sancho?" asked Steven.

Lindsay smiled. "Left-handed."

"Seems to me evidence is still stacking up against him," Steven said.

"Sancho's left hand had been nailed to the mast. The ship's doctor wanted to cut it off," announced Bobbie. "He couldn't have used it."

"That's right," agreed Lindsay.

She handed the mallet and skull back to Carolyn, who returned them to the tanks. John handed Lindsay a bandanna to dry the brine from her hands.

"But that doesn't mean he couldn't have used his right hand and hit him backhandedly" said Steven. "If you can't use one hand, you are forced to use another. And it was López's fault he was nailed to the mast. That gave Sancho a strong motive."

"True, that alone is not proof, but I'm not finished."

"He had the victim's blood smeared on him," Nate added, "the blood he got from contact with the wall where it was splattered."

"Yes, and what does the diary say about that?" Lindsay asked. "Does anyone have a copy of the diary handy?" Trey handed her a notebook. She quickly flipped through the pages, and read the section:

> *Father Hernando and Captain Acosta arrived with the boatswain. As the good father prayed over him, I shook my head at the little halos of his splattered blood. Poor López, for all his desires and aspirations, this was all that was left of him.*

"Blood drops and spatters are thin at the edges and thick in the middle. They dry around the edges first, the middle last. The diarist describes the splatters as halos. When Sancho smeared it, the edges had dried, but not the middle. Sancho smeared the blood after it had time to partially dry. That was well after the murder."

"She is right about the blood," Ramirez confirmed. "Very observant, Dr. Chamberlain."

"He may have returned to the scene of the crime," said Nate.

"He may have, but the evidence against him was the blood, which they thought he got on him during the crime. To say now that he came back to the scene afterward no longer connects him to the event of the murder itself." She stopped a moment to let it sink in. "I think Sancho took the cross when he found the body. I doubt that a man like Sancho could resist."

"I think we have to give Lindsay this one," conceded Steven. "But to be fair, none of us know anything about blood splatter."

"Yes, Chamberlain," said Trey. "You have such an interesting repertoire of knowledge."

"Okay, Lindsay. Who did do it?" Korey asked.

"Any guesses?" Lindsay asked.

"How about the diarist," Gina said. "He risked his life to get the cross, and López took it from him."

"I hope Valerian didn't do it," remarked Juliana. "But he had those dealings with López, and López wouldn't let him keep his servant in his quarters."

"I never liked that captain," Nate joked. "He was a wuss."

"I think I know who did it, and why," said Lindsay. "But all the evidence is circumstantial."

"Circumstantial evidence is very strong in court, if you have enough of it," said Ramirez.

"Okay, give, Lindsay," Bobbie said. "Who did it?"

"I think that Bellisaro did it."

"Bellisaro?" said Harper. "He hardly ever said anything. Why do you think he did it?"

"Yeah, Doc," said Nate, "how do you figure that poor guy did it?"

"I think he had the most powerful motive. The diarist describes that Bellisaro had a broken arm and leg that he got in battle, and that his injuries had healed well. The diary also describes that when the ship went down, Bellisaro fell through the middle of it."

"So?" said Nate.

"Here I have more evidence than you do. I thought HSkR4 was Valerian because the measurement indices indicated it to be from

North Africa. But it has healed breaks in the arm and leg. He was found amidships, and he is left-handed. The diary describes Bellisaro with those former injuries as well as his falling into the well of the ship."

"So what?" repeated Nate.

"So his skull suggests that he is from Morocco," said Lindsay, watching all their faces, waiting for someone to get it. No one said anything. "Bellisaro was not originally in on the plot to change the ship's course. He had to be convinced, and the captain wasn't having any luck. López told the captain not to worry."

"During the dinner that the captain hosted, we learn that López knew a lot of people. The diarist mentions that López knew Bellisaro's grandfather. He also hinted that Bellisaro might be offended by the salted pork, and wasn't it good of the captain to order chicken instead. López also asked if Bellisaro was offended when Valerian and the diarist played chess. Each of those times, Bellisaro either refused to engage in conversation, or left the room."

"I don't get it," said Juliana.

"North Africa was primarily Muslim. Spain was still under the euphoria of the Reconquista, reclaiming Spain for the Christian Spanish and driving out the Muslims who had ruled the country for several hundred years. Military societies arose to award the faithful Christian soldiers who fought for Spain, like the Order of Santiago—one of the most honored and powerful, of which our diarist was a member. He recounted some of the privileges derived from being a member, such as exemption from certain punishments. There were many other more lucrative perks that made membership very important if you were to get along well in a highly stratified bureaucratic society like Spain. Bellisaro was also a member of the Order of Santiago, according to the diarist. There were also strict rules about who could become members."

"Oh," said Bobbie. "You had to have pure Spanish blood."

Lindsay nodded. "In particular, Christian blood."

"But Bellisaro had Muslim heritage," said Bobbie.

"Yes, he did. It was common for men to forge their genealogy. The payoff was big. And the loss for Bellisaro would be equally big were he to be discovered. López knew, and he was blackmailing Bellisaro to get him to change course. He knew Bellisaro's grandfather and said so at dinner, probably for Bellisaro's benefit. He also mentions the pork, which Muslims don't eat, another reference to the fact he knows about Bellisaro's lineage and is rubbing his nose in it. It didn't matter that Bellisaro was Christian himself, it mattered that his grandfather was not."

"What about the chess game?" asked Juliana.

"The chess set had a detailed image of a queen—an image of a woman. López mentioned it as a backhanded reference to the Muslim prohibition against images of women in their art. Just another suggestion to Bellisaro that López knew. I believe López wore Bellisaro down until he agreed to change course.

"Bellisaro was basically an honest and honorable man. He struggled hard to save the ship, and he tried to save the children first when the ship was sinking. But López found his weak spot. Bellisaro didn't take the cross because that was not the motive for the murder and he wasn't a thief. The motive was to save his career and his family's position. It was the difference between wealth and poverty. López could hold Bellisaro's secret over him forever, and that's why Bellisaro killed him—to be free of the extortion."

"Wouldn't López have told someone, like the captain?" asked Sarah.

"To a man like López, secrets are power, and he would only share power when he had to. He didn't have to tell the captain. Bellisaro probably knew that. But, as I said, this part is circumstantial."

Lewis clapped his hands. "You've convinced me, Lindsay."

"Me, too," Steven said. "I didn't think you could do it."

"Good job, Doc. I confess, you got a lot more out of the diary than I did. I'm going to have to read the thing again," said Nate.

Lindsay sat back down. "Good job, Rabbit," John whispered in her ear.

Ramirez made his way through the crowd to where Lindsay was sitting. "You put on quite a show. I enjoyed every minute of it. When the solution to our current problem surfaces in your brain, I hope you will call."

"I will indeed. Thanks again for the flowers. They're lovely. You going to take the cross?"

"Ah, the cross. The police asked me to get it for them. It's supposed to be evidence in an attack. However, there are problems. Is this the cross that was stolen? Who knows? I would have said, how many crosses could there be? But apparently, you have discovered potentially a whole shipful. Then, I wonder, is this the cross in the diary, and therefore an artifact of the *Estrella*? Who knows that, either?" He grinned mischievously. "You archaeologists present me with nothing but problems, and only solutions to very old crimes. You go get some rest. I would not describe your appearance in so unflattering terms as that fellow, but you do look like sleep would be welcome."

"I think I'll take your advice."

Lindsay went up to Harper's room and lay down, but couldn't sleep. The reality that someone here, an archaeologist, had tried to kill her, weighed on her so heavily she felt she couldn't breathe. She stared into the darkness trying to remember who was on the skeleton crew. It was so dark, the wind made her eyes water and her vision blurred. Trey could tell her who he had selected.

Trey—it wouldn't have been Trey. He was a friend and wouldn't have done this to her. Would he? No. The attacker was probably the murderer. John was there. John loved her. He wouldn't hurt her. Who else? Someone from John's crew? She knew only Luke. Could one of his crew have known about the treasure all along? That was a dead end. She didn't have enough information to even guess.

Who else was there? Sarah and Juliana? She couldn't see either of them doing such a thing. Steven, Nate? Why? What did she know about Nate? He was shot at, and he was looking for the treasure. Two facts, but what had they to do with anything? What had they to do with her? Steven? Steven was on the scene when they found the rifled sea chest. But as she had just demonstrated in the meeting, being there after the fact proves nothing. Korey was at the dam helping attend the artifacts. He stayed and helped to secure the site. But why would he try to kill her? No reason she could think of.

Lindsay turned over, trying to find a comfortable position to lie. Jones, the person whom she was most suspicious of, wasn't even in contention. Or was she? It was dark. Someone from Jones's crew could have climbed the stairs and secreted themselves in the dam. No. Lindsay hadn't seen any ships on the sea, certainly not Eva Jones's sailing ship. They could swim underwater from the shore—no, the minisub. They could have come in the minisub, come aboard the dam, hid until they saw their opportunity, knocked her out, covered her up, and left the same way they came.

But why? Did she know something she didn't think she knew? Did someone think she knew something? Did she let something slip at her meeting with Jones? Was it something so important that Jones would go to all that trouble?

Lindsay again flipped over on her back. What could she know? Or, what had she seen? As she puzzled over the question, she thought she saw a form coming toward her in the dimness of the room. Lindsay didn't think very long, she flipped over and off the bed and scrambled under it, feeling around for a weapon. The lights went on.

"Lindsay, it's me, John. Are you all right?"

Lindsay crawled out from under the bed, hoping the redness in her face wouldn't show up under her bruises. "I'm fine."

John helped her to her feet. "I'm sorry. I didn't mean to scare you. But I'll have to say, hurt or not, your reflexes are fast."

Standing up in the bright light, Lindsay realized that under the bed was not the best of hiding places.

"I suppose I'm a little skittish."

"More than a little, but I can't say as I blame you. I came up to tell you that Bobbie and Luke are going to pick up some dinner. Harper thought you might want some time to get dressed."

Lindsay looked at herself in the dresser mirror. Her hair was a tangled mess, her face was black and blue, and she had put on her baggiest nightshirt.

"Are you sure you want to go off somewhere with me?"

"Well, when the bruises go away, you comb your hair and put on some nice clothes, you won't look too bad." Lindsay picked up a pillow and threw it at him as she went into the bathroom.

⚓

"Are you sure you feel up to this?" Harper asked, as she set up TV trays around the room for everyone.

"If I get to feeling bad, I'll just go back to bed. But I wasn't getting very much rest. My mind is too restless. And I ache so many places, I can't find a comfortable sleeping position."

"Want a sleeping pill?"

Lindsay shook her head. "No. I'm trying to get my brain back. It doesn't seem to be working too well."

"It was going pretty strong during debriefing," Harper said.

"That was fun. I was thinking, for the book, why don't you write up your scenario and let me put it in as an appendix?"

"I'll do that."

Bobbie and Luke brought back a bucket of fried chicken, shrimp, french fries, slaw, fried apples, mashed potatoes, and more varied desserts than they could possibly eat. Lindsay curled up on the corner of the couch and nibbled at her food, listening to the others talk.

"Aren't you hungry?" asked Harper.

"Not much. I wish I were."

"You feeling nauseated?" Harper asked. John looked up, concerned.

"No, I'm just not hungry. I'll just sit here and listen to you guys." She wanted to ask them not to monitor her, but they were being kind, and that would be ungrateful. "My front teeth are a little loose, too," she said. "Hitting the ship face-first knocked the regulator out of my mouth."

"Oh, no," said Bobbie. "And we got fried chicken."

"That's fine. I've enjoyed the shrimp. Please, I've enjoyed what I've eaten. I just don't feel like eating very much. Lewis, tell us about the museum."

Lewis was not a man who planned small things. Really, his plans sounded fun—they also sounded as though he would have to do a tremendous selling job to the Board of Regents.

"Why don't you build a replica?" asked Lindsay.

"What?" asked Lewis.

"A full-size replica of one of the galleons, filled with reproductions of the things in it. One that people could go in and look around—turn the capstan and work the pumps."

Lewis didn't say anything for a long time. "I like that idea. After I talk them into the museum, that may be my next project. What made you think of that?"

"Standing on the deck of the *Concepción*. As decayed as she was, there was something, I don't know—it was an exciting feeling, as brief as it was."

"Good idea, Chamberlain." Even Trey was catching Lewis's enthusiasm.

"I doubt the university will go along with it," said Lindsay.

"Maybe and maybe not," Lewis said, with just a hint of a twinkle in his eye.

Lindsay lapsed into listening mode again as Lewis told John about Nate's project. "We found the ship before we got a chance to plug in the data for the gold coins Lindsay found on the beach."

Lindsay was curious how the program worked. He "found" the *Estrella* in experimental trials using data for the cannons and other items. But those items were thrown from the ship. How could his program predict which way the storm carried the *Estrella* after the crew ditched the cargo? Meteorologists couldn't predict the last storm. Artifacts that were thrown overboard before the wreck should be treated differently from artifacts that washed away after the wreck. She imagined that Nate accounted for that in defining his variables. He'd have to. She asked Lewis about it.

"How the artifact was lost figures into the program. He's adapted his own model from other models explaining how different objects travel through a cultural system and become a part of the archaeological record—adding natural underwater current activity as a component in the model. Of course, he has to also take into consideration the shape and mass of the object. It's very complex."

So is bullshit, thought Lindsay. But she didn't say it.

"Looks like he'd need a lot of data on small-current vectors." Luke had his forehead wrinkled as if he was trying to think of how much data that would be.

"He has notebooks full of data he's been collecting and keying into the system," said Lewis. "I'm almost sorry we found the wreck before he could try it. Almost. It is a relief to know that we have it and not Jones. I've sent several notebooks of his unrecorded data to be keyed in by graduate students. It ought to be done in a couple of weeks. We can test his program on the coins Lindsay found. If he turns up the site, we're in the money, so to speak."

"Did you ever figure out what that thing was I found?" Bobbie asked Lindsay.

"No. I asked Steven Nemo if it could be used to catch fish or anything and I'm afraid I've let myself in for a lifetime of fishing jokes." Lindsay paused. "If you guys don't mind, I'd like to go to bed. Please don't leave. You won't bother me at all. In fact, it will be comforting to hear your voices out here. Besides, it looks like we still have food left."

Lindsay crawled into bed, sleepier than when she napped earlier. She wouldn't tell Lewis that, he might take offense. She smiled as her head hit the pillow. She almost drifted off to sleep, but awoke with a start.

She knew what the coins were for. Keith was staking the coins out on the ocean bottom on a length of fishing line and letting them drift with the current. He'd go back later, measure and record the place where the coin drifted, put the stake in the new spot and start over. He would repeat that until he had a description of the path the coin took reaching the shore. And he had done this for years. It probably worked. He had found at least three ships that we know of. Maybe more. He probably wouldn't have told his father, afraid Boote would give out his secret. All he had to do was to take all the data and work an average approximation of how the coins moved through the water. That's why he searched the beaches, especially after a storm. Looking for coins from shipwrecks. If he could find coins, he could find the ship. He didn't need to go all the way back 440 years ago. Just the last storm would do.

It was really a better experiment than Nate's convoluted program because he was taking a direct measure of an object and applying the conclusions to that same object. Keith Teal, in effect, had taken Occam's razor to Nate's program—variables shouldn't be multiplied needlessly. Keith used only coins—he only needed coins. And he didn't need all the other data, just his average vectors. He didn't need all Nate's fancy complex variables.

Lindsay sat up in bed, struggling to remember all those things in her head that made shadows but would not show themselves. She got out of bed quickly and dressed. Harper was asleep on the couch. She took her key and tiptoed to the door and locked it behind her on the way out. As she descended the stairs, she thought she heard voices. It sounded as though Dale the security guard and William the meteorologist were talking by the front desk.

She went down to the lab to her desk to search for Keith's post card that Boote had loaned her. It must have fallen out of her notebook. She searched every drawer. She went to Carolyn's and Korey's desks, thinking that perhaps the card had fallen on the floor and either Korey or Carolyn might have picked it up. Nothing in Korey's drawers or around his workplace. Carolyn had a phone message from the Smithsonian weighted down with a book about the Chinese box. Lindsay gave it a brief glance— "lacquer's main ingredient from Oriental lacquer tree is urushiol. Ha . . ."—the rest was covered up. Lindsay searched the desk drawers. Nothing. She looked on the floor.

"Hi. Dr. Chamberlain, isn't it?"

Lindsay started and looked up. It was one of the new security guards. "Hi. Yes, I'm Dr. Chamberlain. I'm sorry. I forgot your name."

"Tom Bowers. Shouldn't you be in bed? The last time I saw you—"

"I know, I looked half dead. I lost a post card and felt the need to find it. How is everything here?"

"Fine. Our friend Dale is manning the front desk just fine; Robert is at the warehouse. It's all very quiet."

"This job must be quite a change of pace for you guys."

"You can say that again. Is archaeology always this exciting?"

"It's always exciting, just not usually so—adventurous."

"Robert and I are gearing up for a lot of treasure hunters. I'm glad we've got a few National Guardsmen here."

"Me, too. I can't find my post card, so I think I'll go on up to bed."

"I'll lock up," said Bowers. "Oh, there's some stuff pinned to that bulletin board in the kitchen. Someone may have found it and stuck it up there."

"That's a good thought. I'll go look."

Lindsay walked back to the kitchen. The board was filled with pieces of paper. She began looking through them for the card. The back door opened and Nate entered.

"Nate," said Lindsay, "what are you doing here?"

"Looking for an opportunity to get you alone. I need my notebooks back."

"You mean Keith's notebooks, don't you? The ones he recorded his coin data in, the ones that match the handwriting on the postcard I got from Boote."

"Whoever's, I want them."

"I don't have them."

"No one else would take them."

Lindsay eased back toward the hallway door. It opened and Bowers entered. Lindsay sighed.

"I'm glad to see you. Will you walk me back to my room?"

"No, Dr. Chamberlain. I can't do that."

Chapter 33

Lᴉɴᴅsᴀʏ ʀᴇᴍᴇᴍʙᴇʀᴇᴅ Wɪʟʟɪᴀᴍ Kuzniak saying that Nate was after Lewis to get new security guards. Of course—why couldn't she have remembered that while she was upstairs working out all those other things?

"You and Robert are the divers who shot Nate aren't you? Did you mean to hit him, or were you simply giving Trey a reason to call the Coast Guard to maintain a close presence and harass Evangeline Jones to keep her out of the running for the galleon?"

"You're right, Nate, she's quick," said Bowers. He looked at Lindsay. Tom Bowers was one of those people who looked friendly no matter what he was doing. "Too bad about the concussion. I'll bet if you had been thinking straight, you would have been quicker and avoided this situation." He walked over to the cabinet and got a bottle of whiskey.

"I was thinking the same thing," Lindsay said. "Nate, for the record, it was you who hit me and left me in the dam, wasn't it?"

"Yes. Who would have thought you could get away in a hurricane? But I'm glad you found the galleon."

"I'll bet you are. You wouldn't have found it with that lame program of yours. You've been dry-labbing your data, haven't you? How long did you think you could get away with that? There would come a time when Lewis and your committee would examine your data closely and realize you were faking your successes."

"Lewis. All this is his damn fault," Nate swore. "He wants results, all the time, results. It's a good program. I'm just not finished."

"It's not Lewis's fault. He pushes all of us—me, Harper, Carolyn, Trey—even John. We just tell him our boundaries and he backs off. You didn't have to kill people, for heaven's sake."

339

"Kill people? Nate, what's she talking about?"

"Who do you think's generating all these dead bodies?" Lindsay asked.

"You said it was the pirates," said Tom, looking uncertainly at Nate.

"No. It was Nate," said Lindsay. "That must have really infuriated you, Nate—Keith, the man everyone referred to as a beach bum, coming up with a better method than yours for finding wrecks."

"My program is a simulation of ocean dynamics. Finding wrecks is just part of it. His was just a bunch of observations."

"Your program is a hodgepodge of incomplete data. You thought enough of Keith's observations to steal them from him. Was that what you argued about with Keith the night Mike Altman saw you?"

"Keith wanted me to guarantee him a cut, a big cut. I couldn't give him a guarantee that would satisfy him."

"So you killed him. And you attacked Boote when you went to steal the rest of Keith's notebooks—and the cross."

"Shut up."

"Look, Nate—" said Tom.

"She's lying."

"She's got some of it right," Tom said. "Look, we agreed that we'd just get her drunk and leave her somewhere so people would think she was crazy, or hit on the head too hard."

"He killed Denton, too." Lindsay wished William or Dale or someone would come to the kitchen for water. But everyone went to the break room when they wanted something in the night. She thought about screaming, but she was too far away from everyone—no one would hear and it would force them into action.

"Nate, tell me, did you kill those two?" Bowers asked.

"No. Can't you see what she's trying to do?"

"You found Denton here getting copies of diary pages from Mike—who stole them from us. Denton was giving them to Eva Jones. You couldn't have that, could you? Denton told you Jones was close, that she had something. She had a letter addressed to Valerian, didn't she? It was in code, the code the pilot of the *Concepción* wrote in to Valerian, telling where the ship was. Jones found out that the diary from the *Estrella* mentioned the name Valerian and that it was written in code. She thought it was the same code. That's why she wanted the translation and a few pages of the diary—a little Rosetta stone to allow her to translate her letter."

"Nate," said Tom, "what the heck is she talking about?"

"She's just delirious. I told you, it will be easy just to make her look drunk. Come on." He grabbed her arm.

"Denton didn't just tell you about the letter," she yelled as he pulled her across the kitchen. "You had to hold his head under water in the warehouse to force him to tell you. You know, don't you, they found sugar water in his lungs?"

"Shut up." He started to slap her and she ducked, pulling away.

Tom came up behind her and held her. Lindsay kicked at his shins and screamed. He put a hand over her mouth.

"Hush now. I don't want to kill you, but I will hurt you to save myself. I know what you are going to say next. You're going to tell me that I haven't killed anyone, so now would be a good time to cut my losses. After all, I only took an underwater shot at Nate and that was for a good cause—to keep looters away from the area. I'm right, aren't I? That's what you were going to say?"

He was right. That was exactly the argument she was going to present to him.

"But you see," he continued, holding her so tight her ribs ached. "That's a lot of money on that ship. And Nate says he can see to it that we get a share. I know there are all kinds of guards there now, and a big portion has already been packed up by you guys, but Nate here is on the inside. He also tells me that there is a king's ransom still on the bottom that the ship dropped before it washed ashore."

Lindsay tried to break away again. Tried to stomp his feet. He squeezed her around the middle so hard she thought she would pass out from the pain.

"I have a sister like you," Tom said. "I love her. She's a great sister. She's smart like you. She values her brain more than any part of her body. I'll bet you're like that. I won't kill you, but I can put you in a choke hold and cut off the blood supply to your brain for just a few seconds. Do you know what that will do?" Lindsay nodded. "Good. You aren't going to struggle any more, are you?" She shook her head. He let go of her mouth, but held her upper arm in a hard grip, her injured arm, which was now throbbing from lack of circulation.

"See, Nate, you don't have to kill people."

"You can't let her go," began Nate.

"Dammit, Nate. I've never killed anyone and I'm not going to. I don't really want to hurt her. Now, our original plan will still work. She has no proof of anything."

"You don't understand. She is very persuasive. You should have heard her today. She convicted the pilot of the *Estrella* after 440 years."

"That's interesting, isn't it?" asked Lindsay.

"What?" said Nate.

"Both you and Bellisaro had the same motive for murder—your careers."

"You are such a bitch. Why couldn't you take that message to heart?"

"Stubbornness, I suppose."

"I'll bet you wish you had."

"Considering how things are right now, yes."

Lindsay was searching her brain for a plan. She had none. Help was so close—several people were in the house, the National Guard was down the beach, the Coast Guard was patrolling the water, and she might as well be in the middle of nowhere. Each of them took an arm and escorted her out the back door. The moon was waning and there were clouds. It was dark, but not as dark as pitch, not as dark as a cave. But dark. Perhaps she could do something with the dark. Her gaze roved over the area. They were on a wooden walkway that led to the second-floor kitchen. She and Bobbie had carried groceries in that way. There was a parking lot ahead just beyond the shrubbery. To the right was sand and palmettos. To the left were a ten-foot expanse of sand and the alligator pond.

"You won't be able to get any treasure," said Lindsay. "It will be so well guarded that even Nate can't get to it. I've talked with Lewis and it's all spoken for."

"That's a little lame," Tom countered.

"Nate is not an expert in artifacts. He's an excavator and a diver. His academic speciality is geography—that's what his master's is in. There's no reason whatsoever for him to have access to the treasure. If he tries too hard to gain access, Lewis will become suspicious. If any turns up missing, he'll know. Don't think for a minute that it won't be inventoried and Nate won't be a suspect. You can still get out of this."

"Will you please just do that choke hold thing and shut her up?" said Nate.

"Nate knows I'm telling the truth. He's stringing you along so you'll do what he wants. But now you know about the murders. That makes you an accessory after the fact."

"Then I've got nothing to lose by killing you?" Tom rasped at her. He was losing patience. That was a bad sign.

"Yes, you do. Simply turn him in—then you're not an accessory and not a murderer."

"I'm also not rich."

"You're not going to get rich. You can forget that."

Nate swung his fist to hit Lindsay in the face. She ducked her head, and his fist connected with Tom, knocking him sideways and loosening his grip on her arm. Lindsay bolted. Nate grabbed her and started to swing again. Nate wasn't a fighter. He took a lot of time swinging his arm back to get momentum for his punch. Lindsay kicked him in the groin and he doubled over. Tom rushed for her. She ran. He was about to grab her, she felt his hand on her shirt. She ducked sideways through the railings, sprinted across the ten feet of sand, slipped into the alligator pond, dove under, and swam.

She came to a clump of vegetation and surfaced just long enough to take a breath and in time to hear Tom call Nate an idiot and tell him to get Robert to help them hunt. She thought about swimming to the front to get Dale. But Dale might not believe her and let Nate drag her off, telling Dale they were taking her to the hospital. Or worse yet, Dale could be in on it with them.

Where could she get help? The meteorologists? Could she dash past Dale and get to William, or lock herself in Lewis's office and telephone the barge? Or dash up to Harper's room? Could she be fast enough? Would they come after her? Would they kill everyone, or simply run away? She hurt—her ribs, her legs, her arms. She hurt so bad she shook. Her brain was growing dull again from the pain. She surfaced. It was quiet. A flashlight, like a spotlight, swept across the water. She ducked just in time and swam farther into the pond, waiting until she could hold her breath no longer before she surfaced. She heard them. Someone was around in front of the house. Robert? Tom was still sweeping the flashlight back and forth in a search pattern. She heard the splash of a boat and the rhythmic splashing of oars. Nate had put a rowboat into the water, probably the one he used to move the bodies. No doubt he was armed and dangerous—and had a flashlight.

Think, think, think. The National Guardsmen were just a couple of miles down the beach. A couple of miles—they may as well have been a hundred. She couldn't make it. Could she? What if she went through the woods?

She heard the boat and went under the water again, swimming farther into the pond. How big was it? It was fairly deep where she was. Around the front of the house it had come up to John's chest. The marsh was shallow where Harper took a bath after falling in the quicksand. She wished one of them would fall into a pit of quicksand.

She heard the boat coming and saw another light sweeping the water. She ducked the light, hoping the ripples wouldn't give her away. When she had surfaced last, she saw a clump of marsh grass to her left. She swam for it until she felt vegetation, and resurfaced. Perhaps she could just avoid them until daylight. It was more shallow here. Her feet touched the bottom. Her eyes were getting better adjusted to the darkness. She rubbed the water from them. And looked for the light.

That's when she discovered she was face-to-face with an alligator. It lay in the water not four feet away, its nose and brow ridge above the water. She started shaking so hard, the water quivered. She never thought she would prefer to be back in the ocean in a hurricane. Stay still, don't move. Alligators are active at night. She knew that about them. Please have already eaten. The alligator didn't move, but stared at her, or seemed to. How many more were in here? This was not a good plan.

She heard the *splash, splash, splash* of oars in the water. Nate coming for her with a gun. Surely he couldn't hope to get away with killing her? Maybe he would—"*saw her leave the house and followed her. She fell in the water and was attacked by an alligator, meant to shoot him, not her. Sorry.*" What kind of story would that make? The question was, would Nate think it would make a good story? Yes, he would. He had two witnesses to back him up.

Splash, splash, splash. He was closer, shining that light. Light was death if it fell on her. Lindsay was afraid to move, close to panic, terrified. Surely the alligator must hear her heart beating, surely Nate must, it was so loud in her ears. It pounded up in her throat, in her ears. *Thump, thump, thump, splash, splash, splash.*

Nate was almost upon her. The light would hit her in a moment, the alligator would attack, she would die a terrible death. She slowly ducked under the water, trying to make nary a ripple. She felt the boat move over her, felt an oar just miss the top of her head. She came out of the water under the left side of the boat and pushed with all her might, capsizing it. Nate fell into the water, splashed, cursed, yelled, then screamed. She heard running, saw the wiggling beams of the flashlights that Robert and Tom carried.

Where could she go? She swam away from the commotion, trying to filter out the screams and the enormous splashing of the water, which she knew was the alligator. Suddenly she was hauled out of the water and a hand clamped over her mouth. She struggled.

"It's me, Mike Altman—and James Choi."

They pulled her back into the brush, into the sharp palmettos, away from the lights. She heard gunfire and grimaced. Mike led her through the brush and down a narrow trail until she thought she would faint. She saw lights ahead and pulled back.

"It's all right," said James.

It was the ranger station. They rushed her up the stairs and into the kitchen.

"My God, what happened to you?" Lindsay looked up at Tessa.

Gretchen came into the kitchen. "What was that shooting!"

"Don't shout," Lindsay whispered. "Lock the doors."

"What's going on?" asked Tessa.

"Nate's gone berserk," said Mike, going to all the outside doors and locking them.

Tessa left the room a moment and came back with a blanket and put it around Lindsay's shoulders.

Lindsay's teeth chattered and she started shaking uncontrollably.

"Can we move to the interior of the house?" she asked.

"Good idea," said Mike, returning from his rounds.

"What is going on?" asked Gretchen.

They took her to what appeared to be a den, with no windows. Lindsay briefly explained what had happened.

"He was trying to kill you?" Gretchen asked. Lindsay nodded.

"Call the ranger station on Cumberland," Mike told Tessa. Tessa picked up the phone and dialed.

"Thanks," said Lindsay. "You saved my life."

"You were doing okay," James said.

"What were you two doing out there?" asked Lindsay. Then she saw that James held a pair of night goggles.

"I'm observing the night animals—alligators, too. We would have helped sooner, but we couldn't figure out what was going on."

"I'm sorry about the alligator," said Lindsay.

"He might make it. They're hard to kill."

"You killed an alligator?" Gretchen looked incredulous.

"No, she fed him Nate," said Mike.

"Please point me to the bathroom," said Lindsay. Tessa showed her the way.

Lindsay made it to the commode and threw up. When she finally came out, there was a sudden loud knocking at the door.

"Stay here," Mike said. He opened a closet and got a gun off the top shelf and went to the door.

"Yes," he yelled through the door.

"My name's Tom Bowers. I'm looking for one of our archaeologists. She was hurt in the hurricane and suffered a concussion. I'm afraid she may have wandered away."

"Is it that Chamberlain woman?"

"Yes, that's her. Is she here?"

"No, but if she comes, I'll shoot her head off. The bitch cost me my job."

"If you see her, please give me a call. My name's Tom Bowers."

"Yeah, sure. What's that shooting I heard? You're not supposed to be shooting on the island."

"I think that was Miss Chamberlain. She's really in a bad way."

Mike came back into the room. "I guess you heard that?"

"I didn't really cost you your job, did I?" asked Lindsay.

Mike looked at her a moment. "No, I just made that up."

"Do you think they'll break in?" asked Gretchen.

"I don't know. What did the rangers say?" he asked Tessa.

"They're coming. They're calling the National Guard."

"The National Guard?" said Gretchen, wide-eyed. "Is it that bad? Who are those people?"

"Gretchen just got back from the mainland," Mike told Lindsay, with a hint of a smile. "The National Guard is here guarding that big ship that washed ashore. Those guys, if my guess is right, are treasure hunters."

"Yes. Lewis hired them as security guards, not knowing they were in with Nate."

"Nate killed those people?" said Tessa.

"Yes," said Lindsay. "Apparently, pressure over his dissertation, if you can believe that."

There was a knock on the door again. "Can we come in? We have an emergency."

They looked at one another, not knowing what to do. Lend assistance, or possibly let Nate die. James Choi went to the door.

"What is the nature of your emergency?"

"We've had a man attacked by an alligator."

"I'll call the ranger station on Cumberland and get help. You take him to the archaeologists' house. We are quarantined until the CDC gets here. One of our tropical animals has come down with flulike symptoms. It's probably nothing, so don't worry, but we can't take chances. I'm very sorry."

"Oh, that's all right, you don't need to call the rangers. We can take care of it. This was just the closest house."

Gretchen put her hand over her mouth to keep from laughing. Lindsay heard them leave. She was still shaking.

"Can I use your phone?" Tessa nodded. Lindsay called John. "John, the people in the Magdalena House may be in danger." She told him what happened.

"What! Are you all right? I'll call the National Guard and tell them to go to the house. I'll be right over. Stay where you are. Don't do anything."

Lindsay hung up the phone. "The National Guard's going to think we're all nuts." They laughed nervously.

"What happened to you?" asked Gretchen. "Did they beat you up?"

"Nate tried to kill me at the cofferdam when the hurricane was coming. He left me there. I got all this trying to get to shore." Lindsay told them the entire story. They listened openmouthed.

There was more pounding on the front door. No one moved. It reminded Lindsay of *The Haunting of Hill House* where the inhabitants huddled together and watched the door distort from the pounding and malefactions of the evil presence.

"Mike, Tessa!"

Tessa let out a breath. "It's the rangers."

Mike went to the door and let them in.

Nate, as it turned out, was mangled, but more or less intact. He was attended by one of the rangers. The other park rangers, with the help of the Guard, had Tom and Robert in custody, waiting for the FBI. The alligator, too, appeared to be okay.

Their plan, indicated by their statements to the rangers, was to cast doubt on Lindsay's rationality. She, after all, had a concussion and had misinterpreted their intentions.

They were all in the lobby when Ramirez arrived with the paramedics. Harper stood in a robe, holding herself against the chill of the night and the evil that had occurred while she slept.

"Are we going to have to hire her a keeper?" she whispered to John, who stood with his arms wrapped around Lindsay.

"I reckon we are going to have to," he whispered back. Lindsay leaned back against him and he tightened his arms around her.

Lewis, Trey, Carolyn, and the others stood looking from one person to the other, confused.

"We were only trying to help," said Robert and Tom. "She obviously was released from the hospital too soon."

"We saw you trying to help," said James and Mike.

"It was dark and confusing out there," said Tom, still looking friendly.

"I didn't hear a thing," said Dale Delosier. "No one came by the front door."

Lindsay briefly gave Ramirez her rationale for Nate as the murderer.

"You can't prove it." His voice was hoarse.

"Yes I can. You thought I took Keith's notebooks. It was Lewis. He was having the data keyed in. I'm sure examination will show they are in Keith's handwriting."

"That proves nothing."

"Look at the poison ivy on your hands. Only you and Carolyn have it."

Carolyn looked at her hands "You have it, too?" she asked Nate, glaring at him.

"So?" said Nate, wincing from pain from the alligator attack as the paramedics gave him an IV drip.

"The Chinese box is lacquered with sap from the Chinese lacquer tree as a main ingredient. It contains the same substance as poison ivy—urushiol. It took me a while to remember that that is one of the things archaeologists have to be careful of, working in certain tombs—Chinese lacquered objects. I'm sure the Smithsonian advised Carolyn to handle it with care."

"Yes, they did," she said, still glaring at Nate.

"You were the one who broke into the warehouse and vandalized the chest. You recognized Valerian's crest. After Hardy Denton confessed that Eva Jones had Valerian's coded letter, you hoped that there would be a clue to the whereabouts of the treasure galleon tucked away in Valerian's belongings. You were so desperate to show Lewis some results."

"Damn you, Nate," said Carolyn. "That scroll was completely destroyed. The books are so damaged I don't know if I can salvage them, and I think one is by Roger Bacon. You piece of turkey shit."

"You can't prove anything. You need proof." Nate moaned in pain.

"There're the notebooks, the poison ivy, the fights with Keith, and my testimony that you tried to kill me tonight. Mike and James witnessed it and saved my life—despite the hard time we archaeologists have given them since we got here."

"We didn't know about this," said Tom Bowers.

"You came to the door and told us it was Lindsay shooting a gun on the island. She was with us when the shots were fired. The other guy, Robert, told us not to call the rangers."

"It was a misunderstanding," said Tom. "It's all circumstantial."

"Well, all these circumstances are piling up to make a stinking mess, and you guys are starting to smell," said Mike.

"It's your gun that's been fired," commented the ranger. "How did you think this woman fired it?"

Tom said nothing.

"We need to get this man to the hospital," said the paramedics.

Nate went to the hospital; Tom and Robert were taken into custody by Ramirez and the rangers. Lindsay took a hot shower and went back to bed.

⚓

"Tom and Robert are trying to weasel out. Nate's trying to make a deal," said Lewis. He, Lindsay, John, and Harper sat in Lewis's office, debriefing the latest. "Did I really push him into killing people? Do I push people?"

"You push," said Lindsay. "But you don't hound. There's a difference. Nate and Nate alone is to blame for his behavior. Neither I, Harper, Trey, Carolyn, nor Steven went on a killing rampage."

"I agree," said Harper. "You jump to conclusions about who's to blame about certain things, but you don't drive people to murder."

"Thanks for your endorsement," Lewis said.

As they spoke, Lindsay eyed the papers on Lewis's desk. "What's this?" She picked up a letter.

Lewis looked. "It's a letter from King-Smith-Falcon, the third bidder. They're dropping their query into the bidding process for the dam in view of recent events."

"And you didn't notice it? Neither you nor Trey?"

"What are you talking about? We read it," Lewis said.

"For archaeologists, I just don't know about the two of you," Lindsay said.

Harper looked over her shoulder and gasped, then a grin spread across her face.

"What?" said Trey.

"I'm going to use your phone," said Lindsay. She picked up the phone and dialed the number on the letterhead.

"May I speak with Mr. Beck, please? This is Dr. Lindsay Chamberlain from the Archaeology Department at the University of Georgia."

The receptionist put her through.

"Dr. Chamberlain. We sent a letter dropping our query."

"I know. This is not related to the query. Can you tell me a little about the history of your company?"

"What? Sure. We are one of the oldest companies in the United States, founded in the middle 1700s by Nathaniel Smith and his family. They built bridges and were one of the first companies to work underwater. We have some literature on it. May I ask why you're asking?" Lindsay told him.

The next day Jerome Beck, president and CEO of King-Smith-Falcon, and Lenton King, vice president in charge of design, arrived at St. Magdalena. After complimenting John on his cofferdam design, they were escorted by Lindsay, Francisco Lewis, Trey Marcus, and John West down to the conservation laboratory where Carolyn, Harper, Bobbie, and Korey were laying out the artifacts.

Eva Jones had been forced to turn over the diving bell to them.

It was six feet in height, part wood, part encrusted metal, half of it missing. But the crest stood out in relief. The chest was sitting on the floor soaking in brine, the carved crest on the lid showing beautifully.

"May I?" asked Jerome Beck. Carolyn nodded and he put his hand in the water and stroked the wooden relief of the falcon sitting in the middle of a *V* holding a scroll in his beak.

"And we didn't notice your logo on the letterhead," said Trey. "I can't believe it."

Jerome stood up. "Our company obviously has roots farther back than the mid-1700s." Carolyn showed them the other artifacts that were in the trunk.

"If you can provide the proper environment," Lewis offered, "we can give you the artifacts on long-term loan to display."

"We would like that," Lenton King said, obviously moved.

"Now, we have something to show you," said Beck. "It has been handed down from Nathaniel Smith. It was a family heirloom as far as we could determine." Beck put his briefcase on the desk and took out a small box. He opened it and took out the contents and handed it to Lindsay, his eyes twinkling. It was a gold ring. She caressed it, then slipped it on her finger. It was much too large, but she was wearing the ring with Valerian's crest— Valerian's ring. He had survived the wreck and had apparently done quite well.

OIC 1 5 '99

Connor, Beverly, 1948-
Skeleton crew : a Lindsay Chamberlain novel

FIC CON

Delafield Public Library
Delafield, WI 53018

DELAFIELD PUBLIC LIBRARY

3 0646 00103 1503